Dragon Scroll of Nepthali

B.L. Madole

Dragon Scroll of Nepthali

Copyright © 2017 by B.L. Madole

All rights reserved. No part of this book may be reproduced or transmitted in any form or by any means without written permission from the author. Unauthorized reproduction of any part of this work is illegal and punishable by law.

ISBN: 978-0-9987338-0-7

Printed in the USA

Dedication

This book is dedicated to my amazing husband, Darrin, who has loved me for over a quarter of a century and encouraged me to pursue a lifelong dream. To my four children: Jacob, Joshua, Hope, and Jesse who tolerated countless nights of late dinners after I had lost track of time while writing. To the greatest editor and cheerleader anyone could ask for, Beth O'Keefe; who also happens to be the best sister in the world! Lastly, to our dog Rusty who faithfully snuggled beside me during long hours in front of the computer with merely a pat on the head as thanks. Rest in peace sweet girl, you are sorely missed!

Contents

Chapter 1
The Dragon Brothers — 1

Chapter 2
Death of a Dream — 13

Chapter 3
A New Life at the Castle — 37

Chapter 4
Treacherous Plans — 61

Chapter 5
An Evil Alliance — 81

Chapter 6
Traitor in the Midst — 105

Chapter 7
Haunting Resemblance — 133

Chapter 8
I Thought I Might Find You Here… — 147

Chapter 9
The Coming Storm — 171

Chapter 10
Return of Narok — 195

Chapter 11
Escape into the Forest — 225

Chapter 12
A Grassy Knoll — 241

Chapter 13
Resolve for Revenge — 259

Chapter 14
A Shocking Discovery — 289

Chapter 15	Friends Reunite	307
Chapter 16	An Unlikely Spy	323
Chapter 17	Army of Farmers	341
Chapter 18	Mistaken Identity	363
Chapter 19	A Bride for Narok	385
Chapter 20	Up to the Challenge	405
Chapter 21	United Resolve	427
Chapter 22	Renewed Strength	447
Chapter 23	One Shot	469
Chapter 24	Heartfelt Plea	491
Chapter 25	Sworn Allegiance	513

Chapter 1

The Dragon Brothers

Throughout every generation a story can be found of a poor maiden with exceptional beauty who falls in love with a handsome prince. Although the stories go by different names, each of them can be traced back to one that begins with dragons.....

Long ago and faraway, the Kingdom of Nepthali was ruled by dragon brothers named Orpheus and Natas. The dragons were covered in scales of purest white and stood taller than the rolling hills of Irvania. Their powerful wings spanned nearly as wide as Lake Placia, and one roar put the loudest rolls of thunder to shame. Yet, the people had no fear of their unconventional rulers because this was a time when a dragon's sole purpose was to protect humans; especially from goblins.

Like all goblins, those in Nepthali were characterized by towering height, unusually large noses, and pointed ears. The goblins were gold-seeking creatures that terrorized people on their quest for the sparkling treasure. Orpheus and Natas kept the goblins contained to the forest until one day a proud and foolish goblin king started what became known as The Great Goblin War. The war lasted longer than the dragons expected because of the goblins' ruthless fighting technique of using people as shields when the dragons tried to attack. The goblins advanced until they overtook the entire province of Haliel. Never before had such a thing happened to the Dragon Rulers, and it enraged Natas. The young dragon insisted that Orpheus use his magic, which only the elder dragon possessed, to destroy Haliel and be rid of the troublesome creatures. Although Orpheus agreed this would put an end to the goblins, the wise dragon reminded his brother that his magic could never be used to harm another dragon or humans. Since the goblins had already demonstrated their unscrupulous ways, Orpheus feared they would somehow use his magic to harm the people, therefore, he refused. His refusal further enraged Natas, and for the first time the younger dragon resented being bound to submit to his brother's authority.

The powerful Dragon Rulers eventually defeated the goblins under Orpheus' direction serving as another blow to Natas' already wounded pride. A seed of resentment was planted which fully bloomed when Orpheus ordered the younger dragon to take the remaining goblins into the woods and kill them while he tended to the traumatized people. As Natas led them away, the goblin king keenly recognized a prideful heart in the young dragon and cleverly appealed to it. He deceived Natas into believing that by sparing his life, and the lives of his fiercest warriors, Natas would have a newfound power over Orpheus. Natas found the king's smooth speech irresistibly enticing, and the young dragon started down a path that would forever change the way dragons are remembered.

The Dragon Brothers

******

Following The Great Goblin War, Natas intentionally avoided Orpheus and kept to his new lair within Og Mountain where only the goblin king and what remained of his men were allowed. Unaware of what Natas had done, or the company he was keeping, Orpheus focused his attention on the hurting people of Nepthali. To help them re-build their broken kingdom, the good dragon used his magic to bestow lavish gifts upon each province. The western province of Nepthali received rich soil to grow fine crops, and shipping ports to allow for trade across The Great Sea. The eastern province of Haliel was given an abundance of diamonds as large as a man's fist sprinkled throughout the mountainous terrain. The northern province of Belzeeb received sandstone and limestone to be used for the building of grand castles locally and across The Great Sea. Finally, because he believed the goblins were gone, Orpheus filled the Cherith River and surrounding hillsides in the southern province of Irvania with more gold than a man could find in a hundred lifetimes.

Because of these gifts, the people adored Orpheus more than Natas. Things worsened when Orpheus announced his decision to appoint a king, an act only the eldest dragon brother had authority to do. Natas seethed with envy and allowed it to consume him to the point that his eyes suddenly turned green. Legend has it that because of what happened to Natas, jealousy is known as the green-eyed monster. A black spot also appeared on one of his white scales as another outward sign of the change within the young dragon's heart. Fueled by resentment, envy, and pride; Natas vowed to turn the people against Orpheus as he foolishly believed Orpheus had done to him.

Oblivious to the horrific change occurring within his brother's heart, Orpheus established the royal bloodline through a man from the kingdom's namesake province of Nepthali. Jeptha had a head full of golden curls and eyes as blue as the summer sky. He was a craftsman of wood with a humble heart who also possessed exceptional sword skills for someone of his trade. The entire kingdom, including Natas, attended Jeptha's coronation. The young dragon easily concealed his black spot, but could do nothing to disguise his piercing green eyes. Orpheus noticed the change at once, but the festivities commenced before he could inquire. Sensing his brother's pensive gaze throughout the ceremony, Natas slipped away before the festivities concluded. He burned with jealousy after watching the people shower Orpheus with praise and adoration as Natas flew until he found himself over the Cherith River. He looked down into the gold-filled waters expecting to see his glorious reflection, but instead saw a hideous creature looking back at him. The gold revealed the ugliness within the young dragon's heart, which Natas found intoxicatingly wonderful.

******

Natas continued to avoid Orpheus throughout King Jeptha's reign and the reign of Jeptha's son with the help of a Royal Scribe named Ganu. The young dragon promised to establish a new royal bloodline through Ganu if the scribe deflected Orpheus' inquiries concerning Natas, and his whereabouts. Natas was able to promise such a thing knowing that once Orpheus was removed from the kingdom he would have ultimate authority. Ganu readily agreed to do the dragon's evil bidding, and began his own legacy of treachery and deceit.

The Dragon Brothers

With Ganu in place to deal with Orpheus, Natas and the goblins were free to devise a way to rid the kingdom of the good dragon. In exchange for their help, Natas promised the shifty creatures gold and powerful positions under his rule. This offer was agreeable to the goblin king and his warriors now living at the base of Og Mountain. The grotesque creatures took women for themselves from Haliel to continue their evil bloodline and created a new half-breed race. The part-goblin, part-humans called themselves the Bara and soon rivaled the fierce and ruthless fighting style of their goblin forefathers. Eventually, thieves and bandits throughout the kingdom flocked to the camp and the term Bara expanded to include all who joined the feared enemy of the good people of Nepthali.

As the years marched on, Natas evolved into the hideousness creature the gold had previously revealed. His scales turned as black as a starless night, and the ears which once listened for the cries of the people turned into twisted horns as hard as the young dragon's heart. No human recognized Natas as one of the Dragon Rulers on the rare occasions the beast was seen. With his metamorphosis complete, Natas was ready to execute his plan to permanently turn the hearts of the people against Orpheus, and then have his brother banished from the kingdom.

Under the cover of night, the black dragon breathed down fire from above while Bara soldiers stole diamonds and gold. Reports of the raids involving a dragon-like creature and his goblin-like accomplices reached the now reigning King Thaddeus, grandson of Jeptha. The king had his grandfather's same golden curls, crystal blue eyes, and exceptional skills with a sword. King Thaddeus summoned Orpheus to share the disturbing news which the people had relayed. When the good dragon arrived he assured Thaddeus that such actions could never be true of a dragon. He also reminded the king that the goblins had been annihilated years earlier not knowing what his brother had become, or had done. To put the king's mind at ease, Orpheus took flight in search of the mysterious creature and bandits as a steady rain began to fall.

The white dragon eventually caught sight of a black, winged creature. Orpheus' chest glowed as he prepared to shoot his deadly fire, but he stopped suddenly when the beast turned around. Orpheus stared in disbelief at the piercing green eyes looking back at him, and knew at once it was Natas. Orpheus allowed his brother to escape into the storm and returned to the castle with a heavy heart.

******

When Orpheus landed in pools of water collecting in the courtyard, he found an angry mob gathered demanding the dragons be removed from the kingdom. Orpheus tried to reassure the people that he had nothing to do with the raids, but Natas had succeeded in turning their hearts against even the good dragon. Unable to dissuade their fears, the white dragon took flight in search of Natas hoping to reason with his wayward brother. As Orpheus approached Og Mountain, Natas swooped down and tore through Orpheus' wings with his deadly talons to render his brother unable to fly. He carried Orpheus through the storm to his lair.

Once inside, Natas dropped Orpheus onto one of the many mounds of gold and diamonds. The treasures meant nothing to Natas, but he allowed the Bara to store them in his lair since that was the only place large enough to hold everything the Bara stole from the people. It is because of his treasure-laden lair that dragons gained their reputation of being creatures obsessed with gathering gold, when in truth it was the Bara. The treasures gave off an eerie glow within the darkened cave as Natas cackled with delight while smoke drifted from his blackened nostrils. Thunder crashed overhead and the heavy smell of sulfur filled the lair as the beast revealed his longstanding resentment towards his brother, and the truth about not killing all of the goblins. He also told Orpheus about Ganu, and how the treasonous scribe was doing the dragon's evil biding within the castle.

When Natas finished his confessional, he slithered like a serpent behind a large rock and emerged with a scroll in his twisted claw. When Orpheus saw the scroll he knew that Natas was beyond saving, and that the beast intended permanent harm to the people of Nepthali. Natas stood over his crippled brother and, without warning, ripped a scale from Orpheus' chest. The pain of flesh being pulled out with the scale was excruciating, but Orpheus never flinched. Natas' green eyes glared with contempt as he handed his brother the blood-soaked scale and ordered Orpheus to write down everything he said with the threat of killing the humans if Orpheus refused. Having no choice, Orpheus moved the scale up and down in eloquent strokes across the scroll while Natas dictated.

With his evil demands complete, the black dragon insisted that Orpheus place his seal upon the scroll. The good dragon knew this was his chance to thwart his brother's evil plan and offer hope to the people. Orpheus channeled his magic through his paw to embed an inscription into his seal which negated all but one of Natas' demands. Unaware of what Orpheus had done,

Dragon Scroll of Nepthali

Natas quickly snatched the scroll and placed his mark beside his brother's to make it binding for all time. The beast believed the goblin king's promise of having a greater power over Orpheus had finally come to fruition until Natas saw the smile spread across his brother's face. Natas looked at the scroll and, to his horror, saw what Orpheus had done. He lunged to attack, but while in mid-air Natas fell into a deep sleep and collapsed onto a mound of gold. The moment Natas' body touched the sparkling treasure it turned to coal, and Og Mountain became a volcano.

Orpheus snatched the scroll from Natas' twisted talons and staggered from the lair as a bolt of lightning illuminated the night sky. Although uncertain if he could fly, Orpheus had to try so he could get back to the castle. He mustered what strength he had left and floundered against the raging storm with his tattered and torn wings. The Bara soldiers watched Orpheus leave Natas' lair then hurried inside only to find lumps of coal where the gold had been, and their leader trapped in timeless slumber.

******

Orpheus landed within the expansive courtyard as morning dawned and the skies cleared. The Chief Royal Scribe, Carmi, was in his study when he heard the familiar violent rush of wind caused by the dragon as he landed. Orpheus lowered his massive neck until his head was level with the balcony as Carmi came out to greet the Dragon Ruler. From the hallway, Ganu also heard the rush of wind and hurried to gather information for Natas. When Ganu slyly entered the study, he saw Orpheus use his magic to reduce a scroll in size before handing it to Carmi. Ganu then listened with dismay as Orpheus explained Natas' current state of slumber within his lair until an appointed time. The dragon's voice was muffled, but Ganu managed to hear that the foretelling sign of this appointed time was the birth of twins. Although Orpheus did not say so specifically, Ganu presumed this meant the birth of twins to the Royal Family. The evil scribe tingled with excitement as Orpheus continued to explain that the scroll in Carmi's hand possessed great power. Ganu envisioned himself ruling the kingdom even without Natas' help, yet his fanciful thoughts were quickly interrupted when Orpheus exposed Ganu's treacherous ties with Natas. Orpheus warned Carmi never to allow Ganu, or his descendants, access to the scroll lest its power be used for evil. With his treachery exposed, Ganu fled the study before he was seen and thrown into the dungeon…or worse.

Moments after Ganu slipped away, King Thaddeus joined Carmi on the balcony where Orpheus told the king that he must leave. This was the one demand which Orpheus had not altered with his magic because he knew that for a love to be true it can never be forced. The good dragon loved the people more than life itself, but would never insist on their love in return. Orpheus explained that he would return at the appointed time only if a member of the Royal Family still believed in the good dragon and wanted him back in the land. As Thaddeus pondered the wise dragon's words, Orpheus lifted the king's left forearm and kissed it. King Thaddeus felt a sting like that from a bee before he saw the mark. To the untrained eye it appeared as nothing more than a birthmark, but the heart-shaped imprint left by the dragon's kiss was really a Mark of Royalty which has appeared on those of royal blood ever since.

Next, Orpheus used his magic to fashion a sword out

of the scale Natas had plucked from his body to remain even in the dragon's absence. Orpheus handed it to King Thaddeus stating that the sword would one day save the kingdom, but it must never be present when the scroll is open until the appointed time lest their power be unleashed too soon. The king was perplexed by what he heard, however, he trusted Orpheus enough to do as the dragon had instructed. Hours later with a plan in place to ensure the safety of the Royal Family, Orpheus left the castle.

The white dragon labored to fly over the kingdom he loved so dearly through the darkness of night. When he reached a remote farm near the edge of Nepthali, Orpheus saw a small boy standing alone in the moonlight. Boaz and his parents had moved to the farm earlier that day from the castle, and the child was unable to sleep in his new surroundings. He wandered outside to gaze at the full moon but instead saw the glorious dragon. Orpheus landed near the lad and spoke to him briefly. Minutes later, Orpheus left not knowing if he would ever return to his beloved kingdom.

******

The people of Nepthali rejoiced believing that the dragons were gone, but became angry to see their gifts were gone as well. Only the Royal Family mourned Orpheus' departure more than the loss of treasures. Their sorrow was so deep that no one saw them for nearly a year. The once prosperous kingdom became a shadow of its former glory, and despair became commonplace. Yet Carmi remained hopeful as he studied what he called the Dragon Scroll. He shared this hope with any who would listen and traveled far and wide to spread it. One day the scribe happened upon Boaz's farm, and soon became a regular visitor after learning of the boy's encounter with Orpheus. Carmi taught Boaz about the hope offered in the Dragon Scroll, and it took root in the young boy's heart.

******

One day as Carmi prepared to leave for the farm and tell Boaz about the Mark of Royalty, Ganu suddenly appeared in his doorway. The deceitful scribe hadn't been seen since Orpheus' departure because he was hiding out with the Bara soldiers. They waited together for Natas to awaken and fulfill his promises, but Ganu had grown tired of waiting. He returned to claim the scroll which he believed contained the power to rule the kingdom, and insisted that Carmi give it to him. The Chief Royal Scribe was shocked to learn that Ganu knew of the Dragon Scroll, but adamantly refused his request.

The treacherous young man became enraged and reached out to grab hold of his former mentor. When he did, Ganu knocked over a candle on the cluttered desk igniting the many maps and scrolls. Carmi turned to flee the spreading flames, but Ganu grabbed hold of his long robe. The old man pulled back with surprising force and Ganu lost his grip. When he did, Carmi stumbled backwards from the shift in force and tripped over his robe and crashed through the window. Horrified by what he had done, Ganu fled the study empty-handed. Carmi's body was found at the base of the tower, but no one suspected foul play thinking the old scribe had merely jumped from the window to escape the flames. The Dragon Scroll was miraculously found unscathed inside Carmi's robe, but those who found it were unaware of its significance. The scroll written by Orpheus was placed in a temporary storage room above the Royal Library along with other documents recovered from what became known as The Great Fire. With Carmi dead, Ganu resumed his position as a Royal Scribe without fear of retribution. His long absence was explained away as having conducted studies of ancient writings in faraway lands. But even after his return to the castle, Ganu continued to meet regularly with the Bara.

******

The kingdom was in a terrible financial crisis without the gifts from Orpheus, which caused the necessary repairs to take decades to complete. Therefore, those who knew of the temporary storage room had either died or forgotten about it by the time the castle was restored. The Dragon Scroll was presumed lost in The Great Fire, when in truth it sat on a shelf collecting dust.

With time, the goblins and Dragon Rulers faded from the hearts and minds of the people until they became nothing more than characters in a children's tale. Although Boaz never knew why Carmi stopped coming to the farm, or of the Mark of Royalty, he clung to the hope in the Dragon Scroll. It became as much a part of Boaz's legacy as his golden curls and eyes of crystal blue.

Chapter 2

Death of a Dream

Four-year-old Mitzy's golden curls and crystal blue eyes peered above the thick, woolen blankets as shadows from the fire dance along the cottage wall.

"Papa!" called her muffled voice anxiously. Mitzy couldn't bear another moment of silence, and didn't know what she would do if her father was asleep like her mother and two brothers. Mitzy sighed with relief after hearing the familiar thump of her father's boots as he walked across the old wooden floor. Her father, Amalek, was the great-great-great grandson of Boaz and shared his ancestor's batch of golden curls and crystal blue eyes just like his daughter. Amalek sat on the edge of her bed and Mitzy immediately crawled into his lap and deeply breathed in the familiar scent of sweat, freshly cut wood, and hay. The women in their village thought Amalek possessed features of a nobleman, and often said as much to Mitzy's mother, Meridia. Mitzy adored her father, and agreed with any who thought him the most handsome man in the kingdom.

"What are you doing still awake at this hour, Miss Mit?" he whispered.

"I can't sleep, Papa. I don't want you and the boys to leave," she managed before bursting into tears.

"Now, now, Miss Mit, don't cry," said Amalek softly as he held his only daughter. Although surprised by her tears, Amalek had learned after fifteen years of marriage to never question the emotions of a female.

"What if something happens to you...or Joab...or Gideon? What shall Mama and I do?" sobbed Mitzy.

"You've nothing to fear, Miss Mit, for we're traveling with other farmers this year," said her father reassuringly. Mitzy took comfort from his words as Amalek tried to conceal his own fears. Hay was a valuable commodity in these lean times, and the journey to Haliel was riddled with Bara soldiers. The bandits with goblin origins remained the most feared enemy of the good people of Nepthali.

"Papa, are you going past Og Mountain?" asked Mitzy as she wiped her nose.

"Yes; but have no fear, the volcano shan't erupt," he said playfully. This time Mitzy took no comfort in her father's words since that wasn't her concern.

"Is Natas still there?" she whispered. Amalek suddenly understood his daughter's fear.

"He is, but Orpheus promised that Natas shall remain asleep until the appointed time," he reminded her.

"I know, but hasn't he been asleep since even before you were born?" asked a wide-eyed Mitzy. Amalek smiled at his daughter's exaggerated perception of his age.

Death of a Dream

"It has been a long time, but the promise of a dragon is the one thing you can be certain of in this world," he answered with absolute certainty.

"Papa, please tell me the story of the dragon brothers. It always helps me fall asleep," begged Mitzy.

"Very well, Miss Mit, but if your mother awakens I shall claim this was all your doing," he teased. Mitzy giggled with delight as her golden curls bounced up and down while she situated herself in her father's lap.

Her fears immediately melted away with the deep, soothing sound of her father's voice as it floated over the crackling fire. She imagined what it would have been like to live when dragons ruled the kingdom, and what it would be like to be a part of the Royal Family. She and her father shared in this habit of allowing their thoughts to take them away to wonderfully far off places where anything was possible. They also shared an unwavering hope in the return of the good dragon Orpheus. Mitzy soon drifted off to sleep and Amalek kissed his daughter gently on the forehead. He was halfway across the room when he stepped on a loose floorboard and shattered the silence with a loud *Squeak*!

"Where're you going, Papa? You're not done yet," called Mitzy's sleepy voice. Amalek winced and silently scolded himself for not having fixed the loose board weeks ago when Meridia had asked.

"I thought you'd fallen asleep, Miss Mit," he whispered as he resumed his place at the edge of her bed.

"I was just resting my eyes; keep telling," she said with a yawn. Amalek knew they should both be asleep, but he was happy to continue. He picked up where he had left off just before Orpheus was captured by Natas.

"How could the people want a good dragon like Orpheus to leave?" asked Mitzy.

"Well, Miss Mit, they were afraid, and fear can be a terrible thing. It can make a person forget things he should remember, and remember things he should forget," answered her father wisely. As he continued and got to the part when Natas plucked a scale from Orpheus' chest, Mitzy threw off her blankets suddenly and sat straight up.

"Poor Orpheus!" she exclaimed.

"What's going on over there?" called Meridia's sweet voice through the darkness.

"Nothing, my dear," answered Amalek sheepishly. "Miss Mit couldn't sleep, so I was just telling her a story." His wife smiled knowing exactly what story it was, and only hoped he was close to the end.

"Try to finish up soon; you've a big day ahead of you," she reminded him tenderly. Meridia and Amalek were poor by worldly standards but shared a love worth more than all the gold which once filled the Cherith River.

"Yes, my love, we're nearly finished," he assured her. Amalek waited a few minutes before turning to his daughter with a child-like grin. "Now, where was I?"

"In the lair, Papa," she said in a loud whisper. Amalek nodded as if she had told him something he didn't know and continued with the drama between the dragon brothers. Mitzy refrained from further outbursts until the story was nearly over and she could no longer contain her excitement.

"Is this when greatestest-grand-papa Boaz sees Orpheus?" she asked anxiously.

"Yes, Miss Mit," he said with a chuckle at the mispronunciation of her ancestor. Amalek closed his eyes for a moment and remembered the expression on his mother's face each time she re-told this part of the story. "When my great-great-great-grandfather Boaz was a young lad, a little older than you are now, he saw Orpheus as the dragon left the kingdom."

"Where did greatestest-grand-papa Boaz see Orpheus?" asked Mitzy eyes filled with wonder.

"On the hill just outside of this window," replied Amalek as he pointed into the darkness. He paused again and pondered anew what it must have been like to see the glorious dragon.

"Keep telling, Papa," insisted Mitzy with her voice interrupting his thoughts. Amalek ran his calloused fingers through his golden curls and sighed before continuing.

"Orpheus spoke to Boaz, and the lad remembered every word the dragon said for the rest of his life," he explained.

"Tell me what he said, Papa," begged Mitzy.

"He said, 'Things are not as they appear, Young Sire. When the night is dark and dreary; never give up, nor grow weary. The lion is wounded but may be saved by the youngest one so brave,'" said Amalek.

"What does that mean?" asked Mitzy.

"I wish I knew for certain, Miss Mit. I was told it speaks of the king who shall be saved from Natas by the youngest member of the Royal Family," answered her father. Mitzy found this very exciting.

"I'm the youngest in our family, Papa. Do you think I could ever do something that important?" she asked.

"Of course, you can do anything you put your mind to," he said with certainty.

"What else did Orpheus say?" asked Mitzy. Amalek's eyes twinkled as he and his daughter repeated the familiar phrase together.

"A hope which is pure and true shall not disappoint," he said as Mitzy giggled with delight.

"What's so important about hope, Papa?" she asked with a yawn.

"Hope is what keeps a person from despair, Miss Mit, no matter what life throws at you," he answered. Although too young to understand her father's words, Mitzy sensed their importance.

"Is that why you and Mama believe in Orpheus even if it won't bring the great dragon back?" she asked innocently. Amalek had often asked himself this same question over the years, but each time something inside refused to let go.

"I suppose. You see, a poor farmer like me has little control in this world, Miss Mit; but I can control what I believe in. Your mother and I believe in Orpheus and the

Dragon Scroll, even if our belief won't bring the great dragon's return. We cannot make you or your brothers believe; the choice shall be yours alone to make one day. The same is true for members of the Royal Family," he explained. Her father's words felt alive to Mitzy and touched a special place in her heart.

"Do King Daven and Queen Lydia believe in Orpheus, Papa?" she asked.

"I'm certain they do, but remember it is King Daven's eldest son, Shem and his wife Ashter, who are the new king and queen," corrected her father. Mitzy had forgotten but trusted her father that they also believed in Orpheus.

"I believe, Papa, and I always shall," she vowed.

"I hope so, Miss Mit," he said. Amalek wanted this to be true for his daughter, but knew all too well that people could change. Isabella, his aunt on his mother's side, once believed in the hope found in the Dragon Scroll like the rest of Amalek's family. However, she forsook her belief after both her husband and son died from the plague. Isabella blamed Orpheus, and concluded the Dragon Scroll was nothing more than a foolish story for old women and children. She found employment at the castle, left her village, and severed all ties with her family.

"Papa, why don't more people believe in Orpheus?" asked Mitzy innocently returning her father's attention to his little girl.

"Perhaps it's because we no longer see him, or the Dragon Scroll. It takes a special person to believe in something that can't be seen," he said while rubbing his tired eyes. "But, just because you can't see something doesn't mean it isn't real."

"Why can't people see the Dragon Scroll, Papa?" she asked.

"It was destroyed in The Great Fire," answered Amalek sadly.

"But if the Royal Family doesn't have the scroll, how can they learn about Orpheus? And if they can't learn about Orpheus, how can they believe in him? And if they don't believe, Orpheus shall never return!" exclaimed Mitzy with growing anxiety.

"Easy now, Miss Mit, I'm certain the Royal Family has someone to teach them just as you have me," he said.

"Can we go to the castle and tell them?" she pleaded.

"Perhaps someday, but it's very late now and time for both of us to get some sleep," said Amalek. He pulled back the blankets for Mitzy and she crawled beneath them. He then tucked in the corners nice and snug just the way she liked them. "Goodnight, Miss Mit."

"Goodnight, Papa," she said softly.

Amalek slid into bed next to his beautiful wife and tried to sleep, but found himself staring at the ceiling wishing that his belief was enough to bring about Orpheus' return.

******

Amalek, Joab, and Gideon rose earlier than usual the next morning to load the wagon with hay. Meanwhile,

Meridia and Mitzy worked alongside one another in the cottage preparing sliced ham, cheese, fruit, and fresh bread for the journey. Once the hay was loaded and the horses were hitched to the wagon, Amalek jumped down and the family started their goodbyes. Meridia handed the basket filled with food to Joab before hugging Gideon, while Mitzy ran to her father.

"Please don't go, Papa!" she cried. He scooped Mitzy into his arms and held her tightly.

"If the boys and I don't go, who shall sell all this hay?" he said with a smile.

"But, Papa, I shall miss you so," she moaned. Amalek saw the anguish in his daughter's eyes and reached into his torn pocket. He opened Mitzy's clinched little hand and placed something inside.

"Hold onto this for me, Miss Mit. I was planning to work on it while I was away, but I suppose I can finish it when I get back," he said. Mitzy was too sad to look at what he'd given her as she held onto her father's neck.

Amalek hugged his daughter one last time then set her down next to her mother. Amalek hated to leave Mitzy and Meridia, but knew he must reach Haliel early in the harvest season to get the highest price for his hay, and hopefully avoid the Bara soldiers. He tried not to think about the dangers he and his boys would likely encounter as he wrapped his arms around his wife's small waist and gazed deeply into her dark brown eyes. To him, the years of hard work and lean times hadn't aged Meridia a bit. He thought she was even more beautiful today than the day they had married, but Amalek recognized the worried look in his wife's eyes.

"Why the long face, my love? You know the boys and I shall return in little more than a fortnight," he said hoping to cheer her. But as he held her close, Amalek had a strange feeling it would be for the last time. Meridia rested her head on his broad shoulder and breathed in the familiar mixture of hay, sweat, and wood. It was his scent, and it reminded her of home.

"I have a bad feeling about this trip, Amalek," she whispered. "Must you go today?" Amalek felt a stab of guilt as she looked up and he saw her eyes fill with tears.

"We've been over this, Meridia, you've nothing to fear. Besides, we shan't even be gone long enough for you to miss the extra cooking and cleaning with us around," he teased. Meridia wanted to believe him, but her female intuition told her otherwise.

"Without Joab here, who shall finish harvesting the corn fields? And, do you really think Gideon is ready for such a journey; he's only nine?" asked Meridia. In truth, she knew Gideon was ready and the corn could wait until they returned, but Meridia was searching for any excuse to keep them home.

"Trust me; this crop is exactly what we've been waiting for. If we reach Haliel ahead of the other farmers, the boys and I should return with enough money to clear our debts, and maybe even have a little extra to save for a payment to buy this land," said Amalek. Looking at her husband, Meridia remembered why she'd fallen in love with him in the first place. It wasn't because of his strikingly handsome features, but rather for his unrelenting hope that better times were coming. His positive attitude was as contagious as it was irresistible, and Meridia often wished she was more like him.

"Trust me, my love, everything shall be fine. Remember, a hope which is pure and true shall not disappoint," he said with a twinkle in his crystal blue eyes. Meridia smiled because he knew she could never argue with him when he quoted Orpheus.

"Yes, I know…and I remember," she answered softly.

"That's my girl," he said and then turned to Mitzy. "I want you two to take good care of each other, and don't forget that you're my best girls." Amalek gave a gentle pat to the mound of curls atop Mitzy's head before kissing his wife long and hard.

Amalek climbed into the front of the wagon as a soft rain began to fall. When they pulled away, Joab and Gideon called out their last goodbyes as Mitzy ran alongside them. She stopped at the edge of the farm but waved in the rain until the swaying pile of hay became nothing more than a speck.

"Come along now, Mitzy, and help me finish cleaning the vegetables," called Meridia from the cottage as she wiped away her tears.

"Coming, Mama," answered Mitzy.

As she walked through the gentle rain, Mitzy suddenly remembered the object her father had placed in her hand. She unclenched her fingers and stared at the small piece of wood with a smoothed-out center and delicate etchings along the edges. It was far from finished but Mitzy could tell it was going to be a doll. She squealed with delight and tucked the precious treasure into her skirt pocket. The child ran through the rain with an even greater anticipation for her father's return.

Mitzy named the unfinished doll Polly. Each night before she went to sleep, Mitzy told Polly about Orpheus and how the good dragon would someday return to make Nepthali a wonderful place, just as her father would return to make Polly into a beautiful doll.

******

The first few days of their journey to Haliel were uneventful for Amalek and the other farmers. He was pleased with their steady pace, especially considering the heavily loaded wagons and mixture of young boys and old men in their company. Although he hated to be away from his wife and daughter, Amalek enjoyed the time with Joab and Gideon. He marveled at how much both had grown, and was proud of the fine young men they were becoming. On the second day of travel, they reached the border of Nepthali and Haliel in the late afternoon where it was decided they would stop for the night.

"Let's get to work men. The horses need to be unhitched and watered. Boys, I need you to gather wood for a fire," instructed Amalek.

"Must we be in such a hurry? I think we deserve rest more than these beasts," complained Laban. Laban was a lazy, lanky fellow who, much to everyone's surprise, had recently completed training to be a Royal Guard. The young man was making this trip with his father for the last time before moving permanently to the castle. Laban despised Amalek for taking charge, and believed he shouldn't have to take orders from a farmer now that he was a Royal Guard.

"Unless you want to walk the rest of the way, Laban, I suggest you help take care of these so-called beasts," replied Amalek firmly. Laban sensed the other men were on Amalek's side, so he quickly came up with a solution to keep from following any orders.

"These woods are crawling with wild animals, and possibly bandits. I think that I, being the most qualified, should provide protection for the boys as they gather the wood," he suggested slyly. Although fully aware of Laban's true intentions to get out of work, Amalek agreed it was a good idea.

"All right, Laban, go with them," he replied. Laban smiled broadly knowing he'd won this battle.

"I shall watch them as if they were my own," he replied sarcastically.

"It's Laban who needs to be watched," whispered Joab as he and Gideon led the other boys into the woods.

After traveling a short distance, Laban announced that he had something in his boot and sent the boys ahead without him to collect the wood. As only a fool would do, Laban applauded himself for having outwitted children and found a soft patch of grass beneath the trees to take a nap.

******

When the boys returned to camp with enough firewood to last the night, Amalek noticed that Laban wasn't with them.

"I wonder where Laban is?" he said to himself.

However, Amalek was too busy mending a loose shoe on one of the horses to concern himself with the whereabouts of the lazy young man. But what Amalek didn't realize was that the boys weren't the only ones who'd returned to the camp from the woods. A group of Bara soldiers followed the boys back to their camp and quickly surrounded the unsuspecting farmers.

"Wait for my signal," whispered Cain.

Cain was a direct descendant of the goblin king who started The Great Goblin War generations earlier. Cain was the fiercest warrior who believed he should be the leader of the Bara. His prideful natured caused Cain to mistaken the fear other men had of his unmatched sword skills and impressive height as respect. But Lemuel, the Bara leader, saw in Cain the same irrational behavior which could be traced back to his vile ancestors. Cain saw Lemuel as the one man standing in his way to becoming the leader. Because of this, the young warrior waited for the right opportunity to kill Lemuel just as he waited now to attack the unsuspecting farmers.

As Amalek finished mending the horse's shoe, he heard a branch snap at the edge of camp. He looked up expecting to see Laban, but instead his eyes met with those of a Bara soldier as a battle cry called out from the trees. In an instant, the camp was flooded with the fierce men whose screams mixed with those of the startled farmers. The commotion was so loud it woke Laban, who initially believed he was having a dream. But as the cries continued, the coward realized it was real and crouched on his knees then looked between the natural gaps of the bushes. The first thing Laban saw was a Bara soldier running a sword through his father. The sight was too terrifying for Laban to comprehend and he passed out, hitting his head on a rock as he landed.

Death of a Dream

Inside the camp, Amalek frantically searched for Joab and Gideon amidst the chaos. As he ran, a Bara soldier charged after him. Amalek pulled a sword from the belly of a fallen neighbor to defend himself. He hoped to remember the training his grandfather had given him as a boy as the Bara raised his sword to strike. Amalek blocked his assailant's first blow then readied himself for the next. Although unaccustomed to using a blade, Amalek's natural skills were undeniable. His enemy advanced and thrust, but Amalek successfully blocked each move as if knowing where the man would strike. The soldier became enraged at his inability to kill a farmer. He charged again, but this time Amalek pierced the man in the chest. The bandit's final expression was one of disbelief as he fell to the ground dead. Amalek spun around in time to see another soldier coming straight for him. The farmer ducked, then jabbed, twisted, and thrust like a seasoned Royal Guard. Amalek's skills were raw, but deadly accurate; enough so to capture Cain's attention.

While Amalek fought, he repeatedly called out, "JOAB!! GIDEON!!" The terrified boys recognized their father's voice in spite of the noise around them. Joab grabbed Gideon by the arm and ran towards Amalek. They were only a few feet away when Cain's impressive figure stood between the boys and their father. The ruthless warrior rightly surmised that these must be the sons of the skilled farmer who'd killed some of his best men.

Amalek was in the midst of fighting another Bara when he turned around to see Cain with his sword raised over Joab. The terrified father swiftly kicked his opponent in the knee to dislocate it before sprinting for his firstborn. Cain lowered his blade, but Amalek dove through the air and extended his body between the sword and his son. The blade pierced through Amalek's abdomen while Joab and Gideon watched in horror. The brave farmer collapsed on the ground and blood trickled from his mouth.

"NO!" screamed Gideon.

"FATHER!" yelled Joab as both boys rushed to his side. Amalek's shaking hands took hold of each boy as he knew that his life was slipping away.

"A hope which is pure and true shall not disappoint," he whispered. A blast of thunder suddenly rolled through the cloudless sky as Amalek took his last breath.

Cain approached the grief-stricken boys with a sword in each hand. The cold and calculating killer drove one through Joab's back and the other through Gideon. The boys fell on either side of their father as another blast of thunder rolled and the ground shook. Amalek and his sons died as they had lived...together...side by side.

"There's something unnatural about this, Cain," warned an old Bara soldier named Gilgal. Gilgal knew well of Natas and Orpheus for he had goblin blood running through his veins just like Cain.

"You sound like a foolish old woman," snapped the brazen young soldier.

"Maybe so, but even foolish old women can be right," warned Gilgal. "The skies are clear, yet thunder rolls the moment you killed the farmer and his two sons. It's dragon magic I tell you." But Cain refused to heed Gilgal's wise warning.

Death of a Dream

"Enough of this nonsense! Make sure there are no survivors then take these wagons back to camp. Lemuel shall be pleased," boasted Cain. Although Gilgal did as he was told, the old man feared what evil may befall them as he passed the bodies of Amalek, Joab, and Gideon.

******

Laban regained consciousness after the Bara soldiers had gone and slowly got to his feet while holding his throbbing head. As he stood, Laban remembered the attack and stumbled into the campsite. He found it emptied of all the wagons and only the lifeless bodies of men he had known his whole life remained. Laban also noticed many Bara corpses and wondered who among these farmers possessed the skills to accomplish such a feat. Instead of checking for survivors as every Royal Guard was trained to do, Laban ran away in terror.

******

Laban ran all night and arrived at his small village by midday. News quickly spread of his return and everyone gathered to learn the fate of their loved ones. Laban stood before them recounting a tragic, yet extremely altered, tale in which he was the hero. He claimed to have single-handedly slain multiple Bara soldiers, when in truth it had been Amalek. Laban attributed his survival to the bandits believing he was dead, and showed his head covered in dried blood as proof. The villagers never questioned Laban's account since he was not only one of their own, but also a Royal Guard.

Meridia felt like she was in a dream from which she couldn't awaken as Laban spoke. The young widow would never know how bravely her husband had fought, or that he died trying to save their sons. After Laban finished his account, Meridia and Mitzy walked home in a silent daze. When they entered the cottage, Meridia burst into tears after seeing the bed in the corner Amalek had made as a wedding gift, the rocking chair he made after Joab was born, and the boots that would forever be empty. Although she was too young to fathom just how drastically her life had changed, Mitzy did understand her mother's tears and the ache she felt in her own heart. The child cried as she clung to her mother and the doll which would remain unfinished.

******

Days after relaying the tragic news to his fellow villagers, Laban and his mother departed for the castle where he would begin his new life as a Royal Guard. Like others, Meridia received correspondences offering condolence, but the most surprising one came from Amalek's aunt, Isabella. Still living at the castle, Isabella learned of her nephew's tragic death from Laban's mother upon her arrival. She also learned that Amalek was survived by a wife, who happened to be a wet nurse, and a young daughter. A master in the art of gossiping under the guise of concern, Isabella approached Queen Ashter with Meridia's sad story. She was careful to include that Meridia was a wet nurse knowing of the king and queen's desire to have children.

Isabella, therefore, was writing to inform Meridia of Queen Ashter's offer to make Meridia a personal attendant, and later serve as a wet nurse, should she accept. It was a generous offer including not only wages, but also private living quarters for her and Mitzy. Although Meridia hated to leave the farm, she knew it would be too difficult to manage alone. The young widow believed this was her best option to provide for Mitzy, and wrote back to accept. Meridia shared her decision with Mitzy that night before bed.

"Mitzy, my darling, I have some exciting news," she said trying to sound cheerful.

"What is it, Mama?" asked Mitzy absentmindedly while playing with Polly.

"You know how you've always wanted to see the castle?" continued Meridia.

"Yes," answered Mitzy.

"Well, by this time next week you shall. In fact, you shall see it every day because we are going to live there," Meridia announced. She held her breath and waited for Mitzy to respond. The child looked up with a bewildered expression and tilted her curly head to one side.

"But, how can we live at the castle if we live here?" she asked innocently. Meridia took a deep breath and continued.

"I'm afraid that without Papa and your brothers, there's too much work for just the two of us to stay," answered Meridia honestly. She choked back tears knowing the dream she and Amalek shared of one day owning this land had to die along with her husband.

"I can do the boys' chores," offered Mitzy enthusiastically. Her daughter's determined spirit reminded Meridia so much of Amalek.

"Yes, I'm certain you can, but don't you want to live in a castle?"," she said. Meridia wondered how she could possibly explain adult worries to a four-year-old child as she gazed into her daughter's eyes so full of innocence.

"I want to stay here… at home," answered Mitzy as her eyes filled with tears. Meridia scooped her daughter into her loving arms.

"I wish we could, Mitzy, and I don't expect you to understand, but we simply cannot. Your father's Aunt Isabella has arranged a position for me at the castle where I shall be close to you all day. We can make new friends and see new places. Besides, I hear the queen is as kind as she is beautiful," said Meridia.

"Can I bring Polly?" asked Mitzy as the child wiped her nose with her sleeve.

"Of course you can!" exclaimed Meridia brushing a tear from her daughter's cheek. It was the first time Mitzy had seen her mother smile in weeks, so the child quickly decided things would be fine as long as they were together. Mitzy also realized that if she was at the castle she could make sure the Royal Family knew about Orpheus and the Dragon Scroll.

******

There was much to do before Meridia and Mitzy were expected at the castle. Meridia gave away furniture which would no longer be needed, and said many goodbyes. On their last night at home, the rain tapped upon the roof as Meridia tucked Mitzy into bed. Meridia stroked her daughter's golden curls and marveled again at how much Mitzy looked like Amalek.

"Are they really gone, Mama?" asked Mitzy softly.

"Yes, darling, I'm afraid that Papa and your brothers are gone," answered Meridia sadly.

"But, who shall call me Miss Mit now?" asked Mitzy. A tear came to Meridia's eye at the thought of never again hearing the special name Amalek gave to Mitzy as a baby.

"Well, darling, I'm sure that someday you shall meet a wonderful man, and perhaps he shall call you Miss Mit," replied Meridia. Her answer brought Mitzy no solace, so Meridia offered something she knew Mitzy loved. "Would you like to hear the story of Orpheus and Natas?" Mitzy immediately curled into a tiny ball and pulled the wool blankets over her head. Seeing her daughter's reaction, Meridia regretted having asked.

"No, Mama, I don't ever want to hear that story again," whispered Mitzy.

"I understand, darling, try to get some sleep," replied Meridia kindly. She kissed Mitzy's forehead and walked across the empty cottage.

Meridia sat on the rocking chair in the darkness listening to the rain against the roof. She looked around in amazement at how large the cottage seemed now that it was empty, and how odd. Only a few weeks earlier every space had been filled with furniture, boots, piles of laundry, and a complete family. Yet, the emptiness of the cottage was nothing compared to the emptiness in Meridia's heart. Tears rolled down her pretty face as another wave of despair washed over the young widow. Meridia wanted to be strong for Mitzy's sake, but wondered if she could be. Suddenly, she remembered what Amalek always said about hope being the very thing which kept one from despair.

"A hope which is pure and true shall not disappoint," she whispered. Saying the words Orpheus spoke to Boaz all those years ago brought Meridia comfort and she brushed away her tears.

On the other side of the cottage, Mitzy lay awake feeling guilty and ashamed. Unable to stand it any longer, the child cried out.

"Mama!" she called. Mitzy listened to the soft click-click of her mother's shoes as they touched the wooden planks and thought how differently they sounded from her father's heavy boots. When Meridia sat on the edge of the bed, Mitzy sprang out from beneath her blankets and wrapped her arms around her mother's neck.

"Mama, I'm sorry for telling you that I didn't want to hear the story of Orpheus and Natas," she sobbed.

"Oh, darling, I understand," said Meridia. "The things which were special with someone can often be the most painful to remember once that person is gone, but that doesn't mean they should be forgotten," replied Meridia as she held Mitzy close.

"I know, Mama," continued Mitzy between sobs. "I promised Papa that I would always believe, and I do. I want to hear the story again, and again, and again!" Meridia looked into her daughter's crystal blue eyes and smiled.

"Very well, then I shall tell it to you as often as you would like. But, it's much too late now," she said. Knowing her mother was not as easily swayed as her father, Mitzy resigned to the next best thing.

"Can you at least sing me the lullaby?" she asked.

"Of course, but you must close your eyes," answered Meridia with a smile. Mitzy was happy to comply and drifted off to sleep to the sound of her mother's soft, soothing voice as she sang the familiar lullaby.

"Hush little one with eyes so bright,
Mama's gonna keep you safe through the night.
Hush little one with cheeks so red,
Mama's gonna cradle your sleepy little head.
Hush little one with curls of gold,
Mama's gonna tell you the legend of old.
Hush little one the scroll is true,
The kingdom shall be saved by someone like you..."

Dragon Scroll of Nepthali

Chapter 3

A New Life at the Castle

The next morning streaks of sunlight shot like arrows through the blanket of fog which lingered after the heavy rains from the night before. Meridia found the gloomy weather fitting as she and Mitzy said their final goodbyes and left their home for a new life at the castle.

The two walked in silence alongside the small cart carrying their few belongings. Meridia listened to the sound of leaves crunching beneath the wheels as she wondered what was in store for them, and if she was doing the right thing. The young widow took a deep breath and pressed ahead leading them by faded memory from the one time she and Amalek had gone to the castle, combined with the few directions Isabella had provided in her letter.

******

After walking for hours, they reached the top of a small hill where the fog suddenly lifted. Mitzy had a strange sense that she was finally home as she looked down at the quaint cottages surrounding the grand castle below. It was the most beautiful site Mitzy had ever seen with its stained glass windows and tall towers reaching like fingers into the sky. Yet for Meridia, the tranquil scene was not enough to prevent a fresh wave of uncertainty.

"You can do this...for Mitzy," she whispered to herself. Mother and daughter descended the hill and followed the well-trodden path leading to the castle's enormous outer gates. Although quite lovely, up close one could see the castle was in need of many repairs. Times were hard for everyone in the kingdom, even the Royal Family.

Mitzy felt smaller than usual as she and her mother entered the expansive inner courtyard covered with cobblestones. Street vendors were selling goods, Royal Guards rode on horseback, and children were chasing stray chickens in every direction. Mitzy held tightly to her mother's hand and to Polly. Everything about this place was different from her quiet life on the farm, but Mitzy instantly loved it.

"Isn't it wonderful, Mama!" she exclaimed.

"Yes, darling, I suppose it is. Now stay close so you don't get lost," warned Meridia.

They arrived at the Servant's Entrance where Isabella was to meet them, but no one was there. In desperation, Meridia looked around and happened to see Laban walking with a group of Royal Guards across the courtyard.

"Laban!" she called out. The young guard turned around in surprise to hear someone calling his name. Laban saw a woman waving and recognized Meridia as she and Mitzy approached.

A New Life at the Castle

"My lady, what are you doing here?" he asked nervously having never expected to see Meridia again. Her sad eyes filled his soul with guilt, and reminded Laban of his true cowardice behavior during the Bara attack.

"I can't tell you how wonderful it is to see a familiar face," said Meridia cheerfully. "Amalek's aunt found me a position as one of the queen's personal attendants, so it looks like we shall be neighbors again."

"I see…," replied Laban with little emotion. Meridia sensed his hesitation, but attributed it to his many responsibilities as a Royal Guard.

"We were supposed to meet Isabella at the Servant's Entrance, but as you can see she isn't there," explained Meridia as she pointed to the empty doorway. Her brown eyes pleaded for help and Laban cursed his predicament under his breath.

"I can see you get inside the castle, my lady, but I'm afraid I can do no more as I'm running late for a meeting," he said coldly.

"Thank you, Laban, I would be most appreciative," answered Meridia with relief.

Laban did as promised and escorted Meridia and Mitzy into the castle where he quickly excused himself. Meridia had no idea where to go, but started walking with the hope they would find Aunt Isabella, or perhaps another servant who could direct them to their living quarters. Mitzy hid behind her mother's long skirts as their every step echoed against the stone walls. The child stared in wonder at the enormous stained glass windows and tapestries hanging along the walls. Meridia paid no attention to the many luxuries as she soon feared they were hopelessly lost. They turned a corner and entered a long hallway lined on either side with portraits of Nepthali's former kings and queens. Halfway down, Mitzy let go of her mother's hand and stopped in front of one.

"Come along, Mitzy," said Meridia impatiently. She turned around and repeated herself, but Mitzy remained unmoved. Meridia walked back to her daughter then followed her gaze until both mother and daughter stood transfixed. Meridia felt as if she might faint looking at the portrait of a man with golden curly hair and eyes of crystal blue.

"Is that Papa?" whispered Mitzy. Meridia was speechless as she stared at the former king of Nepthali who looked exactly like her dead husband.

"May we be of any assistance?" asked a deep voice. Startled, Meridia turned around to see two ruggedly handsome Royal Guards walking towards them.

Ithamar and Uriah were on their way to the same meeting Laban had mentioned to Meridia when they came upon the newcomers. Ithamar was older than Uriah by nearly a decade; however, the two were the best of friends after going through training together. It had been difficult for Ithamar to change professions at his age, but Uriah encouraged him from the day they met to fulfill his dream of becoming a Royal Guard.

"May we be of assistance, my ladies?" asked Uriah.

A New Life at the Castle

"Oh yes, thank you, my name is Meridia and this is my daughter Mitzy. I'm Queen Ashter's new personal attendant. My late husband's aunt, Isabella, was supposed to meet us at the Servant's Entrance to show us our living quarters, but I'm afraid she wasn't there," she replied nervously.

"Pleased to meet you my ladies, Meridia and Mitzy. My name is Ithamar, and this is Uriah," said the guard who was only a few years older than Meridia with a smile and a bow. "We've been expecting your arrival. Your quarters are located near the kitchen where Cook bakes the finest delicacies in the kingdom. It would be our pleasure to escort you." Ithamar couldn't take his eyes off Meridia. There was something about the sadness in her eyes mixed with a sparkle from happier days that intrigued him. However, Uriah's elbow to his side quickly brought Ithamar's attention away from the maiden's eyes.

"Ordinarily, I'd agree with Ithamar, but I'm afraid we're late for a meeting," stated Uriah with a cockeyed brow.

"Oh yes, Laban mentioned it; I understand completely," replied Meridia.

"Did you say, Laban?" inquired Ithamar.

"Yes, he's from our village. I saw him in the courtyard and he was kind enough to show us inside the castle. But, he was late for a meeting so he couldn't show us to our quarters," explained Meridia. Ithamar and Uriah knew the new guard, and his braggadocios claim of being the lone survivor in a Bara attack. Neither believed Laban's tale, and if Ithamar had known the truth about his cowardice, he never would've allowed Laban to wear the uniform of

Dragon Scroll of Nepthali

a Royal Guard. "If you would be so kind as to tell me the way, I'm certain I can find it," continued Meridia.

"No one knows the castle better than Ithamar, not even the Royal Family," boasted Uriah with a grin. "You see, Ithamar comes from the family of Master Craftsmen who designed the castle. He nearly broke his poor mother's heart when he left the family trade to become a Royal Guard." Meridia smiled politely, but Ithamar sensed her disinterest.

"It's quite easy from here, my lady. Simply follow this hallway until it ends. When it does, you shall see a small staircase. Take it all the way down until you reach the lowest level of the castle. Once there, go straight past the main kitchen and your quarters shall be the first door on the right," explained Ithamar.

"Thank you very much," replied Meridia with a curtsy. Mitzy imitated her mother with a curtsy of her own producing broad smiles from the handsome guards. Meridia took hold of her daughter's hand and looked once more at the portrait. She started to walk away, but stopped and turned around. "Excuse me, but do either of you gentlemen happen to know who this is?" she asked.

"Yes, that's King Thaddeus, my lady," replied Ithamar. Mitzy's eyes grew wide.

"Mama, he was the king when Orpheus left!" exclaimed the child.

"Yes, dear, he was," whispered Meridia. "He looks just like my husband, I mean my late husband. He and my sons, Joab and Gideon, were recently killed by Bara soldiers." Although unnecessary, Meridia felt she owed the men an explanation for her inquiry. The two guards were silent as each realized this must be the same massacre about which Laban spoke of.

"You know about the great dragon Orpheus?" asked Uriah with surprise. He came from a family of Royal Guards who had passed down the story to him, but never imagined a child from the country would know of the good dragon.

"Papa used to tell me the story of Orpheus and Natas," replied Mitzy sadly. Uriah knelt down to make himself eye level with her.

"My father used to do the same with me. You're a very lucky young lady," he said sincerely. Mitzy smiled shyly at the handsome guard who spoke so kindly to her.

"Thank you again, gentlemen," said Meridia. She curtsied once more before leading her daughter down the hallway. When they were out of hearing distance, Uriah turned to his best friend.

"It's tragic to think that someone so young could be a widow. Do you think her husband and sons were killed in the same attack Laban claims to have been a hero?" he asked.

"Most likely since she said they come from the same village," replied Ithamar. He found himself uncharacteristically captivated by the beautiful new maidservant with the saddest eyes he'd ever seen.

"Come on, we're going to be late. I can't wait for this to be over so I can go home. Jenae finally decided on a name for the baby, but won't tell me until tonight," said Uriah as he slapped Ithamar heartily on the back.

"Speaking of your son, when are you going to let me see him?" asked Ithamar.

"Anytime, but tonight I'm riding Starlight home which means you'd never be able to keep up," teased Uriah. Starlight was the fastest horse in the kingdom, and the most stubborn. Because of this, the Queen Mother Lydia insisted the filly receive additional training before Prince Jeru be allowed to ride her. The former queen's brother had been killed in a riding accident as a child which left her with a permanent fear of horses.

"You? Do you know how many guards wanted to train that beauty?" exclaimed Ithamar.

"I sure do, but I guess I'm just the best," replied Uriah in jest.

"Only in your mind; but don't forget we're on King Shem's escort detail leaving first thing in the morning for Irvania," said Ithamar.

"Don't worry, I remember," laughed Uriah.

As the two friends continued on to their meeting, Ithamar's mind returned to the new maidservant with the saddest eyes and most beautiful face he'd ever seen.

******

Meridia and Mitzy reached the lowest level of the castle thanks to Ithamar's directions. When they passed the large kitchen, Mitzy looked with awe at the colorful fruits and vegetables hanging from large baskets as wonderful aromas floated into the hallway. It was almost magical until Mitzy suddenly saw a large figure standing in front of an equally large black pot which frightened her.

"Mama!" she cried. Meridia bent down and scooped Mitzy into her arms.

"I'm here, darling," she said hoping to conceal her own nervousness as they continued down the hallway in search of their living quarters.

They soon reached the first door on the right after passing the kitchen and Meridia slowly turned the knob. It opened to reveal a bare room with a fireplace against the back wall. As Meridia entered, the reality of this being permanent closed in on her like the darkness at the end of a sunny day. Mitzy followed her mother inside and walked across the open room to another door. She opened it and found a room with another fireplace and a small window.

"Look, Mama, we've a room just for sleeping!" she exclaimed. Before Meridia could respond, a deep voice called out from behind.

"I hear we're going to be neighbors," he said. Meridia and Mitzy turned around and saw the same large man who'd been standing over the black pot in the kitchen holding his hands behind his back. Mitzy ran to her mother's skirts in fear. The man wore a stained apron and stood six feet five inches tall with arms as thick as tree trunks, and head as bald as an egg.

"Greetings, my ladies," he said with a bow. "My name is Cork Xavier, but everyone calls me Cook. I wanted to introduce myself since we are going to be neighbors. Your cart is being unloaded as we speak, and your belongings shall be brought here directly. In the meantime, I was hoping you could do me a favor."

"Of course, what is it?" replied Meridia without hesitation.

"I seem to be in need of someone to look after this kitten," he said. Cook brought his arms around from behind his back and revealed a tiny ball of black fur curled up in his large hands. Mitzy squealed with delight and every fear she had of the extremely large man vanished. She learned at that moment that the only thing bigger than Cook's stomach was his heart.

"Thank you, Mr. Xavier, that's very kind of you. My name is Meridia, and this is my daughter Mitzy. Mitzy, what do you say to Mr. Xavier?" coached Meridia. Mitzy's golden curls bounced up and down as she skipped around the empty room cradling the soft kitten.

"Thank you…thank you, very much!" she exclaimed.

"You're most welcome, Mitzy, but please call me Cook. What are you going to call the kitten?" he asked. Mitzy held it out and examined the animal carefully.

"Ashes, because he looks like the ashes at the bottom of our fireplace at home," she answered. Meridia choked back tears as she placed her hand over her mouth to conceal her grief. Cook noticed and understood their heartache better than most. His wife and daughter had died years earlier after a terrible sickness swept through the kingdom.

A New Life at the Castle

"Ashes...I like it...I like it very much," he said with a broad smile. "I shall leave the two of you alone to get settled. But, if there's anything you need, you know where to find me." Cook left with a wave and Meridia felt forever indebted to their very large, and very kind, new neighbor.

******

Cook was as accurate about their belongings arriving as Ithamar had been with his directions. Within minutes, servants appeared carrying Meridia and Mitzy's few possessions. Meridia started to unpack hoping to make this strange new place feel more like home. Meanwhile, Mitzy played quietly with Ashes and Polly in the corner.

"Well, there you are!" cried a high-pitched, shrilly voice. Mitzy looked up and saw a slender old woman with the tightest bun the child had ever seen. Isabella's greeting startled everyone, but none more than Ashes who sprinted from the room. Mitzy followed after her frightened kitten as both disappeared before Meridia ever saw them go.

Mitzy ran past the kitchen and up the same flight of stairs she and her mother had taken earlier in pursuit of Ashes. Their chase continued down long hallways and up more stairs until the exhausted kitten finally stopped in front of a partially opened door.

"Now I've got you," said Mitzy with a smile. She bent down to pick up the kitten, but stopped when she saw rays of sunlight coming in from behind the door. Curious, the child pushed on it then stared in wonder at the most enchanting place Mitzy had ever seen. There were endless rows of exotic flowers with intoxicating aromas and brilliant colors. She slowly walked into the gardens King

Shem had made for Queen Ashter as a wedding gift and was so captivated by its beauty that Mitzy forgot all about the wayward kitten.

******

Up in the east wing of the castle, six-year-old Prince Roffius and sixteen-year-old Prince Jeru were having an adventure of their own. Although ten years spanned their ages, the royal brothers were very close. Naturally, little Roffius idolized his brother and wanted to be just like him. Their current adventure was really more of a quest to find a birthday present for Kleiko, the Chief Royal Scribe and descendant of Carmi. Prince Jeru knew how much Kleiko loved the ancient writings of Nepthali, but the old scribe had difficulty walking up the narrow staircase leading to the Room of the Ancients where they were stored. Therefore, Jeru decided to retrieve one as a gift for Kleiko's seventy-fifth birthday.

"Hurry up, Ro! You're as slow as Kleiko," teased Jeru.

"I'm right behind you, Brother," panted Ro. The little prince tried to gain some ground after watching his brother disappear around a corner. When he rounded the same corner, however, Ro hit something and found himself flat on his back. He looked up to see Mezrah, Lott, and Narok scowling down at him. Each man alone was frightening enough, but to see them together terrified the little prince.

Lott was the eldest among them and a direct descendant of Ganu. Along with a legacy of deceit, the evil scribe of long ago had passed down what little knowledge he possessed of the Dragon Scroll. Because of this, Lott knew of the ancient scroll and that the birth of twins to the

Royal Family was the foretelling sign for Natas' awakening. Like his treasonous ancestor, Lott was a masterful manipulator and equally skilled liar who served as a Royal Scribe by day and conspired with the Bara to overtake the throne by night. Lott was short and slender which made his unusually large nose even more pronounced; especially against his pale skin and thinning grey hair. Lott had waited a lifetime for the Royal Family to produce twins, but sensed his patience would soon pay off with King Shem's recent wedding to Ashter.

Unlike his father Lott, seventeen-year-old Narok was blessed with a tall frame and strikingly handsome features. Narok was a brilliant young man well on his way to continuing the family tradition of becoming a Royal Scribe, and in diplomacy matters with the Bara. He possessed extraordinary skills with a cat o'nine tails given to him by his father as a gift after the mysterious death of Narok's mother when the lad was a mere nine-years-old. Servants within the castle, however, claimed the only mystery surrounding his mother's death was Lott not being in the dungeon for it. Narok's only weakness, aside from his pride, was Queen Ashter. He attempted to win the heart of the renowned beauty with black hair and green eyes prior to her recent marriage to King Shem but, title or no title, Ashter's heart belonged only to Shem.

Mezrah was the bastard son between Lott's father and a peasant woman. His illegitimacy made the thirty-four-year old exempt from Natas' promise to be part of a new royal bloodline as long as Lott and Narok were alive. Mezrah had a stocky frame, bulging eyes, and hair as unmanageable as his personality. He was denied an apprenticeship to become a Royal Scribe because of his unruly behavior, so he settled on becoming a Royal Guard.

Mezrah's heart was saturated with jealousy, and the mutual hatred he and Lott shared for one another was the only thing the half-brothers agreed upon. Deception and mischief followed Mezrah, Lott, and Narok as closely as a shadow, and young Prince Roffius' eyes grew wide with fear when Mezrah lifted him by the shirt.

"Watch where you're going, you little brat!" scolded the unconventional guard. At that moment, Jeru reappeared from around the corner.

"Unhand him!" shouted the prince with regal authority. Lott elbowed Mezrah and the bulgy-eyed man released the boy.

"Excuse him, Your Majesties, I'm afraid that my half-brother's ignorance caused him to mistaken Prince Roffius for the cobbler's son accused of stealing bread," lied Lott hoping to diffuse Jeru's anger.

"As you can see, my brother is most certainly not the cobbler's son!" exclaimed Jeru. "Are you all right, Ro?"

"I'm fine," answered Roffius feeling more embarrassed than hurt as Jeru straightened his brother's shirt.

"My, my; the two of you seem to be in quite a hurry. I hope nothing's the matter," continued Lott with more curiosity than concern.

"We're merely having a little race. Come along, Ro, let's go," said Jeru while grabbing hold of his brother's hand.

A New Life at the Castle

"That sounds like fun, perhaps Narok can join you?" offered Lott. Narok shot his father a glare which said he would do no such thing.

"No, we're quite fine," replied Jeru firmly.

"Very well," answered Lott.

"You may leave us now," continued Jeru. The three bowed out of duty rather than respect as Jeru and Narok locked eyes. Jeru despised Narok for many reasons, but none more than Narok's blatant desire for his sister-in-law. Jeru promised himself that when he turned eighteen and became Captain of the Royal Guards he would find a way to lock these three in the dungeon. Little Prince Roffius tugged on his brother's pant leg as they started down the hallway.

"Why did you tell them we were playing tag? I thought we were going to the Royal Library to find a gift for Kleiko," he said preferring to play tag than go to the library.

"It's none of their business where we're going," replied Jeru sharply. He and Ro disappeared around the corner as the men watched them go.

"King Shem needs to make use of his beautiful queen," Lott said crudely.

"What do you mean?" asked Narok.

"When the queen conceives, there shall be the possibility of twins, and the birth of twins marks the appointed time for Natas to awaken. Once that happens, the castle shall finally be ours," stated Lott with a sinister grin.

Dragon Scroll of Nepthali

******

Jeru was the first to reach the Royal Library where streaks of sunlight magically transformed into brilliant lines of color as they passed through the large stained glass windows. He took the narrow steps two at a time until he reached the door to the Room of the Ancients.

"Come on, Ro, we don't have all day," urged Jeru.

"I'm coming!" called Roffius as he hurried up the last few steps.

The boys entered the small room where the walls were lined with old books. Jeru picked up one after the other and gently flipped through their tattered pages. Roffius stayed close to his brother since the room was ordinarily off limits to the little prince. He didn't like the musty smell, or how old everything was, but Roffius imitated the careful way Jeru handled the books.

"What about this one?" asked Roffius while struggling to lift a large book.

"Careful, Ro, these aren't your nursery rhymes; they're important," scolded Jeru. He was beginning to wish he hadn't taken Ro along when suddenly, a mouse jumped down from a shelf and landed on the open page.

"Aaahh!" yelled Jeru. He threw the book and it smashed against the wall.

"I thought you said to be careful with these," laughed Roffius.

"It was a mouse…," started Jeru. However, he stopped in mid-sentence when the opposite wall slowly started to move. The book had hit a stone which acted like a switch to open a secret door. Boards creaked and puffs of dust floated up as the door slowly swung inwards.

"You're in trouble now," whispered Roffius.

"Only if you tell someone," threatened Jeru. "Wait here while I see where this goes."

"I don't want to stay here alone," whined Ro. Jeru knew he shouldn't leave his brother, but he also knew that taking Roffius could be even worse. Jeru cleverly thought of a way to keep his little brother out of danger without hurting his feelings.

"You can't come because I need you to stand guard," he explained. This sounded very important to Roffius so he happily took his post in the doorway. Jeru grabbed a torch from along the wall before entering the dark tunnel then parted ways with Roffius.

After a short walk, Jeru discovered a small door. It opened to expose a room where the air was damp and smelled of stale paper. Quite by accident, Jeru had discovered the temporary storage room built after The Great Fire. Jeru held the torch high and saw books and scrolls covered with thick layers of dust. He gently slid his fingertips across the old parchments but stopped when he got to a scroll having an elaborate casing with intricate markings. Jeru carefully pulled it out from the pile thinking it would be the perfect gift for Kleiko. He tucked the ornate scroll into his vest and turned to leave. But as he did, another scroll fell from the top of the pile and landed at Jeru's feet. He picked up the simple scroll intending to return it to the top of the pile, but something told Jeru that this was the gift for Kleiko.

"Looks like you fell at the right time," he said aloud. Jeru exchanged the decorative scroll in his vest for the simple one before hurrying back to Ro.

"Come on, I found what we came for," he declared as he emerged from the dark tunnel. The little prince followed after his brother, happy to be leaving the library.

The boys elbowed one another as they approached Kleiko's study with each wanting to be the first one the old scribe saw.

"Happy Birthday Kleiko!" they exclaimed in unison as they entered. Kleiko's wrinkled face looked up in surprise from behind his large desk cluttered with books and maps. The wise scribe immediately burst into a smile after recognizing his royal guests.

"Your Majesties, how kind of you to remember an old man on his birthday!" he said with genuine pleasure.

"We found a present for you in a secret room!" announced Roffius.

"A secret room?" repeated Kleiko, "My, that sounds intriguing!"

"I know how much you love the old writings, so we went to the Room of the Ancients. While we were there, we discovered a secret door which led to another room where I found this," explained Jeru as he produced the scroll from his vest.

"Now, let's see what we have here," said Kleiko. The old scribe took the scroll and his aged fingers slowly unrolled it. When he did, his eyes grew wide with disbelief and his hands began to tremble. "The Dragon Scroll…"

"Have you seen this scroll before?" asked Jeru with a mixture of surprise and disappointment.

"No, Your Majesty, and never in my wildest dreams did I think I would see it with my own eyes. This is the Dragon Scroll written by Orpheus, a Dragon Ruler of long ago," answered Kleiko with reverence. "I thought it was destroyed in The Great Fire. Where did you say you found it?"

"There was a mouse, so Jeru threw a book and the wall opened up. He went into the tunnel and found a secret room!" exclaimed little Roffius. Kleiko nodded, and thought this explained why no one had seen the Dragon Scroll for generations.

"Did you say something about a fire?" asked Prince Jeru.

"Tell us more," begged Prince Roffius happy to at last hear something that sounded interesting.

"Long, long ago there was a great fire which nearly destroyed the castle. Many people died, including a relative of mine; and many precious documents, including this one, were presumed lost. You boys have done our kingdom a great service by finding it," said the old scribe.

"What makes this scroll so special, Kleiko?" asked Jeru.

"My dear Prince Jeru, the Dragon Scroll contains the very thing which separates mankind from the beast," answered Kleiko while reaching for his walking staff.

"What's that?" pressed Jeru.

"Hope…" replied the old scribe. "Now if you'll excuse me, Your Majesties, I must take this to your brother, the king."

Kleiko left them and walked at an unusually brisk pace for the Throne Room. As he went, the old scribe remembered the warning which had been passed down for generations within his family that Ganu and his descendants must never gain access to the Dragon Scroll lest the power it contains be used for evil purposes. Kleiko knew this meant that Lott and Narok must never be allowed to study the ancient scroll, and sighed with relief at the good fortune of Prince Jeru and Prince Roffius being the ones who found the precious scroll. Lost in his thoughts, the old scribe failed to notice that he was being followed.

******

Lott remained unseen but positioned himself within hearing distance when Kleiko entered the Throne Room. Kleiko found King Shem with the queen and respectfully waited in the corner as he watched the two interact. Kleiko had known Shem since the king was a baby and approved wholeheartedly of Shem's choice in a wife. Ashter's stunning beauty was renowned throughout the kingdom; however of greater importance to Kleiko was her inner beauty. Ashter was genuinely kind to everyone, regardless of rank or pedigree, and possessed a level of compassion and understanding rarely found in those of privilege. Shem and Ashter made a striking couple with her beauty and his distinguished features. When King Shem looked up, he smiled when he saw the old scribe standing in the corner.

"Kleiko, to what do I owe this honor?" asked the ruler of Nepthali light-heartedly.

"Forgive my intrusion, Your Majesty, but I must speak with you privately," replied the Chief Royal Scribe with a bow.

"Of course," said King Shem as he turned to his wife. "My dear, please excuse us."

"Certainly, but don't keep him too long, Kleiko. The king is leaving first thing in the morning for Irvania, therefore, he must retire early tonight," stated Queen Ashter with a beautiful smile.

"As you wish, My Queen," said Kleiko. He bowed again as she passed leaving the men alone.

"My King, your brothers have made a great discovery," proclaimed the old scribe. King Shem was intrigued by the look of absolute delight on Kleiko's face as he produced a scroll from beneath his long robe.

"Tell me, what sort of discovery have Jeru and Roffius made which brings you such joy?" asked King Shem as he reached for the scroll.

"They've found the Dragon Scroll, Your Majesty," answered Kleiko reverently. The king looked at him with surprise, and suddenly felt unworthy to be holding the scroll.

"The one written by the ancient Dragon Ruler?" he asked.

"Yes, My King," answered Kleiko. "It is believed to possess great power." Shem immediately understood the importance of such a discovery as he handed the scroll back to Kleiko.

"I am leaving in the morning for Irvania as the queen mentioned, however, upon my return I wish for you to teach me everything you know about this scroll," instructed the king.

"Of course, Your Highness, it shall be an honor," replied the old scribe.

From his vantage point, Lott quivered with excitement, for he too, believed the Dragon Scroll had been lost in The Great Fire. Lott wanted nothing more than to obtain its power and quickly disappeared to devise a plan to get the scroll out of the hands of the Chief Royal Scribe.

******

In the kitchen, Cook pulled out a fresh batch of cookies from the large brick oven to welcome Meridia and Mitzy.

"My, it smells wonderful in here," said a familiar voice. Cook turned around and saw the Queen Mother Lydia accompanied by Prince Roffius. The servants nervously bowed and curtsied before their unexpected royal guests.

"Your Majesties, my apologies I didn't see you," said Cook. He quickly bowed and brushed off a layer of flour from his apron.

******

As the sun dropped lower in the horizon, Mitzy suddenly realized that she didn't remember the way back to her mother. The child reached into her pocket for Polly but the doll was on the floor where Mitzy had dropped her when she chased after Ashes. Feeling frightened and alone, Mitzy sat beside a beautiful pink rose bush and started to cry. She cried for what seemed a very long time until suddenly, Mitzy felt a gentle touch on her shoulder. She looked up and saw a little boy two years older than she offering her a cookie. Mitzy wiped her nose and slowly reached for the delicacy. As she took the cookie, the boy extended his other hand and helped Mitzy to her feet.

"You must be new here," he said. Mitzy nodded in reply as she took a bite. "Come with me, I shall take you back to the kitchen where we can have another cookie." As Mitzy followed the boy, she noticed that he walked with a confidence and certainty similar to her father. "What's your name?" asked the boy casually.

"Mitzy," she replied.

"It's nice to meet you, Miss Mit. My name's Roffius, but my brother calls me Ro," stated the young prince. Mitzy stopped and looked at him in disbelief. "Is something the matter?" Mitzy hadn't been called by that name since her father died. Her cheeks flushed and Mitzy suddenly felt nervous and shy as she slowly shook her head.

When they entered the kitchen, Mitzy saw her distraught mother talking with Cook. The large man was doing his best to console his new neighbor when he saw the children walk in. He smiled and whispered something to Meridia who turned around and burst into tears at the sight of Mitzy.

"Where have you been? And why did you run off without telling me?" cried Meridia. She rushed over to her daughter and scooped Mitzy into her arms.

"I'm sorry, Mama," replied Mitzy. "I was in the most wonderful place, and I wanted to find you but I didn't remember the way until Ro helped me." Meridia placed Mitzy down and the child gestured to the little boy. As she did, Meridia noticed that all of the other servants were bowing. She looked at Cook who motioned for Meridia to do the same. Meridia knew at once that the boy was royalty and immediately curtsied, which Mitzy again imitated.

"Forgive me, My Prince, I didn't know," explained Meridia nervously. "Thank you for the safe return of my daughter." Although accustomed to such formalities, Prince Roffius felt them unnecessary from Mitzy.

"The pleasure was all mine," he replied honestly. "I happened to be playing in the Royal Gardens when I heard someone crying. That's when I found Miss Mit beneath Mother's favorite rose bush." Cook tried not to laugh at the boy's formal speech, but Meridia stared in disbelief just as Mitzy had after hearing the endearing nickname.

"Cook, I promised Miss Mit another cookie upon our arrival at the kitchen. I fear I'd be a terrible disappointment to Father if I went back on my word," continued little Ro in his most dignified manner.

"Of course, My Prince," replied Cook with a wink. He gathered a fresh plate of cookies and handed it to Roffius. The boy took two of the baked goods then offered the largest to Mitzy. As she reached for the cookie, Mitzy looked into his hazel eyes and knew that her heart would forever belong to Ro.

Chapter 4

Treacherous Plans

Uriah arrived at his cottage nestled in the village just outside the castle wall feeling very troubled. His wife Jenae greeted him at the door excited to tell him the name she had chosen for their infant son. However, Jenae stopped herself after noticing her husband's unusually pensive expression.

"Uriah, what's wrong? You look as if the fate of the kingdom was on your shoulders," she said with concern while handing Baby Obed to their oldest daughter. Their nine-year-old son Aykin leaned over the loft railing when he heard his father's voice to see his reaction to the baby's name. Yet like his mother, Aykin saw at once that something was troubling his father.

"Division and mistrust continue to build amongst the guards, as do the rumors surrounding Lott. They say he's promising riches and position to those who agree to conspire against the king," whispered Uriah as he ran his fingers through his dark hair.

"You've heard those rumors for years, Uriah. I'm certain there's nothing to worry about," replied Jenae as she moved a strand of brown hair that had come loose from her long braid.

"Perhaps, but this time feels different," continued Uriah. "On my way to fetch the carrots and apples for Starlight from the kitchen, I overheard voices in the Throne Room."

"What's so unusual about that?" asked Jenae.

"Typically nothing, but because I'm on the detail traveling with the king to Irvania in the morning I knew he had retired for the night," explained Uriah looking increasingly anxious. "When I went to investigate, I found Narok seated upon the throne as Lott boasted that they would soon rule the kingdom using the power within the Dragon Scroll." The color left Jenae's cheeks and Aykin leaned further over the railing at the mention of the ancient scroll.

"That's impossible!" exclaimed his wife as the guard paced the room. "The scroll was lost in The Great Fire."

"I thought so as well, but apparently Prince Jeru and Prince Roffius found it today," explained Uriah.

"I can't believe it. What did you do?" asked Jenae.

"I panicked and ran away before they saw me," he confessed with shame. Jenae was now as disturbed as her husband.

"You must return to the castle at once to warn the king," she urged him. Although they spoke in hushed voices, Aykin sensed something was terribly wrong.

Treacherous Plans

"I shall never get an audience with the king at this hour with my rank," snapped Uriah.

"What about the Chief Royal Scribe, can you tell him?" pressed Jenae. Uriah wondered why he hadn't thought of Kleiko, and smiled knowing how lucky he was to have such a beautiful and clever wife.

"That's a wonderful idea, Jenae!" he exclaimed.

"Please be careful, Uriah," begged Jenae. He embraced his wife and looked up to see Aykin leaning against the loft railing. The two looked more like brothers, and Aykin dreamed of becoming a Royal Guard one day just like his father. The boy started to speak, but Uriah turned and ran out the front door. Baby Obed started to cry as it shut and Aykin crawled out the loft window. He grabbed hold of the vine-covered wall and scrambled down but not in time to speak with his father before he sped past on Starlight.

"Father!" he yelled. "Father!"

Aykin chased after them, but all that remained was a cloud of dust. Instead of going back inside, the lad decided to wait for his father's return in the tall oak tree in front of their cottage.

******

Uriah reached the castle in record time thanks to Starlight's unparalleled speed. The guard was intent on finding Kleiko as quickly as possible, and nearly jumped out of his skin when someone called out from behind. Uriah turned around with his hand on his hilt.

"Ithamar, you scared me!" exclaimed Uriah as he released his hand from his weapon.

"You didn't you come back just to tell me the baby's name, did you?" teased Ithamar.

"What? No, I came to find Kleiko," replied Uriah. Ithamar found his friend's answer intriguing, especially since Uriah seemed unusually nervous.

"It must be of great importance for you to leave Jenae and the kids," he continued with a raised brow. Ithamar was like a bloodhound once he suspected something was amiss and Uriah knew it. So to protect his friend from getting involved in something potentially dangerous, Uriah lied.

"Jenae and I had a little disagreement and I was hoping Kleiko could settle it; otherwise I may have to sleep in the barn," he said with a nervous laugh. Although Ithamar thought this an odd reason, the thought of Uriah lying to him never crossed his mind.

"If you say so, but it seems this could've waited until morning," stated Ithamar plainly.

"You shall understand one day when the right woman comes along," answered Uriah.

"I don't think so," replied Ithamar shaking his head.

"Who are you trying to fool? I saw the way you looked at that maidservant today," teased Uriah. Ithamar now appeared nervous.

"You mean Meridia?" he asked casually.

"Oh, so you remember her name?" chuckled Uriah.

Treacherous Plans

"A gentleman always remembers the name of a beautiful woman," answered Ithamar with a grin. Until that afternoon, his focus had strictly been on his duties with no time for the distractions which naturally accompanied a woman. However, since meeting Meridia, Ithamar could think of nothing else. "Aren't you supposed to be looking for Kleiko?" he asked to change the subject.

"Yeah…sure…see you tomorrow," answered Uriah pensively. He walked away promising himself that he would explain everything to Ithamar in the morning. Ithamar watched his friend disappear and shook his head at the strange things a man was willing to do for the woman he loved.

******

Kleiko sat at his desk in the highest room of the east tower feeling like a child again as he unrolled the Dragon Scroll with great anticipation.

"I have much to learn from you, Orpheus," he said. But as Kleiko read, his expectations of finding hope were dashed. The scroll read just as Natas had intended of a list of horrific things starting with Orpheus' exile, and ending with Natas' promise to kill the established royal bloodline so he could begin a new one. The scribe's aged hands trembled as Kleiko sat in stunned silence before he placed the Dragon Scroll down. He wondered how this could be the same parchment his family had spoken of with such joy, but his thoughts were interrupted when Lott suddenly appeared in the doorway.

"The king has requested your presence in the Throne Room," announced the descendant of Ganu.

"At this hour? Whatever for?" asked Kleiko. He found the request strange knowing that King Shem had retired for the night.

"I'm merely the messenger, Your Grace," replied Lott as he removed his headpiece and approached his superior. Lott quickly scanned over the maps and scrolls scattered across Kleiko's desk for the Dragon Scroll, and smiled slyly when he saw it resting against Kleiko's fingertips. "He is waiting for you in the Throne Room," continued Lott. As he spoke, Lott casually dropped his headpiece behind a chair cluttered with more books and scrolls.

"Very well," answered Kleiko. He would never refuse an order from his king, so Kleiko grabbed his walking staff and followed after Lott in his typically slow pace. As they neared the staircase, Lott suddenly stopped.

"Forgive me, Master, but I left my headpiece in your study. As you know, I am forbidden to be seen by the king without it, therefore, I shall retrieve it and catch up with you shortly," stated the deceitful scribe. Kleiko absentmindedly agreed and continued towards the Throne Room forgetting about the Dragon Scroll lying on his desk, and the ancient warning.

******

The descendant of Ganu hurried down the long hallway and found Mezrah waiting outside of Kleiko's study as expected.

"Keep watch and make sure he doesn't return until I've retrieved the scroll," ordered Lott. Mezrah nodded and walked around the corner where he would be unseen yet could easily see if anyone was coming. Lott slipped inside the study and picked up his headpiece before going to the desk for the Dragon Scroll. With his back to the door, Lott froze in place when the voice spoke behind him.

"Your Grace, may I have a word?" asked Uriah assuming the man behind the desk was the Chief Royal Scribe. "I apologize for my unexpected visit at this late hour, but my wife encouraged me to come. I overheard something very troubling in…" But Uriah stopped in mid-sentence as Lott turned around. "Excuse me, I thought you were Kleiko. Is he here?" Beads of sweat formed on the young man's forehead and his heart beat wildly as Uriah took a step back. Lott put down the Dragon Scroll and casually walked around the large desk. He knew far too well of Mezrah's incompetence, but even he had to have seen Uriah enter the study. Therefore, Lott sought to stall the young guard until his half-brother arrived.

"I'm afraid you just missed him. Perhaps, I may be of assistance," offered Lott. "You mentioned something about a troublesome conversation, wasn't it?"

"It can wait until morning," answered Uriah firmly. The guard turned to leave, but found himself face-to-face with Mezrah.

"What's your hurry, Uriah?" sneered Mezrah. The two locked eyes briefly before Uriah shoved Mezrah aside and ran towards the door. Lott was prepared for such a move and swiftly struck Uriah on the back of the head with a candlestick. Uriah dropped to the floor unconscious.

"He knows too much, dispose of him," said Lott coldly.

Mezrah despised his subservient role to his half-brother, yet his fear of the Bara soldiers compelled Mezrah to comply every time. As he dutifully dragged the young guard across the room, Uriah started to regain consciousness. Unfortunately, Uriah was unable to do so in time to defend himself when Mezrah picked him up and threw the guard out the tower window. As he fell, Uriah's last thoughts were of his wife, his children, and the king he had failed to protect. Lott looked out the window while Mezrah wiped his hands as if soiled with physical evidence of the murder he'd just committed.

"His family must be killed as well," said Lott.

******

Ithamar had just stepped outside the castle on his way to the Guard's Quarters when a body suddenly fell from the sky. He jumped over the waist-high wall and ran down the ravine to investigate. To his horror, Ithamar found Uriah's lifeless body lying on the jagged rocks. Although the sight was nauseating, the soldier composed himself and signaled the alarm. Within minutes, a flood of Royal Guards swarmed the area with others ensuring the safety of the Royal Family. Amidst the chaos, Ithamar remembered what Uriah had said about being on his way to speak with Kleiko and immediately raced inside the castle to find the Chief Royal Scribe.

******

Ithamar was surprised to find two men standing at the open window when he arrived in the east tower at Kleiko's study.

Treacherous Plans

"What's going on here?" he demanded. Lott turned around with equal surprise to see the impressive guard, especially since he hadn't yet retrieved the Dragon Scroll. Since lies came as easily as breathing for Lott, it took little effort on his part to create one which explained his and Mezrah's presence.

"I don't know what came over him...he seemed to have such promise," wailed the scribe while choking back fake tears.

"What do you mean?" asked Ithamar.

"I returned for my headpiece when Uriah suddenly appeared insisting that he speak with Kleiko. I told him that Kleiko had just left and the young man went mad. He forced his way in to see for himself while rambling on about not being able to live a lie anymore," said the crafty scribe.

"What are you talking about?" pressed Ithamar.

"It was dreadful I tell you; Uriah confessed his plot to assassinate the king! I tried to reason with him, but he jumped out the window before I could stop him," cried Lott.

"No, it can't be true...not Uriah," whispered Ithamar. He heard everything that Lott had said, but none of it made sense. Admittedly, Uriah had acted strangely when Ithamar saw him earlier, but not plotting-to-kill-the-king kind of strange. Ithamar's gut told him that Uriah had stumbled upon something treacherous which Lott didn't want Uriah to share with Kleiko, or anyone else. Just then, King Shem burst into the study surrounded by Royal Guards.

"What happened? Is it true that one of my guards has died?" he demanded. Ithamar bowed at once in the presence of his king.

"Yes, Your Majesty, a most valiant man has died," he said sadly. But Lott quickly stepped forward to repeat his false account.

"O King, Uriah may have once been the man whom Ithamar described, however, that was not the man I saw moments ago. Uriah intended to take your life, but I thwarted his evil plan," boasted Lott.

"It's true, Your Majesty, I heard it as well," added Mezrah. Although Ithamar had no proof to discredit their claims, he refused to remain silent.

"With all due respect, My King, I believe a complete investigation is warranted," he said.

Seconds passed like hours as the wise king considered Lott's damning account. The shifty scribe became increasingly anxious to get away in order to kill Uriah's family, therefore, he formulated a plausible excuse to allow his leave.

"There's something else, Your Majesty," said Lott. "Before Uriah took his life, he mentioned his family whom I now fear shall be in great danger when the town's people discover that a traitor was living among them. Since I was the last to see him alive, I beg Your Majesty's permission to allow me and Mezrah to go at once to ensure their safety." Ithamar was surprised by such an offer coming from the selfish man, and became increasingly suspect of Lott's true intentions. However, before the guard could press the matter, the king spoke.

Treacherous Plans

"My heart goes out to the innocent who have been placed in harm's way because of Uriah's foolish choices, and I agree it is our duty to protect them. Lott, you may take Mezrah with a squadron of Royal Guards to retrieve the family and bring them back to the castle," proclaimed King Shem.

"Certainly, Your Majesty," replied Lott with a shrewd smile. He and Mezrah bowed and left at once to find Laban and a handful of other guards whose allegiance lay with Lott. But in his haste to go, Lott left the Dragon Scroll on Kleiko's desk.

******

Ithamar remained in the study to wait for Kleiko after the king was escorted back to his chambers. The devastated guard walked to the window and looked into the night sky. He didn't believe a word of Lott's account, and vowed to discover the truth.

"My boy, what has happened? Is it true that a guard has died tonight?" asked the visibly shaken Chief Royal Scribe as he entered the study. Ithamar spun around and thought Kleiko looked as pale as Uriah had when Ithamar last saw his friend alive.

"Yes, Your Grace, it was my close friend, Uriah. I'm here because he told me that he had returned to the castle to speak with you," explained Ithamar.

"Me? Whatever for?" asked Kleiko.

"He said it was something about needing your help to settle a disagreement he and his wife were having, but I don't believe that was all," admitted Ithamar.

"What do you mean, my boy?" asked the old scribe.

"I'm not sure, but if you don't mind my asking, where were you?" asked Ithamar.

"Lott arrived not long ago with word that I'd been summoned to the Throne Room by the king. I thought the request unusual since King Shem had retired for the night, but I left at once. However, when I arrived, the Throne Room was empty," answered Kleiko. His statement confirmed Ithamar's suspicion that Lott was lying, but the guard still needed solid evidence.

"Did you say Lott told you to go to the Throne Room?" repeated Ithamar.

"Yes," answered Kleiko.

"Why did he not accompany you there?" pressed Ithamar.

"He did, that is until he remembered that he'd left his headpiece in my study. We parted company before we reached the staircase so he could retrieve it," replied the old scribe before he suddenly looked ill. "Oh no..."

"What is it?" asked Ithamar. Kleiko was silent as he walked at an unusually quickened pace to his desk. When he saw the Dragon Scroll lying where he had left it, Kleiko sighed with relief.

"I feared Lott may have taken this," he said as he held the precious scroll.

"What's so special about that scroll?" asked Ithamar.

Treacherous Plans

"This scroll was written by Orpheus, the great Dragon Ruler of long ago. It was given to my ancestor with the warning to keep it from Ganu and his descendants lest they obtain the scroll's power," explained Kleiko. Ithamar pursed his lips sensing his hunch about Uriah having stumbled onto something big was right. The guard knew he must speak with Lott before the scribe left for Uriah's.

"If you'll excuse me, Your Grace," said Ithamar with a bow before running out the door.

******

Ithamar reached the courtyard in time to see Lott and Mezrah speed past on horseback accompanied by a squadron of Ithamar's least favorite guards, including Laban. Ithamar suddenly feared that Jenae and the children were in greater danger with these men than a mob of angry villagers. He sprinted toward the stables, but was stopped by his commanding officer.

"Where do you think you're going? I need you back at the murder scene," said the man.

"But Sir," begged Ithamar, "I must get to Uriah's home. I fear his family may be in grave danger."

"Which is why a squadron has just left," said the commander. "Look Ithamar, I know you and Uriah were close, which is why I need you here. You and I both know Lott's story is hogwash, so get out there and find the truth!" Unable to disobey a direct order, Ithamar reasoned that although Lott and Mezrah were unscrupulous they would never harm a woman and children.

"Yes, Sir," replied the dutiful guard.

Ithamar's only consolation as he made his way back to the base of the tower was that he would check on Jenae and the children first thing in the morning. He also planned to have a very serious discussion with Lott as soon as the cunning scribe returned.

******

From their window in the west wing, Prince Jeru and Prince Roffius watched the squadron of Royal Guards speed away on horseback.

"Where do you suppose they're going in such a hurry?" asked little Roffius.

"I'm not sure, but I saw Lott and Mezrah among them which means trouble," replied Jeru.

******

With a fire crackling in the fireplace of their cozy new living quarters, Meridia searched for the perfect place to put the rocking chair. Mitzy was sound asleep after her adventure in the Royal Gardens, and Ashes had returned and was curled up beside the child. But the tranquil scene was disrupted when Cook burst into the room.

"Have you heard the news?" he shouted.

"Ssshhh! Mitzy's sleeping. What news? What's the matter?" asked Meridia with concern.

"A Royal Guard is dead!" exclaimed the large man.

"How terrible!" gasped Meridia.

Treacherous Plans

"Yes, I thought Uriah was a respectable family man, but they say he was plotting to kill the king," continued Cook.

"Did you say Uriah? He was one of the guards who helped us this afternoon," said Meridia in disbelief. "Is the king safe?"

"Yes, he's fine, but the queen is very upset. King Shem is worried about her and has ordered for all of her handmaidens to attend to her at once," reported Cook. Just then, Mitzy emerged from the bedroom rubbing her sleepy eyes.

"What's going on, Mama?" she asked with a yawn. Meridia scooped her daughter into her arms.

"There's been an accident, darling, and I must go to the Queen's Chamber," she said.

"Please don't go, Mama," cried Mitzy. Cook could see the look of distress on Meridia's face and quickly offered to help.

"If it's all right with your mother, I could use an extra pair of hands in the kitchen," he said with a wink. Meridia felt a wave of relieve at his kind offer.

"That would be wonderful, as long as she's back in bed before long," she said. Cook lifted Mitzy out of Meridia's arms and placed her atop his broad shoulders.

"Of course; now, my lady, let's roll some dough," he said. Mitzy squealed with delight as her golden curls bounced up and down with each of the large man's steps.

******

Aykin drifted in and out of sleep in the oak tree waiting for his father's return. With his head rested against one of the large limbs, the boy was startled by vibrations from the approaching horses. He sat upright with a burst of energy thinking his father had finally returned, but soon realized he was wrong. A trail of Royal Guards soon appeared led by Mezrah and Lott. The lad easily recognized the half-brothers from his numerous trips to the castle with his father.

"Surround the house!" shouted Mezrah as his finger made a circular motion above his head. Aykin's heart pounded as he watched Lott dismount and walk to the front door sensing something terrible had happened to his father for these men to be here.

The boy started to climb down, but his pant leg caught on a branch. As Aykin struggled to free it, his mother opened the door with Baby Obed in her arms. Aykin pulled at his pants as Jenae and Lott exchange a few words. Her expression suddenly changed from a cheerful smile to a look of disbelief and Aykin knew he'd been right about the men having bad news. Yet the boy never expected to see Lott shove his mother aside, or the Royal Guards to storm inside the cottage. Aykin listened helplessly to the screams of his mother and sisters as they mixed with the cries of his baby brother while guards set fire to his home. Terrified, Aykin yanked violently and tore his pant leg free. The lad scrambled down the tree and found himself running in a panic for the castle.

Treacherous Plans

******

The cries from Aykin's family awakened other villagers, and before long lanterns could be seen drawing near.

"Laban, tell them Uriah's wife became hysterical after hearing of her husband's plot to kill the king and accidentally knocked over a lantern which started the fire," instructed Lott.

"I don't know if I can, Sir," said the coward.

"You can, and you shall!" snapped Lott.

Although Laban did as he was told, the villagers insisted on extinguishing the flames to prevent the fire from spreading. Once it was out, Laban and the other guards ordered the concerned neighbors to leave under the guise of needing to investigate. With any witnesses removed, Lott demanded for the bodies to be dragged outside. It was a gruesome sight, but one Lott willingly tolerated to make certain they were dead to prevent any loose ends in his tapestry of treachery. As he walked past the charred bodies, Lott heard a faint cry coming from Jenae. He rolled over her smoldering body with his boot and saw that she was clinging to a bundle which she'd managed to shield from the flames. Curious as to what was so precious to her, Lott crouched down and Jenae slowly lifted her head.

"Please have mercy, he's just a baby. His name is Obed...," she whispered before dying. To his surprise, Lott found himself moved by her courage; however, the feeling quickly passed. Lott stood and walked away from the screaming baby still in his dead mother's arms.

"Is this all of them?" he shouted.

"Yes, they're all accounted for," replied Mezrah covering his nose from the repulsive smell of burnt flesh.

"Isn't there a young boy? Where is his body?" demanded Lott. The guards looked with dismay at the charred corpses knowing it would be impossible to identify gender.

"Here he is," said Laban as he pointed to what remained of one of Amalek's sisters. Lott inspected the remains before exploding with rage.

"This is a girl you fool!" he shouted. Lott feared if the boy had escaped he may one day grow into a man seeking revenge, but his scheming mind soon came up with a solution. Lott walked back to the hysterical baby and picked him up. "Well, young one, it looks as if your mother's plea for mercy shall be granted."

"What are you doing?" asked Mezrah.

"I'm merely collecting some insurance. Take the baby and I shall meet you at my home later. Tell King Shem that the woman set fire to the house after learning of her husband's demise and there were no survivors," ordered Lott. "And the baby's name is Obed."

"Wait a minute, where are you going?" insisted a frustrated Mezrah.

"I need to pay someone a visit," replied Lott sharply as he handed the screaming infant to his half-brother. "We shall get the Dragon Scroll in the morning." With that, Lott mounted his horse and rode off towards Og Mountain.

Treacherous Plans

******

When Aykin reached the castle, he immediately knew something was wrong seeing the circle of torches at the base of the east tower. He assumed this was the reason his father had left in such a hurry, and why Uriah hadn't returned. The boy was careful to stay out of the way as he drew closer, but Aykin wasn't prepared for the shocking sight of his father's body smashed against the rocks.

"NO!" he screamed.

Ithamar turned around at once recognizing the lad's voice. However, Ithamar saw only the faces of other guards. Aykin had disappeared into the night not knowing where to go or what to do as rain began to fall and sobs wrenched his young body.

Dragon Scroll of Nepthali

Chapter 5

An Evil Alliance

Lott's cloak flapped violently in the wind as he urged his horse through the storm to the Bara camp to meet with Lemuel. Lemuel was still the leader of the vile mix of half-breeds and low-life criminals who called themselves the Bara. Few knew of the camp's exact location because of its goblin origins, but since Lott was a descendant of Ganu, he knew the way well.

When he arrived, Lott was met by Gilgal as usual. The old man who had been present when Mitzy's father and brothers were brutally murdered was responsible for tending to the horses of all who came into camp. Since Lott was a frequent visitor under the cover of night, Gilgal never questioned his arrival.

"Where's Lemuel?" asked Lott above the howling wind.

"In his tent," replied Gilgal.

"Make sure to give her some extra oats," shouted Lott as he ran through the rain.

Lott's mood was as foul as the weather, and only worsened when he saw Cain as he entered Lemuel's tent. The two were like oil and water sharing an equal distain for each other.

"Lott, what brings you out on such a night as this?" asked Lemuel.

"I bring good news; may we speak privately?" answered the scribe. Lott didn't want Cain around when he told Lemuel about the Dragon Scroll being found by children. He shivered and removed his cloak then draped it over a stool by the fire.

"You may speak freely in front of Cain," replied Lemuel. Cain was amused by the scowl Lemuel's remark created on Lott's face.

"The Dragon Scroll has been found," stated Lott plainly. Lemuel and Cain looked at one another with surprise.

"Congratulations old friend," said Lemuel as he heartily slapped Lott on the back. Lott's frail frame was not accustomed to such masculine expressions of approval, and the scribe nearly crumbled beneath its force.

"Unfortunately, it was not I who found it, but rather Prince Jeru and Prince Roffius. The fools discovered it by accident and gave it to Kleiko as a birthday present," he confessed with shame. Lemuel and Cain were silent for a moment until Cain burst out in boisterous laughter.

"You mean to tell me that the scroll which holds the answers to when Natas shall awaken, and the power to rule the kingdom, was found by children?" he mocked.

An Evil Alliance

Lemuel could see that Lott's humiliation was now surpassed by his anger. The Bara ruler wanted to keep peace between the two men since he understood the delicate relationship between the Bara and the descendants of Ganu. Cain, on the other hand, still had much to learn.

"Enough of this Cain; it's not important who found it, only that it has been found. Do you have it?" asked Lemuel.

"Not yet, Kleiko won't let it out of his sight. But mark my words, I shall have it first thing in the morning," promised Lott.

"How can you believe this man, Lemuel? He's a failure," accused Cain.

"Perhaps, but Natas promised to establish a new royal bloodline through Lott's family, which means we're bound to stand by him. To sever our ties now would forfeit the promises of riches and position made by the black dragon to our kin," said Lemuel firmly. Lott smirked knowing Lemuel would never challenge him, and wanted to establish that same level of respect with Cain.

"I know all about you, Cain. You are the last living descendant of the goblin king whose pride led to the annihilation of his race. It wouldn't surprise me if the only thing Natas puts you in charge of is shining my boots," sneered Lott. Without warning, Cain grabbed hold of Lott by his shirt.

"Let's see how well you succeed in taking the throne without our help," threatened the brash young solider.

"Do you dare to threaten me?" snapped Lott. He pushed Cain back and foolishly reached for his sword. But Cain's reflexes were far superior to Lott's and his blade pierced Lott through the heart before the scribe's sword ever cleared its scabbard. Lott dropped to the floor and Lemuel looked at Cain with disdain.

"You imbecile!" he shouted. "What have you done?" He rushed to Lott's body but it was too late, the wicked scribe was dead.

"He was the imbecile thinking he could best me with a sword," boasted Cain.

"You're a fool. He was part of the Chosen Family, and had access to the Dragon Scroll. Now we shall have to deal with his son, Narok, who is even less tolerable than Lott," said Lemuel with disapproval. "Get rid of his body, and make sure no one sees you. Narok's sure to come looking for his father, and when he does we must say that we haven't seen him."

******

The castle was far behind him, but the haunting cries of his mother, sisters, and Baby Obed urged Aykin onward. The boy believed he was the sole survivor of his family not knowing that Obed was being taken to the castle at that very moment. A streak of lightning flashed across the sky and Aykin was reminded of the stories his father used to tell about a good dragon named Orpheus. The lad never doubted the existence of such a dragon until tonight. After everything he had seen, Aykin's heart hardened and his belief in Orpheus became as dead as his family.

An Evil Alliance

******

Mezrah hated his half-brother more than ever as Baby Obed screamed the entire ride back to the castle through the raging storm. If Mezrah had known that Lott was dead, he would've abandoned the infant along the way. Fortunately for Obed, Mezrah didn't know, and by the time they reached the castle the baby had finally cried himself to sleep. Mezrah quickly dismounted and ordered one of the guards to put his horse in the stables while he ran through the rain to Lott's house. Mezrah was exhausted from his many acts of treachery and eager to leave the baby with his nephew.

A trail of water followed Mezrah from the door to the bed in the corner where he laid Baby Obed. Mezrah then removed his cape as he walked over to the fire to warm himself.

"Father, where've you been?" called Narok from the next room. He had heard noises and assumed it was his father. Narok entered the main room where he was surprised to see Mezrah standing by the fire and a baby lying on the bed. The infant woke from Narok's voice and immediately resumed his screaming.

"Now you've done it!" snapped Mezrah.

"Done what? Whose baby is that?" asked a bewildered Narok. Mezrah picked up the infant and began pacing the room. The movement calmed Baby Obed some, but he was more than frightened, he was hungry.

"He's the son of Uriah; your father thought we should take him," answered Mezrah over Obed's wails.

"Why would Father do that, and where is he?" insisted Narok.

"Follow me to the kitchen so I can find some milk to feed this thing. I shall explain everything on the way," snapped Mezrah fearing his head may explode. He grabbed his cape and returned outside into the storm with the crying baby and Narok.

******

Once inside the castle, Mezrah told Narok about the events of the past few hours, starting with Uriah's murder. However, when he finished, Narok still had questions.

"You still haven't said where Father is, or why he's not with you," said the deceptively handsome young man.

"I'm not sure, but I think he rode out to the Bara camp," replied Mezrah. Narok had a bad feeling but they arrived at the kitchen before he could press the matter. The baby's cries were amplified against the stone walls which brought Cook rushing in.

"What's going on here?" demanded the large man. When Mezrah turned around, Cook saw the hysterical baby in his arms. He sensed something was amiss, but Narok wasted no time in fabricating a story.

"Cook, just the man we were hoping to see; perhaps you can help us. A very distraught young woman stopped by our house and begged for my father and me to care for this poor babe, but we've nothing to feed him," he said. Even Mezrah was impressed with the ease and believability of Narok's lie. But Cook was not easily swayed and eyed them suspiciously. He started to question the tale, but Meridia burst into the kitchen on her way back from the Queen's Chamber.

"I thought I heard a baby crying," she said.

"My lady, this poor child is hungry so Cook here was about to help us get something for him," said Mezrah. Meridia looked at him and tried not to laugh.

"How do you suppose Cook would help you feed this baby?" she asked with a raised brow. Although Meridia knew nothing about these men, it was clear by their appearance they had no woman looking after them.

"This is the kitchen, is it not?" replied Mezrah ignorantly.

"Yes, but he is just a baby. Without his mother, he is in need of a wet nurse," stated Meridia matter-of-factly. She wondered what kind of mother would leave her child with such incompetent men, not knowing of the mother's true unparalleled bravery. Mezrah and Narok stared at Meridia with blank faces and her heart went out to the innocent baby. "Oh, the poor dear! Please, let me hold him," she insisted.

Mezrah was happy to oblige and placed Obed in her arms. The baby calmed down as if knowing he was safe for the first time since being taken from his mother. Narok noticed Meridia's natural touch, and wasted no time preying upon her obvious compassion.

"My father and I would like nothing more than to care for this precious cherub, however, since the loss of my mother, our home is without the tender care which only a woman can provide," he said shrewdly. Meridia looked at the baby's tear-stained face and knew she must help.

"Well, gentlemen, it just so happens that I'm a wet nurse. I would be happy to assist in caring for this baby," she volunteered. Mezrah suspected Lott would be angry, but quickly decided his half-brother had no choice in the matter since he wasn't here.

"You are too generous, my lady; we humbly accept your offer," he said before Meridia could change her mind. The two men turned to leave, but Meridia call out to them.

"Wait! You forgot to tell me his name," she said. Once again they looked at her with blank faces. "Surely his mother told you his name when she left him in your care, did she not?" Mezrah suddenly remembered what Lott said before he left for the Bara camp.

"Obed…his name is Obed!" he exclaimed.

"Obed," she said softly. The baby smiled at Meridia as Mezrah and Narok left the kitchen relieved to be rid of the baby. The men went back to Lott's house to wait for his return, but that would never occur.

******

A dusting of puffy clouds was all that remained of the terrible storm as the sun came up the next morning. Narok grabbed his cat o'nine tails and left for the Bara camp not knowing if he would ever see his father again. Regardless of whether or not Narok found his father, the young man vowed to get his hands on the Dragon Scroll upon his return to the castle.

An Evil Alliance

Although it had been a while since his last visit, Narok arrived to find the Bara camp in its usual disarray. The handsome young man looked around with disgust and wondered how his father tolerated dealing with such barbarians. Gilgal approached Narok and made ready to take his horse.

"Narok, what brings you here during daylight?" asked the old soldier.

"I'm looking for my father. I was told he may have come here last night and wondered if perhaps he chose to stay due to the storm," replied Narok. Gilgal remembered Lemuel's strict instructions to deny Lott's visit the night before, so the old man lied.

"I haven't seen him, but at my age I can be forgetful," he replied gruffly.

"If it's all the same to you, I shall check with Lemuel," said Narok in his usual snobbish tone. He started off for Lemuel's tent, but stopped when he saw Cain. Narok shared his father's disdain for the hot-tempered barbarian.

"What brings you here without your father?" asked the soldier with goblin blood running through his veins.

"Funny you should ask since that's why I'm here. Have you seen him?" asked Narok.

"I haven't seen him for days, and no one's come in or out of camp," replied Cain with an icy stare. But Narok noticed a twitch in Cain's upper lip as he spoke and suspected he was lying.

"I see; nevertheless, I shall check with Lemuel. Perhaps the two of them met without your knowledge," suggested

Narok. The intentional insult was meant to trip up Cain in his lie, and Narok was pleased to see how quickly it worked.

"Lemuel's not here. He had business in town and shan't return until nightfall," answered Cain sharply.

"I thought you said no one has come or gone from camp?" pressed Narok shrewdly. Cain furrowed his brow and glared at the young man who'd out-witted him so easily.

"It seems you've caught me, my friend," he replied awkwardly. "I didn't want to tell you the truth for fear of what you may do."

"Try me," stated Narok coldly.

"Your father was here last night," answered Cain.

"Well, where is he?" demanded Narok.

"Follow me," said Cain. The muscular man placed his hand upon Narok's shoulder and led him to the edge of camp. Narok kept his eye on Cain, and his hand on his whip. After walking a short distance, Cain stopped and pointed to a fresh grave.

"He's right there; Lemuel killed him last night after learning that the Dragon Scroll had been found by Prince Jeru and Prince Roffius. I tried to stop him," said Cain hoping to pass off this lie better than the last.

"Why should I believe you?" asked Narok.

"You of all people know that if I'd done it I'd say so," said Cain falsely.

An Evil Alliance

"I'll kill him!" threatened Narok through clinched teeth. He turned towards Lemuel's tent, but Cain abruptly grabbed hold of his arm.

"Don't forget where you are, Narok. If you kill Lemuel here, you're sure to end up beside your father. Let me take care of this. I shall say that Lemuel was cursed for killing a member of the Chosen Family, that way we both get what we want," suggested Cain. Narok pondered the offer briefly before realizing that his desire for the throne was far greater than his desire for revenge.

"Very well, but if you fail, I shall see to it that you end up beside my father," he threatened. Cain considered killing the young scribe for his arrogance, but was in too good a mood knowing he would soon take his rightful place as the Bara leader. Therefore, Cain allowed Narok to live.

"I thought you might want to have this," said Cain. As he reached into his shirt, Narok stepped back and took hold of his whip thinking Cain was reaching for a weapon. But the only thing Cain produced was Lott's cloak.

******

Narok left the Bara camp in Haliel as Ithamar was leaving the castle in Nepthali to check on Uriah's family. The guard heard rumors of the family's death, but until Ithamar saw the trail of smoke drifting into the sky he had refused to believe they were true.

"NO!" cried Ithamar while springing from his horse.

The gruesome scene of charred bodies lined up in a row forced even the seasoned guard to look away. Ithamar was deprived of both sleep and food which, combined with his insurmountable grief, created an overwhelming sense of despair. It was nearly more than he could bear, yet Ithamar composed himself and began the somber task of burying the dead.

Tears flowed freely as Ithamar carried each body one by one for burial. When he lifted Jenae, pieces of blanket dropped to the ground and the guard winced thinking this was all that remained of the baby he had never met. After lifting the last body, Ithamar realized there was one missing. He couldn't be sure, but the guard thought the missing body belonged to Uriah's oldest son, Aykin. Ithamar suddenly remembered hearing what he thought was the boy cry out the night before and felt a glimmer of hope.

"Aykin!" shouted Ithamar.

His heart raced as he ran inside the smoldering cottage and looked through the rubble for signs of the lad. Finding nothing, the guard ran back outside where he noticed a child's footprints in the mud. Ithamar followed the tracks past the cottage, but soon lost them in the foliage.

"Aykin! Aykin!" he repeated. "Answer me if you're out there!" A deafening silence engulfed Ithamar as the exhausted guard fell to his knees. The ache in his heart was greater than anything he had ever experienced, and Ithamar vowed to find Aykin as well as the truth surrounding Uriah's death. He never imagined that both Aykin and the baby were still alive, or that the infant was in the safe-keeping of the woman who had stolen the guard's heart.

An Evil Alliance

******

Mezrah entered the courtyard just as Narok returned from the Bara camp. The bulgy-eyed man saw his nephew and followed him into the stables.

"Where's your father?" asked Mezrah as Narok dismounted. The strikingly handsome young man glared at his uncle.

"He's dead thanks to you," snapped Narok as he walked his horse to its stall. "My father went to the Bara camp where Lemuel killed him. But, I've arranged for Cain to kill Lemuel." Mezrah thought such rash behavior sounded more like Cain's doing rather than Lemuel who had worked peacefully with Lott for years. Mezrah feared all Bara, but none more than Cain. Yet, he didn't care who had killed his half-brother as long as Lott was dead.

"Can you be certain?" asked Mezrah attempting to sound distraught.

"I saw his grave myself," said Narok. "And don't think you can fool me; I know the two of you despised one another. But have no fear, I shall soon get my hands on the Dragon Scroll and use its power to take the throne." Mezrah listened half-heartedly to his nephew's declaration since he viewed Lott's death as one step closer on his own quest for the throne.

"What shall we tell the king?" he asked. Narok thought for a moment.

"We shall say that he was attacked by wild dogs which left nothing but bones," replied the cunning young man.

Mezrah nodded in agreement and the two left the stables to relay the false story to King Shem. Unbeknownst to them, Laban overheard their entire conversation from adjoining stall where he was polishing his boots.

******

Ithamar's rage towards Lott as the guard returned to the castle after burying his best friend's wife and children had reached a dangerous level. He suspected the shifty scribe was somehow responsible for their deaths, and was anxious to prove it. However, before Ithamar sought out Lott, he stopped by the kitchen for carrots as a reward for his faithful horse. As he walked down the hallway, the guard heard Obed's cries echoing from Meridia's quarters. Ithamar never imagined they could be the cries of Uriah's youngest son as he choked back tears and grabbed the carrots before hurrying away.

When Ithamar entered the stables, Laban was just leaving. The impressive guard decided to ask Laban a few questions remembering he had been with Lott and Mezrah the night before.

"Laban, I need a word," said Ithamar sternly.

"Is something the matter?" asked the guilty guard.

"That depends…why did Lott and Mezrah chose someone like you to accompany them to Uriah's last night when there are guards with far more experience?" inquired Ithamar.

"How should I know? I was around when they said they needed a squadron of guards, so I went," he said as tiny beads of sweat formed along his upper lip.

"Why so nervous, Laban?" asked Ithamar with a raised brow.

"If you saw what I did, you'd be jittery too," answered Laban.

"I did, but I had the decency to bury them!" exclaimed Ithamar. "Now, if you'll excuse me, I need to speak with Lott."

"Lott's dead," stated Laban.

"What?" asked Ithamar in disbelief.

"Narok and Mezrah were here not long ago," answered the traitor. For a brief moment Laban considered telling the truth, but the moment passed. "I overheard Narok say that Lott was killed by wild dogs. Now if you'll excuse me, I'm late for my rounds." Laban slipped away as Ithamar stood in stunned silence. He could barely fathom the idea of never knowing the truth surrounding the deaths of Uriah and his family.

******

While on his rounds, Laban happened to see Mezrah and Narok leaving the Throne Room after the half-brothers had told King Shem the false story surrounding Lott's death. Laban nodded with respect to the man who'd lured him into joining a treasonous conspiracy against the king. Mezrah offered false promises of riches and power to the lazy young man in return for service, to which Laban foolishly agreed.

Aykin collapsed near an old farmhouse in the province of Haliel not far from the Bara camp. He woke up to the afternoon sun shining through tattered curtains lying on a bed in a strange room with a boy his age staring back at him.

"Where am I?" asked Aykin bolting upright.

"My name's Eliab, and you're in my house," replied the boy. Eliab stepped closer with a welcoming smile. The boy's eyes and hair were the same dark brown as Aykin's father. When Aykin noticed the similarity, his mind was instantly flooded with images too painful to recall. He looked away before Eliab could see his tears.

"Are you okay? Where'd you come from?" asked Eliab with concern.

"Near the castle in Nepthali, but that doesn't matter. Where's this house?" asked Aykin.

"Haliel," replied Eliab. Aykin was shocked to learn how far he had traveled believing Haliel was a full day's journey from the castle. However, in reality a swift horse could easily make the trip in two hours. "Where's your family?" continued Eliab.

"I don't have a family...at least not anymore," whispered Aykin dropping his eyes to the floor. An awkward silence fell over the room.

"Wait here," Eliab finally said before leaving faster than an arrow shot from a bow. He returned a few minutes later looking very pleased accompanied by another boy slightly younger than he and Aykin. "Ma says you can stay here as long as you help out with the chores and farming," announced Eliab proudly. "And this is my cousin, Kenan; he lives here too."

"Hello," said Kenan softly. He avoided eye contact with Aykin sensing somehow that the stranger would change their lives. Uncertain of where else he would go, Aykin agreed to stay. From that day on, Eliab and Aykin were inseparable. Although the older boys always included Kenan, a seed of resentment was planted in his heart because Aykin had taken away the undivided attention his cousin once gave to Kenan.

It didn't take Aykin long to realize that Eliab and Kenan's home on the dilapidated farm in Haliel was nothing like the one he was used to. The men were belligerent drunkards, while the women were vile and abusive. Beatings were commonplace, and yelling was the preferred form of communication. Aykin's strong-willed temperament, which had been a source of frustration for his mother, was now the source of his survival. Yet, because of what he had seen happen to his family, and from living in such terrible circumstances, Aykin changed. Gone was the boy who dreamt of becoming a Royal Guard like his father, replaced by one whose only dream was revenge.

******

Following Lott's death, Narok became increasingly moody and irritable. His behavior was largely excused as grief-related, but in truth it was because Kleiko repeatedly denied Narok's requests to study the Dragon Scroll. Kleiko held firm to the warning which forbid Ganu, or his descendants, access to the precious document. Narok nearly went mad from frustration, and was forced to fabricate details about the Dragon Scroll for Cain to prevent the irrational Bara leader from discovering the truth about his never having seen the scroll. Like his forefathers, Narok perfected a double life of serving as a dutiful scribe by day while plotting with the Bara to take the throne by night.

******

Four years passed following Meridia and Mitzy's arrival at the castle. Kleiko spent those years studying the Dragon Scroll in a relentless pursuit to find hope buried within the despair. He was ecstatic when his perseverance finally paid off late one night. While studying the scroll, Kleiko happened to notice a slight difference between the dragon brothers' seals. Natas' mark was fine and smooth, yet Orpheus' appeared bumpy and irregular. Curious, Kleiko retrieved his magnified looking glass to examine the marks more closely. While doing so, the scribe noticed tiny etchings within Orpheus' seal which were actually words. After Kleiko read the hidden inscription made by dragon magic that had been lost for centuries, he could hardly contain his joy. He wasted no time sharing his discovery with King Shem, as well as with the former King Daven and Queen Mother Lydia. The current and former monarchs shared in Kleiko's excitement, but instructed the scribe to keep this monumental discovery a secret lest the descendants of Ganu should learn of it.

******

Thirteen-year-old Aykin was still living with Eliab and Kenan's dysfunctional family in Haliel. The past four years had been the most miserable of his young life, and Aykin knew he must leave. He finally got his chance while the teenagers were in town one day. As they passed the mercantile shop, Aykin noticed some men loading a wagon.

"I still say it was Cain who murdered Lemuel," said one.

"That was four years ago, let it go!" exclaimed another.

"Maybe, but I agree with Gilgal. Cain's cursed," added a third who had been there when Cain murdered Mitzy's father and brothers.

"Don't be such an old woman!" snapped the first. "Just keep loading that grain so we can get back to camp."

Aykin knew by their clothing that the men were Bara soldiers. He remembered his father's warnings to keep away from this ruthless band of warriors, but after living as he had Aykin didn't care who they were. He approached the men while Eliab and Kenan stayed back and watched Aykin take the first step to change each of their lives.

"Excuse me, Sires, but it seems you've quite a load to get into your wagon. Would you like some help?" he asked.

"You're quite the little gentleman. Where's your mother?" asked one of the scruffy men.

"She's dead, as is my father. I'm in need of shelter, and am willing to work to earn my keep," replied Aykin. His blunt answer surprised them, but one saw this as an opportunity to get out of loading the wagon.

"Today's your lucky day, lad. It just so happens that we're in need of some extra hands to help around our camp, what'd you say?" he asked.

"Thank you, Sire. What about my friends here, can they come too?" asked Aykin as he pointed to Eliab and Kenan.

"Sure, why not?" replied the man. "You can start by loading this grain into the wagon while we gather the rest of our supplies." The men were pleased to get out of loading the wagon, but not as pleased as Aykin. He was lifting one of the heavy sacks of grain when Eliab and Kenan joined him.

"Are you crazy? Do you know who those men are?" asked Eliab.

"Bara soldiers, but frankly I don't care. Any place is better than with your Pa…or yours," said Aykin gesturing to both Eliab and Kenan. They knew Aykin was right; especially since their backs still stung from the whippings each received the night before.

"The two of you can stay if you want, but this is my chance and I'm taking it," stated Aykin firmly.

"I'm going with Aykin, you can do what you want, Kenan," said Eliab to his cousin. Kenan thought for a moment, but soon joined Eliab and Aykin in loading the wagon.

The teenagers never returned to the dilapidated farm on the edge of town, and sadly, no one noticed or cared. Aykin knew his decision to join the Bara soldiers would change his life, but never imagined it would lead him to the son of the man responsible for killing his family.

The Bara soldiers welcomed their newest recruits, and to Aykin's surprise made good on their promise to provide them with food and shelter in exchange for work. It was not the life Aykin had envisioned for himself, but since the loss of his family nothing had been as he expected. Happiness was a memory, and dreams were a luxury he couldn't afford; especially the dream of becoming a Royal Guard. But Aykin was a hard worker and did as he was told, while making sure Eliab and Kenan did the same. His natural leadership, along with his exceptional swordsmanship, quickly caught Cain's attention.

"The lad shows much promise," Cain said to Gilgal after watching the boy in a mock duel one afternoon. Gilgal agreed. Aykin reminded the old man of the farmer's sons Cain had killed four years earlier. He only hoped the lad wouldn't meet their same fate at the hand of Cain since that image still haunted Gilgal at night.

******

In the four years since moving to the castle, the ache in Mitzy's heart of losing her father and brothers lessened as the eight-year-old's beauty increased. Her golden curls fell past her shoulders, and her crystal blue eyes sparkled with a hint of mischief just like her father's.

At nearly five years old, Obed lived as a member of Meridia and Mitzy's little family. He adored Mitzy and, like Ashes the cat, followed her everywhere. With each passing day the boy looked more like his mother but there was no mistaking that Obed wielded a sword, even one made of wood, just like his father.

One day as Ithamar walked through the courtyard, he stopped suddenly at the sight of Obed in the midst of an imaginary duel. Ithamar was struck by the boy's haunting resemblance to Jenae, but shook his head and quickly rationalized away the obvious. Yet as the guard continued on his way, Ithamar felt a fresh sting of failure for not having found Aykin, or the truth surrounding Uriah's death.

******

Mitzy and Obed spent their carefree days helping Cook in the kitchen, playing in the Royal Gardens, or brushing the horses in the Royal Stables. It was a wonderful season in their young lives, especially as the entire kingdom anxiously awaited the birth of two royal babies. Meridia happily attended to both Queen Ashter and Princess Tamar, Jeru's wife. Jeru was the Captain of the Royal Guards and waited for his opportunity to make good on his vow to throw Narok and Mezrah in the dungeon. The queen and princess were due in the same month, and possibly even the same day according to Lamech, the Royal Physician. Lamech had faithfully served the Royal Family nearly as long as Kleiko and the two men were lifelong friends.

Kleiko wanted to share in the joy of the upcoming births with the rest of the kingdom; however, he was deeply troubled. Hidden within Orpheus' inscription on the Dragon Scroll, Kleiko had found that the foretelling sign of Natas' awakening was the birth of twins on the night of a terrible storm. Like Ganu had done generations earlier, Kleiko assumed this meant to a member of the

Royal Family. The scribe rightly concluded that the risk of twins was far greater with both the queen and princess expecting babies. He shared his concerns with King Shem who wisely heeded Kleiko's council by placing extra guards along the castle wall and scouts around the perimeter to keep watch for the black dragon.

Sadly, Kleiko's fears proved to be true, yet not as he, or anyone else ever expected. Shortly after giving birth to a son, Tamar developed a fever and died. She lived just long enough to name the baby Julean, which means joy, because when she looked upon the infant her heart was filled with joy. Queen Ashter was in labor when Julean was born and she, too, gave birth to a son they named Stefano. The happiness the young king and queen wanted to feel after years of waiting for a child was lost to sadness upon hearing the tragic news of Tamar's death. The entire kingdom mourned the passing of the young princess, and ached for Prince Jeru and his newborn son who unexpectedly found themselves without a wife and mother.

Meridia served as the wet nurse for both royal babies, and Mitzy and Obed were eager helpers. Even as an infant one could see that Prince Stefano was blessed with his mother's striking features, while Prince Julean proved true to his name by exuding a contagious joy. Meridia often said that Tamar must have known Julean's personality in the womb to have given him such a perfectly suited name.

Chapter 6

Traitor in the Midst

During the weeks following Tamar's death, ten-year-old Prince Roffius became increasingly cynical of Kleiko's teachings from the Dragon Scroll about a good dragon. The young prince doubted this could be true since Orpheus had abandoned the people of Nepthali, and allowed such terrible things to happen. Roffius escaped his emotional pain by riding Starlight for hours throughout the kingdom, or practicing his sword skills. He also frequented the Royal Gardens in hopes of seeing Mitzy. Although not yet old enough to recognize it as love, the young prince understood that he felt empty inside if a day passed without seeing the girl with golden curls and sparkling blue eyes.

******

One afternoon, Prince Roffius was in the kitchen eating an apple atop a barrel when Mitzy and Obed came in followed by Ashes the cat. Cook saw them and smiled.

"Good afternoon, my lady and young sire, what can I do for the two of you?" asked the large man as he picked up Ashes.

"Hello, Cook, I was wondering if you had any scraps left over from supper. Obed claims to be starving," replied Mitzy with a twinkle in her eyes. As she spoke, the young prince hopped down from his perch on the barrel.

"Hello, Miss Mit," he said casually. Mitzy was startled to see Ro and quickly curtsied and bowed her head to hide her blushing cheeks. Her heart still belonged to the extremely handsome boy with wavy brown hair streaked with highlights from many hours of riding, and hazel eyes which reminded her of the soil in springtime.

"Forgive me, Your Highness, I didn't see you," she said politely. Cook chuckled at the two children obviously smitten with one another as he placed Ashes down.

"I'd be happy to give Obed a snack if he helps me pluck the feathers off this chicken while I send you on a little errand," said the large man with a smile. "I've prepared Queen Ashter's favorite pastries, and I need someone to deliver them for me. Perhaps Prince Roffius can escort you, if he doesn't mind?" Mitzy looked at Cook nervously and he gave her a playful wink. She reached into her pocket for Polly as was her habit whenever Mitzy felt in need of courage. To Mitzy, holding the piece of wood was like holding a piece of her father.

"Can I, Mitzy?" pleaded Obed.

"I'd be happy to escort you, Miss Mit," answered Roffius before she could refuse. "Let's go, we wouldn't want to keep the queen waiting." The young prince grabbed the basket and strolled out of the kitchen.

"Yes, of course," she replied and followed him after one last nervous glance at Cook.

Traitor in the Midst

******

As the young prince and servant girl walked along in silence, Mitzy thought about how much she enjoyed spending time with Ro, especially in the Royal Gardens. She wished her father was alive because she was certain he would have liked the boy as well. Mitzy nearly ran into the prince when he stopped suddenly in front of her.

"I said, 'How are you today, Miss Mit?'" he repeated with a smile knowing he had caught Mitzy in another daydream as her cheeks flushed with embarrassment.

"I'm sorry, Your Highness; I was just thinking about my father," she said softly. He started walking again and the two continued on towards the south wing. Roffius knew the story of her father and brothers, and now understood the pain of such loss.

"What was your father like?" he asked. A smile spread across Mitzy's face and her eyes got a faraway look in them as sweet memories filled her mind.

"He was tall, and his skin was browned from working in the fields. I remember he smelled of hay, sweat, and wood. His hair was just like mine, and Mama says I have his eyes. He also had the strongest arms I've ever seen," she answered. The prince looked at his pre-pubescent arms and casually moved them behind his back.

"He sounds very special; I wish I could have known him," he replied thoughtfully.

"I think you would've liked him. He knew a great deal about your family," she continued.

"What do you mean?" asked the prince curiously.

Dragon Scroll of Nepthali

"My father told me all about King Jeptha, King Thaddeus, and the Dragon Scroll. It must be quite wonderful to know that your family shall bring the return of Orpheus at the appointed time," she said with a sparkle in her blue eyes. Roffius stopped again after being astonished by the history lesson he had just received from the daughter of a maidservant.

"You sound like Kleiko when he teaches us from the Dragon Scroll. Jeru and I think it is just a silly story," he replied honestly. Mitzy giggled thinking he was toying with her.

"How can Kleiko teach from the Dragon Scroll when it was lost in The Great Fire?" she asked.

"That's what everyone thought until Jeru and I found four years ago," announced the young prince proudly. "Kleiko loves that old scroll. He thinks it shall save the kingdom."

"I can't believe it's actually here and you've seen it!" squealed Mitzy with delight. The boy hadn't expected such an enthusiastic reaction from her. In truth, the scroll frightened Roffius with its warning of a black dragon that would awaken to kill his family. Even still, he took great pleasure in Mitzy's delight.

"It's just an old scroll," said Roffius casually with a shrug of his shoulders.

"No it isn't," continued Mitzy eagerly. "My father taught me all about the hope it contains, and hope is what keeps us from despair. You must believe in Orpheus, Ro, because you could be the one!" He liked it when Mitzy forgot protocol and called him by his nickname, even if she could be thrown in the dungeon for it.

"What do you mean?" he asked.

"My father told me that Orpheus once said, 'When the night is dark and dreary; never give up, nor grow weary. The lion is wounded but may be saved, by the youngest one so brave,'" explained Mitzy. "You're the youngest in the Royal Family, Ro, so you could be the one to save the kingdom from Natas!" She was so certain of what she said that Roffius never thought to ask how Mitzy could know of something the great dragon once said. He only wished he shared her same belief, but Roffius just couldn't.

"Maybe that's what the scroll means to you and Kleiko, but not to me. If Orpheus cares so much about the people of this kingdom, where is he? And why did Tamar have to die, or your father and brothers for that matter? You can think what you wish, but the Dragon Scroll is just a silly story," he said sharply and walked away. Mitzy was disheartened by his response as she hurried to catch up.

"I'm sorry about Princess Tamar," she said softly. Roffius appreciated the thoughtful remark, but he didn't feel like talking.

"Thank you," replied the boy dutifully. An awkward silence followed and Mitzy reached into her pocket for Polly.

As the young prince and servant girl approached the Throne Room, they heard raised voices. Roffius immediately recognized two of them as belonging to his brothers.

"It sounds like they're going at it again," he said while quickening his pace.

"Who?" asked Mitzy. Roffius placed his finger to his lips and grabbed her hand. He ran with Mitzy across the hallway, and then let go to flatten himself against the wall adjacent to the Throne Room. After listened longer, Prince Roffius identified the third raised voice as Narok's.

"Your Excellency, as I've said before, I believe I can uncover mysteries within the Dragon Scroll which Kleiko has missed if you would simply allow me the opportunity to examine it," pleaded the scribe. Narok was desperate to obtain the power within the scroll after being denied access to it for years. He was once again pleading his case before King Shem and Prince Jeru hoping for a more favorable outcome, but the royal brothers agreed wholeheartedly with Kleiko's warning to keep Narok from it.

"The great dragon Orpheus left the scroll in the hands of a Chief Royal Scribe, and that is where it shall remain," answered Jeru sharply. His contempt for Narok had only increased with time, and King Shem sensed tensions were escalating between the young men. The wise king quickly settled the matter.

"I agree with my brother, the Dragon Scroll belongs with Kleiko. If he deems it best to keep you from it, then so be it," stated Shem plainly. Narok seethed with anger at the king's unequivocal ruling.

"As you wish, My King," he replied through clinched teeth. Narok bowed and turned to leave, but couldn't refrain from making one last remark. "Give the queen my deepest, and most sincere, affections," he said. The scribe's words dripped with double-meaning and Jeru knew it. The prince stepped forward filled with rage, but Shem stopped him.

"Not now, brother," whispered the king as he tightened his grip on Jeru's arm.

******

From their vantage point, Prince Roffius and Mitzy heard Narok coming and quickly hid behind a large stone column. Narok was both furious and humiliated as he stormed away to find his uncle. Mitzy and Roffius remained out of sight until the treacherous scribe was gone.

"Do you think he saw us?" whispered Mitzy.

"I don't think so," answered Roffius. "But, we'd better get these pastries to the queen."

Mitzy agreed and followed the young prince up the grand staircase while King Shem and Prince Jeru continued their heated discussion in the Throne Room.

"Why have you not thrown that contemptible man with his treasonous comments in the dungeon?" fumed Jeru.

"Since when has it been an act of treason to pay one's respects to the queen? Besides, if I were to throw every man into the dungeon who finds Ashter attractive it would be filled before morning," stated King Shem. It was often difficult, but the wise king understood that it was both a blessing and a curse to be married to a beautiful woman. Jeru considered the truth in his brother's words, yet his concerns remained.

"Yes, but rumors continue to grow of Narok's intent to take the throne," he stated. King Shem walked across the expansive room and filled a goblet with wine. The golden treasure was a reminder of better days for Nepthali, and the king often felt guilty for having such luxuries knowing his people lived in poverty.

"I seem to remember such rumors surrounding his father, yet nothing ever became of them," replied King Shem. "You know as well as I that only fools begin and believe rumors." He raised the goblet to his lips, but as Shem did Jeru noticed a slight tremble in his brother's hand.

"Perhaps, but you would be wise to heed them; especially since Narok seems increasingly desperate to see the Dragon Scroll. If what Kleiko says is true, we can't allow such power to fall into his hands," warned the young captain. His comment surprised Shem since Jeru made it no secret of his abandoned belief in the Dragon Scroll since Tamar's death.

"I thought you'd forsaken your belief in the Dragon Scroll," remarked Shem.

"I have, but when it comes to your safety I shall take any precaution necessary, even the warnings from a child's fable," snapped Jeru bitterly.

"Take courage, Jeru, my belief shall be enough for the both of us," declared King Shem.

"I admire your faith, Brother, but it's my sworn duty to protect you and that can't happen on mere belief. Narok is like a snake in the tall reeds just waiting for an opportunity to strike," warned Jeru. King Shem could see Jeru was resolved to put his concerns into action.

"Very well, assign a special detail to Narok, but make sure you choose someone trustworthy who shall be discrete. If Narok is plotting something, we don't want him to think we are suspect," said Shem.

"Consider it done, Brother," answered Jeru firmly. As the king looked at his younger brother, he suddenly felt very emotional.

"I'm proud of you, Jeru. In spite of all that has happened in your personal life, you've fulfilled your duties with honor and respect. You even look out for me better than you look after yourself," he said with a smile. "Now go home, see your son, and get some rest; all shall be well." Jeru wanted to believe Shem, but he sensed he would lose Shem just as he had lost Tamar if Narok wasn't thrown in the dungeon soon. Because of this, Jeru disobeyed a direct order from the king for the first time since taking his oath as Captain of the Royal Guards. Instead of going home to see his son, Jeru went to the Royal Stables in search of his most trusted Royal Guard.

******

Ithamar had climbed in rank during the four years since Uriah's murder without blemish to his record. Yet, the guard wrestled with feelings of failure for not having found the truth surrounding Uriah's death, or Uriah's son Aykin. To compensate for these feelings, Ithamar poured himself into his work. When Prince Jeru was appointed Captain of the Royal Guards, he quickly singled Ithamar out and placed him in command of the king's most elite squadron. It was an easy decision for Prince Jeru to seek

Ithamar's assistance with a task as important as the one at hand. As expected, he found the guard in the Royal Stables polishing his saddle.

"I thought I might find you here," said Jeru. Ithamar immediately stood at attention in the presence of his captain and prince.

"Sir," he said with a bow.

"At ease, soldier, I've come on unofficial business," answered Prince Jeru as he closed the stable doors.

"What do you mean?" asked Ithamar.

"I need your help with something," answered Jeru.

"Of course, Captain," replied Ithamar without hesitation. Jeru strolled past Ithamar to Starlight and stroked his horse's soft mane.

"Easy, girl," said the captain calmly. "It seems your colt shall come any time." Ithamar watched Jeru standing beside the pregnant horse and remembered when Uriah was asked to tame the animal. He also remembered that it was Starlight who carried Uriah back to the castle the night he was murdered. Ithamar tried to stop the flood of memories before they became unbearable until he suddenly realized that he hadn't heard a word his captain had said.

"Ithamar?" asked Prince Jeru sensing the guard's lack of attention.

"Forgive me, Captain, I'm afraid my simple mind wandered for a moment. It shan't happen again," admitted Ithamar with shame. The prince knew Ithamar well enough to know his lapse of attention wasn't a sign of disrespect, so he continued.

"As I was saying, I believe Narok may try to steal a certain scroll and I need you to ensure he doesn't," explained Jeru. The prince grabbed a currycomb from the grooming tools and started gently brushing Starlight's torso.

"Why would Narok steal a scroll when he has access to them as a scribe?" asked the confused guard.

"He doesn't have access to this one, and the Dragon Scroll is no ordinary scroll," explained Jeru. Ithamar recognized that name from the many times Uriah spoke of it, and remembered seeing it on Kleiko's desk the night of Uriah's murder.

"I once had a friend who talked of the ancient scroll as you do. If you think King Shem may be in danger, I shall do everything in my power to protect him," proclaimed Ithamar. Prince Jeru was pleased to receive the response he had both hoped for and expected.

"Excellent, I need you to watch Narok's activities and report your findings directly to me. Meanwhile, I'm going to Kleiko's study to check on the Dragon Scroll," said Jeru.

"Of course, Captain," answered Ithamar.

Jeru returned the currycomb to its place and gave Starlight a pat as Ithamar gave a final bow when the prince passed by. After Jeru had gone, Starlight became increasingly restless. She snorted and stomped at the ground then paced back and forth nervously in her stall.

"Easy, girl," said Ithamar as he tried to calm the anxious horse. He reasoned that Starlight's behavior signaled the early stages of labor rather than the warning she had meant for Jeru.

******

When Prince Jeru arrived at Kleiko's study, he found the Dragon Scroll where it always was on the desk. The Chief Royal Scribe had retired for the night, so Jeru decided it best to take the scroll back to his quarters for safe-keeping with the intent to return it in the morning. As he tucked the scroll beneath his vest, Jeru had the feeling someone was watching him. His eyes scanned the room, but he saw only shadows of the fire dancing along the floor and up the wall.

Suddenly, a long, eerie cry cut through the silence. Prince Jeru spun around with his sword drawn and saw a black figure jump down from the window. He lunged at his unknown assailant but struck only air. Jeru spun around again and still saw nothing. His heart raced from the rush of adrenaline flowing throughout his body. Then, Jeru felt something rub against his leg. He looked down and saw Ashes the cat. Ashes had been napping on her favorite ledge when Jeru disturbed her slumber. The cat strolled between his legs and through the open door before it turned around to give the prince a snobbish glare as only a cat can do.

"Ashes! You nearly lost one of your nine lives!" scolded Jeru as he laughed at himself for being spooked by a cat. However, Ashes wasn't the only one surprised by Prince Jeru in Kleiko's study, and the cat wasn't the only one following Jeru as he made his way over to the north wing of the castle.

Jeru arrived at his quarters and kindly greeted the maidservant who'd been keeping watch over his son before excusing her for the night. Once she was gone, the soft glow from the hearth beckoned Jeru to its warmth. He removed the Dragon Scroll from his vest and set it beneath his cloak on a small table near the fire. Jeru was exhausted, but started for the bedroom to check on Baby Julean. As he did, someone suddenly grabbed the prince from behind. Jeru started to reach for his sword, but before he could grasp it Jeru felt a sharp pain in his chest as a blade pierced through his heart.

Mezrah smirked with satisfaction as he looked at the lifeless body of the man who was next in line for the throne. The evil guard then removed a Bara shirt from inside his cloak and attempted to rip it apart, but he was hindered by the sword in his hand. Mezrah cursed Narok for leaving him to do the dirty work alone as he absentmindedly placed his blood-covered sword on a bookshelf. With both hands now free, Mezrah easily tore off pieces of the shirt and scattered them around the room. As he did, Mezrah admitted to himself that Narok's plan was brilliant.

Following Narok's humiliating exchange between King Shem and Prince Jeru in the Throne Room, the scribe had sought out Mezrah. He ordered for his uncle to kill Prince Jeru, but assured him that Cain would be blamed for it. For this to work, Mezrah was to leave pieces of a Bara uniform at the scene of the crime so King Shem would dispatch Royal Guards to the Bara camp. Being among them, Mezrah would then hide the murder weapon inside Cain's tent where he would happen to find it. The plan was brilliant and would result in Narok being rid of both the prince and the troublesome Bara leader. For once Mezrah willingly participated in his nephew's devilish scheme because it eliminated two obstacles in his own quest for the throne.

The bulgy-eyed man smiled shrewdly as he smashed dishes and overturned furniture to create the façade of a terrible fight. Yet Mezrah never anticipated that the noise would awaken Baby Julean. The infant's cries echoed from the bedroom and into the hallway. Cursing as he left in haste, Mezrah left the murder weapon lying on the bookshelf.

******

Ithamar started his search for Narok on the lower level of the castle. When he didn't see the scribe there, Ithamar decided to check Narok's home before going to the castle's upper levels. As he entered the inner courtyard, the guard saw Mezrah entering Narok's house. Ithamar positioned himself beneath an outside window where he was careful to remain unseen. Although unable to hear their conversation, Ithamar peered inside and saw that Narok was very pleased by what Mezrah had to say. With Narok's whereabouts now known, Ithamar disappeared into the darkness to report his observations to Prince Jeru. However, if he had stayed a few minutes longer, Ithamar would have seen Narok become enraged after Mezrah realized he had left the murder weapon in Jeru's room.

******

After washing the dinner dishes with her mother, Mitzy left for the Royal Stables to check on Starlight. When she arrived, Mitzy found Prince Roffius with the Master of the Horse and a stable boy assisting the beautiful mare as she birthed a pure white colt with a striking black mane.

Roffius named the colt Moon Chaser stating that the combination of black and white reminded him of the way the moon's brilliant light chases away the darkness. He and Mitzy giggled and laughed at the wobbly new colt unaware of the treachery happening within the castle.

******

When Ithamar arrived in the hallway of the north wing, he immediately knew something was wrong as Baby Julean's screams resonated off the stone walls. The guard sprinted ahead until he nearly collided with a maidservant rushing to the same cries. Ithamar stopped and instructed her to remain outside as he entered the open door of Jeru's quarters.

Once inside, Ithamar saw what looked to be the aftermath of a terrible fight with Prince Jeru's body lying in a pool of blood. The sight was eerily similar to the one four years earlier when Ithamar had found Uriah's body at the base of the east tower. The seasoned guard pushed aside the terrible memories and rushed to his captain. Ithamar felt for a pulse, but there was none. He looked around and thought it strange that his captain's sword was still in its scabbard with a fight as fierce as this one appeared to have been.

Ithamar's thoughts were suddenly interrupted by the screams of the maidservant who had disregarded his request to remain in the hallway. He quickly removed the hysterical woman from the room and went back to retrieve the screaming infant. When he emerged, Ithamar handed Prince Julean to the maidservant.

"Take the baby to Meridia at once!" he said with urgency.

This time the frightened maidservant did as she was told while Ithamar left to sound the alarm. Within minutes, Ithamar was back at the murder scene where he was surprised to find Narok and Mezrah. The two came to retrieve Mezrah's sword before it was discovered, and Narok managed to slip it beneath his robe seconds before Ithamar returned.

"What are *you* doing here?!" demanded the guard. His question was directed specifically at Narok.

"I was with my uncle when we heard the alarm. I thought perhaps my services may be of help," replied the cunning scribe as more Royal Guards rushed into the room.

"If I'm not mistaken, your services have nothing to do with investigating a murder," snapped Ithamar.

Before Narok could respond, Lamech entered the room followed by a visibly shaken King Shem. The physician knelt beside the dead captain and gently closed his eyes. The king steadied himself against the door frame after Lamech proclaimed what Ithamar already knew. The old physician righted one of the overturned chairs and offered it to King Shem.

"Sit here, Your Majesty," he said. Grateful for the gesture, the king sat before he collapsed in front of his men.

"Who did this?" he whispered.

"It appears to be the work of Bara soldiers, Your Majesty," reported Mezrah as he held up a piece of the evidence which he'd planted.

"Barbarians!" exclaimed Narok with a hint of delight.

"Whoever is guilty of this heinous crime shall pay," answered Ithamar sharply with an equally sharp glare. "But we shan't be hasty in our conclusion."

King Shem ignored their bickering as he scanned the room in disbelief. On the surface it appeared that a great struggle had taken place involving the Bara, however, something about the obvious didn't sit well with the wise king. Although the warriors were ruthless, Shem could think of no real motive for them to kill Jeru. Ithamar shared the same suspicion as he withdrew from the senseless argument with Narok and began combing the room for evidence. The guard was determined to find the truth behind his captain's murder; especially since he'd failed to do that for his best friend four years earlier. Meanwhile, instead of leaving with the murder weapon, Narok and Mezrah remained in the far corner of the room like arsonists compelled to stay and watch their fire burn.

******

After a sleepless night of gathering evidence, Ithamar still had more questions than answers. He felt tired, discouraged, and chilled from the morning air as he walked over to the fire to warm himself. While there, Ithamar saw part of Prince Jeru's cloak sticking out from beneath a small overturned table. He felt a renewed sadness as he lifted the table and bent down for the cloak. To his surprise, when Ithamar lifted the garment a scroll fell out and dropped to the floor. The guard suddenly remembered what Prince Jeru had said the night before about going to Kleiko's study to check on the Dragon Scroll, and wondered if this was it. Ithamar covered the scroll with Jeru's cloak and hurried across the room to King Shem.

As he approached the Ruler of Nepthali, Ithamar noticed the dusting of premature grey sprinkled throughout King Shem's dark hair, and lines forged by stress in the corners of his eyes. When he reached his king, Ithamar bowed with respect.

"Your Majesty, I've found something," he said. Ithamar's deep voice resonated against the stone walls and peaked Narok's interest.

"What is it?" asked the king. Narok walked towards them as Ithamar unfolded the cloak and handed the scroll to King Shem.

"The Dragon Scroll…but, what's it doing here?" asked the king with surprise. Narok's eyes bulged out like his uncle's at the sight of the scroll he'd waited four years to get his hands on, and had killed for.

"I'm not sure, but I think I might know. May we speak privately?" asked Ithamar. King Shem nodded in approval and the two walked to the opposite side of the room where the guard continued. "Last night, Prince Jeru asked me to keep an account of Narok's activities because he believed the scribe might attempt to steal the Dragon Scroll. When we parted, Captain Jeru told me that he was going to Kleiko's study to check on it. Perhaps he decided to bring the scroll here for safekeeping," suggested Ithamar. The king was silent as he recalled his last conversation with Jeru, and felt nauseous thinking he was responsible for his brother's death.

"He was merely doing what I told him to do...I asked him to have Narok followed," whispered the distraught king.

"This isn't your fault, Your Majesty," said Ithamar sincerely. But Shem took little comfort in Ithamar's reassurance.

"Tell me, Ithamar, do you believe the Bara are responsible for Jeru's death?" he asked.

"The evidence suggests they are, but my gut says otherwise," admitted Ithamar.

"What do you mean?" asked the king hoping for plausible cause to avoid conflict with the fierce warriors.

"When I found Prince Jeru, his sword was still in its scabbard. I can't figure out why considering the condition of the room," reported Ithamar. "And, his body had only one wound inflicted by a narrow blade like those belonging to a nobleman, or a Royal Guard. Bara weapons are intentionally crude to ensure their victims die of infection if not from the strike. I think someone merely wants us to believe the Bara are responsible." Ithamar then motioned with his eyes towards Narok and Mezrah. King Shem carefully considered the guard's implication of the two men's involvement. He distrusted them as much as Jeru had, but the wise king knew he mustn't allow his personal feelings to cloud his judgement, therefore, he decided that a visit to the Bara camp was warranted based on the evidence.

"Mezrah! Narok! Come here for a moment," called King Shem. The men scurried towards him and bowed.

"My King, your humble servants are here. Would you like me to take that for you?" asked Narok with his hand extended towards the Dragon Scroll.

"No," replied the king firmly as he covered the scroll with his dead brother's cloak. "I'm not convinced Bara soldiers are responsible for this atrocity, yet I cannot deny the evidence which points to their involvement. It is my understanding that the two of you know the way to their camp."

"Mezrah knows the way, Your Majesty," offered Narok keeping his eyes fixed on the scroll in the king's hand.

"Very well, Mezrah, I wish for you to leave at once," proclaimed the monarch. "Ithamar, you and your men shall follow shortly."

Narok pursed his lips at the news of Ithamar and his elite squadron tagging along, but suspected Mezrah should still have enough time to hide the murder weapon in Cain's tent before their arrival. Mezrah left for the Guard's Quarters expecting Narok to follow him with the sword, however, Narok lingered with the hope of obtaining the Dragon Scroll.

"Such a tragedy, My King, you must be exhausted. Why don't you let me take that scroll to Kleiko for you?" he offered.

"That shan't be necessary, but perhaps you could fetch me something to eat," replied King Shem. Narok was humiliated and infuriated by the degrading order, but had to comply.

Traitor in the Midst

"Of course, Your Majesty," he said coldly. As Narok turned hastily to leave, he collided with a guard and the murder weapon fell out from his robe onto the floor. Narok looked at the sword covered with Jeru's blood in horror, as did Ithamar, King Shem, and the other guards.

"SEIZE HIM!!!" yelled King Shem without hesitation.

Narok tried in vain to flee, but Ithamar stopped him with a solid punch to the jaw. The dazed scribe stumbled backwards and found himself surrounded by Luklin and Perez, Ithamar's most trusted guards. Ithamar picked up the sword and handed it to the king who shook with rage.

"Prepare the guillotine! Narok shall be executed within the hour for the murder of Prince Jeru. TAKE HIM AWAY!" shouted King Shem.

"With pleasure, Your Majesty," replied Ithamar. With merely a nod, his men grabbed hold of Narok and dragged him away.

"No, wait! I didn't kill Prince Jeru; I swear to you!" screamed the traitor. Ithamar was as enraged as the king, and far less controlled. He delivered another punch to Narok' face which knocked the scoundrel out cold before Narok could reveal that it was Mezrah who killed Prince Jeru.

******

Mezrah arrived at the Guard's Quarters to assemble his men and wait for Narok to bring him the murder weapon.

"Get ready to ride, we're going out to the Bara camp," he said to Laban.

"The Bara camp?" asked Laban with a mixture of surprise and fear. Mezrah started to explain, but stopped when a guard suddenly entered calling out his name.

"Mezrah! Mezrah!" exclaimed the man. "You must come quickly; Narok's to be executed within the hour!"

"WHAT?!?" shouted Mezrah in disbelief.

"He was found with the sword which killed Prince Jeru, so King Shem gave the order for his execution," continued the guard. Mezrah's mind raced. Part of him wanted Narok to be killed, but a larger part knew he still needed his nephew's diplomatic skills with the Bara soldiers, especially Cain now that he could no longer be framed for Jeru's murder.

"Where is he?" asked Mezrah.

"They've taken him to the dungeon where he awaits the guillotine," answered the guard.

"Laban, come with me," ordered Mezrah.

******

Mezrah and Laban found Narok in the dungeon where Mezrah was allowed into his nephew's cell to pay his last respects.

"Narok, what happened?!" asked Mezrah.

"Some fool ran into me which caused the sword to fall out of my robe," explained Narok. His face was disfigured and lip swollen from Ithamar's fist.

Traitor in the Midst

"They say you're to be executed within the hour!" exclaimed Mezrah. Narok thought for a moment before he remembered the gift his father had given him as a child to be used in an emergency such as this. He reached into his shirt and pulled out a tiny glass vial.

"What's that?" asked Mezrah.

"This is a potion made long ago by goblins. It can make a person appear to be dead when he is merely in a deep sleep. When I drink it, even a skilled physician such as Lamech shall be fooled," explained Narok. "After Lamech proclaims me dead, you must tell King Shem that the shame of my actions is too great a burden for you to bear so you are resigning from your position as a Royal Guard. Then tell him that you wish to leave the kingdom and take my body with you for a proper burial. Make sure you bring Obed as well since he may yet be of use to us. If anyone objects to your taking the boy, show them the adoption papers in my desk which I forged years ago."

"What about the Dragon Scroll?" asked Mezrah. "Don't you need it to take the throne?"

"We shall claim it later. For now, just get us to the abandoned farmhouse outside of Nepthali, and see to it you do exactly as I've said," ordered Narok. Mezrah nodded as his nephew opened the small vial and drank its entire contents. Within seconds, Narok's body convulsed, and his eyes rolled back into his head. Laban was terrified and turned to go, but Mezrah stopped him.

"Stay here, from now on you shall be my eyes, and ears within the castle," insisted Mezrah before calling out, "Guards!! Something's the matter! Come quickly!" The guards outside of Narok's cell rushed in to find their prisoner thrashing on the floor.

"I don't know what happened. He was fine one minute, and the next he was like this!" exclaimed Mezrah hysterically.

"Get the Royal Physician at once!" shouted one of the guards.

When Lamech arrived, he found Narok lying motionless on the ground. The physician performed a thorough examination while Mezrah played the part of a distraught family member. After Lamech pronounced Narok dead, Mezrah left at once to get the falsified adoption papers from Narok's desk before seeking an audience with the king.

******

Mezrah was permitted into the Throne Room where he found Ithamar with King Shem. Mezrah told them the shocking news of his nephew's death, but naturally, the king and seasoned guard were suspicious so Lamech was summoned at once. When the Royal Physician arrived, he confirmed everything Mezrah had said and assured the king that Narok was indeed dead.

"The shame of my nephew's actions is more than I can bear, Your Majesty. I beg of you to release me of my duties and let me depart from the kingdom with Narok's body so that I may give him a proper burial," pleaded Mezrah.

"Yes, of course," said the king who was happy to be rid of both Mezrah and Narok in the same day.

"I shall leave as soon as I gather my things, and Obed," added Mezrah. When Ithamar heard that, he spoke up.

"The kingdom shall be better off without you, but you have no business taking the boy," he objected vehemently. Mezrah reached into his vest and produced the papers from Narok's desk.

"As you can see, I'm the boy's legal next of kin, which means he belongs with me," stated Mezrah plainly. Ithamar snatched the papers and looked them over. However, King Shem merely wanted Mezrah gone and didn't care who went with the vile man.

"Be gone then, but see to it that I never see your face again lest you end up like your nephew," warned the king.

"I shan't promise that," said Mezrah under his breath as he half-heartedly bowed and hurried away. After Mezrah had gone, Ithamar turned to the king.

"Something about this feels wrong," said the loyal guard.

"I agree; take your men and follow Mezrah to the edge of Nepthali to ensure nothing is amiss…and that he doesn't return," said the wise king.

"As you wish, My King," replied Ithamar with a bow.

******

Mezrah returned to the dungeon where he collected Narok's body and placed it in the back of his wagon before fetching Obed from Meridia's quarters. When he arrived at the cozy home near the kitchen, Mezrah burst inside without warning.

"Get your things, Obed. You're coming with me!" he ordered. Startled by his unexpected entrance, Meridia stood between Mezrah and the frightened children.

"What's going on?" she asked sternly.

"Meridia isn't it?" said Mezrah as she nodded. "The boy's mine, so I'm taking him. Now, as I said, Obed, get your things!" Mezrah produced the false papers which, although Meridia could not read, appeared official. She was helpless to stop him as Mezrah gathered the boy's few belongings and forced Obed out to the wagon.

Ithamar watched the heart-wrenching goodbye from a distance surrounded by his elite squadron. He looked away feeling as if he had failed the boy and, even worse, failed Meridia. It was unbearable to hear Obed ask why he had to leave with a man claiming to be family who was a stranger to him when Meridia had no answers to give. Mitzy and Obed clung to one another until Mezrah pried them apart and lifted the boy onto the front of the wagon.

"Be strong, Obed, and remember that we shall always be here for you," assured Meridia as she wiped a tear from the child's cheek.

Mitzy was heartbroken by the sadness in Obed's eyes and wanted to help, but didn't know how. Suddenly, she thought of Polly. Mitzy reached into her pocket and slowly pulled out the unfinished doll.

"Here, Obed, I want you to take Polly…to remember me," she said softly while handing it to the boy.

"But, your father gave this to you," said the boy with wonder.

"I know, and that's why you must take her. When you feel sad or alone, just hold her and you shall feel better…at least I always do," whispered Mitzy. Although it was difficult to part with her most treasured possession, Mitzy found it worthwhile to see the joy it brought Obed.

"Thank you, Mitzy," he said. He wiped his nose with his arm while clinging to the piece of wood with his chubby little hand.

Their prolonged goodbye only served to worsen Mezrah's foul mood. He had no time for foolish sentiment knowing his presumed-to-be-dead nephew in the back of the wagon wasn't really dead. The bulgy-eyed man finally snapped the reigns and the horses pulled away leaving Mitzy and Meridia to watch them go just as they had watched Amalek and the boys ride off four years earlier. Neither said it, but both feared they would never see Obed again.

******

Ithamar and his men escorted the wagon to the edge of Nepthali where they stopped while Mezrah continued until the wagon disappeared over the ridge. Satisfied that nothing was amiss, Ithamar turned his men around and they started back for the castle. He was thankful for the company of Luklin and Perez, especially as the images of the tearful goodbye between Meridia, Mitzy, and Obed replayed in his mind. He felt like a failure for not having been able to stop Mezrah from taking the boy, but found some consolation in believing that justice had been served for Prince Jeru.

"Is something troubling you, Sir?" asked Luklin.

"I was just thinking about what a scoundrel Mezrah is for taking the boy," replied Ithamar. "I only hope that without the presence of he and Narok the dissension amongst the guards shall cease." Perez and Luklin nodded in agreement believing it would as they rode back to the castle.

Chapter 7

Haunting Resemblance

The effects of the goblin potion kept Narok in his death-like state for nearly two days. When he finally awoke, the young man had a terrible headache to match his throbbing lip from Ithamar's powerful punches. In spite of his discomfort, Narok knew he must ride out to the Bara camp before word reached Cain that he had killed Prince Jeru and tried to frame the Bara for it. If not, Narok was sure to end up as dead as everyone believed him to be. Upon his arrival, Narok's headache only worsened at the sight of the Bara camp in its usual disarray. He sighed and reminded himself that these inferiors were necessary to help him obtain the throne.

"Uncivilized hoodlums," he muttered. Narok dismounted and handed the reigns to Gilgal. "Don't forget the extra oats."

The old man nodded as he stared at Narok's swollen lip. The young man disregarded Gilgal's gawking and walked towards Cain's tent at his typically brisk pace. On his way, Narok passed three teenaged boys whom he'd never noticed before. One in particular had eyes which seemed to pierce right through him. It was Aykin, and he thought there was something familiar about this man wearing the robe of a Royal Scribe.

"Narok, what brings you here in daylight?" called a voice from behind. Startled, Narok turned around to see Cain's impressive figure.

"Cain, just the man I was looking for," answered Narok with a nervous laugh.

"What happened to you?" asked Cain referring to Narok's disfigured face.

"I've come with good news," answered Narok completely disregarding Cain's question. The Bara leader eyed him suspiciously knowing that a face which looked as badly as Narok's didn't usually coincide with good news.

"Prince Jeru is dead," stated Narok plainly. Cain agreed this was good news until Narok continued. "But, whoever did it tried to frame the Bara."

"What fool would dare do such a thing?!" demanded Cain looking ready to kill someone.

"I wouldn't know," replied Narok coyly. "But, I've confessed to the crime."

"Why would you do such a thing?" asked Cain with a raised brow.

"I couldn't risk King Shem waging a fool's war against you when I'm in need of your particular skill sets," said Narok.

"If you confessed to the murder, how is it that you're

Haunting Resemblance

still alive?" pressed Cain.

"I drank a goblin potion which gives the appearance of death," reported Narok proudly." So King Shem and everyone at the castle believe I am dead." Cain's anger started to subside until he remembered the Dragon Scroll.

"You fool! What about the Dragon Scroll? You said we must have it to take the kingdom. I don't tolerate incompetence, Narok!" he exclaimed and reached for his blade. Cain was unaware that Narok never had access to the ancient scroll, so nothing had really changed.

"Wait!" pleaded Narok hoping to save his life with clever rhetoric. "As I've told you before, I know the signs which mark the appointed time, and that's all we need. Once the black dragon awakens from his slumber, we can attack the castle and claim the power from the Dragon Scroll."

"You smell of deceit," scowled Cain. He eyed Narok carefully while keeping his hand on the pommel of his sword.

"The only smell of deceit upon me is that which remains after a lifetime of proclamations of loyalty to King Shem," replied the former scribe slyly.

"What about Queen Ashter? Are you certain you can withstand being away from her?" sneered Cain. Although not the response Narok had expected, he preferred it to being run through by Cain's sword.

"What do you mean?" he asked.

"You're a fool if you think I don't know of your desire for Queen Ashter. The beauty of a woman is nothing new, and has been the downfall of men since the beginning of time. Watch yourself, Narok, and see to it that taking the throne remains your highest priority," warned Cain.

"I can see you are a man of great insight for I've not revealed my forbidden love to anyone. However, make no mistake about my priorities, or my ability to take both Queen Ashter and the throne," boasted Narok.

"You shall have neither without our help," stated Cain plainly.

"Yes, of course," replied Narok thankful to still be alive.

"We shall continue this discussion in my tent," continued Cain. He wanted to kill Narok, but decided that he preferred dealing with Narok over Mezrah. As they walked, Narok and Cain passed the same three teenagers Narok had seen earlier and he once again felt their stares.

"Who are those street rats?" asked Narok motioning towards the boys.

"Afraid of children, are you?" mocked Cain. He slapped Narok on the shoulder and called them over. "Boys, come here! I want you to meet someone." They approached as he continued, "This is Narok; he shall make us all rich some day."

"Charmed," said Narok rudely. The boys on the verge of adulthood stood awkwardly before him, yet Narok's gaze was fixed solely on Aykin. The lad bore a haunting resemblance to the Royal Guard his father and uncle had killed four years earlier.

Haunting Resemblance

"Have I seen you before, boy? You look familiar," probed Narok. Aykin merely shook his head in reply. Without warning, Narok released the cat o'nine tails from his belt and cracked it at the lad's feet. "What's the matter, boy, are you mute?" Eliab and Kenan shook with fear, but Aykin defiantly stepped closer.

"No, Sire, I'm no mute. I just don't know when you would've seen me since, judging by your fine clothes, I'd say you came from the castle and I've never left Haliel," he replied without a flinch. When Kenan heard this, he wondered why Aykin had lied to the stranger.

"That's enough, Narok; I'll not have you intimidating these three. Besides, we have unfinished business," Cain reminded him sternly. Narok re-wound his whip and followed after the Bara leader like a child who'd been scolded. Once they were gone Kenan turned to Aykin.

"Why'd you tell him you were from Haliel when you're from Nepthali?" he asked.

"I told you a thousand times, Kenan, never repeat that!" snapped Aykin. "There's something about that guy I don't trust...and something familiar." Gilgal passed by with Narok's horse as the boys were talking.

"Gilgal, who was the man with Cain?" asked Eliab.

"You mean Narok? He's the son of Lott, and part of the chosen family that will rule the kingdom once the black dragon awakens," answered the old man. He walked away as Aykin's face went pale after hearing Lott's name.

"I'll kill him!" exclaimed the lad. Aykin started towards Cain's tent, but Eliab and Kenan stopped him before he got far. They pulled him to the edge of camp where they demanded an explanation.

"What's going on, Aykin? Do you want to get us all in trouble?" scolded Eliab as he held Aykin down. Aykin didn't hear a word Eliab said as his mind flooded with painful memories of his home burning to the ground while his mother, sisters, and baby brother screamed inside.

"That man's father, Lott…killed my family!" he shouted. Eliab and Kenan looked at one another with disbelief before sitting down on either side of Aykin. Since the day they met, Aykin had refused to speak of his family and now they understood why. Tears flowed down his face for the first time since that tragic night with Aykin being powerless to stop them. "I swear I'll kill him," he vowed through sobs.

"I'll help you, but not now," said Eliab while nudging Kenan to do the same. Kenan nodded, but the young man had no intentions of helping Aykin. Just like Natas, Kenan allowed years of jealousy towards Aykin to make him bitter against the lad who'd shown Kenan nothing but kindness. Kenan was already on his way down a separate path which would lead to his demise.

******

As evening fell upon the castle, Mitzy felt more alone than she had in a very long time. Normally, after the dishes were washed and put away she and Obed sat by the fire and played with Polly, while Ashes curled up beside them. And now, both Obed and Polly were gone. Mitzy tried to forget her sadness by practicing her needlepoint, but that only made the child feel worse. The walls seemed to close in around her, so Mitzy put down her sewing and headed for the door.

"I need some fresh air, Mama. May I please go to the Royal Gardens?" she asked. Meridia was in the chair rocking Baby Stefano, while Baby Julean slept in a basket near the fire. She didn't like the idea of Mitzy wandering around the castle after dark since the murder of Prince Jeru, but was willing to make an exception after seeing the sorrow in her daughter's eyes.

"Take your shawl, darling, and please don't be gone long," pleaded Meridia.

"I won't; thank you, Mama," replied Mitzy.

She grabbed her shawl and gave her mother a kiss on the cheek before leaving for her favorite place. Mitzy disappeared in a swirl of skirts and golden curls leaving Meridia alone with the royal babies, and her thoughts.

"I wish you were here, my dearest Amalek. Things have been so hard, especially for Mitzy," she said aloud. As Stefano cooed in her arms and she looked at his innocent face, Meridia was reminded of the hope each baby represents. Suddenly, her husband's favorite quote came to mind: *A hope which is pure and true shall not disappoint.* Meridia smiled and felt certain that regardless of the pain she and Mitzy were feeling, the hope within the Dragon Scroll was enough to keep them from despair.

******

Mitzy's golden curls bounced freely as she ran along the familiar route to the Royal Gardens. When she entered, Mitzy was instantly carried away to a world filled with beauty and tranquility rather than one filled with sorrow and pain. She followed the torches along the cobblestone path and wandered aimlessly until Mitzy reached the far corner of the garden. She sat down against a blooming hibiscus plant where waves of sadness washed over Mitzy as she recalled her painful goodbye to Obed. With her hands in her head, Mitzy finally let the tears she had been holding back all evening flow freely. Unbeknownst to her, Prince Roffius was on the other side of the same hibiscus plant. He, too, had come to the gardens to cry. Roffius heard Mitzy's sobs and peered through the natural openings of the plant to see who was there. When the young prince saw it was Mitzy, his heart ached even more.

As Mitzy sobbed, she felt a touch on her hand. She looked up and was surprised to see Prince Roffius kneeling beside her. Mitzy felt embarrassed until she noticed his tear-stained face. She rightly assumed his tears were for his brother, and for once Mitzy refrained from making conversation. She simply lowered her head and let her tears continue to flow. Roffius sat beside her and took hold of her hand. The two children understood each other perfectly without saying a word as they cried together side-by-side.

******

Two days later, Mitzy was in the kitchen helping Cook cut vegetables when Aunt Isabella entered with a girl Mitzy's same age.

"Oh, there you are, Mitzy, I've been looking everywhere for you! I want you to meet Cora. Her father is the new Royal Blacksmith," explained Isabella. "Since the two of you are the same age, I thought you should meet." The red-headed girl with green eyes and face covered with freckles twisted her long braid as she looked shyly at Mitzy.

"I'm very pleased to meet you, Cora," said Mitzy with a smile and polite curtsy. Cora smiled in return and the girls stared awkwardly at one another until Isabella broke the silence with her juicy piece of gossip for Cook.

"Have you heard the news about the former King Daven, the Queen Mother Lydia, and Prince Roffius?" she asked.

"What news is that?" replied the large man out of amusement rather than interest.

"They left in the Royal Ship first thing this morning for Hampenstein," she stated matter-of-factly.

"Hampenstein? Why did they go there?" blurted Mitzy in surprise.

"I heard it was because the Queen Mother feared for Prince Roffius' safety after Prince Jeru's brutal murder. Apparently, the poor lad was very upset and all but refused to go," reported Isabella proudly. Cook gave Mitzy a worried glance knowing how difficult the past few days had already been since Obed was taken away.

"Perhaps you're mistaken, Isabella. Perhaps they're simply on a holiday," he suggested.

"No, I'm quite certain since this came from a very reliable source," continued Isabella. "And as far as I know, they've no plans to return any time soon." With that proclamation, she excused herself and Mitzy was left with a new hole in her heart.

"It was very nice to meet you," said Cora as she followed Isabella from the large kitchen.

"Uh-huh," replied Mitzy absentmindedly. By habit, she reached into her pocket for Polly. But Mitzy found her pocket as empty as her heart. Polly was gone just like Obed, and now Ro. Cook hadn't seen Mitzy this sad since the day she and her mother arrived at the castle.

"I'm going to bake some cookies, would you like to help?" he asked hoping to lift her spirits.

"No thank you, Cook. I need to be going now," she replied softly.

******

Mitzy found the clouds covering the afternoon sun fitting to match her gloomy mood as she entered the courtyard for the Royal Stables to visit Moon Chaser and Starlight. She weaved in and out of villagers who were buying and selling goods in a daze. Mitzy felt as if the loneliness she was feeling would suffocate her, and wondered if the hope her father had spoken of from the Dragon Scroll was strong enough to save a life as full of heartache as hers from despair. Although Mitzy didn't want a life of despair, she now believed that was her destiny. She started to run hoping to escape the circumstances she was helpless to change. As Mitzy ran, her father's favorite quote suddenly came to mind: *A hope which is pure and true shall not disappoint.* She stopped in the middle of the courtyard and covered her eyes.

"I know I promised to always believe in Orpheus, Papa, but I don't know if I can anymore. I need a sign to know that the good dragon is real," she whispered.

Mitzy looked up expectantly, yet her hopes were dashed for the countless time when the only thing she saw was the cloudy sky. Even her curls seemed to sag with disappointment as Mitzy sighed deeply and continued towards the stables. She turned a corner and suddenly found herself face-to-face with Cora.

"Hello again," said the redhead while twisting her long braid and smiling shyly.

"Hello," replied Mitzy returning a smile of her own.

"I'm sorry to hear about your friend leaving," continued Cora.

"You must think me quite a fool to consider the prince my friend," answered Mitzy.

"Not at all," said Cora sweetly. Her freckles crinkled together as her smile widened. Mitzy looked up and saw the large blacksmith sign above them.

"Is your father really a blacksmith?" she asked.

"Yes, he's the finest in the kingdom," answered Cora proudly. "King Shem sent for us as soon as he saw Father's work. Father promised to teach me how to use a sword now that I'm eight. What does your father do?" Mitzy was accustomed to the question, but it was still painful to answer.

"My father and brothers were killed by Bara soldiers four years ago," she replied.

"I'm sorry; I didn't know. My mother died when I was five," said Cora softly. Mitzy instantly felt a connection with this girl.

"It seems we have much in common," she said. "Do you think your father would teach me how to use a sword?"

"Oh yes, I'm certain he would. I shall ask him tonight!" exclaimed Cora with delight. "Would you like to come inside?"

"I'd love to," answered Mitzy.

The girls ran up the steps leading to Cora's home above the blacksmith shop feeling happier than either had in a long time. As Cora talked faster than anyone she had ever met, Mitzy was convinced that this red-headed, freckle-faced girl was the sign she had asked for. Mitzy clung to the hope within the Dragon Scroll like never before, and resolved to always believe what she knew in her heart to be true despite difficult circumstances. At that moment, a brilliant ray of sunlight suddenly burst through the clouds.

******

Mitzy and Cora became the best of friends who disagreed only about the Dragon Scroll. Cora believed it was nothing more than a silly tale for small children, while Mitzy was certain that it offered hope for the entire kingdom. Yet, this difference was not enough to come between the girls who spent their days watching after Prince Stefano and Prince Julean, and their evenings in the blacksmith shop practicing their sword skills.

Cora's father was an outstanding teacher, and the girls were equally eager pupils. He taught them proper technique, form, and how to combine the two for deadly accuracy. Although Cora was quite skilled, it was Mitzy who excelled. Cora's father often said that he had never seen anyone outside of the Royal Family possess such natural abilities with a blade.

Dragon Scroll of Nepthali

Chapter 8

I Thought I Might Find You Here...

Eight long summers passed since both Obed and Prince Roffius were unexpectedly taken out of Mitzy's life. During that time, more heartache ensued. Ashes the cat drowned after chasing a mouse too close to the river following a heavy rain, and Aunt Isabella died of pneumonia. More recently, Cora's father was killed in a tragic accident which left the redhead devastated. Mitzy tried to comfort her best friend with the hope from the Dragon Scroll, yet Cora held fast to her belief that it was pure foolishness.

Besides bringing sorrows, the passage of time also brought Mitzy and Cora out of their awkward little girl phase. The sixteen-year-old maidens were now beautiful young ladies. Cora's strange mixture of red hair and green eyes evolved into a mysterious combination, and her freckles all but faded away into a creamy complexion. As for Mitzy, her beauty surpassed that of every maiden in the kingdom regardless of rank or pedigree. Her crystal blue eyes sparkled with a hint of mischief just like her father's, and her golden ringlets hung past her slender waist when not pulled back in her customary braid. Mitzy was the envy of every Lady of Court who thought it a travesty to have such beauty wasted on a maidservant. Cora and Mitzy never allowed jealousy to creep into their friendship, although their beauty caused much envy amongst their peers; especially Nalia. Nalia was a mousy looking maiden who despised Cora and Mitzy for no reason other than they were beautiful and she was not. Nalia was relentless in her bullying and schemes to get them in trouble.

However, for the good people of Nepthali this was an exciting time as they anxiously awaited the birth of a second child to their beloved King Shem and Queen Ashter. The entire kingdom had waited these eight long years for the royal couple to conceive again, and now shared in their joy with the baby's upcoming arrival. Everyone was excited, but none more than King Shem who insisted the castle be decorated from top to bottom with pennants, banners, and flags bearing the Royal Crest to give his child the welcome worthy of a prince or princess. Meridia was asked to serve as the baby's wet nurse as she had done for Prince Stefano and Prince Julean. The boys were now eight years old, and although cousins by blood they lived as brothers. They reminded Mitzy of Obed, whom she still missed terribly. Mitzy often asked farmers selling their goods for news of the boy but, sadly, the most common report was that Obed was living like a slave with Mezrah on an old farm.

******

As the guards finished hanging the banners and flags to welcome the royal baby on this beautiful summer day, a man in his mid-forties with bulgy eyes and unruly hair rapidly approached the backside of the castle on horseback

I Thought I Might Find You Here ...

He pulled back on the reigns and dismounted. Mezrah had finally returned for the Dragon Scroll, but first he must find the key Laban had left for him beneath some shrubs near a seldom-used door. The door led to the dungeon where Mezrah could easily enter the castle. For a moment, the bulgy-eyed man wondered if the coward from Mitzy's village had failed him, but Laban's desire for riches compelled his obedience and Mezrah soon found the key.

"Ah-ha, there you are!" he exclaimed. Mezrah wiped some dirt from the key before placing it into the keyhole. With one turn, the door opened and the bulgy-eyed man slipped into the dark corridors of the dungeon. He snuck past a few guards before bolting up a narrow stairway.

Although Mezrah hadn't been to the castle in eight years, he remembered the way to Kleiko's study with ease. Laban promised to make sure it was empty, and Mezrah counted on that being true as he snuck inside. The study was indeed empty, and the Dragon Scroll was sitting in its usual place on Kleiko's cluttered desk. Mezrah grabbed the scroll and tucked it beneath his shirt.

"Did you find it?" said a voice from the doorway. Mezrah spun around with his sword drawn.

"You fool!" he exclaimed putting down his weapon after seeing it was Laban. "What're you doing here?"

"I just wanted to make sure you found the key," answered the traitor.

"Of course I found it," snapped Mezrah. "I need you to alert Ithamar because we need the help of that bloodhound for our plan to succeed."

"Does Narok know about this plan?" replied Laban.

"Let me worry about Narok. You just make sure you put this key back in the same spot then meet me at the farmhouse after Narok and Cain have been captured."

"Yes, Sire," replied Laban dutifully.

The men parted ways with Laban leaving by way of the front staircase while Mezrah took a lesser-known servant's staircase. The bulgy-eyed man exited from a door within the wall which opened near the apple orchards where Prince Stefano and Prince Julean happened to be playing tag. The boys watched in amazement as a door opened that neither knew existed, and then a strange looking man appeared. Mezrah re-adjusted the scroll inside his shirt before running to his horse never noticing the two figures following after him.

******

Stefano's heart beat wildly as his slender frame sprinted like a deer over the uneven terrain of the forest.

"Hurry, Julean!" he called as wispy strands of blond hair fell across his face. Weighing twice as much as his nimble cousin, Julean struggled to keep up.

"I'm right behind you!" he managed between gasps for air.

Tree branches scratched at their arms, and leaves crunched beneath their feet as the boys chased after the horse carrying a man with bulgy eyes and unruly hair into the quiet countryside. When they reached a small ridge, the boys stopped and watched the man dismount at an old farmhouse. The bulgy-eyed man turned around as if sensing he'd been followed and the boys quickly dropped to the ground.

"Is that who I think it is?" whispered Julean.

"I think so," answered Stefano. Each knew about Mezrah's treachery from King Shem, but neither knew they were looking at the man responsible for killing Julean's father.

The boys peered over the bushes and watched Mezrah lead his horse into the barn. They wondered why Mezrah was at the castle knowing the man had been forbidden to return. When Mezrah emerged, he looked very angry.

"OBED! OBED!" he shouted.

Stefano and Julean watched a lad a few years older than they run in from the pasture. Neither remembered Obed, but both recognized his name.

"Do you think that's the same Obed whom Mitzy talks about?" asked Stefano.

"I'm not sure, but how many Obed's can there be?" answered Julean shrugging his shoulders.

The tall, slender thirteen-year-old lad slouched in front of Mezrah as the older man relentlessly scolded him for leaving the barn door open. Obed was accustomed to such volatile behavior after eight miserable years with Mezrah and Narok. However, the lad was kept from despair thanks to the hope in the Dragon Scroll which he had learned from Meridia.

As Mezrah continued his tirade, Obed reached into his pocket. The lad still kept the gift from Mitzy in his trouser pocket just as Mitzy had kept Polly in the pocket of her skirts. However, Polly was no longer just a piece of wood; she was now a beautiful doll. During his lonely years on the farm, Obed discovered his talent with wood and finished the doll which Amalek had started for his daughter twelve years earlier.

"After you do your chores in the pasture, tend to the horses!" shouted Mezrah before he stormed away. Standing all alone, Obed looked up to the sky.

"I sure hope you come back soon, Orpheus," he said softly. Obed shut the barn door before returning to the pasture. Once he was out of sight, Stefano turned to Julean.

"They're gone; let's go take a look around!" he exclaimed. Julean lacked his cousin's enthusiasm, especially after hearing dogs barking inside the farmhouse.

"I have a bad feeling about this," he said regretfully while following his cousin down the hill. They arrived at the barn and snuck inside to have a look around.

"I'm certain I saw something beneath his shirt when he left the castle. What if he stole something?" asked Stefano. Julean remained near the barn door to keep watch for Mezrah.

"I think we should get out of here before he comes back, or the dogs give us away," he said nervously. Stefano, too, heard the dogs but ignored Julean's suggestion as he approached a row of barrels. He stopped at the second one after noticing its slightly crooked lid.

I Thought I Might Find You Here ...

"This one looks like it has been opened recently," said Stefano. He lifted the lid and found an old scroll lying on top of a bunch of apples.

"Hey! That looks like the scroll I've seen on Kleiko's desk!" declared Julean as he peered over his cousin's shoulder.

"That's because it *is* the scroll from Kleiko's desk. I told you we should follow him," said Stefano. He grabbed the scroll and handed it to Julean.

"Hold this, your shirt is bigger than mine," he teased.

"Very funny, now can we get out of here?" asked Julean.

"Sure, I can't wait to show Father!" exclaimed Stefano.

******

Miles away in Haliel, Gilgal met Narok as usual when the young man arrived at the Bara camp. Gilgal took the reigns and instructed Narok to wait at a small table near the center of camp. The arrogant young man cringed again at the abhorrible conditions these barbarians were content to live in as he sat down beneath tattered strips of cloths failing to shield against the blazing summer sun.

"Sorry to keep you waiting," said a voice. Narok turned around and was surprised to see Aykin standing behind him. Although not as intimidating a figure as Cain, at twenty-one Aykin had matured into quite an impressive young man. He towered above Narok with the rugged appearance of a man accustomed to living outdoors. Aykin was the mirror image of his father, a connection Narok had made years ago. However, what

Narok didn't realize was that Aykin knew who he was and planned to destroy him.

"Where's Cain?" asked Narok impatiently.

"He asked me to get this meeting started," replied Aykin plainly as he sat across from Narok.

"Did he? How can I be sure?" asked Narok suspiciously.

"Because I said so," called a booming voice. Narok turned around again, but this time he saw the man he'd come to meet.

"Cain…I'm sorry, I didn't know if I could trust this young buck," answered a very smug Narok.

"You should know by now that when you speak with Aykin, you're speaking to me," stated Cain. The last man with goblin blood running through his veins heartily slapped Aykin on the back as he joined them at the table.

"Are your men ready?" continued Narok with disregard to the compliment Cain paid to Aykin.

"A better question might be, are you sure this is the appointed time?" snapped Cain. Although Narok was anything but sure, he'd waited long enough to claim the thrown and decided to attack the castle while the king was distracted by the upcoming birth of his child.

"I'm certain," answered Narok falsely.

"Well then, you need only to give the word," added Aykin as the two men glared at one another.

I Thought I Might Find You Here ...

"We shall attack tonight as planned, but Cain and I must first retrieve a key which Mezrah has arranged to have waiting for us. It opens a door within the back wall near the dungeon and shall allow for our entry into the inner castle. In order for us to get back in time, we must leave at once," continued Narok.

"Why not just retrieve the key right before the attack?" asked Aykin.

"Just how do you suppose we find it in the dark, young one?" retorted Narok.

"So, you're going to ride all the way to the castle, retrieve a key, and then just wait around until we arrive to attack?" pressed Aykin.

"Is this too difficult for you to follow, boy?" asked Narok with a raised brow.

"Enough of this!" interrupted Cain like a father of bickering children. "Aykin shall go with you. I've more important things to do than accompany you on your little errand." Aykin hadn't planned for this, but he was too close to crushing Narok's dream of taking the throne to jeopardize years of preparation by objecting.

"Let's go then," he said. Narok walked away in silent frustration as Aykin followed after him. Eliab and Kenan joined their friend before Aykin mounted his horse. "It looks like I'm going with Narok to the castle to obtain a key," said Aykin softly.

"What if he's discovered who you are and this is some kind of trap?" whispered Eliab with concern.

Kenan smiled slyly hoping his cousin was right. Over the years, his unwarranted jealousy of Aykin had clouded Kenan's judgement and blinded him to the true friend Aykin had always been. He managed to conceal his feelings from Eliab and Aykin, but an experienced deceiver like Mezrah saw right through the young man. The two were introduced while Mezrah visited the Bara camp with Narok years earlier, and had been meeting secretly ever since. The bulgy-eyed man preyed on Kenan's all-consuming jealousy, which made the young man easy to manipulate. Mezrah had little difficulty convincing Kenan to betray his friends with false promises of power once Mezrah became king in exchange for his help on Mezrah's quest for the throne.

"I don't think it's a trap, but you know what to do if it is," replied Aykin. Eliab and Kenan nodded their understanding, although only one of them was sincere.

"Are you sure about this?" pressed Eliab.

"I'm sure; and remember, protect the king at all costs," whispered Aykin as he mounted his horse. "See you in a few hours."

"Not if I see you first," replied Eliab with a sideways grin. Aykin laughed as he turned his horse around and sped out of camp in a cloud of dust.

******

Perez, Luklin, and Laban sprinted across the courtyard for the Royal Stables where they hoped to find Ithamar. They soon found their commander quietly polishing his boots in front of Starlight's stall. The past eight years had little effect on Ithamar who still retained his ruggedly

I Thought I Might Find You Here ...

handsome features and muscular frame. The only hints of age were a dusting of grey in his brown hair, and fine lines at the corners of his eyes.

"Excuse me, Sir, but we have reason to believe two riders are approaching from the east with the intent to harm the king," reported Luklin.

"What makes you say that?" asked Ithamar casually. Luklin and Perez looked at one another nervously then Luklin took a deep breath and responded.

"Because, Sir, it's a Bara soldier with the ghost of Narok," he reported sheepishly. Ithamar looked up with a cockeyed brow. He was tired of hearing about the so-called sightings of Narok's ghost riding throughout the kingdom. Ithamar was certain they were nonsense since he'd seen Narok's dead body with his own eyes. "Did you hear me, Sir?" repeated Luklin.

"Yes, I heard you. A Bara soldier, you say?" replied Ithamar purposely omitting the part about Narok's ghost.

"Yes, Sir," added Perez. "By good fortune, Laban overheard their plans last night." He stepped aside to reveal the cowardly guard standing behind him. Ithamar was surprised to see a weasel like Laban in the company of his most trusted guards.

"Tell me, Laban, what exactly did you overhear?" asked Ithamar as he returned to polishing his boots.

"Well, Sir, when I got to the tavern just outside of town last night, Mezrah was there. He was as drunk as a sailor and chatty as an old woman," explained Laban. Perez and Luklin chuckled and nodded their approval as Laban continued, "I overheard Mezrah bragging about the Bara leader, Cain, and Narok coming today to retrieve a key so they could get inside the castle and kill the king." This news gave the men Ithamar's full attention.

"Nonsense! Narok's dead!" he exclaimed.

"Perhaps, but we found the key right where Mezrah said it would be," continued Laban as he produced the key. Ithamar looked to Luklin and Perez who nodded in confirmation. Ithamar sighed and ran his fingers through his hair. He'd spent his whole career trying to keep the good people of Nepthali safe, and knew it was more than coincidence for Mezrah and Narok to be mentioned again on the same day.

"Gather the rest of the squadron and meet me around the back side of the castle. We shall finally put an end to this nonsense, and give whoever those riders are a surprise they shan't soon forget," stated Ithamar firmly. "We shall also find the traitor who left them that key!" Laban lowered his head and his heart beat a little faster as he followed them out of the stables.

"Shall I inform the king?" asked Perez knowing how Ithamar never kept things from him.

"Not until we have two more guests in the dungeon," snapped the commanding officer. He thought it best to wait; especially knowing that Queen Ashter was in the early stages of labor.

******

After their silent ride, Narok and Aykin finally arrived at the castle. They left their horses tied to a tree and traveled the rest of the way on foot. At the back side of the wall, Narok easily found the shrubs and door, but not the key. As he and Aykin searched for it, their tempers flared.

"Do you see it?" asked Aykin impatiently.

"That imbecile; he can't do anything right!" mumbled Narok under his breath.

"Looking for something boys?" called a voice.

Aykin immediately drew his sword and turned around. When he did, Aykin found himself looking at a key dangling from the tip of a sword held inches from his nose. Ithamar's impressive figure stood at the other end of the sword surrounded by a circle of blades belonging to the king's most elite squadron of guards. Aykin hadn't seen the uniform his father wore, or his father's best friend, since the night his father was killed. Aykin wrestled with his emotions and wondered if Ithamar would recognize him. But the stunned expression on Ithamar's face confirmed that he did as the guard stared in disbelief at what he thought were two ghosts.

"Uriah? Narok?" he whispered.

"Well, if it isn't the mighty Ithamar," mocked Narok. "What's the matter? Haven't you seen a man come back from the dead before?" Ithamar quickly composed himself as he realized this was no ghost, and only hoped he could fight the urge to make Narok one right then and there.

"Don't flatter yourself, Narok," Ithamar replied sharply. "I don't know what sort of dark magic you used eight years ago, but I can promise you that nothing shall save you this time. Take him away!"

"With pleasure," answered Luklin. He and the other guards bound both prisoners and started for the dungeon while Laban slipped away to deliver the news of their capture to Mezrah. As the guards forced Aykin towards the dungeon, Ithamar grabbed hold of his arm and stopped him.

"What's your name?" demanded the guard.

"Aykin," answered the young man in barely a whisper. Because his head was bowed, Aykin didn't see the color leave Ithamar's face or the guard step back in shock.

"Is something the matter, Sir?" asked Perez.

For a moment, Ithamar felt as if he'd gone back in time and was looking at his best friend. The resemblance was undeniable, and Ithamar knew that this young man was Uriah's son. Before now, Ithamar believed his greatest failures were never finding the truth surrounding Uriah's death and never finding his missing son. But, to see Aykin wearing the uniform of a Bara soldier surpassed them both to become Ithamar's consummate failure. The guilt was overwhelming, and the only way Ithamar found he could cope was to deny knowing the young man.

"I'm fine; he just looks like someone I once knew; but that boy would never associate with scum like the Bara. Take him to the dungeon!" ordered Ithamar coldly. His words were more painful to Aykin than if Ithamar had pierced him with a sword. The young man walked away in somber silence with hands bound through the dismal corridors of the dungeon. He agreed with Ithamar that no son of Uriah would stoop to the depths he had, and that's

I Thought I Might Find You Here ...

when Aykin allowed himself to remember who he really was.

******

Stefano and Julean stopped suddenly at the barn door when they heard the pounding of hooves from an approaching rider.

"It's a Royal Guard," whispered Stefano after peering through a crack in the door.

"What do you suppose he's doing here?" asked Julean.

"I don't know, but whatever it is, it can't be good," surmised Stefano.

Laban jumped from his horse and ran up the front steps of the farmhouse to inform Mezrah of Narok's capture. The boys watched as both men entered the house. Once they did, Stefano and Julean sprinted from the barn. While Mezrah was closing the door, he thought he saw something and quickly re-opened it.

"What's the matter?" asked Laban. Mezrah looked around, but the boys had managed to hide themselves behind some bushes.

"Nothing, I suppose," he said and closed the door. Laban sensed Mezrah's foul mood and hoped his news would improve it.

"It's done; Narok and the Bara are in the dungeon," he stated proudly.

"Very good, we shall leave at once for Og Mountain," said Mezrah with a sly smile. However, if he had known that the soldier captured with his nephew was Aykin rather than Cain, Mezrah's smile would've disappeared faster than the sun behind the dark clouds gathering overhead.

******

Stefano and Julean ran up the hill and through the forest until they reached the far edge of the meadow filled with wildflowers. Stefano was confident they hadn't been followed, so he stopped for a much needed rest even though they were nearly back to the castle. When Julean caught up to his cousin, the boys burst into laughter and collapsed onto the soft grass.

"I can't believe he didn't see us!" exclaimed Stefano.

"Yeah, or send the dogs after us!" added Julean.

Stefano propped himself on one elbow as the wind tossed his hair in every direction and caused the wildflowers to sway from side to side. His blue eyes danced with delight as he imagined the accolades he would soon receive from his father after showing him the Dragon Scroll. Stefano's decision to follow Mezrah had resulted in a greater outcome than the boy ever expected. He rewarded himself with a long blade of grass which he happily stuck between his teeth.

"Do you really think that was Mezrah?" asked Julean. He then made his eyes as large as possible and twisted his hair around his fingers to impersonate the bulgy-eyed man.

"I think so," laughed Stefano until he saw the black, ominous clouds blowing in from the east. "It looks like the weather is about to turn as fowl as your mood when Cook runs out of pastries." No sooner had the words passed over Stefano's lips did a gust of wind sweep the blade of grass from his mouth.

"Very funny, can't we rest a little while longer?" moaned Julean.

"No, we're almost there. And besides, if you didn't eat so many pastries you wouldn't need to take such long breaks!" teased Stefano.

"Maybe if you didn't get us into these scrapes we wouldn't have to do so much running!" quipped Julean.

"No more fooling, I've got a bad feeling about this storm," urged Stefano. He started off at a quickened pace and Julean found himself lagging behind. "Hurry up! At this rate, Mother shall have the baby and it shall be half grown before we get back," teased Stefano.

"Ha-ha, everybody wants to be a court jester," retorted Julean.

******

Mitzy raised her hand to shield the brilliant summer sun bursting between the clouds as she stepped outside for the first time all day. The hot, moist air was a telling sign of the impending storm, but she wasn't going to allow anything to dampen her spirits as Mitzy entered her favorite place. She deeply inhaled the familiar exotic scents of the Royal Gardens and casually adjusted the basket hanging on her arm. Mitzy had readily agreed when her mother asked her to fetch the ill-feeling queen some flowers, while Cora was sent to fetch the Royal Physician. Mitzy hoped nothing was seriously wrong since she knew how much this baby meant to King Shem and Queen Ashter after waiting so long to conceive again.

Mitzy wished she could stay in the gardens all day as the gentle breeze brushed against her cheek and swept along to orchestrate a delightful dance among the flowers. Her mind happily skipped from one daydream to another until she stopped at the hibiscus plant where she and Prince Roffius had cried together before he unexpectedly left for Hampenstein. Not a day passed in the eight years he'd been gone that Mitzy didn't think of the boy who'd stolen her heart as a child. Prince Roffius was now eighteen and had returned two weeks prior without his parents to assume his position as Captain of the Royal Guards. Mitzy was happy to hear of his appointment knowing it had been his dream since the murder of his brother Jeru. Although she hadn't seen him since his return, Mitzy heard reports from other maidservants that the prince was handsome and tall. She also heard that he was a master swordsman and playfully wondered if she could best him in a match.

"Are you going to stay here daydreaming, or can you come back and help us?" called a voice. Startled, Mitzy turned around. She smiled broadly after seeing it was Cora.

"I was just trying to decide which flowers the queen would like best," replied Mitzy with a twinkle in her eye. But Cora knew her well enough to know what that look meant.

"Did those flowers happen to be six feet two inches tall with wavy brown hair?" she teased. Mitzy blushed and wished her friend didn't know her so well as she put another flower into her basket.

I Thought I Might Find You Here ...

"I'm sure I don't know what you mean, Cora," she replied coyly.

"Prince Roffius has been back for nearly two weeks and you still haven't seen him. If I didn't know better, I'd say you were purposely avoiding him," accused Cora playfully with a raised brow. Mitzy shrugged her shoulders and bent down to pick one last flower.

"Don't be silly. But I've heard maidservants and Ladies of Court say that he's tall, handsome, and generally wonderful. I doubt he even remembers me," sighed Mitzy.

"I'm sure he does. He's just been busy with his new position as Captain of the Royal Guards," reasoned Cora.

"Perhaps," replied Mitzy with a faraway look in her eyes.

"Well, right now you need to get yourself, and these flowers, back to the Queen's Chamber. Lamech said the baby shall most likely come today," continued Cora. As much as Mitzy loved the gardens, hearing this news inspired her to leave.

"Today? That's wonderful!" she exclaimed. Mitzy looked with satisfaction at the colorful arrangement in her basket before glancing over the castle wall into the vast meadow filled with its own array of wildflowers. Instead of noticing the flowers as she usually did, Mitzy noticed the boys running through them.

"Now what do you suppose those two are up to?" she asked.

"Who?" asked Cora.

"Prince Stefano and Prince Julean; it looks as if they're in a frightful hurry. I hope they haven't gotten themselves into any trouble," answered Mitzy while pointing towards the meadow. Cora squinted and nodded her head in agreement.

"I know there's certain to be trouble for us if we don't get back before the queen has her baby. Now hurry up," she insisted. Just then, Nalia appeared in the gardens.

"Here you are, Mitzy! Your mother wants to know what's keeping you," she said while approaching. Mitzy and Cora knew better than to believe this was the only reason Nalia had come. Since Prince Roffius' return from Hampenstein, Nalia went to the Royal Gardens every day after hearing that he had frequented them as a boy. Cora rolled her eyes and turned to leave.

"I'm coming," called Mitzy.

She followed after Nalia and Cora, but stopped for one last look at the boys. While Mitzy was watching Prince Stefano and Prince Julean run towards the castle, Nalia stuck out her foot which caused Mitzy to trip when she turned back around. Mitzy unexpectedly found herself on the ground with the flowers she had chosen so carefully scattered all along the cobblestone path.

"Oh-no!" she exclaimed. Cora turned and saw Nalia grinning over Mitzy.

"Mitzy! Are you all right?" asked Cora with concern. She started back to help her friend, but Mitzy raised her hand to stop the redhead.

I Thought I Might Find You Here ...

"I'm fine, just clumsy," she said through clinched teeth while glaring at Nalia. "You two go ahead and tell Mother I shall be there shortly." Nalia smirked with delight at the thought of the scolding Mitzy was sure to get from Meridia for being late. The jealous maiden found this immensely pleasing as she turned on her heels and followed Cora back inside the castle.

******

Julean and Stefano bounded through the meadow until they reached the well-trodden path leading to the castle. The inner courtyard was filled with the usual townspeople, merchants, and prominent Ladies of Court; however, there was an extra excitement in the air mixed with a sense of urgency. Everyone seemed to know that Queen Ashter was in labor and hurried to finish the final preparations to welcome the royal baby.

"Wow! This looks amazing!" exclaimed a wide-eyed Julean as he looked at the colorful banners and flags bearing the Royal Crest. But Stefano was anxious to show his father the prized scroll, so he hurried Julean inside. They ran down the long hallway until the boys reached the Throne Room.

"We found it! We found it!" they shouted as they burst into the epicenter of Nepthali.

"What is it this time? One of Cook's pastries, perhaps?" asked King Shem in jest. Julean felt his cheeks flush remembering the crème puff in his pocket from earlier that morning. When he reached into his pocket for it, the delicacy was gone. Julean resigned that it had been lost somewhere along the way in their recent adventure.

"No, it's nothing like that," he answered.

"Then tell me, what news warrants such an entrance?" asked the king with a smile. He was in a good mood, and had been for weeks. Most attributed this to the upcoming birth of his child, but those closest to Shem knew it was because Roffius was finally home.

"It's Mezrah, Father, he was here at the castle!" exclaimed Stefano.

******

Mitzy mumbled things she'd like to say to Nalia while crawling on her hands and knees to gather the scattered flowers. She reached out for one, but a hand suddenly appeared and picked it up. She looked up to see who it was, but the afternoon sun shone directly into her face and blinded her. The same hand holding the flower took hold of Mitzy's hand and helped the maiden to her feet.

"Allow me, my lady," said a deep, soothing voice.

"Thank you, Sire…," said Mitzy as she brushed the dirt from her skirts while her eyes adjusted from the sun. However, when Mitzy looked up and saw Prince Roffius she quickly corrected herself. "I mean, Your Highness." She curtsied and tried to keep her heart from beating out of her chest. He was much taller, and his hair was longer than she remembered, but it had the same natural highlights from hours of riding throughout the kingdom. Mitzy never expected him to recognize her, but she was wrong.

"Hello, Miss Mit, I thought I might find you here," he said cordially. Mitzy looked at him in disbelief wondering if she'd heard him correctly.

I Thought I Might Find You Here ...

"Me? In the gardens? Yes, I'm here," she replied nervously. As soon as the words left her mouth, Mitzy wished she could take them back. She had dreamt of this moment for eight years, but seeing Roffius in person caused Mitzy forget everything she'd rehearsed. She regressed to an old habit and reached into her pocket.

"Still holding onto Polly, and those foolish notions of Orpheus?" he teased. Her cheeks turned a deeper shade of red.

"I don't have Polly anymore. I gave her to Obed the day he left, but I shall always have hope in the good dragon's return," answered Mitzy firmly. Roffius hadn't meant to be insulting, although he disagreed with her about the existence of a good dragon.

"Yes, I remember how difficult it was for you when the boy left," he continued. Mitzy was saddened to hear Roffius poke fun of her belief in Orpheus, but his thoughtfulness about Obed warmed her heart.

"It was a difficult time for us both," she said with compassion.

He nodded, yet Roffius was so distracted by her beauty and mesmerized by the sound of her voice that he barely heard what she said. He had intentionally avoided Mitzy since his return, but was unable to resist coming to the gardens any longer in hopes of seeing her. Roffius feared his feelings would be the same now as when he was a child, and looking into her crystal blue eyes he realized they were even stronger.

"I remember you used to come here often when we were children," he heard himself say.

"Yes, it's been my favorite place ever since Mother and I arrived at the castle," she admitted. There were so many things Mitzy wanted to ask, and to tell him, but she knew it wouldn't be fitting. They were no longer children, and the chasm between their two worlds was wider than the canyons in the province of Belzeeb. Mitzy understood that whatever feelings she had, or thought she had, for the prince must be ignored.

"I remember that day. You were crying beside Mother's pink rose bush, and I gave you a cookie," said the handsome prince as he pointed to the spot Mitzy knew so well. She started to respond, but a Royal Guard suddenly appeared.

"Excuse me, Captain, but the king has requested your presence in the Throne Room at once," he said with a bow.

"Duty calls," said Prince Roffius with a dashing smile. "It was very nice to see you again, Miss Mit."

As he handed her the flower, their fingers brushed against one another and Roffius felt as if he'd found a piece of himself which had been missing. He suddenly didn't know which frightened him more: his feelings for Mitzy, or a life without her. Mitzy watched the prince and guard walk away until they disappeared into the castle.

"It was very nice to see you again, too, Ro..." she whispered.

Chapter 9

The Coming Storm

Roffius was distracted with thoughts of Mitzy as he entered the Throne Room where King Shem, Stefano, and Julean stood huddled together.

"What's going on, Brother?" asked the prince. Shem was relieved to see Roffius walking towards them.

"Stefano, tell your uncle what you've told me," encouraged the king.

"Mezrah was here at the castle and we followed him back to an old farmhouse. He went into the barn before going inside the house, so Julean and I decided to check out the barn once Mezrah was gone," explained Stefano.

"You did what?!" exclaimed Prince Roffius.

"We stayed out of sight, I promise, and we left as soon as a Royal Guard arrived," continued the boy.

"A Royal Guard met with Mezrah?" inquired Roffius.

"Yes," answered Julean.

"Do you know who it was?" pressed Roffius.

"No, we were in such a hurry to leave that we didn't get a good look at him," said Stefano.

"You're lucky the two of you weren't seen. Mezrah's not a man to be trifled with by anyone, let alone two boys," scolded Roffius.

"We're sorry, but while we were there we found the old scroll from Kleiko's desk," reported Stefano proudly. Roffius gave a worried look to Shem.

"The Dragon Scroll?" he asked. The king nodded slowly and his usually steady hands trembled when Shem handed the precious parchment to Roffius. "Guards!" yelled Prince Roffius while tucking the scroll deep within his vest. The men posted outside the door rushed in. "Have Ithamar take roll call of the Royal Guards at once!" The men bowed and immediately left to carry out their captain's order. "We shall find who the traitor is and deal with him."

"Yes, but right now we must find Kleiko," whispered King Shem.

Roffius went numb as he realized his brother was implying that this was the appointed time mentioned in the Dragon Scroll. The past eight years hadn't changed Roffius' cynical belief of Orpheus, yet he respected Shem and his belief. Roffius also remembered from Kleiko's teachings that the birth of twins to the Royal Family on a wickedly stormy night marked the appointed time. Just then, a blast of thunder shook the castle as Ashter's screams of labor floated down from the south tower.

"Let's go," said Roffius with urgency. The men started to leave with Stefano and Julean following close behind, but King Shem was quick to stop them.

"Boys, you've done the kingdom a great service by recovering this scroll, however, right now I need you to check on your mother," he said firmly. Stefano and Julean knew that tone well enough to know it meant Shem's mind was made up.

"Yes, Father," replied Stefano dutifully.

The boys watched as King Shem and Prince Roffius quickened their pace upon leaving the Throne Room while rolls of thunder echoed off the stone walls, and dark clouds swallowed up the afternoon sun.

******

The Royal Guards whom Prince Roffius sent to find Ithamar found their commander running through the pouring rain across the courtyard on his way back from the dungeon.

"Commander, Captain Roffius has ordered for an every-man roll call," stated one.

"Now?" asked Ithamar. He found the timing of such a request strange with the queen being in labor, as well as inconvenient given that he was on his way to tell the king the news about Narok being alive and in the dungeon.

"There seems to be a traitor among us and Captain Roffius wants to discover who it is," answered the other guard.

"What do you mean?" pressed Ithamar.

"We only know that Prince Stefano and Prince Julean rushed into the Throne Room, and moments later the king sent for Captain Roffius. Moments after the captain arrived, he gave us this order," continued the first guard.

Although Ithamar didn't have all the information, the seasoned guard had enough to understand the urgency of the situation. He gave the signal for an every-man roll call and the courtyard was eventually filled with Royal Guards standing at attention in the pouring rain. After a meticulous inspection, Ithamar discovered that Laban was the unaccounted guard. Ithamar was outraged as he dismissed the men and sent a squadron to find the traitor while he set out to find the king.

******

Neither Stefano nor Julean wanted to admit it, but both were frightened by the raging storm outside. Yet, Julean's hunger superseded his fear as the boy started for the kitchen.

"I don't know about you but I'm starving. Let's see what Cook's preparing for dinner," he suggested. Stefano agreed as both forgot all about their promise to check on Queen Ashter.

The boys passed by servants lighting candles and torches earlier than usual because of the darkness caused by the storm. Although summer storms were common in Nepthali, nothing was common about the one overhead.

"This storm reminds me of the one Meridia often speaks of; you know, the one that's supposed to happen when Natas wakes up," said Stefano nervously.

"Are you trying to scare me?" accused Julean.

The Coming Storm

"No, but do you think it could be that storm?" continued Stefano.

"I sure hope not, but right now I'm too hungry to care," answered Julean honestly.

"Is your stomach the only thing you think about?" asked Stefano in jest.

"Only when it's empty!" exclaimed Julean. Stefano laughed in agreement as he realized that he, too, was famished.

******

A sense of impending doom filled the castle as Queen Ashter's screams of labor echoed off the stone walls. The wind mimicked her cries with shrieks of its own as the storm took on a supernatural force. Maidservants scurried in every direction to get water and cloths while fearing the storm was a bad omen for their beloved queen and baby. Mitzy and Nalia were two of the servants sent to the kitchen to retrieve more water. As she carried her full bucket, Mitzy noticed an ominous glow at the base of Og Mountain each time she passed one of the many large windows.

"Look, Nalia! The Bara soldiers are gathering," she said. Mitzy felt a chill run down her spine as she recalled the prophecy of Natas awakening after the birth of twins on the night of a terrible storm. A bolt of lightning suddenly zig-zagged across the blackened sky and the castle vibrated from another blast of thunder.

"Hurry up, Mitzy!" snapped Nalia. "We don't have time to gaze out windows when Lamech needs this water for the baby!"

"I'm coming," replied Mitzy. She quickly tucked one of her golden curls behind her ear that had fallen free from her braid before re-adjusting her bucket as Nalia disappeared around a corner.

When Mitzy rounded the same corner, Nalia stuck out her foot just as she had done in the Royal Gardens and tripped the unsuspecting maiden. Water spilled from her bucket onto Mitzy's skirts which produced malicious giggles from Nalia. Just then, King Shem and Prince Roffius rounded the same corner from the opposite direction on their way to Kleiko's study. Both nearly slipped on the water and Roffius almost stepped on Mitzy, but his quick reflexes allowed him to stop in time. He looked down with a smile and extended his hand to the embarrassed handmaiden.

"This is the second time I've seen you like this today, Miss Mit," he chuckled. The handsome prince helped Mitzy to her feet as Nalia watched in disbelief.

"Thank you, Your Highness," said Mitzy with red cheeks and a curtsy.

"Your Excellences'," said Nalia with an exaggerated bow. She hoped to capture the eye of the handsome prince; however, Roffius paid her no attention as he and the king continued on their way. Mitzy wondered where they were going in such a hurry but not more than she wondered how she was going to explain the empty bucket to her mother.

******

When Mitzy and Nalia returned to the Queen's Chamber, Cora immediately noticed Mitzy's wet skirts.

The Coming Storm

"What happened?" she silently mouthed. Mitzy motioned with her eyes to Nalia which was explanation enough for Cora. Mitzy's stockings squished inside her boots as she walked to the queen's bedside with her empty bucket. Lamech was already there speaking softly to the weary queen.

"That's it, Your Majesty, you're doing fine," said the physician calmly.

"AAAAHHHH!" screamed Queen Ashter as another contraction hit. Her face was covered with sweat, and her black hair lay in a tangled mess across her pillow as Queen Ashter struggled to push the baby out. She was in considerable pain and felt strangely anxious for her husband.

"Where's the king? Someone, please, get Shem!" moaned the distraught queen.

"Fear not, Your Majesty, he shall be here soon," Lamech reassured her. Seeing her distress, Mitzy leaned in close to her mother.

"I just saw the king running towards the east wing," she whispered. Meridia looked at Mitzy and noticed her daughter's wet skirts and empty bucket.

"You've got some explaining to do," she said with a raised brow. Mitzy looked down in shame while Meridia walked across the room to Cora.

"Go to the east wing as quickly as you can and fetch King Shem!" she exclaimed.

"Yes, my lady," answered Cora with a curtsy. She passed Nalia on her way out and the two exchanged icy glares.

Meridia resumed her position beside the queen and informed Lamech that a maidservant was on her way to fetch the king. He sighed with relief knowing this would comfort the queen.

"The king is on his way, Your Majesty. Now please, focus on the baby. Just a little more time," coached the physician.

******

Another blast of thunder crashed and streaks of lightning shattered the darkened castle as King Shem and Prince Roffius entered Kleiko's study.

"Kleiko, are you here?" called the king with urgency. Like an apparition, Kleiko suddenly appeared from around the corner.

"I am here, My King," said the Chief Royal Scribe.

"Stefano and Julean have just returned the Dragon Scroll after finding it in Mezrah's possession," stated King Shem. He motioned to Roffius who produced the scroll from his vest. Kleiko looked at the scroll briefly before looking out the open window to the ominous glow at the base of Og Mountain.

"I fear, My King, that this is the appointed time, however, I've discovered something of great importance which may alter everything. May I please see each of your left forearms?" asked the old scribe. Neither Roffius nor Shem understood why Kleiko would ask such a thing at a time like this, but both trusted the old scribe enough to comply. They rolled up their sleeves for Kleiko to examine. When he was done, Kleiko staggered backwards.

"What is it Kleiko? What's the matter?" asked King Shem steadying the old man.

"I'm afraid I've spent so much time in study of the Dragon Scroll that I dare say I've neglected other ancient writings," he answered with a faraway look in his eyes.

"Kleiko, I don't understand. Tell us what you've found," continued the king.

"This morning while reading one of Carmi's journals, I discovered that Orpheus gave King Thaddeus a very special gift just hours before the good dragon left the kingdom," said Kleiko.

"What was it?" asked King Shem.

"A kiss," answered the old scribe.

"A kiss?" repeated Roffius while throwing his hands up in exasperation.

"Yes, the kiss of a dragon onto human skin produces a permanent mark. Carmi called it the Mark of Royalty, and it appears on all those of royal blood," explained Kleiko.

"What does this mark look like?" asked the king.

"Carmi said in his journal that it looks like a small heart. I would show you, but I'm afraid that neither of you possess it. This means that you, Shem, are not the true King of Nepthali," proclaimed Kleiko as another blast of thunder erupted overhead. Roffius and Shem immediately looked down and inspected their forearms.

"This is ridiculous!" snapped Roffius. "Check again!"

Although quite certain of his findings, Kleiko checked again out of respect for the men whom he'd spent a lifetime serving.

"I'm sorry, Captain," said the scribe sadly after completing a second inspection. Shem and Roffius were faced with the reality that they were mere commoners. Roffius found this further proof that the notion of a good dragon was pure foolishness.

"How can this be?" whispered Shem. As quickly as flashes of lightning streaked across the dark sky, everything Shem and Roffius had believed to be true was now a lie.

"But, if we're not the Royal Family, who is? And why aren't they here at the castle?" demanded Roffius.

"Let me try to explain," answered the wise scribe. "You see, as soon as I learned about this Mark of Royalty, I searched through Carmi's other journals. When I did, I found a detailed recording of the last meeting between Orpheus and King Thaddeus. Carmi referenced a secret plan which would ensure the safety of the Royal Family even after Natas awakens," explained Kleiko.

"What plan?" asked Shem,

"According to the journal, King Thaddeus took the queen and their young son away from the castle before Orpheus left. The true Royal Family was replaced with a substitute family sworn to secrecy. The two of you are descendants of that substitute family," explained Kleiko.

"What does this mean?" asked Shem in a whisper.

"It means that you are still very important to the kingdom, for it is the members of your family whom shall protect the real Royal Family from Natas," reassured Kleiko. "It also means that the real heir is safe out there somewhere...for now. However, there is more."

"What more can there be?" sighed Roffius.

"I have learned that the sword you carry, Shem, was made by dragon magic from one of Orpheus' scales," stated Kleiko. Shem looked down at the blade tucked inside his scabbard with an overwhelming sense of unworthiness. It was given to him at his coronation, and had been passed down within his family for generations. "This means it can defeat a dragon, and it was given to your family for that very purpose. Don't you see, the sword possesses a great power which...," but Kleiko stopped when Cora unexpectedly burst into the room.

"Excuse me, My King, but the baby is almost here and Queen Ashter desperately needs you!" she blurted in-between gasps for air. Cora had run all the way from the south wing, and Shem sensed the urgency in her voice. At that moment, nothing else mattered to him.

"Roffius, we must make haste!" exclaimed Shem. Roffius returned the Dragon Scroll to its place inside of his vest as he and Shem burst from the room. Kleiko grabbed his walking staff wishing he'd been able to tell them that the sword possessed even greater power than the Dragon

Scroll, but the only way to unleash it was to unroll the scroll in the sword's presence.

******

Down in the kitchen, Stefano grabbed an apple while Julean looked for pastries. He soon resigned himself to indulging himself with the plate of freshly baked cookies. The boy happily stuffed them into his mouth and pockets. As they enjoyed their snack, Stefano and Julean noticed servants boiling water and ripping cloths instead of preparing their next meal.

"What's going on? Why aren't they making our dinner?" asked Julean.

"This is no time to be thinking about your stomach, My Prince, the queen is having her baby!" answered a familiar voice from behind. The boys turned around to see Cook's large face smiling at them.

"Baby…now? Oh no!" exclaimed Stefano.

He shot from the kitchen like an arrow released from its bow, while Julean grabbed a handful of rolls and added them to the cookies in his pockets before following after his cousin. In the hallway, Julean saw Stefano take a sharp turn and knew he was headed for the secret passageway.

"Hey, slow down!" called Julean. He struggled to keep up without losing the food in his pockets.

******

Up in the south tower, Queen Ashter tried to focus on Lamech's soothing words as her labor pains intensified.

She was exhausted, but gathered what little strength remained to bring her baby into the world.

"Push, Your Highness!" pleaded Lamech as the baby's head crowned. Her cries mixed with the ghostly howls of the wind during each contraction. Ashter pushed as hard as she could and the baby landed in the waiting hands of the trained physician who held up the newborn for everyone to see.

"It's a boy! You've done it, Your Majesty! It's a boy!" he announced with joy. Mitzy sighed with relief knowing that the queen's discomfort was finally over. She soaked a fresh cloth in the basin of cool water and handed it to her mother who then applied it to Ashter's forehead.

"Well done, Your Majesty he looks just like the king," said Meridia softly.

"I'm glad," replied Ashter with a weak smile.

The mood in the room was one of great joy as some maidservants cleaned the wailing newborn while others tended to the weary queen. However, Ashter strangely felt no relief, and fear gripped her as the labor pains continued. She found herself unable to resist the natural urge to push. Lamech heard the queen's groanings and quickly returned his attention to Ashter.

"Lamech, what's happening? Why does the pain continue?" she moaned. After a brief inspection, the physician's face went pale.

"There's another baby...," he whispered. "Your Majesty, you must push a little longer to get the second child out."

Meridia gave Lamech a terrified look since she knew that the birth of twins on the night of a terrible storm marked the appointed time for Natas to awaken. Although she was afraid, Meridia tried to remain calm for the sake of the others; especially the queen. She held Ashter's hand and looked at Mitzy.

"Fetch more water for the queen as quickly as you can, child!" instructed Meridia. Mitzy felt as if someone had removed her legs from beneath her as she realized what was happening. The birth of twins on the night of a terrible storm marked the appointed time for Natas to awaken. Mitzy looked around the room for Cora, but remembered that her best friend had been sent to fetch the king. Mitzy quickly grabbed her empty bucket and left for the kitchen while the story of the great dragon brothers replayed in her mind. Mitzy was gripped with fear at the thought of the evil dragon coming to kill King Shem…and Prince Roffius.

She reached the kitchen in record time where she began to fill her bucket with fresh water. As she did, Cook approached with an arm-full of wood to add to the fire beneath the boiling water.

"What's going on up there? I thought the baby was born? Why are you getting more water?" he asked. Mitzy hesitated for a moment but decided to tell Cook for his own safety.

"There's another baby, Cook. The appointed time has come," she whispered. Although standing beside a warm fire, Cook suddenly felt a cold shiver throughout his body.

She finished filling her bucket and hurried back into the crowded hallway as servants gathered to spread the news of the baby prince. Mitzy struggled to keep the water from spilling out of her bucket as she maneuvered around them since she had finally dried off from her earlier accident. When Mitzy turned the corner at the top of the stairs of the south wing, she saw Prince Stefano and Prince Julean exiting from the secret passageway.

"Your Majesties!" she called. The boys turned around and burst into smiles at the sight of Mitzy.

"Mitzy, is Mother having the baby?" asked Stefano anxiously.

"She's given birth to a son, but a second baby is on the way," explained Mitzy while trying to remain calm. The boys looked at each other with surprise as they followed after the beautiful handmaiden. They entered in time to see the second baby slip into Lamech's waiting hands.

"It's another boy!" exclaimed the physician proudly.

******

Deep within Og Mountain after generations of slumber, thin trails of black smoke and an ominous green glow filled the dragon's lair. Natas breathed in deeply and steadied his enormous frame on legs which had gone unused for far too long. Once he was standing, Natas stretched his mighty wings as wide as the cave would allow. The hideous creature could think of nothing other than killing the Royal Family as he flew out from the cave into the raging storm. He released a roar which belittled the crashes of thunder throughout the kingdom.

******

When Mezrah arrived at the base of Og Mountain with Laban, he scanned the crowd of Bara soldiers for Kenan. When Mezrah spotted the young man, Kenan touched the tip of his hat to signal his readiness for what was about to unfold. Mezrah returned the gesture with a sly smile.

Flames from the large bonfire Mitzy and Kleiko had seen from the castle whipped in every direction with the howling wind. Mezrah continued to scan the crowd and sensed that the unruly soldiers were as hungry for battle as he was for the throne. He was confident that both desires would soon be satisfied until he saw Cain approaching on horseback. Mezrah stared in disbelief at the impressive leader who was supposed to be in the dungeon with Narok. Since Cain clearly was not, Mezrah knew he must now free his nephew and alter his plans.

"I thought you said Cain was captured?" he whispered to Laban.

"He was…at least I thought it was him," replied Laban. Cain eyed Mezrah and Laban suspiciously as he stopped his horse in front of them.

"Something the matter, Mezrah?" asked the intimidating Bara leader.

"I thought you were with Narok," answered Mezrah nervously.

"I sent Aykin with him. Is there a problem?" asked Cain with a raised brow. Mezrah chose his words carefully knowing that his life depended upon the believability of his answer.

The Coming Storm

"My Lord, my surprise in seeing you stems purely from delight over your well-being as this Royal Guard has informed me that Narok and his companion were captured and thrown into the dungeon," he explained. Cain had expected their incompetence, which was exactly why he hadn't accompanied Narok. He glared at Mezrah then raised his muscular arm to silence his men.

"Brothers, I've just learned that our comrade, Aykin, has been captured by the king's guards," he shouted over the storm. The rowdy Bara soldiers erupted in cries of outrage. "Silence! You shall have your revenge, and free Aykin, for tonight we shall claim what was promised to us long ago!" The shouts of men in agreement were deafening as a bolt of lightning flashed across the sky. Yet, Mezrah paid them little attention because he was transfixed on the rapidly approaching large, black shadow. Suddenly, a roar crashed in unison with the thunder and the ground shook beneath them.

"Look! The black dragon has awakened to lead us to victory!" proclaimed Mezrah.

Gilgal was amongst those present, and the sight of the hideous creature was more than his old heart could bear. He dropped dead and his body was trampled by the frenzied soldiers on horseback racing after the beast. Kenan started to mount his horse and join the others until Eliab grabbed hold of his cousin's arm.

"Remember, stick to the plan," he said firmly.

"Don't worry, I know," snapped Kenan. He broke free from his cousin's grip and soon both were riding alongside Cain at the front of the pack.

Dragon Scroll of Nepthali

******

Lamech started to hand the second baby to a maidservant, but stopped when it made no first cries of life. He pulled the infant close and carefully worked to clear his mouth and nose as Queen Ashter watched anxiously.

"What's wrong? Why is there no cry?" she pleaded.

"Easy, Your Majesty; try to relax," encouraged Meridia in spite of her own concerns about the baby.

Lamech did his best to revive the infant; however, it was no use. When he looked at the distraught queen, the kind-hearted physician could not bring himself to say what she already knew. Therefore, Lamech merely placed the stillborn baby boy into her arms as Ashter sobbed uncontrollably. Meridia cried alongside her queen knowing first-hand the pain of losing a child.

In a far corner of the room, Stefano and Julean leaned against Mitzy as they watched in somber silence. Lamech understood this was an extremely difficult time, but he loved the Royal Family too much to remain silent. Like Meridia, the old physician understood the significance of the birth of twins on the night of a terrible storm.

"Your Majesty, the time has come for the courage in both men and women to arise. I know you are weak, but you must make haste and flee with Stefano and the baby while there's still time," urged Lamech.

Queen Ashter sat dazed as she clung to her stillborn baby. She could barely comprehend the weight of Lamech's words, let alone prepare to ride. Ashter desperately wished Shem was with her, and wondered where he could be. The fragile queen felt as if she may suffocate under the weight of despair until suddenly, the doors to her private chamber flew open.

"Ashter, Ashter, I'm here!" exclaimed Shem.

******

As Ithamar crossed the courtyard on his way inside the castle, he felt the ground beneath his feet tremble. Without warning, a ball of fire fell from the sky and made kindling of the outer gates. This blast was immediately followed by another against the west tower. Ithamar looked up and saw an enormous black shadow. Before he even saw the dragon, Ithamar saw the first wave of Bara soldiers flooding into the courtyard. Flank riders jumped from their horses and began scaling the outer wall, while others ambushed Ithamar's men as they scrambled to their positions.

"ATTACK FORMATION!" shouted the guard.

The courtyard became a scene of chaos and panic. Because of the roll call, none of the Royal Guards were at their posts so the castle was completely vulnerable to the attack. Cain dismounted and led the charge on the ground while Mezrah, Laban, Eliab, and Kenan rode towards the main entrance of the castle. Ithamar immediately recognized Laban and Mezrah and chased after them. But Ithamar was quickly surrounded by angry Bara soldiers and the guard found himself in a fight for his life.

******

Laban, Mezrah, Kenan, and Eliab sprang from their horses and bolted up the steps of the castle on their way to the dungeon in search of Narok and Aykin. Eliab and

Kenan eliminated any Royal Guards who dared stand in their way, while Laban swiped the keys from one of his fallen comrades without remorse.

"Narok, Narok… where are you?" yelled Mezrah as they traveled further into the dungeon.

"Uncle…is that you? Back here!" called a voice from the darkness.

Mezrah and the others followed the sound of Narok's voice to the last cell in the deepest corridor of the dungeon. Mezrah motioned for Laban to open the large wooden door, and the bulgy-eyed man was the first to enter.

"Narok, are you in here?" called Mezrah.

"Aykin, where are you?" added Eliab as he followed Mezrah into the cell.

"Aykin's not here," answered Narok as he emerged breathing heavily.

"What's going on? Why are you out-of-breath?" demanded Eliab.

"After the beating I've received, even the slightest movement has me winded," said Narok falsely. "But, as bad as it was for me, Aykin's was far worse. The fool was mortally wounded when he tried to escape. Royal Guards took his body away not long ago." Eliab was speechless, however, Kenan smiled slyly at this fortuitous twist of fate. "We must leave before they return." Narok hurried them from the cell and then shut the large door. As he did, a faint cry called out from the darkness.

"Narok! I'll kill you for this!" said Aykin before he lost consciousness.

Mezrah and Narok lingered behind the others as they made their way back towards the castle.

"You have the Dragon Scroll, right?" whispered Narok.

"Not exactly…," replied Mezrah. Narok stopped at once and firmly grabbed hold of his uncle's arm.

"What do you mean?" he snapped.

"I took it from Kleiko's desk and placed it inside a barrel in the barn. But, when I went to retrieve it all I found was this," explained Mezrah. He reached into his pocket and produced a crème puff. Filled with rage, Narok slapped what Julean had left behind out of his uncle's hand.

"You fool!" exclaimed Narok. "Can't you do anything right? We must have the Dragon Scroll to take the throne!"

"Perhaps not, Nephew," answered Mezrah slyly.

"What do you mean?" asked Narok through clinched teeth.

"The black dragon has awakened and there is no sign of Orpheus, which means this is the appointed time," continued Mezrah. Hearing this, Narok assumed this meant that Queen Ashter had indeed given birth to twins. He gloated in his good fortune but was still angered by his uncle's incompetence.

"You'd better hope so for your sake, but we must still find the king before he escapes!" insisted Narok.

"He's most likely with the queen," stated Mezrah.

"Take those two Bara soldiers with you to the torture chamber and make ready for the king's arrival. Laban and I shall see to it that King Shem arrives shortly," said Narok.

When they caught up to the others, Eliab noticed that Narok no longer showed signs of fatigue from his supposedly brutal beating. But before he could question Narok, Mezrah insisted that Eliab and Kenan follow him as Narok and Laban continued ahead.

"It's up to us to save the king," Eliab whispered to Kenan. The young man consumed with jealousy towards Aykin nodded, but he was already deeply involved with Mezrah in a plan of his own.

******

Like the storm all around them, the fighting between Royal Guards and Bara soldiers raged on. Ithamar killed at least a dozen of the fierce warriors as he battled his way towards the inner castle. He entered the grand foyer at the same time as Laban and Narok did on their way to the south wing from the dungeon. Ithamar noticed that Aykin was not with them, but assumed he'd been freed as well.

"YOU!" shouted Ithamar.

"Get to the Queen's Chamber!" shouted Narok to the squadron of Bara soldiers chasing after Ithamar. The unruly men changed course and started up the staircase as Cain joined Narok and the others in the foyer.

"You'll never succeed," stated Ithamar as another fiery blast from Natas shook the castle.

"I find your perspective amusing considering your current situation," mocked Narok.

"Perhaps, but you know I'm right," Ithamar said with unnerving conviction. Narok tried to remain calm, but Ithamar saw his upper lip twitch. The evil man turned away and called out to Cain and Laban.

"Finish him!" he ordered.

Cain's brow furrowed as he twirled his sword intending to use it on Narok for having the audacity to give him an order, but refrained after looking more closely at the impressive guard. His desire to kill a formidable opponent like Ithamar suddenly outweighed his desire to kill Narok…at least for now. Laban on the other hand knew he could never best Ithamar in battle, therefore, the coward stepped aside and left the task to Cain.

"I'm going to enjoy this," boasted Cain as he continued to twirl his massive blade.

"Not as much as I," replied Ithamar as he raised his standard-issue weapon.

Although Narok wanted to stay and watch Ithamar's demise, killing King Shem and finding Queen Ashter were of higher priority.

Dragon Scroll of Nepthali

Chapter 10

Return of Narok

Shem rushed to his wife's side after bursting into the Queen's Chamber followed closely by Roffius, Cora, and finally Kleiko. Cora could see from the look on Mitzy's face that something was terribly wrong. Shem kissed his exhausted wife tenderly on the forehead, and then he saw the dead baby in her arms.

"I'm so sorry, Shem," sobbed Ashter with a look of absolute sorrow.

"It is I who am sorry that you had to do this alone, my dear," answered Shem while choking back tears of his own.

Meanwhile, Stefano and Julean ran across the room to their uncle. Roffius welcomed his nephews with open arms, but the captain's gaze remained fixed on Mitzy. She looked so beautiful and frightened that Roffius longed to run to her side and hold her in his arms just as Shem had done with Ashter, especially knowing that he was no longer a prince. But Roffius knew that he must continue to conduct himself as a prince for the sake of the true king…whoever he was. His scattered thoughts were suddenly interrupted as Lamech spoke to Shem.

"Forgive me, Your Majesty, but there were two babies born tonight," reported the physician. When Shem heard this, he knew for certain that the legend within the Dragon Scroll was unfolding, and that Natas was coming to kill him and his family. "She's very weak, but you must leave at once," urged Lamech. Shem looked around the room.

"Where's the other baby?" he asked. Meridia stepped forward holding a bundle.

"Right here, Your Majesty," she answered. Shem gathered the healthy baby into his arms and kissed his tiny forehead.

"You must grow to be strong and brave, my son, and whatever happens…know that I love you," he said softly.

Shem returned his newborn son to Meridia as the sound of cries rose up from the courtyard below. Cora ran to the window and released a blood-curdling scream after seeing an endless number of Bara soldiers scaling the castle wall, and fire raining down from the sky. Mitzy ran to her friend's side and saw for herself the terrors coming towards them.

"Run, Cora!" she shouted. Mitzy ran alongside Cora until she suddenly realized that her mother was still in the room. She went back while Cora fled in a panic with the other servants down the long hallway. Within seconds after Mitzy returned, the first wave of Bara soldiers burst into the Queen's Chamber.

The room soon looked like the courtyard below as Bara soldiers yelled and metal clashed in an eerie melody with the crashing thunder. Shem sorely lacked his brother's abilities with a sword, which meant he could manage only one opponent at a time. Roffius, therefore, was left to face the majority of the fierce warriors alone. Kleiko helped the young captain by hitting a Bara in the head with his walking staff after Roffius threw the soldier across the room. Even Lamech did his part by sliding a sword through the chamber door handles to prevent more Bara from entering.

Glass suddenly flew throughout the room when the windows shattered after another fiery blast from Natas struck the castle. Meridia held the infant close and shielded him and Queen Ashter from the jagged pieces. As Roffius turned away from the spray of glass, Mitzy saw a Bara soldier approach the captain from behind. Without hesitation, Mitzy picked up a sword lying beside one of the men Roffius had killed and rushed across the room. As Roffius' attacker lunged towards him, Mitzy thrust her blade through the man's back. Roffius spun around and stared in disbelief as Mitzy pulled her sword free from the dead soldier on the floor.

"Mitzy! Look out!" yelled Stefano. With the skill of an expert swordsman, Mitzy turned around and plunged her blade into the chest of another Bara as he charged at her.

"Hooray! You got 'em!" cheered Julean. He and Stefano knew of Mitzy's exceptional sword skills but Roffius, Shem, and what remained of the Bara soldiers did not. They stopped to marvel at the beautiful young maiden who, without effort, had just managed to kill two men twice her size.

"Uncle, look out!" shouted Stefano. Roffius wisely heeded his nephew's warning and turned around in time to block the strike of another assailant.

The men matched each other blow for blow until Roffius finally delivered a deadly strike through the man's midsection. Shem managed to kill his opponent just as the last remaining Bara soldier charged at Roffius. The young captain side kicked him across the room and the man's head split like a melon when it smashed into the corner of a table holding the vase of beautiful flowers Mitzy had picked earlier. The room fell silent and Mitzy stared at the slain men strewn throughout the room. She dropped the blood-stained sword in her hand and started towards her mother. Mitzy didn't get far before someone grabbed her arm and spun her around.

"Just what did you think you were doing? You could've been killed!" shouted Roffius with his chest heaving from the fight. His grip was firm, yet tender as he pulled Mitzy close. She felt herself tremble from his touch, and Roffius was startled to find that it took more strength for him to fight his overwhelming desire to kiss her than it had to fight off the Bara soldiers. If Shem hadn't interrupted by calling out, Roffius surely would have succumbed to his desire.

"Roffius, you must leave at once with Ashter and the boys!" he ordered. Roffius released his grip and turned to face his brother.

"Don't be ridiculous! I shan't leave you!" he replied sharply.

"Do as I say! I command you as your king!" shouted Shem. Roffius glared at his brother knowing that Shem no longer had the right to say such a thing.

"Listen to him, you must take the queen and children out of here!" interjected Kleiko. The pounding of boots in the hallway grew louder as the next wave of Bara soldiers drew near and another direct hit from Natas struck the castle. Shem steadied himself knowing they didn't have much time.

"Roffius, I'm begging you, *please* go!" he insisted.

"NEVER!" shouted Roffius adamantly. Shem could see that Roffius' mind was made up, so he did the only thing he could think of to save his brother's life. When Roffius turned to make ready for their attackers, Shem rendered him unconscious with a single blow to the back of Roffius' head with the butt of his sword.

"I'm sorry, Brother, I don't envy you the headache you shall have when you awaken, but at least you shall be alive," said Shem as his brother dropped to the floor. "Stefano and Julean, the two of you must take your uncle, mother, and the baby into the forest through the secret tunnel."

"What secret tunnel?" asked Stefano.

"This one," replied Shem. He then took hold of a tiny vase and tilted it back. The vase acted as a lever which opened a hidden door within the wall. It led to a tunnel known only to the king, queen, and Ithamar. "When you get to the end, you must press on a purple stone to open the hidden door. You must get to Irvania as quickly as you can and find the blacksmith, Jesorath. He and Roffius shall

Dragon Scroll of Nepthali

know what to do." The boys nodded and Shem lifted his limp brother. He draped one arm around Julean's shoulder and the other around Stefano's as Queen Ashter staggered towards them.

"Always remember how much I love you," she said weakly. Ashter kissed each boy on the forehead then motioned for them to go as Shem turned to his wife.

"You must take the baby and go with them," he said.

"Shem, I can barely stand, let alone run through those dark tunnels," replied Ashter. Meridia watched as the king and queen spoke in whispers and knew what she must do. She carried the newborn over to Mitzy.

"Take the baby and follow the boys," said Meridia as she placed the infant in Mitzy's arms. "I shall be along shortly."

"Me? I can't! Mother you keep him!" pleaded Mitzy.

"The queen's too weak to travel on her own, Mitzy. You must take the baby so I can help Queen Ashter," continued Meridia.

"I don't think I can, Mother," admitted Mitzy.

"Of course you can," encouraged Meridia. "Your father always knew you were destined for greatness, and this is your chance to prove him right. Perhaps everything happened as it did years ago to bring you to the castle for this very moment."

"But...what if something happens to you," said Mitzy with a lump in her throat.

"Don't worry, my child, I shall be right behind you," answered Meridia. She hugged her daughter and nudged her towards the secret tunnel. Meridia smiled through tears and motioned for her daughter to go when Mitzy looked back from the opening, but Shem stopped the maiden.

"My lady, you must give this to Roffius; he shall need it," he instructed. Shem held out the sword forged by dragon magic, but Mitzy struggled to take it while holding the baby. She looked nervously at her mother who quickly came to her daughter's aid. Meridia cleverly secured the sword beneath Mitzy's second layer of petticoats.

"Don't worry, my child, you can do this," said Meridia. She hugged her daughter once more before Mitzy and the baby disappeared into the dark tunnel.

"It's your turn, Ashter; but before you go, there's something I must tell you," said Shem. She looked so frail, but he knew he must tell his wife the truth. Ashter sensed something beyond their immediate circumstances was troubling her husband.

"What is it, Shem?" she asked.

"Ashter, you know that I love you, and have always told you the truth," he said as he gently moved a strand of hair away from her green eyes.

"Yes, of course," she answered.

"Then, I must tell you that I'm not the man you think I am," he said sadly. As Shem spoke, Narok arrived outside the door with more Bara soldiers. They pounded against it, yet Ashter remained focused on the man she loved.

"What do you mean?" she asked. Shem saw the confusion in her eyes and wondered if he had the strength to tell her.

"Ashter, this is hard for me to say, but...I'm not the King of Nepthali. It seems that everything about myself was a lie, except of course my love for you," he said while choking back tears. Ashter braced herself against her husband and felt the room start to spin, but not because of his confession. She was dying from a hemorrhage caused by the birth of the twins.

"My place is with you, Shem, for you are my husband. This truth has always meant more to me than a title," she said weakly. With those words, Ashter tilted the vase upright to close the secret door before breaking it free from the table. She knew this doomed everyone in the room, but the sacrifice was worth it to Ashter knowing it would save her children. As the hidden door closed, Narok and the Bara soldiers crashed through Lamech's make-shift lock. Narok strolled arrogantly into the Queen's Chamber. Shem and the others stared in disbelief at the man they thought was dead, but only for a moment because Shem soon found himself fighting enemy soldiers alone. Unfortunately, it was a very short skirmish without the help of Roffius and Mitzy. Two fierce warriors quickly pinned Shem against the wall, while others surrounded the women and old men in a circle of blades. Narok smiled upon seeing Queen Ashter after all these years, and thought she looked even more beautiful than he had remembered. He also grinned at the ease with which the castle had been overtaken, and wondered why he hadn't done it sooner. Just then another fiery blast from Natas shook the room as if to remind the prideful man that he hadn't done this alone.

"Well, well, King Shem, it's been a while. You look surprised to see me," sneered the evil man.

"You died eight years ago...," stammered Shem in disbelief.

"So you thought, Your Majesty. But as you can see, I'm very much alive and I've come to claim what's mine," said Narok with a lustful gaze towards Ashter. Shem tried to strike Narok, but was immediately restrained by his captors. Narok laughed in the face of the man he believed was king as he continued, "Don't worry; I have special plans for you, King Shem. But first tell me, where are the babies?" The room became silent as Narok paced around. Impatient with their refusal to answer, he stopped in front of Lamech.

"Tell me, Physician, where are the babies?" he repeated.

"There was just one baby, Narok, and he was stillborn," replied Lamech. Narok was in no mood for games. Without warning, he plunged his dagger into Lamech's chest and the old man fell to the floor.

"NO!" screamed Ashter. She tried to run to the physician's side, but collapsed into Meridia's arms.

"Now...who wants to tell me the truth?" demanded Narok. Kleiko bravely stepped forward.

"It is as he said, Narok. There was just one child born tonight, but sadly, he died in birth. You were wrong about the legend within the Dragon Scroll; it does not speak of this night... or of you!" he said firmly. Narok turned around to face the man who had repeatedly denied him access to the Dragon Scroll.

"I'm afraid you're wrong, old man!" he exclaimed. With that, Narok cracked his deadly cat o'nine tails across Kleiko's midsection. The scribe dropped to his knees as his intestines spilled onto the floor.

"NO!" shouted Shem. Again he struggled to break free, but his captors slammed him against the wall.

"I'm growing tired of this nonsense! Now, who's going to tell me the truth?!" screamed Narok.

"This is insane! Let the women go!" yelled Shem. "Lamech and Kleiko were telling the truth! Can't you see that Ashter has suffered enough tonight?" Narok suspected everyone was lying, including Shem, or stalling as the former scribe took long strides towards the women. Meridia held Ashter to keep her from falling with one arm, and slyly lifted the stillborn baby off the bed with the other. When Narok reached them, he unfolded the linens and saw the dead infant.

"Well, it looks as if your precious Dragon Scroll was wrong about two babies being born on the night of your demise. No matter though, Natas has awakened and you are the doomed king. I am now the Ruler of Nepthali!" boasted Narok as a bolt of lightning flashed and thunder boomed overhead. Meridia started to cover the lifeless baby, but suddenly found herself on the floor beside Lamech after Narok struck her across the face.

"No! Please, Narok, don't harm her!" cried Ashter.

"Now, now, my dear, don't look so distraught. You've nothing to fear for you shall remain the Queen of Nepthali for you and I shall soon be wed," he said.

Ashter looked at him with contempt and tried to step away, but Narok grabbed her by the arm and shoved her onto the bed. She could barely move, but Ashter knew she must do something to stop this madman. Thinking quickly, she propped herself up on one elbow and gave a sultry look to Narok which bid him come closer. Shem tried in vain to break free knowing that Ashter kept a dagger hidden beneath her pillow and feared what she may try.

"Ashter, no!" he shouted.

"Silence him!" ordered Narok. One of the soldiers struck Shem across the face while the other delivered a painful blow to his abdomen as Narok approached Ashter like a dog in heat.

Still in a daze on the floor, Meridia felt a soft touch on her hand. It was Lamech and he motioned with his eyes to a sword beside her. Although Meridia had never used one, she slowly reached for the weapon. Meanwhile, Ashter's breathing quickened as her hand slid beneath the pillow to grab her dagger. She grasped the handle just as Narok sat on the edge of her bed.

"I can give you everything you ever dreamed of and more...," he whispered and pressed his body against hers. Although repulsed, Ashter waited with the patience of a lioness stalking her prey for the right moment to strike.

"Since you put it that way, Narok; I, too, wish to give you something," she said softly. Ashter raised her lips until they nearly touched Narok's, and then she swiftly thrust her dagger into his side. Narok pulled her from the bed as he fell back in disbelief while clutching at his wound. At the same time, Meridia sprang to her feet and stabbed one of Shem's captors in the leg. The man released his grip allowing the former king to quickly grab the sword from his other captor and thrust it into the man's chest. Horrified by what she had done, Meridia dropped the sword as Shem rushed to Ashter who was lying on the floor in a pool of blood.

******

Down in the foyer, the duel between Cain and Ithamar raged on. It was unlike any Laban had ever seen as the coward continued to watch from a distance. Although Ithamar was a worthy opponent, Cain possessed the advantages of size, youth, and goblin blood flowing through his veins. But Ithamar had no intention of dying that day, and matched his younger opponent blow for blow.

"Your skills are quite impressive. Something about them reminds me of a farmer I once killed," said Cain as they fought. It was intended to be as much of an insult as a compliment.

"Do you dare compare my skills to those of a farmer?" snapped Ithamar as he blocked another strike.

"Yes, but this farmer was quite exceptional. He fought unlike any man I've seen before, or since. We came upon him and his companions purely by chance twelve years ago. Naturally, the farmers were no match for us, except the one. He killed some of my best men that day, so I intended to kill him, but not before killing his son. I raised my sword to strike the oldest boy, but the foolish farmer lunged his body between my blade and his son," Cain recalled. Ithamar remembered the story of Meridia's husband and sons being killed by Bara soldiers twelve years ago as he listened to Cain's horrific confession.

"What was this farmer's name?" asked Ithamar as he blocked another jab.

"How should I know? But I shan't ever forget the names of his boys because he wouldn't stop calling for them...Joab and Gideon," boasted Cain. "Pity he didn't live long enough to watch me kill them as well."

His next strike nearly pierced Ithamar as the stunned guard realized Cain was indeed talking about Meridia's husband and sons. Ithamar's surprise was soon replaced by a rage which gave him the strength to advance on Cain like a man half his age. Cain found himself unexpectedly overpowered and backed in a corner.

"Justice shall be served this day, and the innocent shall finally be avenged," declared Ithamar. He raised his sword and in one swift motion, Ithamar ended the wicked goblin bloodline by separating Cain's head from his worthless body. Laban watched in horror as Ithamar turned around and advanced toward him with a scowl. Knowing he could never best Ithamar, Laban decided to inflict what little pain he could before his inevitable demise.

"We killed them that night," said the coward plainly. Ithamar stopped his approach and eyed Laban carefully.

"Killed who?" he asked with a furrowed brow.

"Uriah's wife and children...sometimes I can still hear their screams at night," Laban said with a hint of remorse. Hearing this, Ithamar's rage became beyond measure and he charged for the coward. Yet, Laban refused to give Ithamar the satisfaction of killing him, so he threw himself upon his own sword. Although surprised, Ithamar didn't give the worthless traitor a second thought as he jumped over Laban's lifeless body and hurried up the stairs in search of King Shem.

******

When Ithamar reached the main hallway of the south wing, he heard a woman's screams echoing along with the shrieks of the storm. He stopped outside the Queen's Chamber and flattened his body against the wall then craned his neck to look inside. The first thing Ithamar saw was blood spattered everywhere, and then he saw Queen Ashter lying on the floor with the king kneeling beside her. Although worried for the queen, Ithamar was relieved to see that King Shem was still alive. The seasoned guard knew that if Narok had intended to kill him, Shem would already be dead. Ithamar then looked for his captain, but didn't see Roffius before having to duck back into the hallway when a Bara soldier looked in his direction. Ithamar quickly began to formulate a plan as he listened to the arguing coming from inside the room.

"He's been stabbed!" yelled a man.

"Idiot!" shouted another whom Ithamar soon realized was Narok. "I'm fine! Take the king to the dungeon for his flogging...and kill this insolent servant!" A large Bara soldier immediately grabbed Meridia by the arm and pulled her into the hallway.

When Meridia and the Bara rounded the corner, Ithamar suddenly appeared. The man released Meridia and she backed away as he and Ithamar engaged in a duel. It didn't take Ithamar long to kill his opponent. Once he did, Ithamar turned around to see a terrified look on Meridia's face.

"Are you all right, my lady?" he asked breathing heavily.

"Yes, thanks to you. But....how did you know?" she asked in disbelief.

"Just call it a hunch. Are you sure you're not injured?" he repeated looking at her blood-stained dress.

"I'm fine, but I must reach Mitzy and the others," she answered frantically.

"Others...who?" asked Ithamar.

"Prince Stefano and Prince Julean carried Prince Roffius into a tunnel, and Mitzy took the baby so I could help the queen. I must reach them or the baby shall starve!" answered Meridia hysterically.

"Easy, my lady, tell me what happened to Roffius? Why were the boys carrying him?" he asked fearing the worst.

"The prince refused to leave, so King Shem struck him on the head," she replied. Ithamar was relieved to hear it wasn't serious, and quickly realized that Meridia was speaking of the secret tunnel built off the Queen's Chamber.

"Do you know where they're going once they leave the tunnels?" he asked. Meridia thought for a moment and tried to compose herself.

"King Shem said something about finding a blacksmith in Irvania," she said. Ithamar knew Jesorath from his many visits to Irvania, and agreed with the king's choice to send them there.

"Come with me, I think I can help you reach them," he said. Ithamar grabbed hold of her hand, noticing how soft and smooth it felt against his own, as the guard led Meridia around the rubble. When they reached a door at the end of a hallway which Meridia had never been down, Ithamar released her hand. A gust of wind and rain struck them in the face when he opened the door.

"They shall come out over there," instructed Ithamar as he pointed through the raging storm. "Wait here until you see them."

"I don't know how to thank you," she said breathlessly.

"Just stay alive, that shall be thanks enough," he replied.

"What about you?" asked Meridia.

"Have no fear, my lady, my men and I shall keep watch over the king. But, before I leave you, there's something you must know," said Ithamar.

"What is it?" she asked with trepidation.

"The man responsible for murdering your husband and two sons is dead," he stated plainly. Meridia stepped back in shock.

"How do you know?" she managed in barely a whisper.

"While I was fighting against the Bara leader, he boasted of killing a farmer and his two sons twelve years ago. I wasn't sure if he was speaking of yours until he mentioned the names Joab and Gideon," continued Ithamar. Meridia's face went white and her eyes welled up with tears.

"But, how did you know those were the names of my boys?" she asked.

"Because, my lady, you told me the day you and Mitzy arrived at the castle," replied Ithamar. He smiled sheepishly, and for the first time Meridia noticed his ruggedly handsome features.

"Thank you," she said.

Ithamar tipped his hat before sprinting back down the hallway. In the midst of being surrounded by chaos, the guard took great satisfaction in knowing that he had avenged the deaths of Meridia's husband and sons. This served to lessen the guilt he carried for not avenging Uriah, and for not finding Aykin before he got involved with this whole nightmare.

******

In the kitchen, Cora tried to tell Cook everything that had happened in the Queen's Chamber in-between remorseful sobs.

"Oh Cook, I'm such a coward! I never should've continued on without Mitzy!" she cried. The large man offered what comfort he could, but feared the worst for Meridia, Mitzy, and the Royal Family.

"Don't blame yourself, Cora," he replied. The beautiful redhead appreciated his kind words, but Mitzy was her best friend, like a sister, and Cora had abandoned her. Cora felt an overwhelming sense of shame and doubted if she could ever forgive herself.

******

As Mitzy walked further into the dark tunnel with Stefano and Julean, the baby's cries grew louder. The maiden feared he would give them away and desperately tried to calm him, however, nothing but his mother's sustenance would calm the hungry baby. Mitzy wished she could scream as well, but knew she must be strong for the boys; especially with Prince Roffius still unconscious. Her thoughts were interrupted when Stefano suddenly called out.

"Mitzy, wait! It's Roffius!" he yelled. She turned around and saw that the boys were no longer behind her. Mitzy quickly ran back and found Roffius sitting on the ground with Julean and Stefano standing on either side of their uncle.

"Oh, my head, what happened?" asked the handsome young man groggily. Mitzy sighed with relief seeing that nothing was wrong; although a part of her wished Roffius could stay numb to their situation a little longer.

"You're a lot heavier than you look," complained Julean.

"Did a Bara soldier strike me?" pressed Roffius. The boys looked nervously at one another since neither wanted to tell their uncle that King Shem was the one who had hit him. Mitzy recognized their dilemma, and decided the truth would sound best coming from her.

"King Shem could see that you were firm in your resolve to stay, My Prince, so he did what he could to save you," she said softly. Roffius recognized her voice before her face came into focus as he staggered to his feet.

"What are *you* doing here?" he asked with surprise.

"My mother insisted that I take the baby so she could help the queen. But, the door shut before anyone else could enter the tunnel," replied Mitzy sadly. Roffius suddenly realized the graveness of their situation and knew it was his duty to keep them alive.

"Did your father give any instructions before you entered the tunnel?" asked Roffius.

"He told us to escape into the forest, and then go to Irvania to find Jesorath the blacksmith," answered Stefano.

"Your father is a very wise man. We shall do as he said," said Roffius. Just then the baby let out another wail from hunger.

"Excuse me, Your Highness, but I think we should keep moving," said Mitzy. Roffius cringed at hearing the title which was no longer rightfully his.

"He sure cries a lot," complained Julean.

"He's hungry," explained Mitzy.

"I'm hungry too, but you don't see me crying," replied Julean.

"He's a baby!" snapped Stefano. "That's what they do!"

"Oh yeah," moaned Julean. Roffius rubbed his throbbing head while the boys bickered and the baby cried. He then placed his hand on his side and realized his sword was missing.

"My sword!" he exclaimed. "Where is it?"

"It's still in the Queen's Chamber, but the king wanted me to give you his," answered Mitzy. Roffius understood this meant his brother didn't expect to make it out alive.

"May I have it?" he asked. Mitzy was thankful for the darkness so Roffius couldn't see her blush.

"No, I mean…not now, it's in my petticoats," she replied sheepishly as Stefano and Julean giggled.

"I suppose you shall have to retrieve it for me later," answered Roffius awkwardly.

"I think you should let her keep it!" exclaimed Julean. "Did you see her kill those Bara soldiers back there, Uncle?" Roffius suddenly remembered Mitzy fighting like an expert in the Queen's Chamber.

"I do seem to recall. Where did you learn to use a sword like that?" he asked with a furrowed brow. Before she could answer, Natas struck the castle with another blast of fire. Roffius grabbed Mitzy and shielded her and the baby from the falling debris.

"We've got to get out of here!" he exclaimed. Roffius quickly took the lead through the twisted tunnels until they reached what appeared to be a dead end. "Now what?"

"Father said to press on a purple stone and it shall open a hidden door," said Stefano. Roffius hoped his nephew had heard correctly as he struggled to see in the darkness. He finally located the stone and when he pressed on it, the wall in front of them immediately started to separate. Boards creaked and a cloud of dust floated upwards as the door opened for the first time in centuries.

******

Lamech lay motionless with his face to the floor while Bara soldiers dragged King Shem away from his dead wife. The soldiers spoke in anxious voices, but Lamech overheard them say Narok was going to the Throne Room for his wound to be mended. After waiting what he deemed to be sufficient time in silence, Lamech finally lifted his head.

Although he had witnessed the ravages of war, nothing prepared the physician for the sight of Queen Ashter and Kleiko lying in pools of their own blood. Lamech hurried to the queen and felt for a pulse, but found none. He concluded that she had died from blood loss caused in childbirth after finding no wound marks. Lamech gently placed his aged hands on her face and closed her beautiful green eyes for the last time.

"Rest easy, My Queen," he said sadly. Lamech then went to Kleiko whose intestines lay spilled on the floor from Narok's cat o'nine tails. The physician was amazed to find his old friend still breathing. "Kleiko, it's me,

Lamech; can you hear me?" Kleiko's eyes fluttered and he looked at the physician in disbelief.

"Lamech, you're alive!" he whispered.

"Yes, thanks to my journal here," answered Lamech. He pulled out the thick leather bound book used to record each royal birth and death since the reign of King Jeptha. "How is it possible that Narok has returned? I examined him myself eight years ago, and he was dead!"

"Goblin magic is in the air...but there's something you must know," said Kleiko with urgency.

"Easy, my friend, don't talk," replied Lamech.

"No! You must listen to me!" insisted Kleiko. His shaky hand took hold of Lamech's shirt as the scribe struggled to breathe. "Shem is not the true king of Nepthali..."

"What?" asked the astonished physician.

"It's true; the real king is safe, but he must be found before Natas and Narok discover the truth. There is still hope...," whispered Kleiko before breathing his last. As Lamech held his friend's lifeless hand, he wondered if Shem and Roffius knew.

Suddenly, Lamech heard footsteps approaching from the hallway and feared the Bara soldiers were returning to gather their dead. He grabbed a sword and readied himself for another fight. When the chamber doors opened, Lamech dropped the weapon and fell to his knees with relief at the sight of Ithamar and his squadron.

"Are you hurt?" asked Ithamar as he rushed to Lamech's side.

"I'm fine; this is the queen's blood...and Kleiko's," replied the dazed physician. "Narok is here, Ithamar, I saw him with my own eyes."

"Yes, I know. Mezrah and the black dragon are here as well," answered Ithamar plainly.

"I tried to save the queen, but it was no use," continued Lamech.

"There's nothing more that can be done, Lamech, but we can save you. You must change clothes with this dead Bara so when they return, they think he's you," instructed Ithamar.

"We don't have much time," urged Perez.

Lamech tried to hurry but found it difficult with his trembling hands. As he waited, Ithamar marveled at the fact that only one member of the Royal Family was dead after seeing the inside of the room. He was thankful Meridia told him about Prince Roffius and his nephews having escaped, but hoped to learn more about King Shem's whereabouts from Lamech.

"Do you know where they've taken the king?" he asked the physician.

"I heard something about the dungeon...and a flogging," answered Lamech as he put on the Bara vest.

"He shall be in need of your skills; let's go!" exclaimed Ithamar.

The king's most elite squadron of guards quickly ushered Lamech away, and the old physician found himself struggling just to keep up with the others while maneuvering around debris caused by Natas' fiery blasts. He soon forgot about telling Ithamar the shocking news that King Shem wasn't really the king as the guard led them down corridors and darkened tunnels which Lamech never knew existed.

"Where are the other Royal Guards?" Lamech managed to ask as they ran.

"Those not captured or killed have joined forces with Narok believing he has returned from the dead," replied Ithamar with chagrin.

"The lousy scum," said Luklin under his breath.

"Wait until I get my hands on them," added Perez.

"You shall have your chance, but for now, the king's safety is our only priority," Ithamar reminded them firmly. He knew that he and his men would have to wait to go to Irvania until after King Shem was under Lamech's care. Only then could they risk leaving for the southern province to find Prince Roffius.

When Ithamar at last slowed down, Lamech staggered from the grotesque smell of death and decay. They had reached the dungeon where they continued on to the deepest corridor and stopped at the last cell.

"This is it," announced Ithamar. Perez expected to walk right in, but instead he ran into the cell door.

"It's shut. Why would men who've been freed from a place like this take the time to close the door?" he asked.

"Maybe they wanted to make sure the rats didn't follow them," teased Luklin.

"Very funny; you have the keys, right?" asked Perez. Luklin fumbled with the keys for a moment before opening the heavy door.

"After you, Sire," he said while holding the door open for Lamech. The physician took a deep breath before entering the dark and dreary cell.

"Don't worry, Lamech, you shall be safe here," promised Ithamar.

"Ithamar, wait! There's something I must tell you," said Lamech remembering the news about Shem. Although Ithamar sensed it was important, he had no time for talk.

"Whatever it is, it shall have to wait. We can't risk being discovered," he replied gruffly. "Take this, you should find what you need until I can return with more supplies." Lamech took the small satchel and trusted Ithamar to make good on his promise as the heavy door slammed shut.

"Don't forget to watch out for the rats!" called Perez with a chuckle. Lamech lifted his foot and looked around as his only link to freedom disappeared into the darkness.

Alone in the cell, the physician chose to prepare for Shem's arrival rather than focus on his dismal surroundings; especially if the beating was as severe as Ithamar had implied. Lamech opened the satchel and was pleased to find a small vile of vinegar, herbs, strips of cloth, and a flask of water. While going through the items, Lamech heard a strange sound deep within the cell.

"I say, is anyone there? Show yourself!" he called with a slight tremble in his voice. A muscular figure limped into sight as Lamech felt his legs go weak. "Uriah?" he whispered. Aykin recognized the old physician from his visits to the castle a lifetime ago.

"Lamech, is that you?" he asked. Lamech nearly collapsed, but Aykin caught him.

"Uriah? Is that you?" repeated Lamech with glazed eyes.

"No, it's me, Aykin…Uriah's son. We've not seen one another since I was a child," he answered kindly. Lamech stared in disbelief, and vaguely remembered the young boy who often came with his father to the castle years ago.

"I can't believe it…you look just like him. What are you doing here?" he asked.

"It's a long story," replied Aykin.

"Something tells me we have the time," answered Lamech managing a smile.

******

From where Meridia stood waiting, she could see a door within the castle wall open right where Ithamar said it would. She ran into the storm calling out her daughter's name. Mitzy immediately recognized her mother's voice, and turned around to see Meridia running towards them. The two embraced in an emotional reunion of laughter and tears.

"Mother, you're alive!" exclaimed Mitzy.

"Yes, and so is Narok! He burst through Lamech's lock with more Bara soldiers, and there was a terrible fight! Narok stabbed Lamech and Kleiko, and Queen Ashter stabbed Narok…," blurted Meridia before breaking down in tears.

"You're safe now, Mother," said Mitzy.

"My lady, did you say you saw Narok?" clarified Roffius. Meridia took a deep breath and continued.

"Yes, I saw him as clearly as I see you now. Narok lives; he's the one who gave the order to have me killed, and for the king to be taken to the dungeon. I'm certain I'd be dead if not for Ithamar," she said.

"Ithamar?!" exclaimed Roffius with amazement.

"Yes, he killed my captor and then took me to where I could wait for you. I was so worried the baby would starve if I didn't reach you in time," answered Meridia. Although Roffius could see Meridia was distraught, he pressed her for more information.

"My lady, did you and Ithamar discuss anything other than the baby?" he asked.

"Yes, I told him that you were going to Irvania to find a blacksmith named Jesorath," she answered. Roffius felt a glimmer of hope hearing that his most trusted guard knew where they were going.

"What about my mother and father?" asked Stefano. Meridia's face went pale. She feared the news may be too difficult for the boy to hear, and for her to say.

"Your father was taken to the dungeon, but I fear your mother is dead," she answered softly. Stefano leaned against Roffius who steadied his nephew with his strong arms.

"I never should've left them!" cried the boy.

"You did as you were told, Stefano, and now you must be brave. When Narok learns of our escape, he shan't stop until he finds us," said Roffius. Stefano knew his uncle was right, but the only thing he wanted to do was run back and find his parents. "I know this is difficult, but we must make haste," continued Roffius.

Mitzy's heart raced as she realized they were about to leave the safety of the secret tunnel for the vast, open meadow. The fear which gripped her heart intensified when Mitzy saw an ominous green glow cutting through the storm clouds as Natas passed overhead. She wondered if she would be able to do what was being asked of her, but then Mitzy remembered what Orpheus told Boaz: *When the night is dark and dreary; never give up, nor grow weary. The lion is wounded but may be saved, by the youngest one so brave.* The young maiden knew Roffius didn't believe in Orpheus, nevertheless she felt certain he was the one who would save the kingdom. At that moment, a blinding light suddenly pierced through the darkened sky. Roffius shielded his eyes and stepped into the meadow.

"Run!" he shouted. Mitzy grabbed Stefano and Julean by the hand, while Meridia clung to the baby as they followed Roffius out of the tunnel. The light blinded the Bara soldiers along the castle wall, and Natas. The beast knew this was no coincidence, and who was responsible.

Return of Narok

"Curse you, Orpheus!" roared the black dragon.

Dragon Scroll of Nepthali

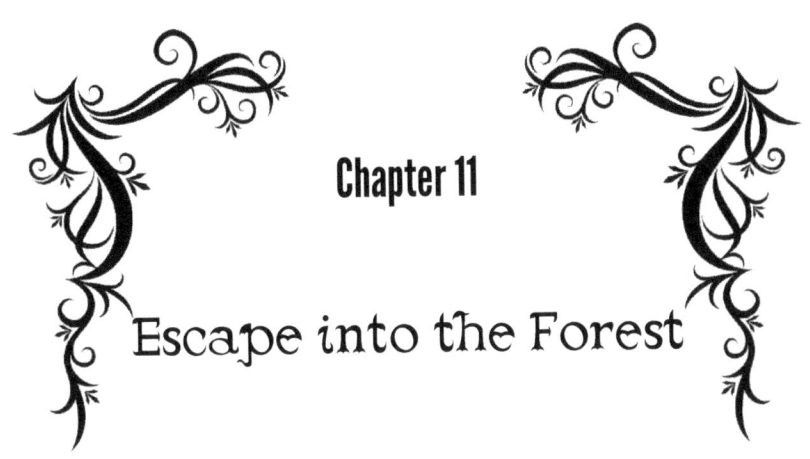

Chapter 11

Escape into the Forest

The mysterious light allowed Roffius and the others to reach the safety of the forest unseen, but it also enraged Natas. He sensed his brother was the cause of the light and was more determined than ever to eliminate every last descendant of King Jeptha to prevent Orpheus' return. After hours of scanning the castle and its perimeter, Natas was finally satisfied that the members of the Royal Family were either dead or captured. The black dragon prepared to land in the courtyard but as he did, Natas noticed that the Royal Ship was missing from port. Natas rightly surmised that some members of the Royal Family weren't present during the attack, therefore, the beast started out across The Great Sea in search of the missing ship.

******

Roffius kept a watchful eye on the sky for the black dragon as he and the others pressed forward. When they reached the top of a hill deep in the forest, the clouds parted just long enough for Roffius to see Natas' silhouette against the full moon as the black dragon flew out over The Great Sea. The young captain instinctively knew where the beast was going, and that he would never see his parents again. Although heartbroken, Roffius dutifully carried on for the sake of the others. Finally, Julean couldn't walk another step and sat down on a tree stump.

"I'm tired and starving!" moaned the boy.

"Me too," added Stefano as he sat beside his cousin.

"I know we've asked much of you both, but we must continue for as long as your uncle sees fit," replied Mitzy thoughtfully. "Why don't you tell me about something you enjoy as we go?" Julean thought for a moment before he began to describe Cook's chicken pot pie in great detail. Roffius was impressed with Mitzy's ability to get the boys moving again, and felt himself falling more in love with her with each moment spent in her presence. Roffius longed to tell the golden haired beauty how he felt, but knew he could not. A prince would never express his love for a servant, and Roffius must continue to conduct himself as such until the true king was found. With a heavy heart, Roffius led them further into the forest. The rain eventually subsided and the full moon broke through the clouds to reveal a small clearing.

"You can rest here while I find suitable shelter," he proclaimed. "Stefano, I'm leaving you and Julean in charge. If I don't return within the hour, follow the southern stars until you reach Irvania. I'm counting on the two of you to look after the women and baby."

"Yes, Uncle; but what if someone, or something, comes?" asked Stefano with concern. Roffius took out one of his daggers from its sheath.

Escape into the Forest

"Take this, but use it only if necessary," he said sternly. Beneath a tree, Mitzy sat shivering beside her mother. When Roffius passed by, he saw her and stopped.

"Take this, Miss Mit, it should help relieve the chill," he said. Roffius then removed his cloak and handed it to her.

"Thank you, Your Highness," she replied with gratitude. As she reached for the cloak, their hands brushed against one another and Mitzy felt a rush of warmth. Roffius felt it too, but quickly pulled away and walked off at a brisk pace.

"Stay together and keep quiet," he called out over his shoulder.

"You can count on us, Uncle," answered Stefano. He and Julean looked at Mitzy.

"Wow! He never lets anyone wear his cloak. I don't even think he takes it off to sleep," said Julean. Stefano shoved his cousin.

"Of course he takes it off to sleep!" he scolded. "You make him sound like some kind of freak." Mitzy smiled happily as she wrapped the cloak around her shoulders feeling warm and safe.

Distant rolls of thunder and water droplets falling off leaves were all that remained of the fierce storm, yet the forest was filled with noises which left the women and boys anxious for Roffius' return. The simple cry of an owl sounded like a secret message, while creatures scurrying for shelter sounded like footsteps approaching. The fugitives stayed close together as the minutes passed like hours until Meridia finally broke the silence.

"Mitzy, may I use the Captain's cloak for the baby?" she asked.

"Of course, forgive me for not thinking of it sooner," replied Mitzy feeling ashamed for her selfishness. She quickly removed the warm cloak and handed it to her mother. Mitzy watched as Meridia swaddled the tiny baby and admired her mother's faithful service to the king and queen even in their absence. Mitzy realized again how lucky she was to still have her.

"I'm sorry, Mother," she said softly.

"For what, my dear?" asked Meridia.

"For not telling you often enough how much I love you," answered Mitzy. Meridia smiled at her daughter.

"I love you too, Mitzy. I know this has been hard, but we must be strong for the young ones," she said looking towards Julean and Stefano. Meridia knew the boys needed a distraction, and soon thought of the perfect one.

"What shall we name him, Your Highness?" she asked Stefano. "The baby needs a name and since you're his brother, I'm certain your parents would want you to name him." Stefano sat in silence for a moment trying to remember the names his parents had discussed. Suddenly, it came to him.

"Zerah, his name shall be Zerah," he announced.

"I think Julean Jr. is better," remarked Julean. Mitzy chuckled and rolled her eyes.

Escape into the Forest

"Zerah is the perfect name. It means dawn, and his birth shall mark the dawn of a new era of greatness for Nepthali," said Meridia. Mitzy agreed, as did Julean after thinking it over. Moments later, they heard footsteps approaching from the forest.

"Quiet," whispered Mitzy. Stefano pulled out Roffius' dagger while Mitzy reached into her petticoats for the sword. They stood waiting for the intruder to come into view.

******

Cora and Cook were held captives along with the other servants in the kitchen. Cora looked around for Mitzy but didn't see her anywhere. She hoped her best friend's unrelenting belief in Orpheus counted for something, and that by some miracle Mitzy was still alive. Cora's thoughts were interrupted when a Bara soldier burst into the kitchen.

"I need water…and someone who can sew!" he shouted. Cora was the best seamstress in the kingdom, but the last thing she wanted to do was help these barbarians.

"She can do it," called a voice. Cora turned around and saw Nalia pointing at her with a shrewd smile across her face.

"Come with me, Red," said the Bara soldier as he grabbed Cora by the arm. She looked to Cook for help.

"Don't worry, just do as they say and you shall be fine," he whispered.

The grungy soldier took Cora to the Throne Room where she saw more soldiers and someone seated upon the throne.

"Your Grace, I found this maidservant to close your wound," announced the man holding Cora. He shoved her towards the throne as Narok carefully eyed the beautiful redhead.

"Don't just stand there, come here!" he shouted impatiently. "Tell me, can you close this wound?" Cora doubted she could as she approached slowly until she saw it was merely a flesh wound.

"I've never done such a thing, but believe I can," she answered nervously.

"Very well then, get to it," snapped Narok.

Cora took a deep breath before grabbing hold of the needle and common thread being handed to her. She steadied her shaking hands as she thread the needle before gently piercing his skin.

"Aaahh! Watch yourself, wench!" exclaimed Narok. Mezrah stood smirking in the far corner of the room after leaving Eliab and Kenan in the dungeon to wait for King Shem.

"Perhaps if you hadn't been so hasty in killing the Royal Physician, a more skilled hand would be doing this," mocked Mezrah.

"Shut up! You're the fool who lost the Dragon Scroll!" shouted Narok. Annoyed with his uncle, Narok returned his attention to Cora. "What's your name?"

Escape into the Forest

"Cora," she replied while starting the next stitch.

"Well, Cora, I've seen women make butter faster than this. I suggest you get on with things before I find you a permanent replacement," he snapped.

"Forgive me, Sire, I'm trying," she said. As Narok watched her, he became intrigued by her rare beauty.

"You're quite a lovely girl. Perhaps, I shall consider you for my new queen," he said as he leaned in closer to Cora. However, just like Ashter, Cora found Narok's advances repulsive and could think of nothing worse than a life spent with him. She made sure Narok felt the next stitch as she thrust the needle into his open flesh.

"I said be careful!" he yelled.

"Forgive me, My Lord," she replied as she lowered her face to conceal her smile.

Mezrah rolled his eyes while marveling at Narok's brief period of mourning for the death of Queen Ashter. His nephew was making a fool of himself over a simple handmaiden, and Mezrah couldn't wait to be rid of Narok. Hoping to divert his attention, Mezrah decided to tell Narok about the second baby.

"I'm not sure if you heard, Nephew, but the queen did indeed give birth to two babies. So, I was correct when I told you earlier that this is the appointed time mentioned in the Dragon Scroll," he said proudly. Cora stopped in mid-stitch and wondered how they found out.

"A second baby?" asked Narok. "Who told you this information?"

"One of the handmaidens we captured said she was present when both babies were born," answered Mezrah. Cora knew at once it must have been Nalia since only she would do such a thing. Narok was as pleased and distracted by this news as Mezrah had intended. But, like his father before him, Narok wanted to make sure there were no loose ends.

"If one has died, where is the other?" he asked. "And for that matter, where is Prince Roffius? Has he joined King Shem in the dungeon?"

"Prince Roffius and the other baby, along with Prince Stefano and Prince Julean, remain unaccounted for," replied a Bara soldier.

"WHAT?!" shouted Narok.

"They were last seen in the Queen's Chamber with King Shem, but they seem to have disappeared," continued the soldier. Cora listened with interest, and even dared to hope that Mitzy had somehow escaped with the missing prince.

"Nonsense, no one vanishes into thin air. They're probably hiding somewhere. Have Cain lead the search; I'm sure he'd be happy to capture a prince," ordered Narok.

"Cain's dead, Your Grace," answered another soldier.

"What about Ithamar, is he dead?" asked Narok with a tremble in his voice.

"He must be, Sire. No one can best Cain in a duel," bragged the first soldier.

Escape into the Forest

"Someone did you fool because Cain is dead!" snapped Narok. "I want every crevice of this castle searched for Ithamar and the missing members of the Royal Family! Don't let me see any of your ugly faces again unless one of them is with you!" A handful of Bara soldiers left at once to carry out their new orders from the man they assumed was in charge believing Aykin was also dead. Narok quickly returned his attention to Mezrah. "I can see why Father loathed you, Uncle. You fail at everything asked of you; even the simplest of tasks," he snapped. As Narok continued with a barrage of insults, Mezrah's thoughts drifted elsewhere. He smiled while picturing himself seated upon the very throne where Narok sat getting the last of his stitches. "Are you even listening to me, Uncle?" shouted Narok.

"Yes, of course," answered Mezrah falsely. "I was just thinking, Nephew, that perhaps the missing royals should no longer be of consequence to you. Events within the legend have come to pass which cannot be undone, yet there is still no sign of Orpheus. The throne is clearly yours as was promised to our ancestor long ago." Narok smiled as he put on his shirt while considering his uncle's words.

"True enough, however, I believe it too early to share in your confidence. I shan't rest until every last member of the Royal Family is dead!" exclaimed Narok adamantly.

"Nephew," said Mezrah, "King Shem is in the dungeon, and it shall only be a matter of time before we find Prince Roffius and the boys. It seems to me that the Royal Family is as good as gone."

Cora returned the needle and thread to the basket while the evil men conspired. She started to walk away, but Narok reached out and grabbed hold of her arm.

"Just where do you think you're going?" he asked. "Guards, take her to the Queen's Chamber along with every other young maiden in the castle. The next few days shall be spent in preparation for my inspection at which time I shall select my new bride." Cora listened with dread and found herself being escorted between two large Bara soldiers to the Queen's Chamber.

******

In the corner of the dungeon reserved for the cruelest of beatings, Eliab and Kenan watched as two of their comrades held down the man they believed was king, while another flogged him. Eliab winced with each lashing as chunks of flesh ripped from Shem's back. Even Kenan flinched at the sight until the soldier delivering the beating finally stopped.

"He's all yours boys," he said while wiping the sweat from his brow. "But I doubt he shall make it to his cell."

Eliab hoped his comrade was wrong as he and Kenan picked up Shem's broken and bloodied body. They carried him through the dark corridors of the dungeon to the same cell where they had found Narok hours earlier. They never noticed Ithamar's impressive figure waiting in the safety of the shadows for Shem to arrive. At the cell door, Eliab heard something and stopped.

"Did you hear that?" he asked. Kenan listened as Ithamar remained perfectly still and held his breath.

"Hear what?" replied Kenan.

"I could've sworn I heard something," answered Eliab.

Escape into the Forest

"The only thing I hear are the moans of the king; now open the door," urged Kenan impatiently. Eliab disagreed, but opened the door anyway. Once inside, Eliab heard the sound again, and this time so did Kenan.

"I heard it," he said.

"Who's here? Show yourself!" ordered Eliab. When the lone figure slowly stepped out from the shadows, Eliab immediately recognized his best friend. He dropped Shem and rushed to Aykin, yet Kenan remained frozen in place.

"Aykin, you're alive!" exclaimed Eliab as the two clasped hands. "Narok told us you were dead!"

"I would've been if Narok was stronger…or had better aim," answered Aykin. "How's the king?"

"He's alive, but barely," replied Eliab.

"We must hope for a miracle," added Kenan in keeping with his role of a supportive compatriot. Aykin looked at him with a shrug of his shoulders. The hardened young man hadn't dared to hope in miracles since his family was killed. Aykin changed the subject by explaining how Narok struck him on the head with a rock as the attack began. Eliab listened intently, yet Kenan remained aloof.

"I don't like this, Aykin. You were left for dead, the queen is dead, and King Shem's nearly dead," stated Eliab. "Narok thinks he's the new king and has ordered a manhunt for someone named Roffius." Aykin recognized that name.

"We've got to get you out of here," added Kenan with false concern.

"Not yet, Narok mustn't know I'm alive. Roffius is the king's youngest brother and Narok mustn't find him. I shall stay here and attend to the king while the two of you find out what you can about Roffius' whereabouts. Narok shan't stop until he's found. The safety of every member of the Royal Family is now our highest priority," explained Aykin. As he finished, they heard footsteps approaching the cell.

"What's taking you so long down there? Narok wants you back in the Throne Room at once," called a voice. The men recognized it was Mezrah, so Aykin continued in a hushed voice.

"We can still succeed, but trust no one; especially Mezrah or Narok," he said. Eliab and Kenan nodded in agreement, although only one was sincere. Kenan hurried ahead of Eliab after leaving the dark cell so he could catch up with Mezrah.

"Aykin's alive," he said under his breath as he passed by. Mezrah's bulgy eyes widened as he cursed his nephew for failing to kill the Bara soldier's next-in-command.

Ithamar remained hidden in the shadows as he strained to overhear their conversation. He wasn't aware that Aykin was still in the cell, or of any details, but Ithamar knew for certain there was dissention amongst the Bara. The guard never imagined that he and Aykin were fighting for the same cause as he planned to leave with his men for Irvania after getting more supplies to Lamech. Ithamar hurried away once he was certain the Bara soldiers were gone.

Escape into the Forest

******

Inside the damp cell, rats scurried in every direction as Aykin dragged Shem's limp body away from the door.

"It's safe for you to come out now," he called to Lamech. The old physician emerged from the shadows and knelt beside Shem. The former king's spirit was as crushed as his body, and Shem gladly welcomed death knowing that his beloved Ashter was gone. He faded in and out of consciousness as recent events replayed in his mind. Did Kleiko really say he wasn't the king, or had that been a dream? Was he in the dungeon? Shem thought he saw a figure approaching and tried to move away, but his attempts were futile.

"Be still, My King," said a familiar voice. Lamech addressed Shem by his royal title fearing that if he failed to do so it could upset Shem in his already compromised condition if he was unaware of the truth. The physician also feared that Aykin would notice and become suspicious.

"Lamech?" asked Shem in disbelief.

"Yes, it is I, My King," he replied.

"But... I saw you die," whispered Shem. He was delirious with pain and didn't know if Lamech was real or a figment of his imagination.

"I most certainly would be if not for my journal," he said. "It seems as though enough babies have been born throughout the years to have kept Narok's blade from..." Lamech stopped after seeing that Shem had passed out.

With Shem unconscious, Lamech checked for broken bones without fear of causing his patient discomfort and was astounded to discover none. Lamech then gathered the scraps of cloth from the satchel Ithamar had left for him and began the task of cleaning Shem's many wounds. The skilled physician understood how critical the next few hours were for Shem's survival. As Lamech worked, Aykin's muscular frame once again emerged from the back of the cell.

"Shall he live?" he asked. Lamech looked up and wiped the sweat from his brow.

"Do you believe in miracles?" he asked.

"There was a time that I did," responded Aykin honestly.

"Well, it's time for you to start again," replied Lamech. "I could use your help here." Aykin had some experience with this sort of thing from his years living amongst the Bara, but never on someone as important as he thought Shem to be.

"What do you want me to do?" he asked with hesitation.

"Soak these cloths in water then hand them to me," instructed Lamech. Aykin watched the physician work with a tenderness that reminded Aykin of his mother when she had cared for his scrapes as a child. Lamech felt Aykin watching him, and sensed there was more to this young man than his exterior rugged appearance.

"Perhaps you can now explain to me how the son of a Royal Guard ended up in the company of Bara soldiers," he said casually.

"Perhaps…," replied Aykin.

Dragon Scroll of Nepthali

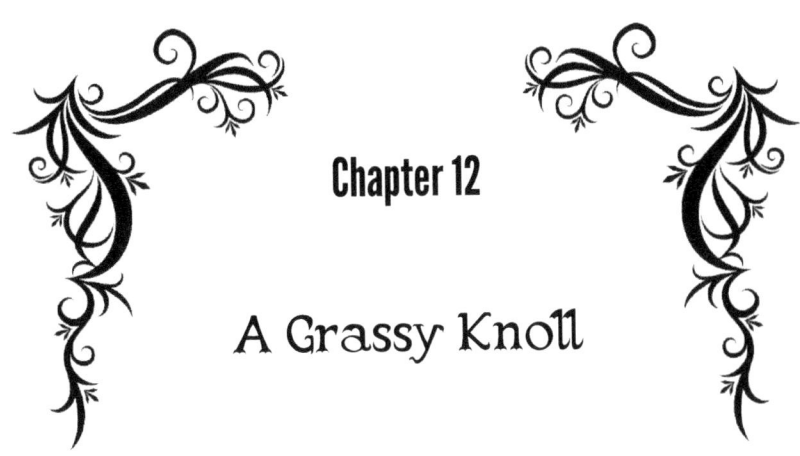

Chapter 12

A Grassy Knoll

In the darkness of the forest, Mitzy and Stefano stood with sword and dagger drawn to face the oncoming intruder.

"What was that?" whispered Stefano.

"Probably my stomach, I'm starving!" answered Julean.

"Ssshhh!" snapped Mitzy. Her heart raced as a muscular figure slowly came into view.

"Do not be alarmed! It is I, Roffius," he called out.

"You scared us to death sneaking up like that!" Mitzy scolded.

"Well, Miss Mit, the point is to remain unnoticed, is it not?" he replied with a dashing smile. Mitzy's cheeks flushed with shame as she immediately realized her impertinence.

"Please, forgive me, Your Highness. It shan't happen again," she said humbly with a curtsy. Roffius cringed after hearing her address him again with a title which was no longer his.

"There's no need for such formalities here, my lady. Please, call me Captain," he insisted. "Stefano, Julean; make haste as I've found suitable shelter for the night."

"Your Highness, I mean, Captain, would you like the king's sword now?" asked Mitzy while extending the blade to him. Roffius looked at the sword with an overwhelming sense of unworthiness in spite of Kleiko's reassurance that Orpheus had given it specifically to his family.

"You keep it for now," he replied curtly before walking away.

Mitzy returned the sword to her petticoats and they started off into the darkness. Stefano and Julean scrambled to catch up with their uncle while Mitzy remained with her mother. The baby finally slept peacefully with a full stomach, which made traveling easier for everyone, but Mitzy was concerned that her mother might slip on the slick, moss-covered forest floor.

"Mother, it's very slippery here so be....AAAAHHHH!" screamed Mitzy as she fell. Roffius heard her cries and ran back to see what was wrong.

"Are you injured, Miss Mit?" he asked seeing Mitzy on the ground.

"It's my ankle; I think I twisted it," she said. Mitzy tried to stand, but started to fall as soon as she put weight on it. Roffius was at her side in time to catch the maiden in his arms.

A Grassy Knoll

"Easy, Miss Mit," he said. "Don't try to walk." Before Mitzy realized what he was doing, Roffius picked her up and tossed her over his broad shoulder. Yet as he did, the sword tucked inside her petticoats fell out and narrowly missed stabbing his foot.

"Oh! I'm terribly sorry, Your Highness, I mean Captain...," exclaimed Mitzy nervously.

"I must commend you, Miss Mit. I dare say I'd forgotten about your unusual place to store a weapon," he teased. Mitzy again felt her cheeks flush and was thankful he couldn't see her face.

"Julean, can I trust you to carry this?" asked Roffius as he motioned to the sword sticking into the ground.

"Sure!" exclaimed Julean enthusiastically. "Let me at those Bara soldiers." The boy pulled the sword free and slashed at the air before parading around Stefano. Roffius' dagger suddenly seemed small and insignificant compared to his father's sword, so Stefano tucked it into his belt.

"Come along, we've tarried long enough," announced Roffius. He started off again with Mitzy dangling over his shoulder.

"You don't have to do this you know, I can manage just fine," protested the maiden.

"As much as I'd like to see you try, Miss Mit, I'm certain it would prove too painful for you, which would slow us down and I cannot risk any more delays," replied Roffius matter-of-factly. They continued on in silence until

Mitzy finally addressed the subject on the minds of all the others.

"I'm very sorry about Queen Ashter. I remember how painful it was after my father and brothers were killed," she said thoughtfully.

"Yes, I remember. It was the reason you came to the castle," he replied. "I also remember how you used to cry when you were left with Cook."

"You remember that?" she said and cringed at the memory of her cries echoing throughout the castle. "But, you must agree that his large kettle can be quite frightening to a child."

"If you say so," answered Roffius with a laugh. He was amazed at how comfortable he felt with Mitzy even after being apart for so many years, and felt as if he could tell her anything. For a moment, Roffius allowed himself to imagine a life with the beautiful maiden hanging over his shoulder. However, the moment passed as soon as Roffius remembered that he had nothing to offer Mitzy once the true king was found. Roffius suppressed his feelings for the countless time and quickened his pace. A short distance later he stopped.

"Here it is!" announced the captain as a fresh rain began to fall.

"Here what is?" asked Julean.

"I don't see anything," said Stefano.

"That's the point," replied Roffius. He gently placed Mitzy down on the soft grass and walked to the bank of a bubbling creek. Roffius then lifted a cluster of low hanging

A Grassy Knoll

branches to reveal a natural cave-like structure within a grassy knoll. "This shall provide us with safe, dry shelter for the night," he said proudly.

"It looks perfect!" exclaimed an exhausted Meridia. She entered the cave with Baby Zerah as Roffius turned to Stefano and Julean.

"I need the two of you to gather some kindling to feed the fire," he said.

"What fire?" asked Julean.

"The one I'm going to start while you're gathering the kindling," instructed Roffius. "Be quick about it, and don't get lost!" Stefano and Julean hurried away on their mission while Mitzy attempted to stand. Before she could, Roffius scooped her into his arms and carried her into the cave.

"Thank you, Your Highness...I mean, Captain, but I can manage," she protested. Roffius was unnerved at hearing the undue title and appreciated her correction.

"I'm sure you can, Miss Mitt, however, duty bids me to help anyone in need, and right now that means you," he answered. As he held her, strands of Mitzy's golden ringlets brushed against his cheek. Roffius thought she smelled of fresh wildflowers, which reminded him of home, and his mind jumped to the many things he could've done differently to change the outcome for his brother and Ashter. Mitzy noticed a sudden sadness come across his hazel eyes.

"Is everything all right?" she asked. Although she had asked with the kindest of intensions, Mitzy could not begin to fathom what he was going through.

"I'm afraid nothing's all right, Miss Mit. Now, if you'll excuse me, I need to start a fire," he said sharply. Roffius placed Mitzy down and left her regretting having asked such a foolish question. Meridia saw the hurt on her daughter's face.

"Don't worry, Mitzy, it's not you; he's been through a great deal tonight. A man of the Captain's position and character must be given time to process things," she said wisely. Mitzy hoped her mother was right as she watched Roffius leave the cave.

After only a few minutes, Roffius returned with some wood which he had gathered earlier. A spark turned into a flame, and in no time a crackling fire was giving off its warmth and light.

"Come now, Zerah, let's get you close to that nice fire your uncle has made," said Meridia.

"Zerah?" repeated Roffius.

"Yes, Captain, that's the name Stefano chose while you were looking for this fine shelter," explained Meridia. Roffius remembered that being one of the names Shem and Ashter were considering, and thought how pleased they would be with Stefano's choice. Meridia held Zerah close to the fire's warmth while Roffius approached Mitzy.

"Forgive me, Captain, I didn't mean to pry earlier," she said softly. Roffius didn't want to talk about it, so he refrained from answering with a quick change of subject.

"How's your ankle?" he asked as he knelt beside her.

"It's nothing to trouble you with, really, I'm fine," she replied.

Roffius lifted her foot and carefully unlaced her boot before attempting to pull it off. He expected to remove it without difficulty, but was hindered by all the swelling. Mitzy tried to conceal her discomfort as he pulled harder. When at last her foot came free, Mitzy sighed with relief. While Roffius examined her ankle by firelight, Mitzy examined his handsome features.

"The swelling is worse than I expected," he said with a furrowed brow. "It shall require a cold compress and rubbing." Roffius placed his strong hands around her petite ankle and began to massage, but she instinctively pulled away from the pain. "Hold still," he said and gently grabbed hold of her foot.

"It's hard to hold still when you're making it hurt more! I'm fine, really. You don't need to do this," she insisted while pulling her foot away.

"Just relax," he teased and grabbed it back again.

"Aren't there other things you should be doing…like tending to the fire, or standing guard, or something," she said through clinched teeth as he rubbed out the swelling. Roffius smiled and found himself staring into her crystal blue eyes. He had always thought she was beautiful, but tonight Roffius felt as if he was seeing Mitzy for the first time.

"It's no trouble, really," he said as their eyes locked briefly. Roffius feared his feelings were becoming too strong to conceal, so he looked away and put her foot down. "I shall get something cold to put on this," he said abruptly and left the cave. As Meridia held Baby Zerah and watched the captain go, she pondered the irony in seeing her daughter look happier than ever on the night of such a terrible ordeal.

"How does it feel?" she asked Mitzy.

"Wonderful," replied Mitzy with a dreamy smile.

"I was talking about your ankle," laughed Meridia at her love struck daughter.

"Oh, it's fine," answered Mitzy absent-mindedly. Although Meridia wanted Mitzy to experience the thrills of young love, she was certain this would end in heartache.

"Mitzy, you know that I have the greatest respect and admiration for Captain Roffius, but you mustn't forget that he's a prince and you're a servant," she warned. "I don't want to see you get hurt."

"What a silly thing to say, Mother," replied Mitzy casually as if Roffius meant nothing to her. Although her mother's concern was warranted, Mitzy held fast to the belief that true love could overcome any obstacle….even a broken heart.

Roffius returned to the cave carrying some large leaves drenched with the fresh rain. He brought them to Mitzy and tenderly wrapped the cool leaves around her ankle.

"These should help with the swelling," he explained. Once the leaves were secured, Roffius left again to watch for Stefano and Julean.

A Grassy Knoll

Inside the cozy cave, the fire crackled as Meridia sang Mitzy's favorite lullaby to Baby Zerah:

> "Hush little one with eyes so bright,
> Mama's gonna keep you safe
> Through the night.
> Hush little one with cheeks so red,
> Mama's gonna cradle
> Your sleepy little head.
> Hush little one with curls of gold,
> Mama's gonna tell you
> The legend of old.
> Hush little one the Scroll is true,
> The kingdom shall be saved
> By someone like you."

******

Stefano and Julean followed the sound of Meridia's angelic voice back to the cave. They added the kindling they had gathered to the small fire and it sprang to life. Stefano sat beside his uncle and asked the question on everyone's mind.

"Are we safe here? I heard men's voices…and dogs," he said nervously.

"It was probably just some of the local farmers. Besides, we have a good head start and they don't know where we're going," answered Roffius. He hoped to sound more confident than he felt since Roffius shared his nephew's same fears.

"Has the legend in the Dragon Scroll really come true?" asked Julean.

"Who told you that?" asked Roffius sharply.

"Nobody, we're just good eavesdroppers," answered Stefano.

"Is Natas coming for us?" asked Julean with trepidation. Roffius wished he could keep the truth from his nephews a little longer, but he knew the time had come to tell them the truth.

"The black dragon shall not stop until he kills every member of the Royal Family, but for now I believe we are safe," he answered honestly.

"What makes you say that?" asked Stefano.

"Because I saw the beast flying out towards The Great Sea," replied Roffius. "I believe he noticed the Royal Ship was missing from port and set out in search of it. Natas would only do such a thing if he thought the rest of us were already dead or imprisoned. Once the beast finds my parents in Hampenstein, he shall kill them and return to do the same to us," stated Roffius plainly.

"You could be wrong, Uncle. Perhaps Natas just wanted to stretch his wings after being asleep in a cave for so long," suggested Julean.

"I've been wrong about a great many things, and believe me when I say that I hope to be wrong about this as well, but I don't think I am," said Roffius. "Yet, as much as this grieves me to say, I'm thankful for the extra time we now have to reach Irvania without worry of Natas." The others considered Roffius' assessment, and realized anew the seriousness of their situation.

Meridia saw the fear on the boys' faces and tried to lift their spirits by reminding them of the hope found in the

A Grassy Knoll

Dragon Scroll.

"Fear not, Young Princes, your father's belief shall bring the return of the good dragon any time now," she said kindly. Stefano and Julean sighed with relief, but Roffius knew Shem's belief no longer mattered even if Orpheus did exist. He knew it was time to tell his nephews the truth.

"I need to speak with the two of you alone," said the weary captain. "Come with me." The boys followed their uncle from the cave while Meridia and Mitzy remained in its cozy warmth. She was accustomed to exclusions from certain conversations amongst royalty; nevertheless it served as a painful reminder of the social chasm separating Mitzy from the young man she loved.

******

The rain subsided as Roffius led the boys to some rocks where he motioned for them to sit. He took a deep breath and ran his fingers through his wavy hair.

"This isn't easy for me to say, but even if Orpheus exists there's a chance he shan't return," said Roffius plainly.

"What do you mean?" asked Julean tilting his head.

"Father believes in Orpheus, so the good dragon must return!" exclaimed Stefano. Roffius paced back and forth realizing just how hard this was going to be.

"Yes, Stefano, he does; but based upon something I've recently learned, your father's belief has no bearing on whether or not the dragon shall return," said their uncle outright.

"What?" asked Stefano.

"Just before the attack, Kleiko discovered that every member of the Royal Family bears a Mark of Royalty on the left forearm... a mark which we do not bear," explained Roffius.

"What do you mean?" asked Julean.

"We have no mark, boys, because we aren't of royal blood," whispered Roffius. The boys quickly inspected their left forearms by moonlight, and found nothing.

"But...if we aren't the Royal Family, who is?" asked a bewildered Stefano.

"I wish I knew, but right now my priority is to get you and the women safely to Irvania. After that, Jesorath and I shall begin searching for the true king," answered Roffius. Even in the darkness he could see the confusion in his nephews' eyes. "I know this is difficult to understand, but you must continue to behave as if you are part of the Royal Family; the life of the true king depends on it."

"Can we tell Meridia and Mitzy?" asked Julean.

"No, we mustn't place them in any more danger than they are already in by being with us," explained Roffius. The boys sat in silence until they heard Zerah's cries echoing from the cave.

"Sounds like Zerah needs to be fed," remarked Stefano.

"I wish I could eat something," moaned Julean.

"We shall look for food at first light," said Roffius. "And, by the way Stefano, I think Zerah is a perfect name."

"Did Meridia tell you?" asked the boy nervously. "Do you really like it?"

"I do," answered Roffius as Stefano sighed with relief. "Now, let's get back to the cave. We wouldn't want to worry the women."

When they entered the cave, Mitzy noticed the somber expressions on their faces. Julean walked over to the fire and lay on his side. When he did, the boy felt a lump in his pocket and reached inside. To his delight, Julean found the rolls and cookies he had placed there just before the attack.

"Hey! Look what I found!" he exclaimed. Julean revealed the precious items and offered some to everyone. These, along with the water Roffius had collected from the creek, made for a satisfying, albeit simple, meal. Mitzy limped over to her mother and gave her more water knowing that Zerah's survival depended upon the production of her mother's milk.

"Here, Mother, drink this," she offered. Meridia welcomed the extra water and drank deeply before addressing the exhausted boys.

"It's been a long day, Your Majesties, try to get some rest," she suggested.

"I'm not tired," complained Stefano.

"I'm still too hungry to sleep," added Julean.

"At least try," encouraged Mitzy as she hobbled back to the boys. They curled up at her feet reluctantly but were soon fast asleep. Roffius knelt beside Mitzy pretending to stoke the fire, but in truth he just wanted to be close to the beautiful maiden.

"I know how difficult this must be for you, Your Highness, but it's clear the boys take great comfort in your presence," she said thoughtfully.

"That's very kind of you to say, Miss Mit, but you couldn't possibly understand what I'm feeling," he said coldly. "Try to get some rest; we shall be leaving again in a few hours. And, please, call me Captain." Although he hadn't intended to sound harsh, Mitzy took his response as a reprimand for speaking to him so informally.

"Yes, of course. Forgive me for being so bold," she replied softly.

Mitzy had never felt more embarrassed, or ashamed. She rested her head against the wall and closed her eyes before Roffius could see they were filling with tears. He walked away sensing that he had hurt her feelings, which was an unbearable thought for Roffius. He stopped at the mouth of the cave and turned around to apologize, but refrained after presuming she was asleep. Like so many things between Roffius and Mitzy, the apology went left unspoken.

******

A heavy rain began to fall as Roffius kept watch feeling more alone than ever. His thoughts drifted like one of Mitzy's daydreams, but without any of the pleasantries. Roffius thought of his parents, Kleiko's discovery, and finally his brother. He wondered if Shem survived the flogging, and struggled to accept the fact that life as he

A Grassy Knoll

knew it was gone forever. Roffius shivered and reached for his cloak to provide shelter from the elements, but then remembered that Baby Zerah was using it as a bed.

"Oh great," he said to himself. Roffius crossed his arms over his chest attempting to keep warm when he felt a lump. He reached in and pulled out the Dragon Scroll. Roffius looked at it somewhat humbled knowing that everything he had believed to be true about himself was a lie, and everything he thought to be foolishness in the Dragon Scroll was true. Yet, he returned the scroll to his vest doubting there was any hope for Orpheus' return.

******

In the earliest hours of morning as the sun crept over the horizon, a thick layer of fog hung over the landscape.

"Wake up!" called Roffius. "It's time to get moving." Julean heard his uncle, but chose to ignore his request.

"Are you sure we can't sleep just a little longer? I was having the best dream about eggs, bacon, and biscuits," moaned the boy.

Mitzy stretched her arms over her head and wiggled her ankle. The swelling was nearly gone, which she rightly attributed to Roffius' treatment of cold leaves and rubbing. Mitzy noticed how refreshed Roffius looked as he approached.

"Good morning, Miss Mit. How's your ankle?" he asked pleasantly.

"It feels much better, Captain; thank you for asking," she replied making sure to avoid using his title. He appreciated her remembering, and nodded with a smile as he reached for Shem's sword resting against the cave wall behind the maiden.

"I'll take this now," he said then slid the weapon into his scabbard.

Stefano put out what remained of the fire and the fugitives followed Roffius out the cave and into the fog. Mitzy did her best to keep up with his quick pace and long strides over the muddy terrain.

"Are you sure you can manage?" he called back to her. Although he was a good distance ahead, Roffius kept a watchful eye on Mitzy.

"I'm fine, Captain, don't worry about me," she answered while trying not to slip.

"I'm glad, because I wouldn't want to carry you around all day," he teased. Stefano and Julean grinned at one another.

"Well, I never asked you to in the first place," she mumbled. Suddenly, a low branch snared the hem of her long skirts and Mitzy found herself hooked like a fish on a line. She stopped and pulled at them to get free.

"Wait, Uncle! It's Mitzy!" shouted Stefano. Roffius feared she had fallen again and ran back to help. However, when Roffius saw her predicament, he just tried to conceal his laughter.

"Shall I come free you, Miss Mit?" he chuckled. Mitzy was embarrassed, frustrated, and confused. One minute Roffius seemed completely disinterested, and the next he appeared to be flirting.

"No, Captain, I'm quite capable. Go on ahead and I shall catch up," she replied.

"As you wish, my lady," he said with a playful bow.

Mitzy tugged at her long skirts and soon freed herself from the branch. Roffius was surprised with her ability to rejoin them so quickly and admired her determination. As they walked along, Mitzy voiced a concern similar to the one Stefano had the night before.

"Are you certain we shall be safe in Irvania?" she asked.

"I've heard my brother speak of Jesorath often and trust him to be a good man. Besides, I doubt the Bara soldiers would think to go that far south," answered Roffius. At the mention of the blacksmith, Mitzy's thoughts wandered back to her best friend still at the castle. Roffius noticed her pace slowing.

"Is your ankle bothering you, Miss Mit?" he asked.

"No, I was just thinking about Cora," answered Mitzy. "I'm terribly worried about her." Roffius had been so consumed with his own worries that he hadn't considered how all this affected Mitzy.

"If she's anything like you, I'm certain she's fine. It's the Bara you should be concerned about," he said hoping to raise her spirits. Mitzy managed a smile and appreciated his thoughtful remark. Meanwhile, Stefano and Julean were deep in their own conversation.

"How are you?" Julean asked his cousin.

"I can't believe they're gone," replied Stefano referring to his parents.

"At least you got to know them; I don't even remember my parents. I wish I had at least one memory of them," admitted Julean sadly.

"We must keep all of them alive in our hearts for Zerah's sake," said Stefano, "I want him to know what an amazing family he had, royalty or not." Julean paused for a moment.

"Where do you suppose we shall live now?" he asked. Stefano had wondered the same thing.

"I'm not sure, but it won't matter as long as we're together," he said with confidence. Julean hoped his cousin was right, but doubted he could live without Cook's pastries.

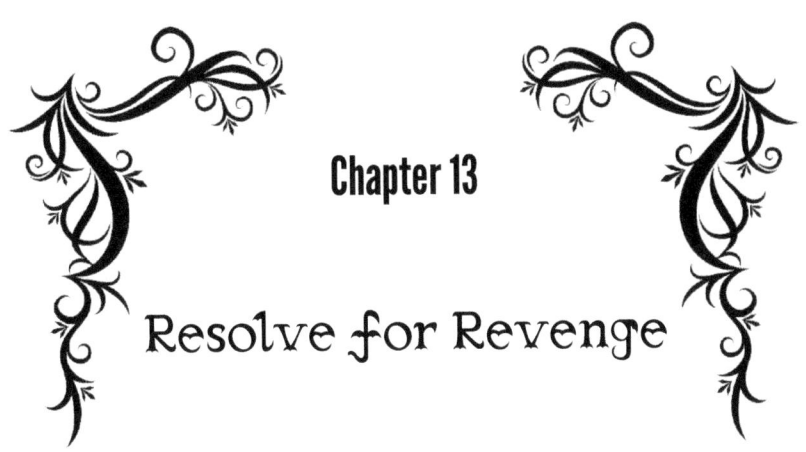

Chapter 13

Resolve for Revenge

As morning dawned at the castle, the former king moaned deep within the rat-infested cell. He continued to slip in and out of consciousness as Lamech and Aykin worked fervently to keep Shem alive.

"I fear he has developed a fever," stated Lamech. While Aykin emptied the last of the water onto a piece of cloth, both men heard footsteps approaching. Within minutes, a small bundle came through the bars of the cell door and Aykin retreated to the back of the cell.

"This is for the king," said a voice. Lamech looked up and saw Ithamar's face peering through the bars.

"Ithamar, you frightened me," said the physician wondering if the guard had seen Aykin.

"How's the king?" asked Ithamar.

"He has developed a fever, and I've run out of water and clean dressings for his wounds," reported the concerned physician.

"You should find everything you need in that parcel; as well as some bread and cheese. I'm counting on you to keep the king alive," Ithamar said in a tone which Lamech thought sounded like an order.

"I shall do my best. Have you any news of the others?" asked the physician. Ithamar thought of Meridia and hoped she was with Prince Roffius and her daughter by now.

"No, but I saw six Bara soldiers ride out a few hours ago most likely in search of them," reported Ithamar. "My men and I shall leave for Irvania after sunset to meet up with them. I shall need you to be on the alert here, for I sense things aren't going as Narok had planned."

From the back of the cell where Aykin was listening, he soon recognized Ithamar's voice. He considered revealing himself to his father's best friend, but chose not to after the guard's painful words from the day before replayed in his mind. Aykin remained silent as he strained to hear more.

"What do you mean?" asked Lamech.

"I sense there is division amongst the Bara soldiers," explained the guard. "I overheard pieces of a conversation between the men who brought the king here last night which gave me the feeling that Narok has enemies closer than he knows. Watch yourself, and keep King Shem alive." The physician wanted to tell Ithamar the truth about Shem, as well as about Aykin and his friends, but the guard disappeared before he could. Once Ithamar was gone, Aykin rejoined Lamech beside Shem.

"Wasn't he the man who brought you here last night?" asked Aykin.

"Yes, that was Ithamar," replied Lamech. He picked up the parcel and eagerly pulled out some fresh strips of cloth and water.

"He's smart, but can you trust him?" continued Aykin. He knew what Ithamar was like years ago, but he also knew from experience how time could change a person.

"I trust him with my life. In fact, Ithamar has been the king's most trusted guard since Narok murdered Prince Jeru," replied Lamech. Aykin looked at the physician with surprise. He wasn't aware that Prince Jeru was dead, let alone that Narok was the one who had killed him. Hearing this only heightened Aykin's resolve to exact his revenge.

"Why did you agree to stay in the dungeon?" asked Aykin. Lamech hated to lie, but in this instance he felt he must since he still didn't know if Aykin could be trusted with the truth.

"Because he is my king, therefore, I shall do anything in my power to help him," he answered. The young man was bewildered by Lamech's response. Such selfless devotion was foreign to Aykin after having spent the majority of his life in the presence of dishonorable people who used others for their own gain. He hadn't seen this kind of simple, unconditional love since he was a child. Aykin struggled to keep his emotions in check, and was thankful when Lamech continued. "Will you hand me that water flask?" he asked.

"Ashter, Ashter," mumbled Shem deliriously.

"It's the fever talking," Lamech explained. Aykin nodded and remembered Eliab telling him that the queen was dead. Even a heart as hardened as Aykin's ached as he watched the king writhe in pain from the horrible images replaying in his mind.

"I know how difficult it is to lose the ones you love," Aykin heard himself saying as he handed Lamech the water. "I used to think I was going to grow up and become a Royal Guard just like my father."

"I'm certain that can still be true if you wish it to be," answered Lamech kindly.

"I'd like to believe you," laughed Aykin. "But it's too late for me."

Lamech's words started a transformation within Aykin which he tried to ignore, but in truth had wanted all along. He assisted the physician in silence as Lamech worked tirelessly to clean Shem's many wounds. Lamech removed old, blood-soaked strips of cloth and handed them to Aykin who in turn handed the physician clean ones. Seeing Shem like this brought back Aykin's most painful memory.

"He reminds me of my father," he said. Lamech continued to change the soiled dressings while pretending to be less interested than he really was to keep Aykin talking.

"I believe Uriah was once a highly esteemed Royal Guard was he not?" he asked. Aykin appreciated the kind words about his father.

"He served for a short time under King Daven and Queen Lydia, and then for King Shem and Queen Ashter," he explained.

"Do you know how your father died?" asked Lamech. It was a rhetorical question since Lamech believed that Uriah had committed suicide. However, when he saw the look on Aykin's face, the physician wondered if perhaps he was wrong.

Aykin took a deep breath and began the tale which had been bottled up inside for far too long. He shared with Lamech the last conversation his parents had in hushed tones about the Dragon Scroll and a plot to kill the king. Aykin then told Lamech how he had waited outside for his father to return only to watch as Lott set fire to his home with his mother, sisters, and baby brother trapped inside. Aykin finished by telling Lamech how he had returned to the castle to get his father, but instead found Uriah's dead body at the base of the east tower. The physician thought it nothing short of a miracle that Aykin hadn't turned out worse than what he appeared.

"I can understand your hatred toward Lott, but why must you exact revenge on his son?" asked Lamech.

"Narok shares his father's obsession to obtain the throne, and because of that my family's dead. And don't forget that he tried to kill me last night," stated Aykin bluntly. Although Lamech disagreed with the idea of revenge, he wholeheartedly agreed that Narok deserved the most extreme punishment for his crimes.

"Why would Narok do that to you?" asked the old physician.

"He's hungry for power and wishes to share it with no one. I believe that, like you, Narok recognized me as the son of Uriah and saw me as a threat," answered Aykin.

"Is that why you aligned yourself with the Bara, to get close to Narok?" asked Lamech.

"No, the Bara were just my way out of the hellhole I was living in after my family was killed," Aykin replied sharply. He then turned around and lifted his shirt to reveal a morbid canvas of scar tissue caused by countless whippings from Eliab's drunkard father. "You must believe me, Lamech, my intentions in all this were to destroy Narok's dream of taking the throne, never to harm the king," continued Aykin as he turned back around. Lamech suddenly realized that this young man was a victim of circumstance rather than a ruthless killer.

"I believe you, Aykin," he replied honestly. For the first time since his father was killed, Aykin had someone who believed in him, and it was life-changing.

******

After delivering the parcel filled with supplies to Lamech, Ithamar made his way through a labyrinth of tunnels back to the long-forgotten room carved out for the bricklayers during the castle's construction. When Ithamar reached the room, he knocked three times on the door then quickly slipped inside the moment it swung open.

"What took you so long?" asked Perez.

"I had to ensure I wasn't followed," replied Ithamar.

"How is he?" asked Luklin referring to the man they believed was king.

"Not well, but if anyone can save him, it's Lamech," answered Ithamar.

"Why are we still here if we know Prince Roffius has gone to Irvania?" asked Perez anxiously.

"Make no mistake, Perez, no one wants to leave more than I, but we must wait until after sunset to have the cover of night. We shall then take the old fisherman's route to ensure we aren't followed," stated Ithamar.

"Won't that add nearly two days to the journey?" asked Luklin.

"Yes, but it is the best way to ensure we aren't being followed. The last thing we want to do is lead Bara soldiers straight to Prince Roffius," answered their commander firmly. Perez and Luklin nodded in agreement and waited anxiously with the rest of the squadron for sunset.

******

The late morning sunshine was a refreshing change from the ferocious storm the night before as Roffius and the others emerged from the dense forest. Roffius was exhausted after not having slept all night, but he dutifully pushed ahead for the sake of the women and boys to reach Irvania before nightfall.

"Keep moving!" he called out.

"I'm starving! The grumbling from my stomach shall lead the Bara straight to us!" complained Julean.

"Try not to think about it," said Mitzy.

"I can't help it. I haven't gone this long without a meal my whole life!" complained the boy.

"We can look for fruit trees...or nuts and berries," suggested Stefano. He bound ahead and soon found animal tracks which led them to a luscious berry bush. Although Roffius wanted to keep moving, even he agreed they were in need of nourishment.

"These are delicious!" exclaimed Julean. He shoved the fruit into his berry-stained mouth one handful after another.

"Well done, Stefano, you've found us a bountiful feast," Mitzy said cheerfully. Stefano was happy to help by doing something which came so naturally to him, and the extra attention from the beautiful maiden was a bonus.

"You can sit here, Mitzy," he said while dusting off a rock.

"Thank you, Your Highness," she replied politely. Mitzy gave the lad an exaggerated curtsy and more golden curls escaped from her braid. Stefano thought she was the most beautiful maiden he'd ever seen, and he wasn't alone in that sentiment.

"I think he's smitten with you, Miss Mit," whispered Roffius from behind.

"Don't be silly. Besides, such a thing is forbidden since he is a prince and I am but a lowly servant," she said playfully. Roffius walked around to face the maiden whose crystal blue eyes danced with mischief and wondered if she was toying with him. He wanted to take her into his arms and profess his love, but he knew he mustn't until the true king was found. Even then Roffius wondered if Mitzy would have him since he would have nothing to offer. Frustrated with the hand which fate had dealt him, Roffius insisted they press on.

"We've lingered long enough. It's time to get moving," he said abruptly.

"I beg your pardon, Captain, but I must feed the baby first. If I don't, travel shall be difficult for us all," said Meridia apologetically.

"Yes, of course, my lady. Take all the time you need," he replied feeling like a louse for not considering the baby's needs. As he turned to walk away, Roffius suddenly felt vibrations beneath his feet and heard a distant rumbling. Stefano heard it as well.

"What's that?" he asked. Roffius knelt down and put his ear to the ground.

"Horses!" he exclaimed. "Quickly, hide!" Roffius helped Stefano and Julean start up a tree, while Mitzy and Meridia hid behind another tree with Baby Zerah. Moments later, five Bara soldiers appeared over the ridge.

"Wait for my signal then drop as many pine cones on them as you can," Roffius instructed the boys. Once they were high enough, Roffius bolted away and positioned himself behind a large boulder between the riders and the women. Mitzy and Meridia watched anxiously as the horsemen drew near, and hoped the hungry infant wouldn't give them away.

"Dismount men! By the looks of these tracks they can't be far," called one to the others. The unkempt men left their horses to search the area on foot as the baby started to squirm. Meridia gently rocked him, but Zerah had waited long enough to be fed.

"WHAAA!" screamed the infant. Within seconds, the women found themselves surrounded.

"Well, well, what do we have here? Where are the others?" demanded one of the soldiers.

"I don't know what you mean; we're traveling alone. My baby has dysentery and we're in search of a village willing to take us in," replied Meridia calmly. Roffius was impressed with her quick thinking as he listened from behind the boulder.

"I don't believe you," said the soldier glaring suspiciously at Meridia.

"She's telling the truth," Mitzy interjected. The man turned his attention to the beautiful maiden and stepped towards her.

"I think you're lying," he accused. "But, what I don't know is why the prince would leave someone like you behind." The man reached out and slid a dirty finger down Mitzy's cheek. She turned away, but the Bara immediately grabbed hold of her face and turned it back towards himself. Seeing this, Roffius could think of nothing but Mitzy's safety as he charged out from behind the boulder. Stefano and Julean assumed this was the signal their uncle had spoken of, so they began to hurl pine cones at the soldiers.

Resolve for Revenge

"Mother, run!" yelled Mitzy.

Meridia fled with the baby while Roffius delivered a solid punch to the man holding the beautiful maiden. The grungy soldier fell to the ground unconscious as his comrades rushed towards Roffius and Mitzy. Roffius quickly pushed her out of harm's way before he found himself surrounded by the fierce Bara. Knowing she could help, Mitzy lifted her skirts to get the king's sword. When she did, the men stopped fighting to gawk at her shapely legs. As much as he hated to turn away, Roffius used her timely distraction to fatally stab one of their attackers. After realizing the weapon was no longer there, Mitzy dropped her skirts and picked up the sword from the man Roffius had just killed.

Two of the soldiers immediately returned their attention to Roffius, while the third approached Mitzy with a lustful grin. He expected to easily disarm the maiden and have his way with her, but the soldier was grossly mistaken. Mitzy dodged his strikes and delivered thrusts with the skill of a master swordsman. Her abilities enraged the man and he managed to slice Mitzy's arm. She continued to fight in spite of her injury, and cleverly lured her opponent over to the tree where Stefano and Julean were perched. When the soldier was below them, the boys pelted him with pine cones. The last thing the Bara saw before blacking out was a large branch coming straight for his head.

"Did you see that?" exclaimed Julean.

"Nicely done boys!" called Mitzy from below. "Can you see your uncle?"

"He was over there," said Stefano pointing to where Mitzy had been.

She returned to the spot, but all that remained were dead Bara soldiers. Mitzy scanned the area until she saw two men fighting atop a small hill. As she sprinted towards them, one man ran his blade through the other.

"RO!" she cried out in anguish fearing he'd been killed right before her eyes. Mitzy waited breathlessly as the survivor turned around. As he did, the morning sun streamed in from behind and prevented Mitzy from seeing whether or not it was Roffius. Unaware if the man approaching was friend or foe, Mitzy stood with her sword in the ready position.

Roffius hadn't heard the name used by only his brother Jeru and Mitzy since he was a child. More than ever Roffius wanted to embrace Mitzy and profess his love as he walked toward her, but he restrained himself after remembering his bound duty to protect the king. The growing conflict between desire and duty created tremendous inner tension which was misconstrued as anger at her when Roffius saw Mitzy's blood-stained sleeve.

"Why must you continue to put yourself in harm's way?!" he exclaimed. Mitzy's relief in seeing him alive dissipated with his harsh response.

"I would've thought by now, Captain, that you'd know I'm perfectly capable of taking care of myself," she replied defensively. Mitzy turned to leave, but Roffius grabbed her and pulled her back.

"Who taught you how to use a sword like that?" he demanded. Mitzy found his abrasive tone more painful than the wound on her arm, and she was tired of his ingratitude. Mitzy was not going to be scolded again by him for helping…royalty or not.

"If you must know, Your Highness, Cook wasn't the only man with whom I've spent time since you left," she said coldly. Her remark hit Roffius like a slap in the face.

"I see…," he said stunned. Roffius immediately released her arm assuming she was referring to a male suitor, which left him feeling monumentally humiliated. Mitzy stormed away as the boys ran up.

"Did you see us? We showed them!" exclaimed Julean.

"Yes, well done boys," replied their distracted uncle. However, Roffius heard nothing more of their excited chatter as he watched Mitzy run to the large tree where her mother stood with Zerah.

"Mother, are you all right?" asked Mitzy as the two embraced. Meridia was frightened and the baby was still screaming, but they were otherwise fine.

"Yes, thanks to you and Captain Roffius," remarked Meridia with a smile until she saw her daughter's arm. "You're bleeding!"

"It's nothing," answered Mitzy as the boys joined them.

"Did you see us? We clobbered those Bara soldiers!" boasted Stefano.

"Yes indeed, the two of you did a fine job. We're forever in your debt," answered Meridia with a curtsy. The boys smiled proudly, but Mitzy hurried away as Roffius approached.

"Boys, I need your help with these sorry excuses for men. We shall tie them to that tree and take their horses for the remainder of our journey," ordered their uncle. Julean was delighted to hear they would no longer be walking, but not more than Meridia. The boys each grabbed an ankle of the man they knocked out and dragged him to the tree, while Roffius followed after Mitzy. Although completely humiliated, Roffius knew he must extend an apology for his behavior. He found Mitzy beside a large tree.

"Forgive me for scolding you, Miss Mit; and for prying. Your suitor must be a Royal Guard to have taught you so well in the art of sword fighting," said Roffius awkwardly. Mitzy looked at him with surprise.

"Suitor? I haven't any suitor," she replied with a crinkled up nose. "Cora's father was the Royal Blacksmith; he taught me everything I know." Roffius barely heard the last part of her sentence as he tried to conceal his elation.

"Yes…I can tell…your form is perfect," he said stumbling over his words. "I mean… you're very natural with a sword."

"Thank you, Captain," said Mitzy with a twinkle in her eyes. "Now, if you'll excuse me, I was about to place this in my favorite hiding place." After she walked behind the tree, Roffius craned his neck to catch another glimpse of her shapely legs. Sensing his gaze Mitzy looked up, but the handsome captain had already gone.

Resolve for Revenge

******

Roffius hoisted the final unconscious Bara soldier over his shoulder and carried the man to the tree where Stefano and Julean were waiting.

"You boys get the women and wait for me with the horses," he said. Roffius dropped the man as Stefano and Julean eagerly ran to select a horse for themselves. As Roffius finished securing the last knot, the soldiers started to regain consciousness.

"Does the king still live?" demanded Roffius.

"For now, but Narok's only keeping him alive to watch you die!" said one with contempt. News of Shem being alive provided Roffius with greater strength than sleep or food ever could, and hearing Narok's name confirmed what Meridia had previously told them.

"We shall see about that. In the mean time, I'd like to thank you for the use of your fine horses. Be sure to tell your comrades that you were bested by a maiden and two boys," mocked Roffius. The soldiers struggled to free themselves, all-the-while yelling obscenities unsuitable in the presence of women and children. Mitzy blushed as Meridia covered the boys' ears. "Where are your manners?" asked Roffius before striking each on the head with the butt of his sword to prevent them from seeing which way they went.

"This is more like it!" exclaimed Julean from atop a fine animal as Roffius joined them.

"Now we shall reach Irvania in no time!" added Stefano as he mounted his horse. Mitzy wrapped the infant securely within Roffius' cloak before tying it around her mother to keep Baby Zerah safe as they rode. Roffius then helped Meridia onto the horse. Although unaccustomed to riding, Meridia welcomed the idea compared to walking the rest of the way with the baby. Once Meridia and Zerah were settled, Roffius turned to Mitzy. Her heart fluttered as Roffius placed his hands on her slender waist and lifted her with ease. She was lost in his hazel eyes as Mitzy looked down from atop her horse to thank him.

"Thank you, Captain," she said softly.

"Please, call me Ro," he replied.

Mitzy's eyes grew wide as she realized Roffius heard the impertinent way in which she had addressed him back at the hill. To do such a thing was punishable by death, and Mitzy feared the retribution which was sure to follow. However, her only consequence was a wink and a sideways smile as Roffius mounted the last horse in one smooth motion. He then turned the animal around and sped south towards Irvania with the others following through his dust.

Mitzy was speechless after her mind-boggling exchange with Roffius as she rode alongside her mother. They were in the rear while Stefano and Julean rode ahead with their uncle. With the tree still in sight where the Bara were tied, Mitzy suddenly felt a sharp pain in her shoulder. She assumed it was from the wound on her arm, but it quickly worsened. When Mitzy reached to rub it, to her horror she felt an arrow. Her head spun and Mitzy called out to her mother.

"Mother!" she managed to yell before fainting. Meridia turned around and saw her daughter falling from her horse.

"MITZY!!" she screamed in terror.

Roffius knew something was wrong after hearing Meridia's cry, but all doubt was removed when Mitzy's horse speed past him without a rider. He turned around to see the maiden lying motionless on the ground as a Bara soldier raced towards them wielding a crossbow. Roffius urged his horse towards the man and kicked the crossbow just as the dirty soldier fired another arrow. The arrow shot into the air and the crossbow spiraled out of the Bara's hand. Each turned his horse around in pursuit of the weapon. Roffius rode alongside the soldier and jumped from his horse onto the man, which caused both to fall tumbling to the ground.

The Bara was the first to his feet and he wasted no time delivering a swift, solid punch across Roffius' jaw. While the dazed captain stumbled backward, the man managed to take one of Roffius' daggers from his belt. The grungy soldier tried to slice him, but Roffius dodged his strike then drew his other dagger. The Bara threw dirt into Roffius' eyes and kicked his weapon from his hand while the captain was blinded. Roffius lunged at the man and tackled him to the ground. They wrestled through the dirt for control of the blade until Roffius head-butted the soldier and kicked the dagger free. Roffius sprinted after one of the loose weapons, but the Bara grabbed his legs and tripped him. With Roffius on the ground, the man pounced on him and pinned Roffius down. The soldier then reached over the captain's head and took hold of a dagger.

A smug smile crossed the grungy man's face as he raised the dagger to deliver a fatal strike. But before the blade lowered, a strange look suddenly crossed the man's face. Roffius watched blood trickle from his mouth before he collapsed face-first onto Roffius. The captain pushed the Bara off, and then stared in disbelief at the arrow protruding from the man's back. Roffius looked up in surprise to see Stefano with the crossbow propped against his shoulder standing behind the dead Bara soldier.

"Nice shot," said Roffius chest heaving.

"Thanks," replied Stefano with a broad smile.

Roffius quickly got to his feet and retrieved his daggers before running back to Mitzy. He was thankful to see she had landed on her side so the arrow wasn't forced in deeper.

"Is she dead?" cried Julean. Roffius placed his head on her chest and listened for a heartbeat while Meridia handed Baby Zerah to Stefano.

"She's alive," he answered with a sigh of relief. His face went pale, however, after remembering Mitzy's hidden sword. "Meridia, I need you to make sure the sword hidden in her skirts has caused no injuries." Meridia lifted her daughter's skirts and was thankful to see none, so she pulled the sword free and handed it to Julean.

"There is no sign of injury down there," announced Meridia.

"Good," said Roffius. "Now, I shall need you to hold her still while I remove the arrow." Meridia held her

Resolve for Revenge

daughter as Roffius carefully pulled the arrow free from Mitzy's flesh.

"You did it!" exclaimed Julean.

"Will she be all right, Captain?" asked the distraught mother.

"These arrows are made with the intent to kill; if not from the strike then from infection. We must get her to Irvania for proper care. She shall ride with me the rest of the way," declared Roffius. He lifted Mitzy's limp body into his arms and they mounted together as smoothly as if he was doing so alone.

As they rode away, Roffius was too consumed with guilt over what happened to notice that the Bara soldiers tied to the tree had regained consciousness. The delay in their departure allowed for the grungy men to gather their senses and watch the man they believed was a prince ride south.

******

After hours of riding, Mitzy started to burn with fever. Roffius urged the exhausted horse onward and desperately wished Lamech was with them, not knowing the old physician was keeping Shem alive back at the castle. As the sun sparkled brilliantly off the Cherith River, the quaint village of Irvania finally came into view. Roffius slowed his horse to a walk knowing the animal was close to collapsing after running so long bearing two riders.

"What's the matter, Uncle?" asked Stefano.

"I fear my horse shall soon collapse if I don't slow down. You and Julean must ride ahead and fetch Jesorath.

Tell him that I sent you, and that we are in desperate need of the local physician," ordered Roffius.

"Yes, Uncle," replied Stefano.

When they reached the blacksmith's shop, Stefano and Julean sprang from their horses and burst through the large doors. The boys looked in awe at the newly crafted swords on display in the turning wheel, and the many pieces of steel in the large brick fireplace for softening.

"Jesorath! Jesorath!" called Julean.

A deep voice answered, "I'll be right out." A very large, muscular man soon emerged. Jesorath was surprised to see his royal guests, and looked around for King Shem.

"Jesorath, are we glad to see you!" exclaimed Julean.

"Uncle Roffius sent us to find you," stated Stefano.

"The castle was attacked, and Queen Ashter's dead!" continued Julean.

"And we must have a physician!" added Stefano.

"Now hold on a minute; one at a time," said Jesorath. It was impossible for him to understand either boy with them talking at the same time.

"Bara soldiers attacked the castle and Queen Ashter is dead, but we escaped with Uncle Roffius," replied Julean. Jesorath braced himself against one of racks of swords as he tried to process such terrible news, but he did catch one thing which offered him hope.

"Did you say you escaped with Prince Roffius?" he asked.

"Yes, and with Meridia and my new baby brother. Mitzy is with us too; she's the one who needs the physician," answered Stefano. Jesorath pursed his lips and thought for a moment.

"Go upstairs to the house and stay there until I return," he instructed.

"What about the physician?" insisted Stefano.

"Don't worry, I shall fetch him before I meet up with your uncle," replied the blacksmith. "Now go!"

The boys hurried up the staircase which led to Jesorath's home above the blacksmith shop while Jesorath saddled his fastest horse to retrieve the local physician.

******

Far across The Great Sea, Natas soared through the air and an evil smirk crossed his face as he spotted land in the distance. The former King Daven and Queen Lydia were oblivious to the impending danger, and to the horrors occurring in their homeland, as they boarded the Royal Ship. They had decided to surprise everyone with an early return after becoming lonesome for family since Roffius had gone.

When Natas reached port, he easily recognized Nepthali's royal crest on the ship's flag flapping in the wind. The black dragon unleashed his deadly fire and watched with satisfaction as King Daven and Queen Lydia were crushed by a mast after it fell upon them. The two joined countless others in a watery grave as their burning ship was swallowed up by the sea. With his goal accomplished, Natas circled and started his long flight back to Nepthali.

******

At the top of a hill looking over Irvania, Roffius watched Jesorath's unmistakably large frame riding towards them. He only hoped the blacksmith would prove to be as trustworthy as Shem professed.

"Greetings, My Prince, you've grown since I last saw you!" exclaimed the blacksmith. "It does my heart good to see you alive; especially after what Prince Stefano and Prince Julean have told me."

"It has been a long time, Jesorath. I only wish our reunion was under better circumstances," replied the weary captain.

"I see the boys didn't exaggerate about the need for a physician," said Jesorath seeing the beautiful maiden in Roffius' arms. Trying not to stare, the blacksmith turned to acknowledge Meridia. "Greetings, my lady; have no fear for the physician is awaiting our return."

Relieved to hear this news, Meridia managed a smile before the blacksmith led them down the hill and through the quiet streets of Irvania. When they arrived inside his stables, Jesorath dismounted and helped Meridia with Baby Zerah before turning to Roffius.

"Allow me, My Prince," offered Jesorath. Roffius started to object, but the burly blacksmith was too quick in lifting Mitzy into his strong arms. "You must be exhausted from your long journey." Jesorath started for the staircase, but was stopped by a firm grip upon his shoulder.

"It's no trouble at all; I shall take her," insisted Roffius. The stern look on the young captain's face told Jesorath it was best not to object. Roffius scooped Mitzy into his arms and nodded for the blacksmith to lead the way.

He led them up a rickety wooden staircase which stopped at a landing in front of Jesorath's small home. When the blacksmith opened the door, they were met with a warm greeting.

"You made it!" exclaimed Stefano

"We thought you'd never get here!" added Julean. Although happy to see his nephews, Roffius was happier to see a man standing in the corner whom he presumed was the physician.

"Bring her back here," said Jesorath. Roffius followed the blacksmith into a small room and gently placed Mitzy on the only bed. Meridia handed the baby off to Stefano so she could assist the physician who looked at Mitzy with concern.

"Roll her onto her stomach and remove the clothing around the wound," he said. Roffius did as the man asked and Meridia tore away the back side of her daughter's dress. With Mitzy's wound fully exposed, the physician's concern increased.

"She'll be all right, won't she?" asked Roffius.

"Hand me the plant in my bag, my lady," the physician instructed Meridia. The man purposely ignored Roffius' question since he had no answer yet as Meridia handed the physician the strange looking plant.

"What is this?" she asked.

"This is the Liaspot plant; it's found only in Irvania along the banks of the Cherith River. If the Liaspot cannot bring healing, nothing can," he replied honestly.

"Was it a gift from Orpheus?" asked Meridia. This time it was Meridia whom the man ignored because he, like most people in the kingdom, knew nothing of Orpheus. While he tore off the bushy leaves and crushed them into Mitzy's wound, Jesorath answered Meridia.

"I was told it was a gift from Orpheus, my lady," he said kindly. Meridia smiled at him in thanks, and then noticed Roffius watching anxiously from the foot of the bed.

"Captain, we could use some water. Perhaps you and Jesorath could fetch some?" she suggested. Roffius gladly accepted the task and left the room with the large blacksmith. When they closed the door, Stefano and Julean were eager for news of Mitzy.

"Is she going to be all right?" asked Stefano anxiously.

"She's in good hands," answered Jesorath. But he, too, was worried about Mitzy having seen stronger men die from a lesser wound once fever developed.

Jesorath and Roffius gathered the water and returned it to the tiny room. When they entered, Mitzy was on her back and Roffius cringed to see her covered with sweat and blood. After delivering the water, the men returned to the sparsely furnished front room where Roffius began to pace in silence. Jesorath pitied the young prince and sensed there was something much more than just concern for the beautiful maiden.

"You're going to wear a hole in my floor if you keep that up, Your Majesty," he said hoping to lighten the mood. Just then, the physician emerged from the back room.

"I'm afraid I haven't been able to bring her fever down as I had hoped. If she makes it through the night, I expect she shall recover," he said plainly. The physician's words hit them all hard, but Roffius was devastated.

"What do you mean *if* she makes it through the night?" he demanded.

"Fever is a mysterious thing. I've seen it leave as quickly as it came, or be the death of a healthy fellow within a matter of hours," replied the physician honestly. "Keep her cool and as comfortable as possible. I've done all I can for now. Send for me if she worsens." Roffius stared at the physician in stunned silence as the man quietly gathered his things. Although Roffius had renounced his belief in Orpheus years ago, he found himself blaming the good dragon for allowing harm to come to someone like Mitzy whose belief had never wavered.

Jesorath showed the physician out, and could see upon his return that Roffius was in need of a distraction.

"Her mother's with her, Your Highness. Why don't you come down to the stables with me while I feed and water the horses?" he asked. "We won't be gone long and the boys can fetch us if anything changes." Roffius reluctantly agreed and felt numb as he followed the blacksmith down the rickety stairs which led to the stables.

When they arrived, Roffius insisted on helping Jesorath in hopes of distracting his thoughts away from Mitzy. The large blacksmith scooped mounds of hay onto the pitchfork while Roffius spread it around the stall for the weary horses. They worked alongside one another without speaking as the sun slowly disappeared from the sky. Finally, Jesorath could take the silence no longer.

"Are you all right, My Prince?" he asked. Roffius pondered the question for a moment before answering.

"In little more than a day's time, Jesorath, my life has changed in ways I never imagined possible. I no longer even have a home," he said sadly. The blacksmith merely assumed Roffius meant because the castle had been overtaken, never guessing it was because Roffius could no longer live there even if he wanted to.

"Nonsense, we shall gather some men and take back the castle in no time," replied Jesorath with confidence. Roffius looked at the blacksmith and understood why his brother spoke so highly of him, but wondered if Jesorath's conviction would change after he learned the truth.

"I fear I've lost hope due to something which has recently come to light," stated Roffius.

"Take heart, Captain, hope may disguise itself, but it never truly goes away. Besides, you've made it this far," Jesorath said with an encouraging smile.

"Jesorath, my brother holds you in the highest regard, therefore, what I am about to tell you must be kept in the greatest of confidence," said Roffius sternly. Jesorath stopped scooping the hay and leaned against his pitchfork.

"I give you my word, and that's as solid as the iron I work with," he replied. Roffius took a deep breath and ran his fingers through his hair just as he had done before telling his nephews.

"Prior to the attack, the Chief Royal Scribe shared a discovery with Shem and me," he said.

"What was it?" asked Jesorath.

"Apparently, every member of the Royal Family bears a Mark of Royalty… one which neither Shem nor I have," he said plainly. Jesorath braced himself against the pitchfork fearing he may collapse without it.

"What?" he asked. "I can't believe it!"

"Trust me, I'm still trying to comprehend such a thing, but it's true," continued Roffius.

"If Shem isn't king, who is?" asked the stunned blacksmith.

"I don't know which is why I need your help. We must find the rightful king before Narok or the black dragon discovers the truth," said Roffius. "But, even if there is such a thing as a good dragon, I fear the true king doesn't believe since Orpheus has yet to return." Jesorath didn't think anything could be more of a shock than what Roffius had said about not being royalty until the blacksmith heard Narok's name.

"Narok? Isn't he dead?" he asked.

"We all thought so, but according to Meridia and the Bara soldiers we encountered, Narok's alive and seeks the Dragon Scroll," replied Roffius.

"What does he want with that?" asked Jesorath.

"Narok believes the scroll possesses some sort of power which has yet to be unleashed," answered Roffius.

"Is he right?" asked Jesorath.

"I'm not sure, but Kleiko believed the same thing," said the captain.

"Too bad you don't have the scroll; perhaps it contains a clue," continued Jesorath. Roffius suddenly remembered the ancient scroll tucked within his vest.

"Jesorath, you're a genius!" he exclaimed. Roffius pulled out the Dragon Scroll and began to unroll it, however, as he did, the scroll lifted from his hands and Shem's sword shot out from his scabbard. Both items hung suspended beside one another for a moment until the words penned with Orpheus' blood suddenly lifted off the scroll. They formed a thread which spun rapidly around until it wrapped itself around the sword.

"What's happening?" whispered Jesorath.

"I wish I knew," answered Roffius.

A blinding light then filled the stables and the men shielded their eyes as the thread fully encased the sword. When the light dissipated, the blank scroll dropped to the floor and the sword floated back to Roffius. The bewildered young man took hold of the weapon and marveled at its perfect fit to his grip.

"It must be from Orpheus," declared Jesorath. "Which means the good dragon *has* returned!" Before Roffius could respond, a violent gust of wind blew open the stable doors. The men exchanged worried glances as another blast of wind struck followed by a thunderous roar.

"Natas...," whispered Roffius. He took off running with Jesorath following close behind with the pitchfork.

An eerie black shadow passed overhead as Roffius and Jesorath emerged from the barn. Natas was in need of rest after his long journey back and forth from Hampenstein. The evil dragon intended to go straight to his lair, but had sensed the presence of royalty, and Orpheus, as he flew over Irvania. Natas circled the quaint province, yet saw nothing even as he passed directly over Roffius wearing his cloak bearing the Royal Crest, and the sword crafted by dragon magic. In frustration, the black dragon shot a blast of fire across the sky and released a roar so powerful it shook the entire kingdom. The hideous creature circled the blacksmith's shop one last time before disappearing into the darkness.

"How did he not see us?" asked a baffled Jesorath.

"Perhaps because of the sword," answered an equally amazed Roffius.

"Or, perhaps it's as I said and Orpheus has returned," said Jesorath. "The sword was most assuredly crafted by dragon magic for you, Captain, which proves you are still of great importance to Nepthali."

"I'm not sure I share your opinion, my friend, but I am sure that we must set out at first light to check every villager for the mark," replied Roffius. "For now, however, we'd best check on the others." Jesorath agreed and went back into the barn to return the pitchfork, while Roffius lingered to scan the skies one last time for Natas.

Dragon Scroll of Nepthali

Chapter 14

A Shocking Discovery

Inside the rat-infested dungeon, Lamech and Aykin knew one of them must hide after hearing the sound of footsteps approaching.

"Shall I stay with the king?" asked Lamech. Aykin winced at the physician's mistake of speaking so loudly.

"Aykin, is that you?" a man called out. Aykin recognized Narok's voice.

"Get out of sight! Narok mustn't know you're still alive," whispered Aykin. Lamech quickly disappeared into the darkness as Aykin answered Narok, "Surprised?" Narok signaled for Kenan to open the cell door and the two entered with Eliab while a fourth person waited in the corridor. Mezrah refused to accompany them after learning that Narok intended to keep Aykin alive.

"So, you are alive. My uncle said you were, but frankly I didn't believe him," stated Narok coldly. Aykin wondered how Mezrah found out since only Kenan and Eliab knew.

"Perhaps I wouldn't be if your aim was more accurate, or if you weren't as weak as a handmaid," replied Aykin defiantly.

Without warning, Narok cracked his cat o'nine tails across Aykin's back. Fortunately for Aykin his toughened skin from years of beatings provided some protection, but the deadly weapon tore away chunks of flesh. Lamech was tempted to help his new friend as the force of Narok's whip knocked Aykin to the ground, but the physician wisely remained hidden.

"Insolent fool," snapped Narok. "As much as I'd like to kill you, it seems you may yet be of use to me." Although the pain was excruciating, Aykin refused to give Narok the satisfaction of seeing his discomfort as the young man staggered to his feet.

"What makes you think I'd ever help you?" he retorted.

"Funny you should ask. You see, I have someone here whose life depends upon you doing exactly as I say," replied Narok. "You can come in now." A lad slowly entered the cell.

"What are we doing here, Brother?" asked Obed. He was confused by everything that had happened in the past few days. One minute he was out in the fields, and the next he was being escorted by Bara soldiers to the castle. When he had arrived, Obed was given fine food and a change of clothing before being taken to a room where he was left alone. He was finally brought to the Throne Room to see Narok who then took him straight to the dungeon.

"Narok, please, tell me why we're here," he repeated.

A Shocking Discovery

"Shut up, you fool!" snapped Narok.

"Brother, you're frightening me," continued Obed softly.

"Silence!" shouted Narok as he cracked the cat o'nine tails on the ground. "Tell me, Aykin, do you recognize this lad?"

Time stood still as Aykin stared in disbelief at Obed. Even in the dimly lit cell, Aykin could see the lad's uncanny resemblance to their mother. He instinctively knew this teenager was the brother he believed was dead all these years.

"Obed?" whispered Aykin. Obed's confusion heightened when this stranger called him by name.

"Who are you? How do you know my name?" he asked in amazement.

"Obed, I'd like you to meet your brother…your real brother," said Narok before Aykin could reply.

"But…you said I was an orphan," said the bewildered lad.

"Alas, things are not always as they seem, my boy. It's time you learned the truth about who you are. This man…this scum, is your real brother," stated Narok. Eliab, Aykin, and Obed were noticeably stunned by Narok's proclamation, yet it had no effect on Kenan. Obed reached into his pocket and took hold of Polly for comfort. He had brought the doll with him after learning he was going to the castle in hopes of seeing Mitzy and returning it to her.

"I don't understand," whispered Obed. He didn't know why, but he began to cry.

"Stop that you blubbering fool!" scolded Narok before turning to Aykin. "My father suspected your escape that fateful night, so he kept the boy for leverage. As it turns out, my father was a very wise man."

"I'll kill you!" threatened Aykin. He lunged for Narok, but Eliab stepped between them.

"I see you have your father's foolish temper," said Narok while raising his cat o'nine tails as a warning. Aykin pushed Eliab aside and took a step towards the evil man.

"Leave my father out of this!" he said through clinched teeth.

"You'd better listen to him, Aykin," suggested Eliab.

"He's right; remember, the boy's life depends on you," continued Narok. Aykin saw the fear in Obed's eyes and his only concern now was his brother's safety.

"All right, Narok, you win," replied a defeated Aykin.

"I'm glad to see you have some sense after all. Now, it seems as if the Bara are disgruntled about your rumored death," said Narok. "I need you to send word that you are alive and in the dungeon as part of our plan."

"I'll do what I can," answered Aykin coldly.

"I hope for your brother's sake it proves to be enough," threatened Narok. He turned and left with a final crack of

A Shocking Discovery

his whip. Kenan followed Narok into the corridors of the dungeon, however, Eliab and Obed remained in the cell.

"Narok's preoccupied with finding Prince Roffius and selecting a queen, so the king should be safe for now. I shall return as soon as I can," whispered Eliab. Aykin nodded in reply, but his focus remained on Obed.

"Obed, I know you probably won't believe anything I say, but I shan't let anything happen to you," he said. There was something familiar about this stranger, although Obed didn't understand why. The lad left the cell in silence as a tear rolled down his cheek.

"Don't worry, I shall keep an eye on the lad," said Eliab as he closed the cell door. After they left, Aykin looked down at Shem.

"I need you to wake up, Your Majesty; I can't do this alone," he pleaded.

Once Narok and the others had gone, Lamech emerged from the depths of the cell fully convinced that Aykin could be trusted with the truth about Shem.

"Are you all right?" asked the physician with concern.

"I'm fine," replied Aykin. But Lamech thought otherwise after inspecting Aykin's back, and he quickly got to work on his new patient.

"Aykin, there's something you should know," said Lamech while bandaging Aykin's wounds.

"Is it about the king?" asked Aykin sensing it was important.

"Yes," replied Lamech.

"Is he going to die?" asked the young man with trepidation.

"No, no; of course not," answered Lamech.

"Then, what is it?" asked Aykin.

"Shem is not the true king," said Lamech plainly. Aykin looked at him with disbelief.

"Does Ithamar know?" asked the young man.

"Not yet; I tried to tell him, but until now I didn't know if you could be trusted with overhearing such news," answered Lamech honestly. Aykin nodded his understanding.

"We've got to tell him as soon as possible," he said with urgency.

"I'm afraid that's impossible," replied Lamech.

"What do you mean?" asked Aykin.

"The last time Ithamar was here, he informed me that he and his men were leaving for Irvania after dark. I'm certain they've gone by now," stated the physician. Aykin sat in silence for a moment as he pondered their situation.

"Then we must hope that by some miracle Ithamar finds Roffius before any Bara soldiers do," answered Aykin firmly.

"I thought you didn't believe in miracles?" asked Lamech.

A Shocking Discovery

"Perhaps it's time for a change," stated Aykin with a glimmer of hope in his eyes.

******

Obed was silent as he followed Eliab through the dismal corridors of the dungeon. The lad had always known Narok and Lott weren't his biological family, but aside from Meridia and Mitzy they were the only family he'd known. The painful expression on Obed's face reminded Eliab of the day he met Aykin.

"Don't worry, you're safe with me. I've known Aykin, I mean your brother, for a long time and I won't let anything happen to you. Just stay close and keep your mouth shut," he instructed. Obed wanted to believe this stranger, but found it difficult to know whom to trust.

When they emerged from the dungeon, Eliab and Obed were met by Narok and a handful of Bara soldiers.

"Lock the boy in the west tower!" ordered Narok as he pointed to Obed. Eliab feared what may happen to the lad apart from him, so he quickly thought of a way to keep Obed close.

"Excuse me, Narok, but I could use the boy's help preparing for battle. We have much to do and a pair of young hands would be of great help," suggested Eliab. Narok's piercing blue eyes seemed to look right through the young soldier. On the surface his request seemed innocent enough; however, Narok knew Eliab and Aykin were close. He suspected Eliab may be up to something, yet quickly decided this would be a chance to see where this soldier's loyalty lay.

"Very well, Obed shall be under your charge, but see to it that he doesn't mysteriously disappear," warned Narok. Eliab maintained eye contact with Narok as he nodded his understanding. To Eliab's surprise, Obed suddenly grabbed Narok by the shirt.

"Brother, you only said those things to make that man do what you wanted, right? You'd never hurt me; you and Father loved me, right?" he pleaded. Narok released Obed's grip and straightened out the wrinkle it had made in his shirt.

"You fool! My father never loved you, and I certainly never loved you. In fact, I loathe you. The very sight of you reminds me of your ridiculous father who nearly ruined our plans. The only reason you're still alive is because I need you. If your brother does as he's told, you shall live. If not, you shall die. Either way makes no difference to me," said Narok without remorse. His words cut Obed to the core, and even surprised Eliab. Obed found himself crying again as Eliab put his hand on the lad's shoulder and led him to the stables. Obed reached into his pocket for Polly, but not even that symbol of love could bring him comfort as tears streamed down his face. Eliab felt pity for the lad whose life had been ruined by no fault of his own.

"By the way, my name's Eliab," he said as they drew near to the stables. Obed wiped his nose with the sleeve of his shirt and tried to regain his composure. He was embarrassed for crying at his age in front of this stranger.

"I guess you already know mine," he replied. At that moment, Eliab saw in Obed the same inner strength as Aykin, and he knew the lad would be all right.

"Come, I've much to tell you," said Eliab.

A Shocking Discovery

"I thought I was supposed to help you prepare for a battle?" replied a confused Obed.

"You pay attention, that's good. I only said that to persuade Narok to let you come with me," explained Eliab.

"I don't understand," said Obed.

"You shall. I'm about to tell you the truth about your family, follow me," said Eliab.

They walked to the back of the stables where Eliab told Obed that Narok's father had actually killed Obed's father, mother, and sisters.

"Why did Lott allow me to live?" asked Obed.

"Narok said it best in the dungeon; Lott suspected Aykin had escaped that night and kept you for leverage in case Aykin ever returned for revenge," answered Eliab.

"I guess he was right," said the lad stating the obvious.

"Yes, but don't you see, Obed, your father started something which you and Aykin are destined to finish. Why else would the two of you be brought together again after all these years?" asked Eliab. His words washed over Obed like a fresh rain, and the lad knew in his heart that his destiny was to finish what his father had started.

"So…what's your plan?" he asked. Eliab was glad to see his hunch in taking a chance on the boy had paid off so quickly.

"I want you to use your relationship, as broken as it may be, with Narok to find out what he's planning. We can then give whatever information you gather to Aykin and King Shem," explained Eliab. "Do you think you can do that?"

"I shall try," replied Obed with absolute resolve.

******

Jesorath and Roffius hurried upstairs after seeing Natas. They entered to find wide-eyed Julean and Stefano rushing towards them with Baby Zerah.

"What was that loud noise?" asked Julean with fear. Roffius gave Jesorath a look which said not to tell the boys about Natas.

"Probably just one of Irvania's high winds; they're very common this time of year," answered Jesorath casually. Just then, the baby started to cry.

"I think he needs to be fed," surmised Stefano.

"I shall inform Meridia," offered Roffius knowing this would also allow him to check on Mitzy.

When he entered the back room, Roffius found Meridia sitting in a chair with her head resting beside her daughter on the bed.

"Excuse me, my lady, but it seems Zerah is in need of sustenance," he said apologetically. Meridia sat upright and wiped her tear-stained face.

"Yes, I'm certain he is by now," she replied softly. "Would you mind staying with her, Captain, until I return?"

A Shocking Discovery

"I'm not sure I should be the one, my lady. After all, this is my fault," answered Roffius with head hung low.

"Don't be silly, this is no more your fault than mine. You mustn't forget that the only reason Mitzy came along in the first place is because I insisted she take the baby," Meridia reminded him. "Besides, I shan't be gone long." Roffius appreciated her kind words, yet respectfully disagreed.

"Of course, my lady," he said.

Meridia gave her daughter's hand a gentle squeeze before leaving the room, and Roffius reluctantly took her place in the chair beside the bed. Not knowing what else to do, he dipped a cloth into the basin of cool water and placed it on Mitzy's burning forehead. Suddenly, she grabbed his hand and muttered something about Bara soldiers in her delirious state.

"Easy now; you're safe, Miss Mit," he whispered. She immediately calmed at the sound of his voice and Roffius continued to hold her hand. He noticed how soft it was, and how perfectly it fit into his own. A few minutes passed before Mitzy cried out again, this time clinging to his arm. "I'm here, Miss Mit," he said calmly.

Roffius gently released her grip, but as he placed her arm on the bed he noticed something. It looked like a small heart in the middle of her left forearm, just as Kleiko had described the Mark of Royalty. Roffius shook his head and laughed at the notion of Mitzy being royalty until his curiosity bid him to look again. He picked up the candle from the nightstand and held it above her arm. The flame flickered as his hand trembled once Roffius saw what was undeniably the Mark of Royalty on Mitzy's forearm. He laid his arm beside hers and thought it strange that he had grown up believing he was royalty and she a servant, when in reality the opposite was true. His thoughts were soon interrupted by the sound of footsteps approaching. With haste, Roffius returned the candle to its place before Meridia burst in holding Baby Zerah.

"Is everything all right, Captain? I thought I heard Mitzy cry out," she said anxiously.

"It's nothing, my lady, just the fever talking," he reassured her while trying to keep his heart from beating out of his chest. Meridia approached her daughter to see for herself that Mitzy was fine.

"I heard her yell and I got so frightened," continued the distraught mother.

"She's fine, really; finish feeding the baby and get something to eat for yourself. I can stay with Mitzy until you return," he promised.

"Are you certain?" she asked hesitantly.

"It would be my pleasure," he said. "Before you go, my lady, may I ask you something?"

"Yes, of course," replied Meridia.

"Where did you and Mitzy live before coming to the castle?" he asked.

"On the same plot of land in Nepthali which my late husband's family worked for generations," she said.

"So, he was a farmer in Nepthali?" repeated Roffius. As Meridia nodded she thought he looked ill.

A Shocking Discovery

"Yes, he was. Is something the matter, Captain?" she asked with concern.

"It's nothing, but can you tell me just one more thing?" he asked.

"Of course," answered Meridia unsure of his intentions.

"How did you and Mitzy gain such knowledge about Orpheus and the Dragon Scroll?" he asked. A faraway look crossed Meridia's eyes as she allowed herself to reconnect with old memories.

"You might think this strange, Captain, but my late-husband Amalek was related to the last human to see Orpheus before the good dragon left our kingdom. Amalek's great-great-great grandfather Boaz saw Orpheus as a lad. He learned all about the Dragon Scroll and the Dragon Rulers from a scribe named Carmi. This family heritage was very precious to Amalek, so he passed it along to me and our children. Amalek believed very strongly in the hope offered within the Dragon Scroll. He felt it mustn't be forgotten, even if our belief had no bearing on the good dragon's return," answered Meridia. As she spoke, Roffius recognized Carmi's name from his many hours of study with Kleiko as a child. Roffius knew that a Chief Royal Scribe would never spend such time with a lad on a farm unless there was good reason. Roffius doubted if Meridia had the mark, but he had to check to be sure.

"My lady, would you indulge me just a moment longer and allow me to see your left forearm?" he asked. Meridia looked at him curiously.

"Certainly, Your Majesty, but what's this all about?" she asked with a raised brow. Roffius looked, but as he had expected, found no mark.

"My lady, there's something I must tell you...," he said. Before Roffius could reveal that her daughter was the rightful Queen of Nepthali, Zerah began to cry. Meridia sensed Roffius had something important to say, however, she didn't want the baby to disturb Mitzy.

"Don't worry, Captain, I'm sure whatever it is can wait," she reassured him. Meridia left before he could object and Roffius found himself alone with the Queen of Nepthali.

He knelt on one knee beside the bed with a heavy heart. Instead of recognizing it as a gift to have found the true heir, and one who believed in Orpheus, Roffius chose only to see that he would now be denied a life with the maiden he loved. His frustration towards Orpheus was ever-increasing; nevertheless, Roffius vowed to spend the remainder of his days in humble service to his queen, and love of his life.

******

Meridia finished feeding the baby and returned to the tiny room having forgotten all about her unfinished conversation with Roffius. When she entered, Meridia was surprised to see such affection in his eyes as Roffius looked at her daughter.

"Thank you, Captain," said Meridia softly from the doorway. Startled by her voice, Roffius quickly stood to attention.

A Shocking Discovery

"She's resting comfortably, my lady," he reported and moved aside to allow Meridia her place in the chair.

"I'm in your debt, Captain, for getting her here safely," confessed Meridia.

"I would die for her, my lady," answered Roffius. She didn't know what to say in response to such a bold statement, but Meridia could see he meant it.

Roffius' thoughts remained on Mitzy as he returned to the main room, but he smiled at the sight of his nephews asleep by the fire.

"How is she?" asked Jesorath.

"She's still unconscious, but I believe she's improving," replied Roffius.

"Maybe you should go back…just to be sure," teased Jesorath.

"Very funny," answered Roffius. "Come with me, there's something I must tell you." Jesorath sensed it was serious, but doubted it could be any more shocking than the news of Roffius not being a prince.

Once outside, Roffius took a deep breath and ran his fingers through his wavy hair as was his habit prior to divulging life-changing information.

"I'm not sure how to say this, so I'll just come right out with it…I've found the true heir to the throne," he said.

"Is that all? You had me worried!" exclaimed the relieved blacksmith. "But, how could you find him since you've been in the back room this whole time?" Roffius looked at him with a raised brow. "Are you saying what I think you're saying?"

"If you think I'm saying that Mitzy is the rightful heir then, yes," answered Roffius. "I saw the Mark of Royalty while sitting with her."

"What about Meridia, does she have the mark?" pressed Jesorath.

"I checked, but her arm is as bare as my own," stated Roffius. Jesorath went pale as he remembered taking Mitzy from Roffius when they arrived.

"I could be killed for touching the queen, couldn't I?" he asked nervously.

"Don't be a fool, of course not; none of us knew," said Roffius with an equally nervous laugh since he, too, previously had the same concern.

"Have you told Meridia?" pressed the large blacksmith.

"I started to, but the baby interrupted me," continued Roffius. "Perhaps it's best if they don't know until we free Shem and reclaim the castle." Jesorath nodded in agreement until he realized he was still missing a piece of important information.

"Mitzy believes in Orpheus, right?" he asked.

"Yes, more than anyone I've ever met," answered Roffius firmly. He felt a stab of guilt for teasing her about her belief, and for abandoning it himself.

A Shocking Discovery

"Don't worry, Captain, she's safe here," assured Jesorath.

"Let's hope you're right, for all our sakes," replied the wary captain.

Dragon Scroll of Nepthali

Chapter 15

Friends Reunite

Two long days passed with Meridia caring for Mitzy while Roffius anxiously watched for signs of Natas. Finally, on the third morning Meridia emerged from the back room glowing with happiness.

"Her fever broke during the night!" she exclaimed.

"Can we see her?" pleaded Stefano.

"I can bring her something to eat!" added Julean.

"Come with me boys, but remember, you mustn't be too loud," warned Meridia kindly. The boys practically ran into the back room as each wanted to be the first seen by Mitzy. Roffius never felt more relieved as he hurried downstairs to tell Jesorath the good news. But when he reached the base of the staircase, Roffius heard hushed voices.

"Shall you tell him?" asked one.

"No, we must wait. Get my horse ready," said another man. Roffius recognized it to be Jesorath, and he suddenly wondered if it had been a mistake to trust the blacksmith. Roffius rounded the corner to make his presence known.

"Going somewhere?" he asked. Jesorath and the man in farmer's clothing looked at him with obvious surprise. The blacksmith then nodded to the man and he ran out.

"Who was that? What's going on here, Jesorath?" demanded Roffius with regal authority.

"Settle down, I've just learned what could be very good news, but I wanted to confirm it before telling you," replied the blacksmith.

"I have some good news as well, which is why I came down," said Roffius with a furrowed brow.

"What's your news?" asked Jesorath.

"You first," replied a suspicious Roffius. Jesorath closed the large stable doors and looked around to ensure no one was listening.

"The man you saw me talking to has a farm on the outskirts of Irvania. He came to tell me that riders wearing Royal Guard uniforms were camped in the pasture on the edge of his farm last night," explained the blacksmith.

"Do you suppose it's a trick?" asked Roffius.

"I don't know, but if Royal Guards are this far south it can only mean they're looking for you!" exclaimed Jesorath. Roffius remembered Meridia's account back at the castle and how she had told Ithamar where they were going. He smiled knowing that only Ithamar and his men were daring, and skilled, enough to successfully elude Narok and his thugs. "I was about to ride out myself to meet

Friends Reunite

up with them, but I didn't want to tell you in case the news was bad," continued Jesorath.

"Thank you, my friend, but I'm going with you and we shall face the news together. Let me inform the boys to watch out for the women while we're gone," replied Roffius. He turned to go back upstairs, but Jesorath stopped him.

"Wait, you haven't told me your good news," he said.

"Mitzy's fever has broken. It seems she's out of danger," answered Roffius with a broad smile. Jesorath agreed this was good news as he readied two horses instead of one.

******

"Stefano! Julean!" called Roffius as bound up the stairs and opened the door.

"We're in here," called Stefano from the back room. As he entered, Roffius refrained from showing Mitzy the honor due her as queen for her own safety, but was pleasantly surprised to find her sitting up in bed.

"Well, I see you've finally decided to wake up," he said with a smile. Mitzy returned a weak smile of her own.

"She shall soon be as good as new," announced Meridia beaming with happiness while holding tightly to her daughter's hand.

"I'm relieved to see you're feeling better, Miss Mit," said Roffius. "Boys, I'm placing the two of you in charge while Jesorath and I attend to some urgent business." Stefano and Julean begged to come along, but Roffius insisted they remain to look after the women and baby. He started to leave, but stopped at the sound of Mitzy's voice.

"Thank you, Captain, for everything you've done," she said softly. Roffius turned around and looked directly at her.

"It was my utmost pleasure, my lady," he replied with a bow before leaving the small room. Mitzy watched him go and felt herself tremble as the door shut.

******

Earlier that morning, the Bara soldiers whom Roffius had tied to the tree returned to the castle. They found Kenan and re-counted their tale, and that Prince Roffius was traveling south. However, they chose to omit the part that they were bested by a maiden and two boys. Kenan told the men to keep this to themselves and then found Mezrah to tell him the news.

"Mezrah, two soldiers from the first squadron sent out in search of the missing members of the Royal Family have returned. They claim Prince Roffius is traveling south," said Kenan. Mezrah understood the value of this information and hoped his nephew didn't know.

"Does Narok know?" he asked. Kenan shook his head no. "Excellent, let's keep this between ourselves."

******

Ithamar stopped his horse and took in the view from the top of the hill. The old fisherman's route added two extra days to their journey, but the guard felt it worthwhile to ensure no one had followed them. His squadron of exhausted men watched with Ithamar as two

Friends Reunite

men on horseback rapidly approached. Ithamar had been expecting company since seeing a farmer ride off earlier, but hoped the riders meant no harm. From their viewpoint, Jesorath and Roffius hoped the men at the top of the hill weren't part of a trap.

As the riders drew closer, Ithamar attached his scarf bearing the royal colors to the tip of his sword and held it up. Roffius immediately recognized his family colors and knew at once that Ithamar was among them. The young captain gave his horse a kick and charged ahead as the large blacksmith tried to keep up. Ithamar led his men down the hill and was the first to reach his captain. Both jumped from their horses and approached with broad smiles as the friends reunited.

"Ithamar, it is you!" exclaimed Roffius as the two clasped hands.

"Yes, My Captain," he replied finding himself suddenly overcome with emotion. "I thought we lost you…all of you."

"It shall take more than a few Bara to get rid of me! But tell me, is what Meridia said true about Ashter being dead yet my brother lives?" asked Roffius as Jesorath and Ithamar's squadron joined them. Ithamar was elated to hear that Meridia was with them, but he hated to relay the sad new about Ashter.

"Yes, I'm afraid the queen is dead. King Shem was severely beaten, but Lamech is with him," answered Ithamar. Roffius was both heartbroken and enraged. He wished he had been there to help, but realized if he had been, he would most likely be dead. Roffius stood in silence for a moment before realizing that Ithamar had mentioned Lamech.

"Did you say Lamech is with Shem?" he asked.

"Yes, Captain," answered Ithamar with a nod. "Lamech's alive and tending to the king. But we shouldn't remain in the open, Bara soldiers have been dispatched to find you."

"I know; we ran into a few the other day," stated Roffius. Ithamar scolded himself for taking the longer route as the reality of what could've happened to the prince, or Meridia, hit him.

"You must tell me everything," insisted the seasoned guard.

"I shall, but for now we must return to the women and boys back at Jesorath's house," answered Roffius. Ithamar agreed and the two mounted their horses.

******

From inside Jesorath's house, Stefano and Julean heard riders approaching. They opened the door and stood on the landing at the top of the stairs to see if their uncle was among them. The boys watched with excitement as a stream of Royal Guards filed into the stables.

"They're back!" Julean yelled inside to the women.

"And they brought Royal Guards with them!" added Stefano. The boys ran down to greet the men.

"Did he say Royal Guards?" asked Mitzy.

Friends Reunite

"I believe he did," replied Meridia, "I shall go see what's going on. I shan't be long."

When Meridia arrived in the stables, she found it filled with Royal Guards and horses. The welcomed sight reminded her of the courtyard at the castle and Meridia smiled shyly as the men tipped their hats as she passed by. Roffius saw her from across the barn and called her over.

"Meridia, come here," he said. She made her way through the maze of men and horses until she reached Roffius where he was standing with one of the guards. When the guard turned around, Meridia saw it was Ithamar.

"Good morning, my lady," he said with a broad smile, "I'm glad to see you made it here safely." Ithamar removed his hat and bowed politely as was his custom each time he saw the beautiful woman who had captured his heart twelve years earlier. Meridia felt her cheeks flush.

"It's good to see you as well, Sir. Thank you again for saving my life, I'm forever in your debt," she replied humbly.

"I only wish I'd been there when those blasted Bara soldiers attacked you," answered Ithamar. Meridia found herself staring at the ruggedly handsome guard feeling something she hadn't in a very long time.

"Thanks to Captain Roffius and Mitzy, we managed just fine," she said kindly. "You and your men must be in need of food and water. I shall prepare something fitting for the king's most valiant guards." Meridia curtsied to Ithamar and Roffius who bowed in return as she left.

Ithamar was so relieved to see Meridia again that he found himself unable to take his eyes off her.

"She's beautiful, isn't she? I remember the day she arrived at the castle like it was yesterday," he admitted. Roffius stared at him with surprise to hear something like that from the stoic guard.

"Does she know how you feel?" he asked with a raised brow.

"No, I could never find the right time," replied Ithamar.

"Well, it looks like you shall have to wait a little longer," laughed Roffius as he walked away. Ithamar stole a final glance at Meridia before following his captain to the back of the stables.

Roffius planned to tell Ithamar that he was not of royal blood, but first Roffius wanted to gather more information from the guard.

"How many men does Narok have?" he asked.

"Hundreds I'd say. The castle is overrun with Bara soldiers," replied Ithamar honestly.

"What about the black dragon, have you seen him?" continued Roffius. Ithamar paused as the terrible memory of the many guards losing their lives at the hand of the beast replayed in his mind.

"Not since the night of the attack," he answered.

"The beast was here the other night," said Roffius.

Friends Reunite

"We've got to get Shem out of there," replied Ithamar with urgency. Roffius agreed, but first he had to tell Ithamar the truth.

"Ithamar, there's something I must tell you; and you might want to sit down," he said pulling up a milking stool.

Ithamar eyed his captain suspiciously as Roffius sighed and ran his fingers through his wavy hair. The guard was thankful for the stool when Roffius explained the shocking news that he and Shem weren't members of the Royal Family. Ithamar was especially thankful to be sitting when Roffius showed him the sword fashioned by dragon magic. He sat in stunned silence for seemingly an eternity after Roffius finished.

"Ithamar, please say something," pleaded Roffius. The guard stood and Roffius could see his eyes were moist with tears.

"Captain, you may not be of royal blood, but this sword is proof enough for me of Orpheus' faith in you," said Ithamar. "Mark or no mark, I shall follow you to the ends of the earth." Roffius was humbled by Ithamar's loyalty, especially since it was no longer required.

"Thank you, my friend, I can't tell you what it means to hear you say that," he said.

"So, how do we find the rightful king before Narok discovers the truth?" asked Ithamar while wiping his eyes to remove any evidence of his temporary show of emotion.

"Actually...I already have," replied Roffius casually.

"What? Where is he?" asked the guard with a renewed hope.

"Upstairs, but it's not a he…it's Mitzy," whispered Roffius. Ithamar slowly sat back down on the stool. A thousand thoughts raced through his mind, but none was more prevalent than the one which said he was in love with the queen's mother.

"Do they know?" Ithamar asked referring to the women and boys.

"No, I thought it best not to tell them. She's safe here…at least for now," answered Roffius.

"What do you propose we do?" asked Ithamar.

"Send out your men to gather every farmer and villager within half a day's ride who is loyal to the crown. We shall need their help to free Shem and re-claim the castle for Queen Mitzy," said Roffius in a manner worthy of his title as Captain of the Royal Guards. Ithamar nodded his understanding and left at once to inform Perez and Luklin.

******

Even being in the dungeon, Shem's health had improved dramatically over the past few days. Yet, his heart remained broken over the death of his beloved wife. Lamech could see the pain in Shem's eyes each time a haunting vision of Ashter and his stillborn son crossed the former king's mind.

"Your Majesty, you must drink this," said the physician as he poured the vinegar and herbal mixture into Shem's dry mouth.

Friends Reunite

"Ugh! That's awful!" complained Shem as he swallowed the bitter liquid.

"Yes, the taste is bad, but the results are worth it. I've seen great improvements since your first dose more than two days ago," stated Lamech. Shem agreed as he tried to put events into place.

"I remember telling Stefano and Julean to go to Irvania before they escaped with Roffius into the tunnels. Have you any news of them?" he asked.

"No, but Ithamar and his men left days ago in search of them," said Lamech.

"Ithamar?" asked Shem.

"Yes, Your Majesty," answered Lamech. "After Ithamar saved Meridia from being executed, she told him where Prince Roffius and the others were going."

"Ithamar will find them," whispered Shem. "What about Kleiko?"

"I'm afraid Kleiko's dead," replied the physician sadly. Shem expected as much, nevertheless it pained him to hear. "But before he died, My King, Kleiko told me something of great importance." Shem was silent as he, too, remembered his last conversation with the scribe.

"What did he tell you?" asked Shem hesitantly. Lamech was uncertain of how to word his response which was enough for Shem to surmise that the physician already knew.

"It's all right, Lamech; Kleiko told me as well... I'm not the true king of Nepthali," said the broken man. "I've lost everything...my wife...my crown...and my family. Yet, I shall not see this kingdom lost to evil without a fight." Lamech marveled at the former king who was beaten, bruised, and locked in the dungeon yet still very much a leader.

From the shadows of the cell, Aykin listened in awe of the man who had lost everything but showed no signs of bitterness. It reminded him of his father and it brought Aykin out of the shadows in more ways than one.

"You look to be feeling much better today," he said. Shem looked up and nearly collapsed thinking he was seeing the ghost of Uriah.

"Easy, Shem," said Lamech calmly. "This is Aykin. He's been assisting me in your care."

"But, you're a Bara soldier...and you look just like someone I once knew...someone who wanted to kill me," replied Shem as he leaned against Lamech for support.

"Aykin is indeed a Bara soldier, but his intent was never to cause you harm. His father was Uriah who, as it turns out, died trying to save you," explained Lamech. Shem was listening, but he couldn't bring himself to believe what Lamech was saying about a man tied to those responsible for inflicting so much pain on his family.

"It sounds as if you switch to whatever side most benefits you at the time," replied Shem coldly.

"Forgive me, Shem, but you're mistaken," Lamech interjected. But it was too late; the damage had been done to Aykin.

Friends Reunite

"No, I'm the one who was mistaken to think I could ever be seen as anything but a criminal," answered Aykin. When the broken young man retreated back into the darkness, Shem immediately relaxed.

"Lamech, do you know who that man is?" he asked.

"I know he's the man who has stayed by your side night and day helping tend to your wounds. I also know that fate has dealt him a very cruel hand, so cruel in fact that most men would have crumbled beneath it. Yet, he has maintained some integrity. Besides, the two of you share the same enemy," answered Lamech firmly. Shem was surprised by the physician's boldness and listened as Lamech told him Aykin's tragic story. Although Shem disagreed with Aykin's choices, he now understood them.

"I've not spent the time with him as you, Lamech, but I trust your judgment. If you say Aykin can be trusted then I believe you," he said.

"Thank you, My King, I vouch for him with my life," replied Lamech. Shem winced upon hearing the physician address him as royalty.

"Lamech, you know I'm not the king so please, do not refer to me as such," he said with shame.

"Title or not, Shem, I shall always see you as my king," answered the physician. From the depths of the cell, Aykin was overwhelmed with gratitude to hear Lamech defended him. It compelled Aykin to emerge from the darkness where he was met by Shem's extended hand.

"Forgive me, Aykin; Lamech tells me that I've misjudged you," said the former king humbly.

Lamech's support was more than Aykin had ever hoped for, but to hear Shem apologize nearly moved Aykin to tears. Not since childhood had Aykin been treated with such kindness and respect. He took hold of Shem's outstretched hand a changed man, and at that moment a permanent friendship was forged. Aykin released his grip and reached into the parcel Ithamar had left for them days earlier.

"Eat this, Your Highness, we need you to get your strength back," he said while handing Shem some cheese.

"Thank you, but I'm afraid you're mistaken...I'm not the king," answered Shem softly.

"I know, but if Lamech believes you are still worthy of the title then so do I," replied Aykin firmly. Shem was speechless and nodded in appreciation as he took a bite.

"Tell me, how are the two of you able to get such delicacies down here?" he asked. Lamech smiled with a twinkle in his aged eyes.

"We have Ithamar to thank for these," he said. "But, there's more you must know which I think Aykin should explain." Shem wondered what more could be said until Aykin told him about Obed. The former monarch remembered Ashter telling him years ago how troubled Meridia had been after young Obed was taken away, and was sickened to discover his part in this tragedy. His understanding of Aykin's relentless pursuit of revenge suddenly increased tenfold.

"Is there anyone you can trust who knows you're here?" asked Shem. Aykin hesitated to tell them about Eliab and Kenan, but he quickly realized that he must be completely honest with them if he was to be deserving of the trust these men had shown him.

"My closest officers know. They're waiting for my signal to exact our plan against Narok," said Aykin. Lamech beamed with pride knowing how difficult it must have been for Aykin to be honest, but saw it as confirmation for having defended the young man to Shem.

"Good," said Shem. "Now let's get to work."

Watching the two leaders collaborate, Lamech was filled with hope for the first time since Narok and the Bara had attacked the castle.

Dragon Scroll of Nepthali

Chapter 16

An Unlikely Spy

Two of Narok's henchmen walked briskly across the courtyard to carry out Narok's order to retrieve Obed. They stormed inside the Royal Stables looking for the lad.

"You there, come with us," said one as he pointed to Obed. The frightened lad immediately looked to Eliab for help.

"Narok placed the boy in my care," protested Eliab.

"Well, now Narok wants him back. We have orders to take the lad to the dining hall," stated the man Eliab recognized as a troublemaker from Haliel. Although Eliab didn't want to, he offered no resistance to keep from jeopardizing the plan to use Obed as a spy.

As he watched the lad leave between the two Bara soldiers, Eliab hoped Obed possessed his brother's natural instincts, otherwise they'd all be in the dungeon before nightfall.

******

Obed followed the men into the expansive dining hall with its windows dressed in silk draperies from faraway lands. On the ceiling, an intricately painted scene of floating cherubs seemed to watch Obed as the Bara led him to a corner of the room. Narok and Mezrah were deep in conversation at the large mahogany table covered with delicacies.

"Is everything in place?" asked Narok. Mezrah took a bite of roasted boar and nodded. As he answered, morsels of food flew out from his mouth.

"I told the men that Aykin chose to stay in the dungeon just as you wanted," answered Mezrah.

"Very good, but we mustn't underestimate Aykin…or the king," warned Narok. When he looked up, Narok saw Obed and shouted, "Come here, Boy! I've a proposition for you."

The soldiers on either side of the lad forcibly led Obed across the room until they stood in front of Narok. Although assisting Narok was the last thing Obed wanted to do after the verbal arsenal the evil man had unleashed on him the last time they saw one another, Obed was wise enough to play his submissive role for the greater good.

"What is it?" he asked with a raised brow.

"It has come to my attention that the king is recovering quite nicely, which leads me to believe that he and your brother may attempt some sort of foolish scheme. I need you to find out what it is," answered Narok.

An Unlikely Spy

"What makes you think they'd tell me anything?" asked Obed.

"Because you, my dear boy, are your brother's weakness; and King Shem is a sap. Once he hears your sad story, he shall immediately trust you," mocked Narok.

"I'll do it," replied Obed trying to conceal the humor of Narok asking him to do the very thing Eliab had wanted all along.

"Very well, go at once to the dungeon and report any findings back to me. But remember, I shall know if you're lying," warned Narok.

"I know," replied Obed softly. The Bara soldiers released their grip on the lad and Obed left the dining hall for the dungeon. As he walked away, Obed took great satisfaction in knowing that he was going to help finish what his father had started years ago. Once the lad had gone, Mezrah spoke freely to his nephew.

"Why have we not seen the black dragon since the attack?" he asked. Narok lifted the king's golden goblet to his lips and drank slowly before offering his curt response.

"You should be glad, Uncle. I'm certain Natas would be far less tolerant than I of your abounding incompetence!" snapped Narok while slamming the goblet onto the table. "Speaking of incompetence, have you found Ithamar yet?" Mezrah believed the guard was heading south to meet up with Prince Roffius after hearing Kenan's update earlier, but he would never share this with his nephew.

******

Aykin and Shem fell silent upon hearing the approach of footsteps as Lamech prepared to make a hasty retreat to the back of the cell.

"Go on," whispered Aykin. Shem watched Lamech slip away in what was clearly a well-executed routine. The men looked up with surprise to see Obed's face suddenly appear through the bars.

"Obed! What are you doing here?" asked Aykin.

"Narok permitted me to return, so I've come for some answers," replied the lad whose striking resemblance to their mother took Aykin's breath away.

"I shall do my best to give them," Aykin replied. Obed started with questions about their family in general, and then he wanted to know more about their father.

"Whatever you may think of me, Obed, you must know that our father was a valiant man to be proud of," answered Aykin. Shem had remained silent up until this point, but he now felt he must speak.

"I give you my full assurance that your father was my most loyal guard, and proved as much by sacrificing his life to save mine," he added. Obed's eyes welled up with tears.

"Thank you, Your Majesty," he replied. Aykin was equally thankful for Shem's kind words. Obed took a deep breath and slowly released it before telling them the real reason he'd come.

"There's something I must tell you…Narok sent me here after I agreed to gather information," he confessed. When Lamech overheard this, he stepped into view. "Who are you?" asked Obed with surprise.

"Lamech, what are you doing?!" exclaimed Aykin.

"If we expect the boy to trust us, we must first show our trust of him," replied Lamech wisely. "My name is Lamech and I'm the Royal Physician. I've had the great privilege of spending the past few days in the company of your remarkable brother." Obed shook Lamech's outstretched hand through the bars as the old man continued. "I fear Narok is a terribly deceitful man whom shouldn't be trusted, my boy."

"I know, which is why I promised to give him information, but I didn't promise it would be accurate," answered Obed with a sly smile. Lamech released a sigh of relief fearing the suspense was more than his old heart could bear. "Eliab suggested that I use my connection with Narok to gather information, which I could in turn give to you. So you see, instead of Narok using me, I shall be using him," continued the lad proudly. Aykin appreciated Eliab's intent, but he was more concerned about Obed's safety.

"Narok's no fool, Obed. If he suspects you're lying to him, you shall be in grave danger," warned Aykin.

"I know, but I'd rather die doing the right thing than have to live with myself knowing I had a chance to make a difference and chose not to," he said with resolve. Aykin looked at Obed and wished he was half the man his thirteen-year-old brother had already become.

"Father would be proud of you, but I can't risk your safety as penance for my poor choices. If anything were to happen to you, I'd never forgive myself," he confessed. But Obed refused to take no for an answer.

"You're my brother, my only family, and he is my king. If you're not worth fighting for, who is?" he asked passionately. Aykin never felt more ashamed, unworthy, and loved all at the same time from his brother's response.

"He's right. If we don't act now, we may not get another chance," stated Shem.

"Very well, but you must promise to do exactly as we say," said Aykin firmly.

"I promise," replied Obed. "What do you want me to tell Narok?" Shem thought for a moment and then had an idea.

"Tell him that Roffius went north to Belzeeb, and that we've arranged for riders to leave during the third watch to meet up with him. Explain that they are going to gather men to wage an attack on the castle," he instructed. Aykin agreed this was believable since the northern province of Belzeeb was extremely loyal to the king. Lamech on the other hand wondered who they would find to do something so daring without Ithamar and his men.

"Who shall we find to be the riders?" he asked.

"Eliab and Kenan can go," offered Aykin unaware of Kenan's plans to betray him. "See if you can find a way to get them here." Obed nodded his understanding, but saw the worry still in Aykin's eyes.

"Have no fear, Brother, all shall be well," he said. Aykin hoped his brother was right as he watched Obed disappear into the tunnels. When the lad was gone, Lamech verbalized what Aykin was thinking.

"Do you think he can do this?" asked the physician nervously.

"Of course he can; he's the son of Uriah," answered Shem with absolute confidence.

******

Obed exchanged the dark and dismal tunnels of the dungeon for the lavish and colorful dining hall. Upon his arrival, the lad relayed his false story to Narok and Mezrah about Prince Roffius being in Belzeeb. He also told them that Eliab and Kenan were leaving during the third watch to meet the wayward prince and gather more men for an attack on the castle. Narok smiled slyly thinking this sounded like something Shem would try. And like Aykin, Narok was well aware of the loyalty the people of Belzeeb had to the crown. They would surely come to the king's aid if summoned by Prince Roffius personally. Narok was pleasantly surprised by Obed's apparent usefulness. Mezrah, however, knew the lad was lying but chose to keep silent.

"I knew I couldn't trust Eliab or Kenan, but it seems I was wrong about you, Obed," said Narok menacingly. "Mezrah, send out a rider at once to inform the squadrons searching for our elusive prince to head north for Belzeeb. If those fools think they can outsmart me, they've got another thing coming."

"Right away, Nephew" said Mezrah with no intentions of carrying out the order; especially since he wanted Prince Roffius to be captured and returned to the castle. Obed turned to leave, but Narok grabbed him by the arm.

"Should there be any changes, Obed, I expect you to report them to me at once," warned the evil man. "Remember, I only have need of you while you prove useful."

Obed swallowed hard and nodded his understanding. Narok released his grip and the lad left the expansive dining hall for the stables where he hoped to find Eliab and Kenan.

******

Obed found Eliab in the stables and relayed his conversation with Aykin, Shem, and finally Narok. Eliab was impressed with Obed's ability to carry out difficult orders under equally difficult circumstances.

"Well done, lad!" he exclaimed. "It seems your father's blood runs thick through your veins." Obed smiled and appreciated the compliment. He was also relieved that Eliab was not upset with Aykin for having offered him and Kenan to be the riders.

"So, you're all right with Narok knowing that your allegiance lies with Aykin?" asked Obed with trepidation.

"I'm sure he suspected as much anyway," replied Eliab casually. "Did Narok say anything else which may be useful?"

"He told Mezrah to send out a rider to inform the Bara squadrons searching for the prince to head for Belzeeb," answered Obed. As Eliab listened, he became increasingly impressed with his young friend. Just then Kenan entered the stables and found the two talking.

"Am I missing something?" he asked.

"Kenan, we were just talking about you," said Eliab with a broad smile.

He brought his cousin up to speed on everything that had transpired between Obed, Aykin, and Narok. But Kenan became increasingly agitated as he listened to a plan which could potentially thwart his own plans with Mezrah.

"Nice work, kid," he said awkwardly. Kenan placed his hand on Obed's shoulder, but Eliab noticed Kenan's pensive look.

"Is something wrong, Cousin?" he asked. As Kenan replied, he couldn't look his cousin in the eye.

"I'm just anxious to free Aykin and the king," he said nervously.

"Good, let's go!" exclaimed Eliab.

Kenan followed them with the intent to obtain more information from Aykin and King Shem before finding Mezrah.

When they reached Aykin's cell, Eliab was shocked to find three prisoners instead of two. Aykin made the introductions between Lamech, Shem, and the men he believed were his closest friends.

"It's thanks to the physician here that the king is still alive," said Aykin proudly.

"Nice to meet you," replied Eliab politely. "Thanks to Obed, Narok believes Prince Roffius is in Belzeeb."

"Excellent," said Shem. "One of you must ride south to Irvania to meet up with Ithamar and Roffius, while the other travels north to Belzeeb." Kenan wanted no part in meeting with the formidable prince, so he quickly offered to go to Belzeeb.

"I shall ride north," he said.

"And I shall go with Kenan since Narok expects more than one rider," offered Obed. Kenan looked at the lad with surprise having never witnessed such selfless bravery.

"No, it's too dangerous," snapped Aykin.

"Not if I go along too," suggested Lamech. "Shem's strong enough for me to leave, and Narok shall never suspect me to be one of the riders since he thinks I'm dead."

"You'd do that?" asked Aykin in disbelief. Kenan was equally baffled, and became increasingly uncomfortable to be surrounded by such noble men knowing his hand in betraying them.

"Of course, it would be an honor," replied Lamech as he placed his hand upon Obed's shoulder.

"Once I find him, how shall I convince Prince Roffius to listen to a Bara soldier?" asked Eliab. Shem looked down and suddenly got an idea.

"Give him this," he said while removing his signet ring. "When we were children, our father told us to use this as proof that the bearer comes with a message from the king. Once he sees it, Roffius shall listen to you," answered Shem.

"I'm in," said Eliab without hesitation. Aykin expected as much as he turned to Kenan and placed his hand on his friend's shoulder.

"Kenan, I can think of no one better suited for the task before you, or whom I trust more with the safety of these two," he said referring to Obed and Lamech. Kenan swallowed hard fearing his guilt was obvious to these fine men. Aykin had shown him kindness and support since the day they met, but until now Kenan had refused to see it. Now with Aykin's demonstration of absolute trust, the chains of jealousy which had bound Kenan for so long finally loosened. However, he wasn't set completely free as Kenan held tightly to Mezrah's promises of power. His only response to the undeserved accolades from Aykin was to look away in shame.

"We shall need food for our journey. Why don't I gather some from the kitchen and meet you in the Royal Stables?" suggested Kenan uneasily.

"Good idea; make sure to get some of those delicious cookies," said Eliab with a child-like grin. Kenan nodded and hurried away before anyone noticed the beads of sweat forming on his brow. Eliab and the others started after him, but Shem stopped them.

"Eliab, perhaps you should leave before the third watch. If you cut across the Placia River, you should reach Irvania ahead of the squadrons already out looking for

Roffius. Do you think you can gather enough men to leave within the hour?" he asked.

"Consider it done, My King," replied Eliab. "Besides, Mezrah usually sends a squadron out to secure the perimeter at midday so they should think nothing of our leaving."

"Very well, go then and bring my brother and boys back safely," instructed Shem.

"Yes, Your Majesty," replied Eliab with a bow. He and Aykin clasped hands before Eliab left with Lamech and Obed. Once they were gone, Aykin turned to Shem.

"Do you think we should've told them you aren't the true king?" he asked.

"They shall find out soon enough," replied Shem softly.

******

As he reached the inner castle, Kenan was surprised by the overwhelming sense of guilt he now felt for being involved in Aykin's betrayal. Nevertheless, the misguided young man continued to the Royal Library to find Mezrah instead of going to the kitchen for supplies as he had told the others. When he arrived, Kenan found the man with unruly hair looking out a stained glass window.

"I've just learned that Ithamar and his men are in Irvania with Prince Roffius," he reported. However, Kenan lacked the sense of satisfaction he typically felt while providing Mezrah with damaging information against Aykin.

"Good work," replied the bulgy-eyed man as he walked away from the window. "Anything else?" Kenan paused for a moment as his feelings of guilt wrestled against his long-standing jealousy of Aykin. The moment passed and, for now, his jealousy remained dominant.

"During the third watch Eliab shall ride south to meet up with Prince Roffius and Ithamar while I travel north to Belzeeb with Lamech and Obed," explained Kenan. Mezrah was surprised to hear that the Royal Physician was still alive, although knew he wouldn't be for long. Mezrah smiled at his good fortune in gaining more valuable information which his nephew lacked.

"See to it that Lamech and Obed never reach Belzeeb," ordered Mezrah coldly. Kenan's heart sank knowing he could never to do such a thing, and his jealousy of Aykin suddenly lost its dominance. Although he was powerless to stop things already in motion, Kenan was now determined to slow them down.

"Perhaps we should keep Lamech and Obed alive longer in case Ithamar has made changes which the king is unaware of and we need them for leverage," proposed Kenan. Mezrah considered this surprisingly wise suggestion from the young Bara soldier.

"Very well, they shall live only as far as Belzeeb. Take the old goblin trail to prolong your journey and allow my men time to catch up," instructed Mezrah. "Once you reach Belzeeb, go to Reuben's house at the end of town and tell him that I sent you. Stall there until your comrades arrive, and then dispose of Obed and Lamech." A sinister grin crossed his face as Mezrah imagined the shock for King Shem and Aykin when their reinforcements failed to arrive. Meanwhile, Kenan agreed to the plan knowing he could best help Obed and Lamech by getting them to Belzeeb and away from Narok.

"What shall we do about Prince Roffius if Narok has sent a rider to turn the squadrons north for Belzeeb?" pressed Kenan.

"The only rider sent was by me to Irvania with orders to bring Prince Roffius back to the castle. He's as good as dead… just like King Shem and Aykin. In a matter of days I shall be ruling Nepthali," announced Mezrah proudly.

"Don't you mean *we*?" corrected Kenan. Mezrah scowled at the soldier willing to betray his closest friend on the premise of a lie.

"Of course, my boy, just a simple slip of the tongue," replied the shifty man. However, hearing this, Kenan finally saw Mezrah for the man he was in stark contrast to the man Aykin had always been. Kenan felt nauseous with the realization that his allegiance had been terribly misplaced.

******

It was late afternoon in Irvania when Mitzy emerged from the back room for the first time since their arrival to the southern province.

"What are you doing out of bed?" scolded Meridia upon seeing her daughter. Baby Zerah was sleeping soundly in a basket while she had been preparing food for Ithamar and his men.

"Mother, if I stay in that bed any longer I shall grow roots into it!" exclaimed Mitzy. "What are you up to? It looks as if you're cooking for an army."

An Unlikely Spy

"I suppose you could say that's true," Meridia said whimsically.

"Mother, there's something different about you; you look so….happy," pressed Mitzy.

"Of course I'm happy, you're alive," replied Meridia with a rosy glow in her cheeks. "But, it may also be Ithamar."

"Ithamar?" asked Mitzy with a raised brow.

"Yes, he's the most dashing man, besides your father of course, I've ever seen," continued Meridia with a dreamy look in her eyes.

"Do you mean Ithamar, the Royal Guard?" Mitzy clarified.

"Yes," answered Meridia while adding a block of cheese to a large satchel.

"What made you think of him?" pressed Mitzy with growing curiosity.

"He's here; he and his men arrived a few hours ago. I've been preparing food for them, so you were correct when you said it looked as if I was cooking for an army," giggled Meridia. "Captain Roffius and Ithamar are down in the stables with Jesorath working on a plan to rescue King Shem and take back the castle."

"The king's alive? That's wonderful!" exclaimed Mitzy.

"Yes, it is. The only thing better would be the return of Orpheus," sighed Meridia.

"Perhaps the great dragon has returned and we just haven't seen him. We mustn't give up hope, Mother," replied Mitzy.

"You're right, darling. After all, those who sow in hope shall reap the joys of its fulfillment," said Meridia with a smile. Just then, Stefano and Julean burst into the room.

"Mitzy, you're up!" they exclaimed.

The boys rushed to her side as Mitzy giggled and hugged them with her good arm. A moment later Roffius walked through the door and stopped in his tracks seeing Mitzy out of bed. She was wearing a clean dress that Jesorath had borrowed from one of the women in town, and her golden ringlets hung freely past her waist.

"Well, well; it's nice to see you're finally out of bed," teased Jesorath as he and Ithamar entered behind Roffius. They knew they should bow before their queen, but remembered Roffius' instructions to keep the truth from the women and boys until Narok and Natas were defeated.

"You must be Jesorath. From what my mother has told me, I'm forever in your debt for everything you've done," she said. Mitzy then kissed the blacksmith on the cheek.

"Your mother did most of the work. I'm just happy you survived the journey, my lady," he replied bashfully. Jealous of the attention Jesorath was getting from Mitzy, Roffius cleared his throat and started his announcement.

"I'm afraid that Jesorath and I shall be leaving indefinitely with Ithamar and his squadron as soon as we gather the necessary supplies and men," said the captain with very little emotion.

"We're coming with you," said Stefano and Julean in unison.

"Not this time; you must stay here to watch over Baby Zerah and the women," answered Roffius.

"They don't need us," complained Julean.

"We could use the extra hands, besides the women are perfectly safe here," said Jesorath.

"Remember how we helped you against those Bara soldiers? You need us," added Stefano. Roffius could see he was outnumbered, and reasoned that the women would be safe in the quiet southern province.

"Very well, you may come along; but at the first sign of trouble the two of you are going straight to the rear," he said firmly.

"Hooray!" exclaimed Julean.

"You won't be sorry!" shouted Stefano.

"Come along my young princes," said Jesorath to keep up appearances. "We must enlist every able man in Irvania to help us take back the castle." Stefano and Julean quickly said their goodbyes to Meridia and Mitzy then hurried after Jesorath. Once they had gone, Mitzy turned to Roffius.

"Why must you go now?" she asked.

"I've made a discovery which bids me to leave at once," answered Roffius. "But have no fear, I shall send someone for you, your mother, and Baby Zerah once the castle has been reclaimed." He turned to leave, but Mitzy followed after him.

"I'm coming with you. You know I'm as good, if not better than any man with a sword," she continued.

"It's too dangerous. Besides, you'd slow us down and I can't put my men's lives at risk because of a fool-hearty maidservant," he said plainly.

"I see," she replied softly. Although Roffius saw the hurt his words had caused, Mitzy was far too important to the kingdom for him to be swayed.

"It's settled then," he stated. Roffius left the room and Ithamar tipped his hat and bowed to Meridia before following his captain down to the stables.

Chapter 17

Army of Farmers

Meridia added a block of cheese to the last satchel filled with food supplies for Ithamar and his men.

"I shall take these down to the stables and then return to feed the baby," she said.

"I can take them, Mother. The change of scenery shall do me good," offered Mitzy.

"No, darling, they're too heavy. The physician warned me of the dangers of your wound re-opening. He said that not even the Liaspot plant could save you," replied Meridia. Mitzy saw the worry on her mother's face and didn't want to add to it.

"All right, but I'm not going back in that room," she said adamantly. Meridia laughed at Mitzy's dramatic statement as she picked up the satchels and headed for the door. When her hand touched the handle, Baby Zerah woke up with cries of hunger.

"It looks as if you shall be feeding the baby now, and I shall take the supplies to the men," declared Mitzy with a smile.

"Very well, but just take two. I shall bring the others later," said Meridia as a compromise. Mitzy agreed and gingerly lifted two satchels to take downstairs.

******

When she entered the crowded stables, Mitzy was met with the smells of hay, horses, and men who hadn't bathed in days. Stefano and Julean immediately saw her and rushed over to help the beautiful maiden.

"Let me take those, Mitzy, you shouldn't be carrying anything," scolded Stefano. He took one satchel and handed the other to Julean.

"Thank you, Your Majesties" laughed Mitzy. The boys glanced at one another nervously and hurried away before succumbing to the temptation to tell Mitzy that they weren't royalty.

"Thank you, Miss Mit, these supplies shall be invaluable to us," said a deep voice from behind. "But, shouldn't you be upstairs resting?" Mitzy knew who it was at once and wanted to be angry at Roffius for refusing that she come along. But when she turned around and saw his dashing smile, Mitzy's heart melted.

"You sound like my mother," she said.

"She's a wise woman," replied Roffius. As he looked into her crystal blue eyes dancing with a hint of mischief, his desire became greater than his sworn duty. Roffius had to profess his love, especially knowing he might never see her again.

"Mitzy, there's something I must tell you...," he said softly. As he spoke, Ithamar walked up behind him.

"Captain, the men are ready," reported the guard.

"Yes, of course," said Roffius awkwardly. "Please excuse us, Miss Mit." She curtsied and walked away wondering what the captain had wanted to tell her. Roffius watched her go and marveled at her ability to make something as simple as walking look so attractive.

"She's not bad but personally, I prefer her mother," whispered Ithamar.

"Well, that just goes to show you that my taste is far superior to yours," replied Roffius with a love-struck grin.

******

The sun was setting in the horizon as nearly two hundred men gathered outside of Jesorath's blacksmith shop. Roffius was pleased to see so many as he climbed onto a bale of hay to address them.

"Men of Irvania, I wish to thank you for joining with us in this noble cause. While I cannot promise any of you freedom from danger, I can promise you freedom from tyranny should we succeed. Partaking in this endeavor shall show you if you are the kind of man who tells stories of bravery from the safety of his home, or the kind of whom such stories are told," said Roffius. The men erupted in wild cheers of support. "Come with me now, and let us reclaim what is rightfully ours!"

Vibrations from the army of farmers as they rode away soon rippled throughout Irvania. Meridia held Baby Zerah as she watched from the tiny landing atop Jesorath's stairs. Before leaving, Ithamar stopped his horse beneath her.

"My lady, may I be so bold as to request a token of luck from you?" he asked. Meridia blushed as she reached into her pocket for a handkerchief. She dropped it and the handkerchief fluttered down to Ithamar's outstretched hand.

"Thank you, my lady, I promise to return it," he said with a smile. Ithamar tucked the precious token into his vest and tipped his hat before riding away.

After the men had gone, Meridia entered the house thinking Mitzy was in the back room resting. Although pleased with her daughter for following the physician's orders, Meridia thought it unusual for Mitzy not to have seen the men off. She quickly dismissed it and hummed a sweet lullaby to Baby Zerah as she placed him in the basket near the fire. Meridia then walked to the back room to check on Mitzy, but when she did her heart sank. The room was empty and her daughter's dress lay folded at the end of the neatly made bed.

******

Roffius was distracted with thoughts of Mitzy as he led the procession of Royal Guards and farmers away from Irvania.

"I wish Mitzy was here," said Stefano as if reading his uncle's mind.

"Yeah, she makes every place feel like home," added Julean.

"You shall see her again soon enough," answered Roffius hoping to reassure his nephews as much as himself.

"I'm going to marry her someday," announced Stefano proudly.

"Are you?" laughed Roffius.

"I'd treat her like a queen," continued the boy. Roffius smiled at the irony of his nephew's statement knowing that Mitzy was already a queen.

"What if she marries another before you?" he teased. Stefano hadn't considered that possibility, and his brow furrowed as Ithamar rode up alongside them.

"What are we talking about?" asked the guard.

"Women!" said Julean with a crinkled up nose.

"Anyone I know?" asked Ithamar.

"Mitzy," answered Stefano with a dreamy look.

"Ah, yes, the fair Mitzy. It's a pity your uncle has yet to tell her how he feels," said Ithamar casually.

"What do you mean?" asked Stefano with surprise. Ithamar quickly realized his blunder and tried to cover it up.

"Simply that your uncle believes her sword skills rival those of a Royal Guard, and he has yet to tell her," he replied awkwardly. Stefano and Julean nodded in agreement as Perez rode up.

"Captain, riders are approaching with haste from the west," he reported.

"Stefano, you and Julean get to the rear and stay close to Jesorath," ordered Roffius. "The rest of you spread out into the trees."

The army of farmers and Ithamar's elite squadron quickly melted into the dense forest as the rumble of horses grew louder. Ithamar and Roffius watched from behind the cover of trees as the riders stopped and a voice called out.

"Prince Roffius! My name is Eliab and I must speak with you!" he shouted. Eliab and the handful of men he assembled had taken a shortcut across the Placia River to arrive outside of Irvania ahead of the Bara soldiers sent to retrieve Prince Roffius. To his dismay, however, Eliab saw them making camp over the previous ridge. From his vantage point, Roffius recognized the Bara soldier uniforms and wondered what purpose it served to make themselves known.

"I've a message from your brother the king," continued Eliab. Roffius immediately nudged his horse forward.

"Don't go, Captain! It's a trap," warned Ithamar.

"What if it isn't? I owe it to Shem to see what this man has to say," answered Roffius sharply.

"If you must, but I shall be ready to charge at your signal," replied the protective guard.

"I'm coming out!" called Roffius. As their uncle left the safety of the trees, Stefano and Julean heard the rider behind them gasp.

******

The Bara soldier and Roffius appeared to be riding in slow motion as Ithamar watched anxiously from the trees. Eliab was the first to dismount when they met.

"Greetings, Your Highness," said the young soldier with a bow. "I come with a message from King Shem."

"And why should I believe you?" demanded Roffius while dismounting. He eyed Eliab suspiciously as the two stood within striking distance. When Eliab reached into his pocket, Roffius placed his hand on the pommel of his sword thinking the Bara was reaching for a weapon. Ithamar shared Roffius' assumption and made ready to charge.

"Easy Captain, I'm simply getting the proof you've asked for. The king said you'd know my words come from him once you saw this," he said and opened his hand. Roffius looked at the object for a moment in stunned silence.

"Shem's ring," he whispered as he took the family heirloom. "You have my attention, Sir." Eliab released a sigh of relief before explaining that King Shem was well and had worked out a plan to take back the castle with another Bara soldier named Aykin.

"I don't understand. Your kind have shown nothing but disdain for the crown, and terrorized the people of Nepthali for generations," stated Roffius plainly.

"I cannot deny these shameful truths, but I'm hoping that you, like me, believe the time has come for change…and reconciliation," replied Eliab. Roffius looked at his brother's signet ring and pondering Eliab's words. He finally spoke to break the looming silence.

"Very well, what's the plan?" he asked. His response invoked a respect in Eliab not often given by the young soldier.

"Narok believes you are in Belzeeb, and that the riders leaving during the third watch are going to meet you there to help gather more men," explained Eliab.

"Why does Narok believe I am in Belzeeb?" asked Roffius with a raised brow.

"Because that's what a lad named Obed told him," answered Eliab.

"Obed?" asked Roffius. He hadn't expected to hear the name of a boy who had been like a brother to Mitzy.

"You know him?" pressed Eliab with surprise.

"I once knew a boy by that name taken in by Narok and his father," replied Roffius.

"It must be the same lad, My Prince. In truth, Obed is the son of a Royal Guard named Uriah, and brother of the very same Aykin whom I mentioned is working with King Shem. Obed is one of the riders going to Belzeeb," continued Eliab. "He's really quite impressive for a lad of thirteen."

"Who are the other riders?" asked Roffius.

"One is the Royal Physician Lamech; and the other is my cousin Kenan," replied Eliab. Roffius always knew Lamech to be a selfless individual, yet this act of bravery was exceptional by all accounts.

"What's to become of them if Narok is aware of their intent?" snapped Roffius harshly. He was concerned for their safety; especially knowing how much Obed meant to Mitzy.

"Have no fear, My Prince, Kenan may not have your same reputation with a sword, but I'd vouch for his skills any day," said Eliab not knowing of his cousin's treachery. "They shall succeed in Belzeeb, just as we shall succeed against the Bara soldiers in the morning. Once we do, the rest of you can continue on to the castle to free King Shem and Aykin while my men and I gather more men in Haliel."

"Tell me, Soldier, just what Bara soldiers do you intend on defeating in the morning?" asked Roffius with a raised brow.

"The ones camped over the previous ridge," answered Eliab sheepishly.

"What! You led them straight to us!" exclaimed Roffius. He was unaware that it was the men he'd tied to the tree whom were responsible for leading their comrades to Irvania after breaking free.

"Let me finish, Your Highness," continued Eliab calmly in spite of Roffius' flared temper. "I don't know how they knew you were here, but I can tell you with absolute certainty that those soldiers didn't follow us." Roffius calmed down some, until he thought of the nearly two hundred farmers being asked to engage in battle against the fierce warriors without proper training. Eliab saw his hesitation.

"Prince Roffius, as I've said before your reputation precedes you, and my men and I are at your disposal. Besides, we shall have the element of surprise on our side," he said with a boyish grin. Roffius hated to admit it, but he actually agreed that this plan could work.

From the trees, Ithamar watched in disbelief as the Captain of the Royal Guards shook hands with the Bara soldier. When Roffius returned to his waiting companions, Stefano and Julean rode up as their uncle spoke to Ithamar.

"As strange as this may sound, Shem sent them to help us," explained Roffius.

"Are you sure?" asked Ithamar with a raised brow. Roffius opened his clinched hand in reply to reveal the king's signet ring. When Ithamar saw it, he was in agreement with his captain.

"We shall take shelter deeper in the trees for the night and attack before dawn. With any luck, we may even succeed," said Roffius.

"How do we know he hasn't killed Father and just taken his ring?" asked Stefano with concern. Roffius had wondered the same thing, but something told him that Eliab was telling the truth.

"I know this is difficult, Stefano, but you must trust me. If these men are leading us into a trap then we shall fight with bravery and honor. But if they're telling the truth, as

I'm bound to believe, they shall help us save your father's life and reclaim the castle," answered Roffius. Stefano reluctantly agreed as he and the rest of the men followed Roffius deeper into the woods.

The noise created by the small army on horseback stirred up a colony of bats. The winged creatures swarmed in masses around the riders and spooked the horses. Julean's horse reared and sent the boy sailing into a tree.

"Julean!" shouted Stefano. He jumped from his horse and ran to his cousin's side. The rider beside Stefano was the next to reach Julean, followed closely by Roffius. Julean lay on the ground moaning while holding his arm.

"My arm, my arm!" he wailed. The unknown farmer provided support behind the boy while Roffius examined Julean's arm.

"I think it's broken. Stefano, fetch me two sturdy branches which shall hold his arm in place," ordered Roffius. Stefano hurried away but was quick to return with the branches. Roffius removed his cloak and tore off a strip to use as a dressing. "Take this," he said and tossed the cloak in Stefano's direction. However, instead of landing in Stefano's arms, the cloak landed in the arms of the farmer supporting Julean. "This might hurt a little," continued Roffius. He positioned Julean's arm between the branches then took hold of his nephew's arm and pulled.

"Aaahh!" cried Julean. Ithamar and Jesorath arrived just as Roffius finished resetting the bone.

"What happened?" asked Ithamar.

"It seems as though Julean decided to take a closer look at this tree with his arm," retorted Roffius.

"Don't worry, Prince Julean, we shall get you more comfortable as soon as we set up camp," assured Jesorath.

"He can't ride alone," noted Stefano.

"The boy can ride with me. I've experience with this sort of thing," said the unknown farmer. Roffius looked up and noticed the farmer for the first time.

"Who are you? What is your name?" he asked. The farmer wore a very large hat low on his brow and kept his head to the ground. He paused as if unsure of his own name.

"Amalek, my name is Amalek," he finally replied. Roffius looked at Amalek thinking there was something familiar about this young man, and that name, but he couldn't place it.

"Have we met?" he asked stepping closer.

"No, Captain, I don't think so; but fear not, I shall take good care of the boy," stuttered Amalek as he backed away. Roffius eyed the small rider for a moment.

"It's settled then, Julean shall ride with Amalek. Stefano, stay with them," he instructed.

"Yes, Uncle," replied the boy dutifully.

"Thank you, Amalek, you're a good man," said Roffius. He heartily slapped Amalek on the back as he passed and felt the young man wince. Roffius walked away wondering why someone so frail would willingly join them into battle.

"Don't worry, the young prince shall be safe with me, Captain," answered Amalek in a muffled voice. Roffius merely waved his hand in reply while Ithamar lifted Julean onto Amalek's horse. When Amalek realized he was still holding the captain's cloak, he shoved it deep into his saddlebag then mounted his horse intending to return it once they reached camp.

"Stay to the rear and keep an eye on them!" said Roffius as he rode past Jesorath.

"Consider it done, Captain," replied the burly blacksmith.

The pain worsened for Julean as the horse trotted along and Amalek sensed the boy's discomfort.

"Lean into me so your arm won't bounce around as much," said the farmer kindly. Julean took Amalek's advice and was relieved to discover the young man was right. "You must be hungry," continued Amalek.

"Not really," moaned Julean as he held his arm.

"Since when are you not hungry?" teased Amalek.

"What's that supposed to mean?" asked Julean. The rider gently pulled Julean closer and whispered into his ear.

"It's me...Mitzy," she said. Julean turned around so quickly that he nearly knocked them both from the saddle.

"MITZY!" he cried out.

"Ssshhh! Not so loud, someone may hear you," she scolded. But it was too late; Stefano had heard his cousin cry out and slowed his horse until they were side by side.

"What's the matter, Julean?" he asked. Mitzy gently squeezed Julean's arm.

"Aaahh! My arm!" he wailed.

"I thought you said 'Mitzy'," continued Stefano. Mitzy knew she couldn't tell Stefano with Roffius just a few yards ahead of them.

"I think he may be going into shock, Sire, he's talking foolishness," she said in her muffled voice. Julean played along with it.

"I wish Mitzy was here, she'd never hurt me, or make me uncomfortable," he said sarcastically. Stefano looked at his cousin with a raised brow.

"Are you sure you hit your arm and not your head?" he asked. Julean sighed with relief once Stefano rode ahead to rejoin his uncle.

"Whew! That was close," he said.

"Too close," replied Mitzy.

"What are you doing here? Uncle shall be really mad once he finds out!" exclaimed Julean. Hearing the boy, Jesorath turned around. Mitzy tipped the brim of her large hat to signal everything was fine and the blacksmith returned the gesture before turning back around.

"Keep your voice down," she warned. "Of course Roffius would be mad, which is why you mustn't tell him."

"Okay, but Roffius is smart; he'll figure it out," said the boy as he swayed in the saddle.

"Let's hope he doesn't until this is over. Now, sit back and relax; it looks like they're stopping," she said.

"What about Stefano? Can I tell him?" asked Julean.

"I suppose so, but no one else," she said firmly.

While the small army dispersed into the trees to make camp for the night, Mitzy turned her horse away and found a spot near a small slope. She dismounted first, and then helped Julean down. When he leaned into her shoulder, Mitzy winced with pain.

"Sorry," he said apologetically. She tried to force a smile in spite of the throbbing pain in her shoulder, and regretted having not listened to Roffius when he said her coming along would be a mistake. The weary maiden steadied Julean and helped him over to a patch of soft moss. He sat down and shivered in the brisk night air.

"Let me look for a blanket to keep you warm until I can get a fire going," offered Mitzy. She went back to her saddlebag and looked for a blanket. She soon found one and pulled it out for Julean.

"Can I stay here with you?" he asked when she returned.

"I don't see why not, unless of course your uncle comes looking for you," replied Mitzy while wrapping the blanket around his shoulders. Just then they heard footsteps running towards them.

"What are you doing way over here, Julean? I have a place for us near Uncle Roffius and Ithamar," called Stefano's familiar voice. Mitzy quickly tried to think of an excuse for why they were so far away from the others.

"I thought the prince would be more comfortable next to this slope so he could rest his arm," she answered. Mitzy hoped the absurdity of her response would go unnoticed as Julean smiled nervously and shrugged his shoulders.

"Well, Jesorath's preparing some stew and Uncle Roffius wants you near him," continued Stefano.

"I'm not really hungry," replied Julean. Stefano tilted his head and looked at his cousin suspiciously.

"Did you just say you aren't hungry?" he asked. "All right, Julean, what's going on?"

"Oh, it's no use! I can't do this; besides, you said I could tell him!" Julean exclaimed.

"Tell me what?" insisted Stefano.

"It's Mitzy!" exclaimed Julean.

"Ssshhh! Not so loud!" she scolded.

"What do you mean?" asked Stefano.

"I mean…Amalek is Mitzy," repeated Julean. He nodded at Mitzy and she stepped closer. Stefano squinted and then suddenly recognized her crystal blue eyes beneath the large hat.

"Mitzy! What are you doing here?!" he exclaimed

while throwing his arms around her.

"Easy, watch the shoulder," she laughed. Pleasant as it was, their reunion was short-lived when Mitzy noticed Julean's eyes widen at the sight of his uncle approaching.

"Tell him I'm gathering wood for a fire," she whispered. Mitzy disappeared into the darkness moments before Roffius arrived.

"I've been looking everywhere for you, Julean; why aren't you with the rest of us? And where's Amalek?" he asked with a hint of frustration.

"You just missed him. He left to gather some wood," answered Stefano.

"I see; well, let's have another look at your arm," said Roffius as he knelt beside Julean. His nephew cried out in pain as soon as Roffius touched it.

"Just as I suspected; it's broken. Keep this splint on for support until we reach the castle where it can be properly cared for," instructed Roffius. "Come along with me back to camp so I can keep an eye on you." Julean gave a worried look to Stefano.

"What about Amalek?" he asked.

"He's welcome to come too; now let's go," insisted Roffius. Julean and Stefano dutifully followed their uncle, but glanced back into the darkness with worry.

From behind a tree, Mitzy watched them walk away and trusted the boys to keep her secret. Although she wasn't looking forward to a night alone in the outdoors, Mitzy preferred it to Roffius discovering her presence.

When she was satisfied they were gone, Mitzy returned to her little campsite and started a fire. She enjoyed its warmth while gazing into the night sky and marveled at the brilliant stars twinkling above. A thousand thoughts flooded her mind, including ones about Cora's safety in the midst of a castle overrun with Bara soldiers. Mitzy also lamented over the worry she had surely caused her mother by leaving without telling her.

"Papa, I wish you were here. Your hope was so strong, and we are in desperate need of Orpheus to help us save the king and take back the castle," she said softly.

No sooner had she finished speaking than Mitzy saw a shooting star cast an explosion of light across the night sky. It reminded her of the light she saw as they fled the war-torn castle, but it was quickly swallowed up by a stream of fire. Mitzy felt herself tremble, so she went to her saddlebag in search of another blanket. Instead of a blanket, however, Mitzy found Roffius' cloak. She draped it over her shoulders feeling safe and warm as she returned to the small fire. Mitzy faded off to sleep huddled beneath Roffius' cloak dreaming of him saving the kingdom, and bringing the return of Orpheus.

******

Kenan and Lamech saddled the horses by torch light inside the Royal Stables while Obed changed into the uniform of a Bara soldier. Obed wanted to keep his involvement hidden from Narok, not knowing that the evil man was already aware because of Kenan. Kenan had started a partnership with Mezrah to gain power and position hoping to impress Eliab and humiliate Aykin, but was beginning to realize just how foolish he had been.

Because of this, he chose not to inform Mezrah that Eliab and a handful of men were already on their way to Irvania.

"Is something troubling you?" asked Lamech sensing Kenan's pensive mood. The young man remained evasive as he mounted.

"Nothing, are you ready?" replied Kenan trying to mask his tumultuous emotions inside.

"As ready as I shall ever be I suppose; I've never done anything like this before," confessed Lamech.

"I know what you mean," added Obed as he mounted. "But, somehow this feels right, almost like I was born to do this. Does that make sense?"

"Knowing who your real father was, yes; it makes perfect sense," replied Lamech without hesitation.

"Let's go then!" exclaimed Kenan.

He led them out of the stables and kept the horses to a walk through the courtyard until they reached the large outer gates. Once there, Kenan urged his horse into a full run which the other horses eagerly matched.

Mezrah smiled shrewdly from his vantage point atop the castle wall as he watched the three men ride away. After they had disappeared into the night, Mezrah left at a brisk pace for the King's Chambers. He entered expecting to find his nephew in bed, but was startled to discover that Narok wasn't alone.

"Just what do you think you're doing barging in here at this hour?" demanded Narok. He quickly grabbed the king's robe to cover himself, while Nalia buttoned her

Dragon Scroll of Nepthali

nightgown with equal zeal. To her good fortune, Mezrah's interruption came in time to prevent the wayward maiden from giving herself completely to Narok after being seduced by his promises to make her queen. Nalia scurried away from the room not knowing the cunning man had made the same empty promises to countless other maidens.

"Excuse me, Nephew," said Mezrah awkwardly. "I thought you'd like to know that three riders just left traveling north." Narok's anger subsided with this news.

"Well, well; it seems that Obed has proved worthwhile after all," he said with surprise.

"Obed was one of the riders," continued Mezrah coldly. Narok's surprise increased tenfold as he stared at his uncle in disbelief.

"So, the little brat thinks he can outsmart me, does he?" sneered the evil man. "I want you to personally take care of him…take care of them all, and bring me their heads as a gift!"

"For what?" asked Mezrah.

"My wedding…or coronation, you decide," replied Narok smugly. He tightened the sash on the robe and walked over to the dressing table where he irreverently placed the crown upon his head. Mezrah seethed with jealousy as he watched. "Well, what are you waiting for? Go after them!" shouted Narok. Although Mezrah hadn't planned on going to Belzeeb, he decided anything was better than staying and having to watch his nephew wearing the crown. Mezrah also surmised that killing both Obed and Kenan would make the trip quite satisfying.

Army of Farmers

******

After his uncle left the room, Narok continued to admire his handsome reflection in the stately mirror. As he did a terrifying image suddenly appeared behind his own. Narok turned around to see the black dragon's face as the creature dropped his enormous neck to become level with the balcony.

"Descendant of Ganu, come here!" commanded Natas. Narok mustered what little courage he possessed as he slowly approached the black dragon.

"O Great One, it is I; Narok," he called with his voice cracking. "I feared for your safety since I've not seen your magnificent image since the night of the attack." Deceit came as naturally to Narok as breathing, but his trickery was wasted on a creature like Natas.

"Silence!" roared the dragon. "Do you take me for a fool? Your false flattery has no effect on me!" Narok's mouth turned as dry as the wheat fields in summer, and beads of sweat formed along his forehead as Natas continued. "I've been resting after my long journey to Hampenstein. I destroyed the Royal Ship carrying members of the Royal Family whom you apparently failed to capture. I trust you have the remaining members in the dungeon?"

"King Shem is, My Lord, and my men are in pursuit of the others who have temporarily eluded capture," replied Narok nervously. The dragon's face twisted into a scowl as he stretched his massive wings then tilted back his head and shot a stream of fire into the night sky. This was the streak of fire which Mitzy had seen from the forest at the edge of Irvania.

"Imbecile! Why does the king still live?" demanded Natas.

"Your Excellency, I merely kept the king alive until the others were captured," answered Narok recoiling in fear.

"Why must humans be so filled with excuses? It seems the only thing you've managed to do is fail!" said the black dragon with disdain. "Orpheus is close, I can feel him. And, in spite of your limitless incompetence, even you should know that the entire Royal Family must be eliminated to keep him away!"

"You have nothing to fear, Great One, by this time tomorrow they shall be nothing but a memory," proclaimed Narok.

"I hope for your sake your bold statement proves to be true. Otherwise, you shall be just as much of a memory as the Royal Family," warned the black dragon.

If not bound by his own promise to make an heir of Ganu the king at the appointed time, Natas would've killed Narok instantly. Therefore, fearing what he may do if he stayed, the black dragon took flight in search of the missing members of the Royal Family. Natas was determined to destroy King Jeptha's bloodline not realizing that Orpheus was just as determined to save them; especially after hearing Queen Mitzy's humble plea for help.

Chapter 18

Mistaken Identity

The sun's first rays of glorious light had yet to chase away the darkness as farmers and Royal Guards extinguished fires to make ready to launch their surprise attack. Ithamar walked through the campsite to ensure every man was up and moving.

"Let's go soldier…mount up men!" he shouted. When Eliab passed by, Ithamar stopped the young man to ask the question which had been burning on the guard's mind all night.

"Eliab, yesterday Roffius mentioned that a Bara soldier named Aykin is now assisting the king," he said careful to keep Shem's true identity from this barbarian. "Do you know of him?" A broad smile spread across Eliab's face at the mention of Aykin's name.

"Of course I know him; he's like a brother to me," he replied casually.

"Is he from Haliel?" continued Ithamar.

"No, Aykin's from Nepthali. His father was once a Royal Guard like you. Perhaps you knew him, his name was Uriah." stated Eliab. He eyed the guard old enough to be his father carefully as Ithamar's face went white.

Eliab's reply confirmed for Ithamar that the Aykin he had thrown in the dungeon days earlier was indeed the son of his best friend. Ithamar wondered if he could live with himself knowing the extent of his failure, but even more, the guard wondered if Aykin was truly an ally or if he and Eliab were just pretending so they could lure Roffius back to the castle.

"Yes, I knew Uriah well," he replied softly. "But tell me, how is it that two Bara soldiers suddenly find themselves assisting the very people whom they attacked?" Ithamar's piercing eyes looked right through Eliab, yet the young soldier had nothing to hide.

"Like I told your captain, we've been on the same side all along…you just didn't see it," answered Eliab firmly. He briskly walked away leaving Ithamar to ponder the possible truth of his words, and perhaps if he had been wrong about many things.

******

Still disguised as Amalek, Mitzy kept her distance as she rejoined the small army before anyone came looking for her. Stefano and Julean saw her approaching and were relieved that she'd made it safely through the night. They wanted to greet her, but didn't want to draw unnecessary attention to the maiden disguised as a farmer.

"Where's Amalek?" asked Roffius. Stefano quickly spoke up.

"He's over there," answered the boy.

Mistaken Identity

"There's something familiar about him, but I can't place my finger on it," said Roffius as he jumped into his saddle. "I want the two of you on the same horse, so mount up." He left them to speak with Amalek.

"Amalek, it seems that my nephews have taken a liking to you. Because of this, I'd like you to stay with them. But make no mistake, I expect you to keep them out of harm's way once the fighting begins," said Roffius firmly.

"Yes, Captain, you can count on me," replied Mitzy in a muffled voice. However, instead of riding away as she had hoped, Roffius lingered.

"Have we met before?" he asked eyeing her carefully. Mitzy sensed his gaze and kicked her heels into the side of her horse.

"Certainly not, Captain," she called over her shoulder while riding away.

******

Eliab, Roffius, Jesorath, and Ithamar led the men out from the safety of the trees, while Mitzy stayed with the boys at the rear. They traveled in silence to the next ridge where Ithamar stopped the men and waited for Roffius' signal. The young captain canvassed the area as the rising sun dusted golden streaks across the horizon. It was a beautiful sight, but one which Roffius knew would soon transform into the horrors of war. In the blink of an eye, Captain Roffius dug his heels into his horse and sped away. When they saw Roffius lead the charge down the hill, the rag-tag army of farmers and Royal Guards followed after the man they believed was not just their captain, but also their prince.

Inside the camp, the majority of Bara soldiers were still asleep. However, those who were awake sounded the alarm while scrambling to get their boots on and rushing to their horses. Ithamar's elite squadron started the attack, and soon swords were clashing and bodies were falling. As she watched with Stefano and Julean from a safe distance, Mitzy noticed something strange on the opposite ridgeline.

"What do you suppose that is?" she asked the boys while pointing to a spattering of tiny dots. Stefano squinted, and then his eyes grew twice their normal size.

"More Bara soldiers!" he shouted.

"If we don't do something, they're gonna get slaughtered!" exclaimed Julean. Mitzy and the boys watched in horror as a flood of prepared Bara soldiers charged towards the unsuspecting army of farmers.

"Follow me!" cried Mitzy as she urged her horse into the fighting.

Eliab's sword clashed against those of former comrades as he fought alongside the king's Royal Guards. Ithamar thrust his sword into an enemy soldier as a rider suddenly sped past. He recognized the small frame, but wondered why Amalek would disobey Roffius' order to stay with Stefano and Julean away from the fighting.

"Was that Amalek?" he asked. Eliab plunged his sword through his opponent's midsection then turned to watch the rider race towards Roffius. Ithamar frantically looked around for Stefano and Julean, but couldn't see them until they nearly ran him over as they, too, sped past.

"Watch out! It's a trap! More Bara soldiers are coming!" they yelled as Stefano pointed towards the oncoming men.

By this time, Mitzy had reached the front lines where she saw Roffius on foot battling three Bara soldiers single-handedly. He wielded the sword made by dragon magic as if it were an extension of his own body. But as he fought against the three, another soldier approached Roffius from behind. Seeing what was happening, Mitzy urged her horse towards the man. She raised her sword and thrust the blade into the soldier's back before the man was able to strike Roffius. Mitzy smiled to herself knowing this wasn't the first time she had saved his life. Roffius watched the rider speed past him with amazement. Like Ithamar, he recognized the rider's frail frame, but had doubted Amalek's ability to even hold a sword let alone ride while wielding one. However, Roffius' amazement quickly evolved into anger after thinking Amalek had abandoned his nephews, or worse, led them into the fighting.

"Look out! More Bara are coming!" she yelled as she rode past. Roffius heard the warning and turned around to see the second wave of soldiers spilling over the ridge. His stomach sank with the realization that his men were trapped inside the small valley.

"Prepare for another attack!" yelled Roffius. Eliab and Ithamar were the first to his side.

"I guess they made separate camps," replied Eliab sheepishly.

"Tell Jesorath to remain here while I take Ithamar and his men to greet our new friends," ordered Roffius.

"Consider it done, Captain. I shall catch up with you as soon as I can!" shouted Eliab. As he pulled a former comrade off his horse and used it to ride away to deliver his commander's message, Ithamar was convinced that Eliab was indeed on their side.

Mitzy stopped her horse at the base of the ridge and turned around to see if the men had heeded her warning. She sighed with relief after seeing Roffius and Ithamar rallying the others to prepare for the next wave of soldiers. She knew they were still in for a fight, but at least now they had a fair chance. Roffius was now too thankful for Amalek's warning to be angry with the frail farmer.

"Nicely done, Amalek…now get back to the boys!" he shouted as she sped past. She nodded and urged her horse through the oncoming men in search of Stefano and Julean. Mitzy soon found them with Jesorath.

"You two come with me!" she exclaimed. The boys raced on horseback following Mitzy out of harm's way, and then watched with awe as the farmers from Irvania finished off what remained of the Bara soldiers in camp. Victory was eminent, and the enemy sensed it.

"Find Prince Roffius! Forget about the others!" shouted one of the Bara commanders. Mitzy turned to the boys with a look of horror.

"Did he just say to find the prince?" she asked.

"They must know they can't win, so they're looking for Uncle Roffius," answered Stefano with dismay. Just then,

Mistaken Identity

Mitzy saw five Bara soldiers break away from the others.

"He'll be killed for sure if they capture him!" cried Julean. Mitzy's heart sank knowing the boy was right. She thought for a moment then suddenly had an idea of how to save him. She yanked her saddlebag free and frantically searched through it.

"What are you looking for?" asked Stefano. But his question went unanswered as Mitzy urged her horse back into the fighting after pulling out Roffius' cloak.

"What do you think she's up to?" asked Julean.

"I'm not sure, but whatever it is…I hope it works," replied Stefano.

Mitzy ignored the throbbing pain as she wrapped Roffius' cloak over her shoulders while her horse barreled its way through the fighting. She pulled the hood over her large hat and charged past the Bara soldiers who were searching for the prince. The Royal Crest on the back of the cloak was like a beacon to the evil men, and they immediately chased after it. Mitzy looked back and smiled when she saw they'd taken her bait. With her horse galloping at top speed, Mitzy turned the reigns hard right to lead her pursuers away from Roffius.

"It's Prince Roffius! Get him!" shouted another Bara soldier after seeing the Royal Crest flapping wildly on the cloak speeding away. Rogue soldiers joined in with those already in pursuit of the rider they assumed to be Prince Roffius making his escape. Still in the midst of combat on foot, when Ithamar heard the men shouting he looked at Roffius with a raised brow as Roffius looked back at Ithamar with an equal surprise.

"That's my cloak!" exclaimed Roffius.

"I can see that, but who's wearing it?" shouted Ithamar above the fighting. Suddenly, Roffius remembered throwing his cloak to Stefano the night before. He also remembered asking for it later, but the boy didn't have it.

Eliab urged his stolen horse towards them fearing the prince was in danger. His fears were soon relieved when Eliab found Roffius with Ithamar. Eliab then looked at the rider wearing the cloak and recognized it was the same one who had warned them earlier about the additional Bara soldiers.

"Who *is* that guy?" he asked with respect.

"I think it's Amalek, but what's he doing?" asked Roffius.

"I can't say for certain, but I think he's saving your life, Captain," answered Ithamar. More Bara soldiers joined in the chase after Mitzy believing she was Prince Roffius as Stefano and Julean looked on.

"We've got to help her!" exclaimed Julean.

"Hold on tight!" shouted Stefano. He dug his heels into the horse's side and miraculously rode unscathed through the fighting. Ithamar saw them coming and alerted Roffius.

"Look Captain, it's Stefano and Julean! I think they're trying to help Amalek," he yelled. Roffius couldn't understand why his nephews would do something so foolish for someone they barely knew. He then remembered why the name Amalek sounded familiar…it was the name of Meridia's late husband, and Mitzy's father. Roffius immediately turned around and pulled a Bara soldier from his horse and jumped into the saddle as the animal galloped ahead.

"Looks like we're going that way now!" exclaimed Ithamar.

"What's he doing?" asked Eliab.

"I'm not sure, which is what worries me!" shouted Ithamar. Each found a horse and chased after Roffius who had joined in the pursuit of the rider known as Amalek. When Ithamar caught up to Roffius, he saw a look of absolute terror on the young man's face.

"What's wrong, Captain?" he yelled over the sound of horses running in full stride.

"It's Amalek!" shouted Roffius.

"What about him?" asked Ithamar.

"I thought there was something familiar about him, but I couldn't put my finger on it until now. Amalek was the name of Mitzy's father," answered Roffius. "Amalek is MITZY!" He urged his horse ahead leaving Ithamar behind with the same look of terror as his captain.

"Oh no," whispered the guard as he watched Bara soldiers gaining on the young queen.

Roffius and his companions caught up to Stefano and Julean who were happy to see their uncle, even knowing he would be angry with them for keeping Mitzy's secret.

"Uncle!" shouted Stefano. "There's something I must tell you! Amalek is really Mitzy!"

"He knows!" shouted Ithamar as the men bolted past the boys.

"Who's Mitzy?" asked a bewildered Eliab.

Mitzy's heart raced as she watched the pack of unrelenting Bara soldiers gain on her. She noticed a small creek up ahead and charged her horse towards it hoping to slow them down. Spray shot into the air as her horse sped through the water, which did nothing to deter her pursuers. One of the soldiers rode up alongside Mitzy and grabbed hold of the cloak. He tried to pull her down, but Mitzy untied the garment and kicked her assailant off his horse. The man fell into the creek holding the cloak where he was immediately trampled by his comrades' horses.

Meanwhile, Roffius closed in on two of the riders at the rear of the pack. He pulled out both of his daggers and threw them with deadly accuracy. The men tumbled backwards while Roffius continued ahead towards Mitzy. He soon caught up to another Bara soldier and grabbed hold of the man's shoulder then pulled him from his horse.

Ithamar and Eliab rode up alongside two large enemy soldiers in the rear and jumped from their horses onto them. All four men toppled to the ground as the horses continued on without their riders. Ithamar and his opponent threw punches at one another as they rolled across the dirt. The guard finally grabbed the grungy man in a headlock and struck him on the side of the head with his elbow to knock him out cold. A few feet away, Eliab staggered to his feet after being punched in the stomach by his former comrade. The man then pulled out his dagger and lunged at Eliab. Eliab dodged the strike and grabbed the man's wrist. The two arm-wrestled for the dagger, but Eliab was out-matched. Ithamar suddenly appeared behind the enemy and thrust his sword through the man's back.

"I had him," moaned Eliab as the dead soldier fell to the ground.

"Sure you did," mocked Ithamar. "Now hurry up, we've got to help Roffius!"

Far ahead, Mitzy struggled to remain conscious from the unbearable pain in her shoulder as another enemy soldier rode up alongside her horse. Roffius was right behind them and saw the man lunge for Mitzy, followed by one stabbing the other.

"NO!" yelled Roffius fearing it was Mitzy.

When Roffius recognized her sparkling blue eyes beneath the brim of the large hat as she looked back at him with surprise, he was filled with both relief and frustration. He scowled at Mitzy as he rode up alongside and grabbed hold of her reigns. Roffius led the horses out of the creek before stopping beneath a small tree. He was furious with Mitzy for doing something so dangerous; especially knowing she was the Queen of Nepthali. Although she expected him to be angry, Mitzy hadn't expected to see such fear in his eyes.

"Of all the fool-hearty things I've seen, this surpasses them all! You nearly got yourself killed!" he scolded. Roffius jumped from his horse and stormed back to Mitzy. He reached up and pulled her down, careful of the wound on her shoulder. Once on her feet, everything began to spin.

"Captain, I...," she managed weakly before collapsing

into his arms.

Roffius' anger melted away as an overwhelming desire to kiss her came while looking into the eyes that always saw the best in him. For the first time in his life Roffius allowed desire to come before duty, and gently pulled Mitzy to himself. As he did, a sneaky Bara soldier approached them from the opposite direction.

Like the other enemy soldiers, this one believed Mitzy was the prince after seeing her wearing the cloak bearing the Royal Crest before it fell into the creek with his comrade. The man assumed Roffius was the prince's bodyguard from the attentive manner in which the muscular man tended to the supposed prince. Unaware of the Bara's presence, Mitzy closed her eyes in anticipation of feeling the gentle caress of Roffius' lips upon hers. However, instead of his kiss, Mitzy felt Roffius collapse. The grungy soldier had delivered a crushing blow to the back of her beloved's head before pulling Mitzy onto his horse.

The man held Mitzy in his arms, yet he failed to recognize the obvious physical differences between herself and the formidable Captain of the Royal Guards because of dragon magic. The half-witted man sincerely believed he had Prince Roffius, and burst into laughter as he rode away with his prize. Meanwhile, Mitzy tried not to faint from the pain in her shoulder, or the stench of her captor.

Ithamar and Eliab were too far away to see the rogue Bara soldier abduct their queen; therefore, their only concern was Roffius who lay motionless on the ground. Ithamar was the first to arrive and he jumped from his horse to help his captain while Stefano fetched his uncle's

Mistaken Identity

cloak from the stream. The boy also retrieved Roffius' daggers from the backs of two Bara soldiers.

"Where's Mitzy?" asked Stefano as he returned.

"She's probably back with the others," replied Eliab absent-mindedly. Stefano was hesitant to agree as he handed the cloak to Julean. "How's Prince Roffius?" Eliab asked Ithamar.

"I suspect he shall be fine," answered the guard. "But judging by this lump, I suspect he shall have a terrible headache when he comes to." Ithamar hoisted Roffius over his shoulder and draped the captain's limp body over the rear of his horse.

Jesorath feared the worst when he saw the boys, Ithamar, and Eliab approaching with Roffius dangling over the back of Ithamar's horse. He immediately rode out to meet them.

"What happened?" asked the worried blacksmith.

"He's fine, just a nasty bump which shall leave him with an equally nasty headache," replied Ithamar.

"Mitzy saved him!" blurted Julean.

"But, Mitzy's in Irvania," replied Jesorath.

"No, she's not; she's here! Amalek *is* Mitzy!" declared Stefano.

"Mitzy put on Uncle's cloak so the Bara soldiers would think she was him, and it worked!" continued Julean.

"Mitzy certainly seems to have a way of surprising us, doesn't she?" replied Jesorath while shaking his head. He thought it no wonder that Roffius was in love with such a clever maiden as he turned around and led the men back to what remained of the Bara campsite.

Stefano and Julean forgot about their concern for Mitzy's whereabouts as they followed Jesorath and the others past smoldering fires and dead bodies scattered throughout the camp. After passing the rubble, Ithamar stopped his horse.

"Jesorath, I need you and Eliab to see how many men we've lost," he ordered while dismounting. He lifted Roffius over his shoulder as he continued, "And make sure there are no enemy survivors."

"Yes, Sir," answered the men heartily. The blacksmith and former Bara soldier rode away while Ithamar carried Roffius to the base of the tree. He placed the captain down and turned to Stefano and Julean.

"You boys stay here and look after your uncle. I've enough to worry about without having to keep track of the two of you," said Ithamar firmly. He then re-mounted his horse and left the boys with their unconscious uncle. While they waited, Stefano and Julean remembered Mitzy.

"Where do you suppose Mitzy is?" asked Julean.

"I don't see her, but perhaps she's tending to the wounded," suggested Stefano. Julean shrugged his shoulders and the boys sat down to wait as Ithamar had instructed.

Mistaken Identity

Hours passed without any sign of Mitzy, or change in Roffius. The boys were beginning to worry about both when their uncle finally started to moan.

"What happened? Where's Mitzy?" asked the dazed captain. He held his throbbing head and tried to stand without much success.

"Easy, Uncle," said Stefano as he braced Roffius. "I'm not sure where she is, but I've got your cloak and daggers." The boy proudly pointed to the items as Roffius shook his head and tried to get his bearings.

"What do you mean you don't know where she is?" he demanded. "Where's Ithamar?"

"He's with Eliab and Jesorath inspecting the wounded and making sure there are no Bara survivors," answered the boy. Roffius steadied himself against the tree for a moment hoping it would make everything stop spinning, but it didn't.

"Ithamar!" shouted the angry captain.

He got off to a very wobbly start as Roffius headed towards the cluster of men with Stefano and Julean following close behind. Ithamar turned around and breathed a sigh of relief at the sight of Roffius up and walking, albeit not in a straight line.

"Captain, how do you feel?" he asked. But as Roffius drew closer, Ithamar could see that his captain was as mad as a hornet.

"Where's Mitzy?" demanded Roffius. Ithamar's face went white as he suddenly realized they hadn't seen her since returning to the desecrated campsite.

"I'm not sure, but she must be here someplace," replied the guard with shame for not having a better answer to give his captain.

"Well, find her!" shouted Roffius. His head was pounding as Roffius struggled to stay on his feet and Ithamar took hold of his captain's arm before the young man fell. Eliab came alongside to assist with steadying Roffius.

"Relax, Captain, there's no need to get so worked up about a maiden," he said. Roffius shot him an icy stare.

"You ignorant fool! Mitzy isn't just some maiden, she's the Queen of Nepthali!" he shouted.

"WHAT?!" exclaimed Eliab.

"The queen?" added Stefano and Julean in unison.

"Are you telling me that Amalek is really Mitzy, and Mitzy is really the Queen of Nepthali?!" repeated Eliab in disbelief.

"It's a long story, but yes," replied Ithamar curtly.

"Well, what are we waiting for? Let's find her!" exclaimed Jesorath. The others agreed without hesitation and spread out to find their missing queen.

Hours later as the sun hung low in the late-afternoon sky; there was still no sign of Mitzy. The disheartened search party was forced to accept the unthinkable…Mitzy was gone.

"Tell me again the last thing you remember, Captain," Ithamar said to Roffius.

"I saw her kill a Bara soldier, and then...I scolded her for coming," replied Roffius shamefully. He chose to refrain from telling them the part where he nearly kissed the queen. While Roffius was speaking, Eliab suddenly remembered seeing another horse with two riders.

"Oh no," he whispered.

"What is it?" asked Ithamar.

"I saw a horse with two riders before we reached Roffius, but I just thought they were fleeing the fight," answered Eliab.

"WHAT?!" exclaimed an infuriated Roffius. "Are you saying that a Bara soldier may have taken Mitzy?"

"Easy Captain," said Ithamar calmly. "If he did, it was only because he thought she was you."

"But she's NOT me! What happens when Narok discovers the mistake?" shouted Roffius.

"Narok doesn't know she's the queen, does he?" asked Eliab.

"Of course not you fool, she doesn't even know!" snapped Roffius.

"We can't just sit here if we think the queen has been captured!" exclaimed Jesorath.

"But, that was hours ago; we'd never catch up to them," lamented Stefano. Eliab could see that queen or not, Mitzy was very special.

"I understand the concern you have for your friend, but as long as her captor believes she's the prince, Mitzy shall be safe," he said to lessen their concern.

"And Narok shall be too distracted by Mitzy's beauty to harm her," added Ithamar.

"That's exactly what worries me," replied Roffius through clinched teeth. Although Ithamar was concerned about Mitzy, he was a man of orders and his were to return Roffius to the castle and free Shem.

"Captain, we must focus on getting back to the castle for Shem's sake, as well as for Mitzy's," urged the guard.

"I agree; besides if you take the shortcut across Lake Placia as we did, you shall return before the morrow," stated Eliab.

Roffius heard what they said, but he wasn't listening. His mind was flooded with regrets for having allowed this to happen to Mitzy after everything she'd already been through. Right or wrong, Roffius chose to direct the brunt of his anger at the former Bara soldier.

"Why should we listen to you, Eliab? Wasn't it one of your comrades who rode off with the Queen of Nepthali?" he snapped.

"Let's get something straight, Captain; that man is no comrade of mine!" countered Eliab. "And why did you let the maiden come along in the first place? For that matter, why didn't you tell me you weren't really a prince?" Eliab was just as angry as Roffius. He was accustomed to being treated with respect, even amongst bandits like the Bara, and was growing tired of being treated like an inferior enemy.

"None of us, except Stefano and Julean, even knew she was here," answered Roffius sharply. "And, if you must know, I didn't tell you the truth about my identity because quite frankly, I didn't trust you!" Eliab wasn't surprised by this, and he didn't even fault the former prince for doubting him. Eliab understood that trust was something to be earned and he appreciated Roffius' honesty.

"Look, Captain, I understand why you didn't tell me. I probably would've done the same thing in your position," said Eliab. Roffius took a deep breath and started to calm down. He could see that he'd been wrong about the man slightly older than himself.

"Forgive me," replied Roffius sincerely. "I can see you are a man most worthy of respect, and I am sorry for having misjudged you."

"Thank you, Captain, and regardless of what has transpired, my resolve remains the same. I wish to see Narok destroyed and the rightful heir returned to the throne," continued Eliab. Roffius nodded in thanks then turned to face the men who had risked everything for him. Roffius knew he must remain the focused leader they expected him to be.

"What do you want us to do, Captain?" asked Ithamar.

"How bad are our losses?" asked Roffius with authority.

"We've lost nearly a third of the men, but the rest are ready to ride," reported Jesorath.

"Then we ride!" said Roffius firmly. Ithamar smiled with pride at the young man who was once again conducting himself in a manner worthy of the title Captain of the Royal Guards.

******

At the opposite end of the kingdom, Kenan continued to wrestle with the guilt of knowing that Obed and Lamech were in certain danger because of him. In an effort to arrive in Belzeeb well ahead of Mezrah's men, Kenan chose not to take the old goblin trail as Mezrah had wanted. Kenan would figure out a way to keep Obed and Lamech safe once they got to Reuben's, but for now he just wanted to get them to Belzeeb.

The old physician was exhausted and sore after riding through the night, and most of the day, but he nearly jumped for joy when Kenan finally stopped at a bubbling brook.

"The horses need water and rest. We're almost there, so this shall be a short break," said the soldier. He chuckled as Lamech gingerly dismounted and walked like a duck towards the refreshing water.

"Do you think we're being followed?" asked Obed as he walked alongside Kenan.

"Wasn't that the idea?" replied Kenan unaware that he, too, was being hunted.

"Yes, but how close do you guess they are?" asked the lad anxiously.

"If we're lucky, three or four hours," answered Kenan.

Mistaken Identity

"What if we aren't lucky?" pressed Obed.

"Let me worry about that," snapped Kenan. Obed swallowed hard as he and Kenan joined Lamech beside the cool water.

"What is your plan once we reach Belzeeb?" asked Lamech.

"We shall find a man named Reuben. His house is located at the end of town, which gives us the perfect vantage point to watch for Narok's men," answered Kenan.

"You've certainly thought this through, haven't you?" remarked Lamech with a smile. "We're indebted to you, Kenan. Someday your children and grandchildren shall speak of your bravery, and how it was you who helped save Nepthali from the clutches of evil." The physician's kind words reminded Kenan of those spoken by Aykin, and the soldier knew he was running out of time to figure out a way to spare the lives of his new friends. Lamech noticed the young man's somber expression and turmoil in his eyes.

"Is something troubling you, Kenan?" he asked.

"We just need to keep moving," answered Kenan sharply. He grabbed his water pouch and took long strides back to his horse. Lamech and Obed sensed his urgency and quickly finished refilling their water pouches before hurrying after him. Before mounting his horse, Kenan placed his ear to the ground and feared their pursuers were gaining on them.

******

Stefano and Julean tried not to worry about Mitzy as they traveled toward Nepthali. Roffius expected them to arrive before morning if all went well at their current pace. The wise captain knew this would be the only way to get his small army past the Bara soldiers sure to be standing watch. Roffius intended to lead the men around the back side of the outer wall where they could then enter the castle by way of a hidden ramp built into the wall. The ramp was constructed by one of Ithamar's ancestors during the Great Goblin War for the purpose of transporting horses and men in and out of the castle unseen. The ramp funneled into tunnels which led to a large underground room designed to serve as a wartime command center for the king. When they finally reached Lake Placia, Eliab and Roffius stopped their horses.

"This is where we part ways, Captain," said the rugged soldier.

"I shall leave a scout waiting in the large oak tree on the back side of the castle wall. When you arrive, blow this whistle so the scout knows it is you," instructed Roffius. He blew into the whistle before handing it to Eliab who easily imitated the call.

"Thank you, Captain. Have no fear, Queen Mitzy shall soon be seated on her rightful throne," said Eliab with confidence. "Make sure you don't forget about Aykin when you free your brother."

"Consider it done. See you soon, my friend," said Roffius as the two clasped hands. Eliab turned his horse around and started off with his men.

"Not if I see you first," he called over his shoulder.

Chapter 19

A Bride for Narok

Mitzy watched with dread as the castle became larger as they drew closer. She wondered how this smelly man could still think she was Prince Roffius after holding her for so long, but doubted her good fortune would continue once she was brought before Narok.

"Look there, Prince, you're almost home," snickered the Bara. "I can't wait for the reward I shall get after Narok sees you." Although Mitzy felt strongly that his reward would be nothing short of the guillotine, she wisely kept silent.

His horse was exhausted after running the entire journey with two riders, but the Bara soldier mercilessly beat the animal to ride on. When they finally arrived inside the inner courtyard, the horse collapsed. Mitzy and her captor fell to the ground, but the man quickly grabbed Mitzy by the arm and dragged her inside the castle. The soldier was told he could find Narok in the king's private quarters, so that is where they went.

When they entered the expansive room, Mitzy immediately recognized Nalia among the many handmaidens lined up along the far wall. Mitzy continued to scan the sea of familiar faces for Cora, but stopped when she was suddenly pushed from behind and fell to her knees.

"Sire," said her captor still blinded by dragon magic. Narok turned around visibly frustrated by the unexpected interruption.

"Whatever it is can wait; I'm busy choosing my new queen," he snapped. Narok turned back around to continue his inspection of the maidens.

"My apologies Sire, but I've got him," announced the grungy soldier careful to keep a firm grip on the nape of Mitzy's neck.

"Who?" asked Narok feeling more annoyed than curious.

"Prince Roffius," stated the soldier proudly. Narok immediately spun around to face them.

"Well, well; that *is* worthy of an interruption!" he proclaimed with a sly smile as he approached. "You've been quite a thorn in my side, Your Highness."

However, it was soon clear to Narok that the person crouched on the floor was far too small to be the formidable Prince Roffius. The cunning man drew his sword as a precaution, and stopped directly in front of the Bara and his prisoner. Mitzy's heart raced as she kept her head down knowing the inevitable was about to occur. Narok swiftly removed her large hat with the tip of his sword and a cascade of golden curls toppled to the floor. He stepped back in surprise, while Nalia and Cora gasped at seeing Mitzy. Although Narok hadn't expected to see Prince Roffius, he also never expected to see such a beautiful counterfeit. "Does this look like Prince Roffius to you?" he asked the Bara facetiously. No longer blinded by dragon magic, the stupefied man tried to explain.

"I don't know how this happened, Your Grace. This was the prince, I swear it. I saw the cloak with the Royal Crest and everything...," he stuttered. Narok loathed incompetence and this man was saturated in it.

"Where is this cloak, Soldier?" he asked. The Bara suddenly realized that he hadn't seen it since capturing the rider he believed was Prince Roffius.

"I'm not sure, but she was wearing it during the battle!" he exclaimed. "Our camp was attacked...and the prince was there!" But it was no use, his credibility had been lost and Narok saw him as nothing more than a desperate man trying to save his pathetic life.

"Get this imbecile out of my sight!" shouted Narok. The soldier repeated his claims of while being dragged away, but Narok heard none of them as he helped Mitzy to her feet.

"Is it true that you were wearing Prince Roffius' cloak?" he asked curiously while examining her from head to toe. The clever maiden quickly offered a plausible explanation.

"Yes, I took it in case we were separated to have something of value to sell, and that's exactly what happened during our escape," replied Mitzy casually. "I haven't seen Prince Roffius since that night, but I did hear him say he intended to go to Belzeeb." Narok was intrigued with her beauty, and her response.

"So, where is his cloak?" asked the ever-suspicious man with a raised brow.

"I lost it in the stream when that thug grabbed me," she replied. Mitzy was very convincing; however, Narok wasn't one to trust easily.

"And, what about his claims of an attack on their campsite?" he continued.

"It's true as well, Your Grace. After I was separated from Prince Roffius, I decided to travel south to get as far away from here as possible. Along the way, I came upon bandits who took me as their prisoner. I'd been with them for a few days when they attacked a group of Bara soldiers camped outside of Irvania," answered Mitzy. "I put the cloak on hoping no harm would come to me if it was believed I was the prince, and that's when that vile man grabbed me and brought me here." She had no idea that her quick thinking not only saved her life, but also the lives of Shem and Aykin. Narok eyed her carefully before breaking into a broad smile.

"You shall do just fine," he announced.

"For what?" she asked with trepidation.

"For my queen, of course," he stated.

Nalia heard this and blushed shamefully after recalling what she had been willing to do for that title. However, her jealousy was far greater than her shame, and Nalia was unwilling to accept defeat; even as she watched Narok reach out and gently caress one of Mitzy's golden curls. Mitzy looked away, but he grabbed hold of her face and turned it back towards him.

"Although I like a maiden with a little spunk, you shall learn your place," he said firmly. "What's your name?"

"Her name is Mitzy, Your Grace. She was one of Queen Ashter's personal attendants," offered Nalia spitefully. Mitzy glared at her, which Nalia found quite rewarding. The name jogged Narok's memory and he looked at Mitzy more closely.

"Mitzy? The daughter of Meridia?" he asked with increased curiosity. Mitzy said nothing, but the look on her face spoke volumes. "Well, well; you've certainly blossomed into quite a beauty! I'm surprised Prince Roffius let you out of his sight." Nalia's jealousy boiled over with that remark and the scorned maiden lashed out at Mitzy.

"I'd say it's more like Mitzy who'd never let Prince Roffius out of her sight, Sire, for she's been in love with him since they were children," stated Nalia plainly.

"Is that so?" asked Narok with a raised brow. Mitzy's cheeks flushed and Narok's boisterous laughter echoed off the stone walls. "You *are* in love with him! My poor dear, Prince Roffius would never notice a servant, even one as beautiful as you." Mitzy refused to remain silent and allow Nalia to win this little war of words.

"Sire, I should think that an educated man such as yourself can surely see past the jealous schemes of a maiden willing to say, or do, anything in order to become queen," she said coldly. Nalia blushed while Narok smiled slyly as both recalled their late night rendez-vous.

"Beautiful and brilliant, I like it! Guards, escort my future queen back to her chambers," ordered Narok. "Cora, see to it that she's cleaned up and ready to join me for dinner. I shan't have my bride looking, or smelling, like this. As for the rest of you...get out of my sight!" He spoke those last words directly to Nalia, and the humiliated maiden left with the others.

******

Cora looked down in silent shame as she and Mitzy were escorted to the Queen's Chamber between two large Bara soldiers. When they arrived, Mitzy saw the blood-stained floor and was reminded again of how lucky she had been to escape with her life.

"You may leave us now. I shall make sure to have her presentable by dinner," said Cora. Yet the soldiers remained unmoved, so she quickly thought of an excuse to get them out. "I suppose you could stay, that is if you think it would please Narok to discover that the two of you have spent more time alone with his future queen than he." The men hadn't thought of it that way and looked nervously at one another.

"We shall be waiting right outside the door," said one. Cora closed the door behind them and Mitzy immediately embraced her best friend.

"Oh, Cora, I'm so glad to see you!" she exclaimed.

"As am I, but can you ever forgive me, Mitzy?" pleaded Cora.

"Whatever for?" asked Mitzy in surprise.

"For not going back with you the night of the attack; you could've been killed!" exclaimed Cora through tears. "I shall never forgive myself, but if you could find it in your heart to forgive me, I would be eternally grateful."

"Of course I forgive you, but there's nothing to forgive! Had you returned, *you* would've been killed," replied Mitzy honestly. Cora's burden of guilt finally lifted as she hugged her friend.

"Thank you, Mitzy," she whispered. "But tell me, was everything you said true?"

"Not a word of it," replied Mitzy with a twinkle in her eye. "I had to lie because I knew Narok was told that Prince Roffius went to Belzeeb. In truth, I was with him in Irvania. We escaped from the castle through a hidden door." As Mitzy spoke, she frantically searched for the small vase. "Where is that vase?"

"What vase?" asked Cora.

"It was right here the other night. When King Shem moved it, a door within that wall opened up to a tunnel that we used for our escape and…." Mitzy stopped in mid-sentence when she saw the shattered pieces on the floor. Although Queen Ashter's decision to break the vase had prevented Bara soldiers from following after her children, it now trapped Mitzy and Cora. Mitzy picked up one of the pieces and her eyes welled up with tears as she looked at Cora.

"Was that the vase?" asked Cora slowly. Mitzy nodded and buried her face in her hands.

"Now we shall never get out," she sobbed.

"Fear not, Mitzy, we have each other," said Cora thoughtfully. Mitzy was thankful to be with Cora again, regardless of their dire circumstances.

"Oh, Cora, there's so much to tell you," she said while clinging to her best friend.

"You can tell me everything while I get you ready," answered Cora. Mitzy wiped away her tears.

"I don't want to dine with that man," she replied in disgust.

"I know, but you don't want to upset him, Mitzy. He's crazy," warned Cora. "Besides, Cook shall be there with you the entire time. Now, let's start with getting you out of these dreadful clothes."

Although Mitzy despised the idea of dining with Narok, she was more than willing to remove the soiled clothing which had served as her disguise. Cora followed Mitzy to the dressing screen next to the large tub.

"Just throw those into a pile and I shall have Cook burn them," said the redhead while crinkling her tiny nose.

"Nothing would please me more," replied Mitzy as she threw the soiled clothing over the dressing screen.

Cora filled the large tub with buckets of warm water while listening to Mitzy recount everything that happened since they last saw one another. Cora was astounded by what she heard; especially when Mitzy told her about the prince nearly kissing her friend just before she was abducted.

"How wonderful!" exclaimed Cora knowing Mitzy had been in love with Roffius since they were children. Once the tub was filled, Mitzy emerged from behind the dressing screen and stepped into the soothing water. Cora gasped at the sight of Mitzy's wound.

"Oh Mitzy, your shoulder!" she blurted out. "Is that from the arrow?"

"Yes, but it's nothing," said Mitzy trying to minimize the injury which had nearly killed her.

"If that's nothing, I'd hate to see something serious," answered Cora with a raised brow. Mitzy giggled as she sank into the soothing, warm water. Cora lifted Mitzy's dirty clothing with her fingertips and Mitzy noticed the dark circles beneath her friend's eyes.

"I was so worried about you, Cora. It must've been awful here with Narok and those horrible Bara," she noted. Cora stared into the distance as if seeing a vision she'd rather forget.

"It hasn't been all bad but, Mitzy, I was wrong for not believing you about Orpheus and the Dragon Scroll. During the attack, I saw the black dragon and realized you'd been right all along," confessed Cora. "What if Narok and the evil dragon succeed in taking over the kingdom? What shall happen to us?"

"Don't worry, Cora. Remember, Orpheus said that a hope which is pure and true shall not disappoint. We must believe that the good dragon shall return," answered Mitzy with confidence.

"I wish I could be more like you, Mitzy. You're so sure of what you believe in," said Cora with admiration. This was the greatest compliment Mitzy had ever received.

"I guess my hope comes from my father, and having it is like having a piece of him with me," replied Mitzy. Cora understood how important that was having lost both parents; however, she was suddenly reminded of her task as the sun sank between the hills.

"I must find something suitable for you to wear," she said in a tizzy. Mitzy finished bathing while Cora looked through the many exquisite gowns in Queen Ashter's wardrobe. She finally returned with a beautiful pale blue one to accent Mitzy's eyes.

"Try this one, I think it shall be perfect for you," suggested Cora. She held it up while Mitzy emerged from the large tub and wrapped a towel around herself.

"I could never wear that, Cora; it's the queen's!" insisted Mitzy.

"Yes, but the best way for you to help Roffius is to keep Narok distracted. And trust me, in this dress you shall be a distraction," giggled Cora.

Mitzy hesitated for a moment, but quickly decided her friend was right. She walked behind the dressing screen and Cora handed her the gown. Mitzy slipped it on and, to her surprise, found that it fit perfectly. When she came out from behind the screen, Cora could hardly believe her eyes.

"Mitzy, you look lovely," she said while clasping her hands over her mouth. The gown looked as if it had been made especially for her, and Mitzy looked every bit like the true queen she was. "Now, sit down so I can do something with that hair," continued Cora.

Mitzy sat on a cushioned stool and Cora got to work. She wove Mitzy's long, golden curls into an array of beautiful braids, and then twisted them into a bun atop Mitzy's head. When she finished, Cora stepped back to admire her work.

"You really do look like a queen," she announced proudly. Cora turned Mitzy around so she could see herself in the mirror. Mitzy hardly recognized the reflection looking back at her. She had never been so pampered, nor worn such fine clothing. Mitzy only wished it was Roffius she was dressing for rather than Narok, but her thoughts were interrupted by a knock on the door.

"Narok's ready for you, my lady," called one of the soldiers. Mitzy looked at Cora with dread.

"Don't worry; Cook shall be right there with you. In the meantime, I shall get word to the king about Roffius and Ithamar," said Cora as she gently squeezed Mitzy's hand.

"Thank you," replied Mitzy.

When Cora opened the chamber doors, the two Bara soldiers barely recognized Mitzy as the same young maiden they had escorted here earlier. The men stood in awe of her beauty as Mitzy held her head high and waited for them to lead the way to the dining hall. The soldiers finally composed themselves and started down the corridor while Cora slipped away.

******

Cora went straight to the bustling kitchen where servants were carrying trays of food for Narok's dinner with his bride-to-be. She looked for Cook and soon found him ladling soup. She snuck up behind the large man and tapped him on the shoulder. Startled, Cook dropped the ladle into the black pot.

"You nearly scared me to death!" he teased when he saw it was Cora.

"Cook, I've got some good news and some bad news," she said.

"I've had my fill of bad news lately, so please, tell me the good news first," he replied.

"The good news is that Mitzy's alive!" she exclaimed.

"That's wonderful news!" answered Cook. "What's the bad news?"

"She's here at the castle and Narok wants to marry her," winced Cora. Cook dropped the ladle again after having fished it out of the large pot.

"That's terrible news!" he exclaimed. I heard Nalia talking, but I didn't believe it."

"Well, it's true; I just helped Mitzy get cleaned up to dine with Narok," continued Cora.

Cook steadied himself against a butcher's block as Cora went on to tell the large man about Mitzy's ordeal since the night of the attack. He'd been sick with worry not knowing what had become of the maiden he loved like a daughter, and shuddered to think of her being forced to marry Narok.

"I must get word to the king, but I don't know how to get past the soldiers in the dungeon," continued Cora. Cook thought for a moment then got an idea.

"Take some bread and water with you and tell the soldiers it's for the king. He is being held in the last cell on the lowest level. Make haste, for surely the king shall know what to do," said Cook with confidence. "In the meantime, I shall keep an eye on Mitzy." Cora quickly gathered the items and started out for the dungeon.

The red-headed maiden made it easily past the soldiers with her basket of simple provisions, but nearly dropped them after a large rat scurried in front of her. From then on, Cora walked with trepidation along the darkened corridors to the last cell as Cook had instructed. From inside their cell Shem and Aykin heard footsteps approaching then heard a female's voice.

"I've brought you some provisions, Your Majesty," said Cora nervously while looking back over her shoulder.

"Just leave them on the ground," grumbled Aykin. He walked to the back of the cell without looking at her, yet Shem approached the door.

"Thank you, my lady, we greatly appreciate it," he said kindly. Shem immediately recognized the maiden with red hair as the daughter of his finest blacksmith, and one who often looked after Stefano and Julean.

"I know you; you're the blacksmith's daughter. I'm sorry for your loss," said Shem referring to her father's recent death. Cora stared in amazement that the ruler of Nepthali actually knew her.

"Yes I am, Your Majesty, and thank you," she replied. As she handed him the basket Cora whispered, "I have news."

"What did you say?" asked Shem. Aykin quickly turned around as Cora leaned against the bars.

"Your Majesty, I bring news of Prince Roffius. He and Ithamar are on their way here with a small army from Irvania. More men are expected to arrive from Haliel and Belzeeb before the morrow," she continued in a whisper. As Aykin stepped closer, he was struck by her beauty.

"Did you say they're on their way here?" he asked while trying not to stare into her mysterious green eyes.

"Yes," she replied.

"From where do you get such information, my lady?" inquired Shem. Cora stood on her tip-toes to get her face between the bars on the heavy door.

"It comes from Mitzy, one of the queen's handmaidens. She was traveling with them," she answered softly. Shem was stunned. The last time he saw Mitzy, she was running into the secret tunnel with his newborn son, Stefano, Julean, and Roffius.

"Mitzy is here?" asked the bewildered former king.

"Yes, she was captured by a Bara soldier after disguising herself as the prince to save his life. But, now Narok plans to marry her and make her his queen," explained Cora. "Mitzy's dining with him now, and if I

A Bride for Narok

may speak freely, Your Majesty; I fear what else he plans to do to her." Both Aykin and Shem understood her implication and agreed that her fears were warranted.

"We must help her," said Shem.

"We need to create a distraction to lure Narok away from her," added Aykin.

"What do you have in mind?" asked Shem. Aykin paused for a moment.

"How about a fight?" he asked.

"A fight?" repeated Shem with a raised brow.

"Yes, a fight between Narok's two prized prisoners would surely be enough to draw him away from Mitzy," explained Aykin as he paced around the cell.

"I think that might work!" exclaimed Shem.

"Do you think you can you help us?" Aykin asked turning to Cora.

"Of course, anything for Mitzy," she answered with resolve. Aykin was impressed with this brave maiden, and accurately guessed that she and Mitzy were very close.

"Good, if you can scream to get the guards' attention, we shall take care of things from there," continued Aykin.

"Yes, of course," replied Cora. Their eyes met in the dimly lit dungeon and she instantly felt a connection with the stranger looking back at her. Cora smiled shyly before unleashing the loudest, most blood-curdling scream either man had ever heard. Aykin and Shem were so shocked with her performance that they nearly missed their cue. Cora left for the kitchen through the darkened corridors as Bara soldiers arrived at the cell.

******

Mitzy exuded her royal heritage as she entered the grand dining hall; especially in contrast to her two oafish escorts. She saw Cook standing in the corner holding a tray of roasted boar behind Narok and immediately felt a sense of relief. Cook was struck by her beauty in a fatherly way, and gave her a reassuring wink. Meanwhile, Narok congratulated himself on such a fine choice for his new queen as he gawked at the beauty walking towards him. He stood in her presence, not realizing this was an honor due her as the true Queen of Nepthali.

"You look absolutely stunning, my dear, please be seated," he said motioning to the chair at the opposite end of the mahogany table. Mitzy carried herself with grace and elegance as she took her place at the table covered with enough food to feed an entire village. Nalia was among those present to serve, and savored in Mitzy's obvious misery. The jilted maiden purposely remained close to Narok in hopes of changing his mind about his selection of a queen.

"I know you must be starving, my dear, so please eat. I don't want my bride looking gaunt on our wedding day," he said.

"I shall never marry you," answered Mitzy coldly. Her crystal blue eyes shot daggers of hatred across the table.

"The fact that you think you have a choice in any of this amuses me. Besides, King Shem was kind enough to decorate the castle for the occasion," said Narok referring to the decorations hung in honor of the royal baby.

"Those aren't for you," she replied firmly. Narok looked up from his food clearly annoyed.

"Need I remind you, Mitzy, that as king you must do as I say," he warned. "And I've never met a woman, much less a maidservant, who didn't want to be a queen." Narok had no idea the extent of his ignorance as Nalia leaned in closer to refill his goblet. She was careful to keep her breasts at eye level, which Narok clearly enjoyed since the only things Mitzy had offered were protests. Mitzy, however, was repulsed by both Narok and Nalia's behavior, and found them to be a perfectly suited pair.

"If, to be a queen I must be your wife, then I shall decline wholeheartedly," stated Mitzy.

"As I said before, you haven't a choice in the matter. You shall feel differently after I kill King Shem and Prince Roffius," boasted Narok. At the mention of Roffius' name, Mitzy's expression changed from contempt to fear. Her reaction intrigued Narok and he left his seat to walk the distance of the table. He stopped at her side and towered over the rightful queen.

"My Dear, if you think you can continue to deny your feelings for Prince Roffius, think again. But, know this: the sooner you forget about him, the better. A man like that would never notice someone of your social standings, nor could he ever please a maiden like you," said Narok crudely. The evil man reached out to caress her cheek, but Mitzy turned away. Infuriated by her repeated rejections, Narok raised his hand to slap her. As he did, Cook stepped forward with a butcher's knife behind his back. Before either man could strike, a Bara soldier burst into the room.

"Your Grace, come quickly!" he exclaimed.

"What's the meaning of this interruption?" snapped Narok. The soldier stood in place trying to catch his breath.

"I'm sorry, Your Excellency, but you're needed in the dungeon at once," continued the man. Narok questioned the man's judgment on matters of urgency, but decided to gather more information before sending him away.

"Tell me, soldier, why must I go to the dungeon at once?" he inquired snobbishly.

"It's Aykin…and the king, Sire; they're going to kill each other!" insisted the man. Narok suddenly found himself in agreement with the soldier and started for the door. But before he left, Narok turned to address Mitzy.

"Don't worry, my dear, I shan't be long. And when I return, we shall pick up where we left off," he promised with a smug grin. "Get her back to the Queen's Chamber at once!"

The same two Bara soldiers who brought Mitzy to the dining room quickly appeared on either side of the maiden to escort her. As she passed by, Mitzy made eye contact with Nalia who looked away in shame.

******

Narok arrived at the last cell in the deepest part of the dungeon to the sounds of yelling and fists making contact with flesh. Bara soldiers inside the cell were trying to control the men, but it appeared to Narok that they were merely adding to the problem.

"Enough!" he shouted with a crack of his whip.

The chaos within the cell stopped momentarily until Aykin delivered another punch across the jaw of a Bara soldier. Narok raised his cat o'nine tails again, but this time he cracked it directly onto Aykin's back. Aykin immediately arched back in pain and stumbled to the ground.

"I said enough!" repeated Narok. He walked further into the cell and grabbed Aykin by the hair. "Now, as much as I don't wish for either of you to live, I can't have you kill each other just yet. So, it would appear that I must separate you." He released Aykin's hair and ordered for him to be moved to another cell. Two soldiers dragged Aykin away as blood seeped through his shirt. Shem was left alone with Narok.

"There's still time for you to surrender," he stated in a kingly manner. Narok took a step closer and spit in Shem's face.

"Let's see how much of your pride remains when I kill what's left of your family while you watch," threatened Narok. He abruptly turned on his heels and left the dreary cell. Shem wiped the spit from his cheek and waited until he was certain they had gone.

"Aykin, are you all right?" he called out.

"I'm fine. I barely felt it with the scars I already bear," he lied. "Besides, it was for the best."

"What do you mean? We're now in separate cells," replied Shem.

"Yes, but when they dragged me in here, I swiped the keys off one of the soldiers," said Aykin with a smile.

He jingled them and Shem thought it was the sweetest melody he'd ever heard as the clink-clink echoed throughout the dungeon corridor.

Chapter 20

Up to the Challenge

As the last rays of sunlight clung to the sky; Kenan, Lamech, and Obed finally arrived in Belzeeb. Kenan intended for Lamech and Obed to remain in the safety of Reuben's house while he took care of the men sent to kill them. He knew it wasn't much of a plan, but it was the best he could come up with. The horses seemed to sense the impending danger as they walked with trepidation down the quiet street. When they reached the last house, Kenan stopped.

"Here we are," he said. Kenan and the others dismounted, but he made it a point to be the first one to the door. He knocked three times before it was opened by a middle-aged man of short stature.

"Reuben!" exclaimed Kenan warmly. However, Reuben didn't return the friendly welcome.

"Who are you?" he asked harshly.

"I'm a friend of Mezrah; he sent me," answered Kenan.

"Mezrah never mentioned anything to me," said Reuben with a furrowed brow.

"We're here on official business from the king," interjected Obed enthusiastically.

"What the lad's means is, we need to come inside," corrected Kenan.

Reuben's expression remained suspicious as he allowed the strangers into his home. They followed him back to the small kitchen where Kenan quickly flattened himself against a wall next to the window before slowly pulling back the curtain. His heart raced as Kenan watched a trail of Bara soldiers ride into town.

"Listen to me," he whispered. "You're in great danger, so you must do as I say!"

"Have Mezrah's men arrived already?" asked Lamech seeing the dread in Kenan's eyes.

"Not just his men, Mezrah's here too!" exclaimed Obed as he looked out the window.

"Mezrah?" asked Kenan with surprise. He looked again and saw the man's unmistakable bulgy-eyes and unruly hair.

"How did they get here so quickly?" continued Lamech in disbelief. Kenan wondered the same thing, but he was more concerned with why Mezrah had come with them. The young soldier was now certain he'd been wrong to trust Mezrah, and realized with shame that his mistake could cost them all their lives. Just then, a voice called from outside.

"We know you're in there!" yelled a man. "Come out now and no one shall be hurt."

Up to the Challenge

Hearing this, Reuben became filled with terror and ran out the back door.

"What are we going to do?" asked Obed looking to Kenan. Surprisingly, it was Lamech who answered the lad's question.

"I may not know exactly what to do, but I can tell you what I'm not going to do," answered the old physician. "I shall not hide in fear while evil attempts to take over our beloved kingdom. Like my good friend Kleiko, I believe there is hope in the Dragon Scroll. And I, for one, am not going to give up on that hope without a fight!"

When he'd finished speaking, Lamech drew his sword and charged out the front door. Obed followed after him leaving Kenan alone in shock. He never imagined that he and Aykin would be fighting for the same cause, but now Kenan couldn't imagine things any other way. The young soldier followed after his new friends to face former comrades whose intent was to kill.

Kenan was up to the challenge and easily blocked the strike of the first man to engage him in a duel. Kenan masterfully countered and dodged while delivering solid strikes of his own. But as he fought, Kenan took note that Lamech was struggling against his opponent. The old physician wasn't accustomed to the art of sword fighting, and tried to remember moves from his training as a youth. He was clearly out-matched against the trained Bara, and in desperate need of help. Therefore, Kenan wasted no time plunging his sword through the midsection of his former comrade and hurried to assist Lamech. He approached Lamech's opponent from behind and pushed the man into the physician's sword. Lamech stared wide-eyed at the skewered soldier on his blade as Kenan smiled proudly. He was fighting for the right cause alongside the right people, and it felt good. Kenan looked to see how Obed was managing, and saw that the lad possessed natural skills which allowed for him to handily kill two Bara. Kenan was relieved to see the lad doing so well, but sensed someone behind him. He turned around to see the bulgy-eyed man with unruly hair.

"You double-crossing bastard!" yelled Kenan. "We were supposed to be partners!"

"Sorry to disappoint, but I don't intend to share the kingdom with anyone; especially not an ignorant fool like you!" replied Mezrah with disdain.

His comment infuriated Kenan and sent the young man lunging at Mezrah. The two master swordsmen engaged in a duel which took them down the streets of Belzeeb. Their boots kicked up dust that floated up like tiny stars into the fading rays of sunlight. Kenan delivered a series of powerful strikes which Mezrah blocked and countered with equal force, however, the older man felt himself tiring against his youthful opponent. Mezrah knew if he didn't finish Kenan off soon, he would be the one finished off. Therefore, the bulgy-eyed man cleverly lifted his sword to give the appearance of an overhead strike, and Kenan raised his sword with both hands to block it. But instead of an overhead strike, Mezrah removed the dagger hidden inside his vest and stabbed Kenan between the ribs. The young man cried out in pain and dropped his weapon. Like the scoundrel he was, Mezrah then plunged his sword through the unarmed man's abdomen. Kenan fell to his knees and slumped to the ground.

Up to the Challenge

As Obed and Lamech were rushing towards the two men, Mezrah rolled Kenan over with his boot and knelt down to ensure the young man was dead. When Mezrah drew close enough, Kenan removed the dagger from his ribcage and drove it into Mezrah's arm. The bulgy-eyed man fell back in disbelief just as Obed and Lamech arrived. Mezrah quickly staggered to his feet and took off running towards the stables.

"He's getting away!" cried Obed.

"Let him go!" shouted Lamech. He knelt beside Kenan and saw that his friend was mortally wounded.

"You can't save me," said Kenan with blood trickling from his mouth. "But, you can still save Aykin and the king."

"Kenan, there's something you must know," said Lamech. "Shem is not the true King of Nepthali."

"What?!" exclaimed Obed.

"I would've told you both sooner, but I was sworn to secrecy," answered Lamech.

"Does…Aykin…know?" asked Kenan between gasps for air.

"Yes," replied Lamech.

"And yet…he chose…to remain…in the dungeon?" continued Kenan.

"Much like you chose to help us here," answered Lamech thoughtfully.

"I've been such a fool…" managed Kenan as he struggled to breathe. "You must gather the men…hurry back…to the castle…" A tear rolled down his cheek as Kenan's hand dropped and he took his final breath. The secret of Kenan's betrayal died along with him, but he died a changed man.

"Find peace, my friend," whispered the physician. Obed hung his head as Lamech gently closed Kenan's eyes.

Obed and Lamech knew there was no time to mourn Kenan if they were to carry out their friend's dying request. Therefore, they quickly set out to gather every able man in Belzeeb before nightfall, and hopefully before the kingdom succumbed to the clutches of evil.

******

As darkness fell across the land, Roffius and Ithamar urged their horses ahead at top speed. Seeing the castle he'd known only as home was bittersweet for Roffius knowing it now served as a prison for both his brother and the maiden he loved.

"Are you all right, Captain?" asked Ithamar sensing Roffius' pensive mood.

"How can I be all right? My brother's in the dungeon, and who knows where Mitzy is, or what Narok has done to her!" snapped Roffius.

"Don't worry, Captain, we shall ensure their safety soon enough," replied Ithamar. Roffius wanted to believe the guard, but feared all hope was lost when he saw the black silhouette cross over the moon. He immediately pulled back on the reigns as both he and Ithamar brought their horses to a halt.

"It's Natas," said Roffius. "Mitzy's in grave danger; I must find her at once!" Ithamar knew what Roffius had in mind, and also knew he must be stopped.

"Easy, Captain, how is the dragon's presence any worse for Mitzy?" he asked.

"If Natas discovers Mitzy is the true Queen of Nepthali, he shan't hesitate to kill her to keep Orpheus from returning," replied Roffius with increasing anger and frustration.

"Captain, I know this is difficult considering your feelings for Mitzy. But, if we charge the castle before reinforcements arrive everyone you care about inside is sure to die. We must stick with the plan," urged Ithamar. Roffius wrestled with his emotions as he reluctantly agreed with the wise guard. However, the young captain promised to never again allow his duty to come before desire.

******

When Mitzy and her unkempt escorts reached the upstairs hallway in the south wing, she saw Cora walking towards them.

"Narok sent me to tend to My Lady until he returns," she explained. The soldiers recognized her from earlier, so allowed Cora to enter the Queen's Chamber with Mitzy. Once inside, Cora gave the soldiers a stern look which told them to remain outside as the red-headed maiden closed the door in their faces.

"Were you able to tell the king about Prince Roffius?" whispered Mitzy.

"Yes, he was especially happy to hear the news of Ithamar being with him. When the king heard your plight, he and his cellmate came up with a diversion to get Narok away from you," explained Cora.

Mitzy was humbled beyond words to hear that the king would do such a thing for a servant, not knowing of his true identity…or her own. She walked across the room and stepped onto the balcony which faced south towards Irvania. She wondered if Roffius was close, and remembered fondly the look he had in his eyes the last time she saw him. It was the same look her father had when he looked at her mother. She always dreamed of someday having a man look at her that way, and to have it be Roffius made Mitzy feel as if she could fly off the balcony. Cora joined her friend outside and recognized the faraway look in Mitzy's eyes.

"It may be forbidden, Mitzy, but I'm certain Prince Roffius is in love with you. Fear not, he shall come for you," she said.

"Narok thinks otherwise," replied Mitzy softly.

"That's only because he wants you for his queen. Narok's jealous because your heart belongs to a man whom he despises," stated Cora. Mitzy hoped her friend was right as she gazed at the brilliant glow from the moon's first light. The tranquil scene was disrupted, however, when Mitzy saw the same black silhouette fly across the moon as Roffius.

"Natas!" she exclaimed with terror.

Up to the Challenge

******

Roffius stopped the army of farmers and Royal Guards at the back side of the castle wall. He dismounted and gathered his most trusted companions.

"Eliab warned us of Bara soldiers being positioned along the hillside. Perez and Luklin, I want you to eliminate them," said Roffius. "Jesorath, you shall take some men to hide the horses and keep watch for Eliab and his men. Remember, listen for the whistle." Jesorath nodded his understanding and disappeared with Perez and Luklin to carry out their newest orders. "Ithamar, I need you to open up that ramp."

Ithamar smiled broadly and enlisted help from what remained of his squadron to open the hidden ramp. As they worked, Roffius noticed the soft glow of candlelight in the highest window of the castle's south tower. He wondered if it was lighting the darkness for Mitzy, and fought the urge to abandon their plan. If Roffius had known of Narok's intent to marry Mitzy, nothing could have stopped him from rushing off to find her.

"I hope Mitzy's all right," said Julean as he and Stefano approached their uncle.

"She can take care of herself," answered Roffius. He said that to console his nephew, and to convince himself.

"Yes, but she's injured," added Stefano.

"Have no fear, we shall help her; but we must first free your father," continued Roffius. "Just stay close to me."

It was becoming more difficult for Roffius to conceal his frustration over the situation he was helpless to change as he ushered the boys over to the other men surrounding Ithamar at the ramp. Ithamar lit an old torch to light the way through the dark tunnels. Stefano and Julean entered with trepidation, and happily complied with their uncle's orders to stay close. The small army filed through the underground tunnels like cockroaches until they finally reached a hollowed out room.

"Here we are," announced Ithamar. The weary men packed themselves into the room and along the tunnel.

"Ithamar, how do you know your way through these tunnels?" asked Stefano in amazement.

"I come from the family who built them," answered the guard proudly. "I used to play in them as a child."

"Do they go into the main castle?" pressed Stefano.

"Of course, in fact, it's very simple. If you take the same tunnel we just came from and stay to the right then veer to the left, and then right again; you shall eventually reach a door which opens into the kitchen," replied Ithamar matter-of-factly.

"Enough of this chatter, we're wasting valuable time," snapped Roffius impatiently. Just then Perez and Luklin returned with a report.

"We've taken care of the scouts along the hillside," said Perez with great pleasure.

"Well done," answered Roffius. "Now, I need the two of you to relieve Jesorath and send him here. He shall take charge of the men while Ithamar and I leave to free Shem and Aykin." Perez and Luklin bowed before leaving to find Jesorath.

Up to the Challenge

"We want to come," pleaded Stefano and Julean.

"No, it's too dangerous. Besides, you shall see your father soon enough," said Roffius. He and Ithamar turned and soon disappeared in the darkened tunnels.

******

Roffius was thankful for Ithamar's knowledge of the darkened corridors beneath the castle to get them to the dungeon.

"Here we are, Captain," the guard finally declared. "Be on the watch for Bara soldiers." The two men expected to encounter enemy soldiers once they reached the main dungeon, and they weren't disappointed.

"You take the one on the left, I'll take the ones on the right," whispered Ithamar as they came upon three unsuspecting men.

"Why don't you take the one on the left, and I shall take the ones on the right?" prodded Roffius.

"Age before beauty, Captain," said Ithamar with a wink.

He drew his sword and charged ahead. With their combined skill, and the element of surprise, the fight was very brief. Roffius and Ithamar stepped over the dead men and continued along the dungeon corridors with a sense of urgency to find Shem and Aykin. They were nearly at the last cell when Ithamar tripped over something and fell. Roffius managed to stop himself in time before meeting the same fate, and bent down to discover a pair of legs.

"I think it's a body," he whispered.

"But, we haven't killed anyone here yet," said the befuddled Ithamar as he stood.

"No…but we have," came a voice from the darkness.

"Who's there? Show yourself!" ordered Roffius. Ithamar stepped in front of his captain with sword drawn as a figure emerged from the shadows.

"Since when do you order me around, Brother?" asked Shem. Roffius felt like a lost child who'd been found upon seeing his oldest brother.

"Shem!" he exclaimed. The two heartily engulfed one another in a hug as neither could remember being happier to see the other.

"Easy," laughed Shem as he winced. Roffius pulled back and saw Shem's disfigured face from the beating that nearly killed him.

"Are you all right?" he asked with concern.

"I'm fine, just a little sore," answered Shem.

"I hate to break up this family reunion, but don't we have a war to wage?" asked Aykin as he stepped into view. Ithamar struggled to contain his emotions as Shem introduced them to the young man.

"Roffius and Ithamar, I'd like you to meet Aykin. He and Lamech saved my life," said Shem. "Aykin, this is my brother Roffius, and my most trusted guard Ithamar." Aykin extended his hand to Roffius first.

"I'm forever in your debt for all that you've done for my brother," said Roffius sincerely as their hands clasped.

Up to the Challenge

Aykin nodded humbly then turned to face his father's best friend. It was clear to both Ithamar and Aykin that each recognized the other, but neither knew what to say. Shem broke the awkward silence with a most pressing question.

"How are the boys?" he asked anxiously.

"They're here waiting with the others. You'd hardly recognize them. These past few days have turned them into young men," stated Roffius. "I'm certain if not for their help I wouldn't be here now."

"And the baby, how's the baby?" pressed Shem.

"Stefano named him Zerah, and he's safe in Irvania with Meridia," said Roffius. "But, there's something I must tell you." Shem saw the seriousness on his brother's face.

"What is it?" he asked.

"I've found the rightful heir," answered Roffius. Shem and Aykin looked at one another with surprise.

"Where?" asked Aykin.

"Who is he?" added Shem. Ithamar strategically positioned himself closer to Shem as Roffius continued.

"The heir is here in the castle, and…it's Mitzy," stated Roffius. Shem was thankful for Ithamar's steady hand as the former king stepped back in shock.

"That's unbelievable," he whispered. Shem never considered the possibility of the rightful heir being a servant, let alone a female. "Then we shall find Mitzy and restore her to her rightful place upon the throne. But, to do so we need my sword and the Dragon Scroll. Do you still have them?"

"Not exactly," replied Ro sheepishly.

"What do you mean?" asked Shem with a furrowed brow.

"In Irvania, I unrolled the Dragon Scroll while your sword was beside it," explained Roffius as he removed the sword from his scabbard. "I believe Orpheus transformed it into this." Aykin and Shem were in awe as they looked at the masterfully crafted weapon. Roffius extended the sword to his brother, but Shem refused it.

"Orpheus made this for you, Roffius. Don't you see? Kleiko was right! Our family has a purpose, and Orpheus chose you to save the royal bloodline," he said firmly. Roffius disagreed, but returned the sword to his scabbard for now.

"I've had enough of this lousy place, let's go!" exclaimed Aykin. Roffius and Shem started down the corridor, but Ithamar grabbed hold of Aykin's arm to stop him.

"Aykin, wait, there's something I must tell you," said the troubled guard.

"What is it?" asked Aykin. Ithamar took a deep breath before releasing his grip.

"I know you're the son of Uriah. In fact, I've known since the day I threw you and Narok in the dungeon," he confessed. "I vowed to find you twelve years ago but failed. Because of my failure, you ended up with scum like the Bara. Can you ever forgive me?" The torment in

Ithamar's eyes reminded Aykin of the hatred he had harbored in his heart for so many years. But, like Kenan, Aykin now realized how foolish he'd been.

"Ithamar, I'm the only one to blame for the choices I've made," he said honestly.

"Perhaps, but I recognized you and did nothing. I was so ashamed of who I thought you'd become that I turned my back on the only living son of my best friend," admitted Ithamar. Aykin placed his hand upon the guard's broad shoulder.

"Ithamar, it is because of you that I remembered who I really am, and where I come from. As I see it, you saved me," replied Aykin sincerely. "And I'm not the only living son of Uriah." Ithamar was finally freed from his burden of guilt, but looked at Aykin in disbelief.

"What do you mean?" he asked in shock.

"Obed, my brother, is alive and with Lamech and Kenan in Belzeeb," answered Aykin.

"Unbelievable," Ithamar whispered. He could hardly fathom Aykin not being the derelict he had assumed, let alone that Uriah's youngest son was alive as well. Ithamar felt like a proud parent and quickly wiped his eyes before Aykin saw the tears forming. "Now let's show that pompous miscreant Narok what happens to someone who tries to take something that doesn't belong to him!" exclaimed the guard. With a restored relationship, and strengthened resolve, Ithamar and Aykin hurried away to catch up with Shem and Roffius.

"So tell me, how did the two of you get out of your cell?" asked Roffius.

"It's a long story, but in a nutshell I swiped the keys from a Bara after pretending to kill your brother," replied Aykin casually. Roffius stopped in his tracks.

"You did what?!" he exclaimed with an angry glare at Aykin.

"Easy, Roffius," laughed Shem at his protective little brother. "I shall explain later."

"You certainly shall," answered Roffius while continuing to eye Aykin suspiciously.

"Come now, we must get back to the others," said Ithamar knowing that time was of the essence.

"Is Eliab among them?" asked Aykin.

"No, he has yet to return from Haliel with more men. He anticipated arriving before dawn," explained Roffius.

"What about Obed, Lamech, and Kenan?" asked Shem.

"They, too, should arrive before sunrise," answered Ithamar as the men continued along the dungeon corridors. They soon reached the first Bara soldiers Ithamar and Roffius killed.

"Is this your doing?" asked Aykin while stepping over the bodies.

"I had a little help," quipped Ithamar.

"A little?" answered Roffius with a raised brow.

Up to the Challenge

******

They returned to the command center greater in number than with what they had started after freeing the Royal Guards imprisoned for refusing to join Narok's evil scheme. Roffius knew they would add much needed skill and experience to the untrained farmers. A surge of energy filled the air when the men caught sight of the man they believed was their king. Jesorath made his way through the cluster gathered around his old friend and bowed in respect before Shem.

"Your Highness, it does my heart good to see you," he said holding back tears of joy.

"Please rise, Jesorath. You know I'm no longer worthy of such honor," replied Shem as the two clasped hands. Their reunion was abruptly interrupted by the boisterous shouts of Stefano and Julean.

"Father, Father!" yelled Stefano rushing towards him.

"My boys, I thought I'd lost you!" cried Shem as he embraced the two.

"We were afraid we'd never see you again!" exclaimed Julean.

"What happened to you?" asked Shem seeing Julean's splint.

"I broke my arm on a tree," answered Julean proudly. Shem looked at Roffius who offered a shrug of his shoulders in reply.

"Father, Mitzy's the true queen and she needs our help," continued Stefano.

"Yes, I know, my son," said Shem.

"Last night we created a diversion to get Narok away from her," explained Aykin.

"What do you mean?" asked Roffius sharply.

"Last night, Narok had some unscrupulous plans for Mitzy, so we stepped in to help," continued Aykin. "She's safe in the Queen's Chamber until the wedding." Shem winced before looking nervously at his brother.

"Wedding?" pressed Roffius with a furrowed brow.

"Yes, Narok has chosen Mitzy to be his queen. They are to be wed tomorrow," stated Aykin. He never expected the ardent response his answer would invoke.

"WHAT?!" exclaimed Stefano and Julean in unison.

"I must get her, now!" shouted Roffius. He turned to leave, but Shem immediately grabbed hold of his brother's arm.

"Roffius, you know as well as I that the best way to help Mitzy is to defeat Narok and his army," pleaded Shem. "If you go after her now, it shall only draw unnecessary, and potentially dangerous, attention to her." Roffius heard his brother, but he was too infuriated by what Aykin had said to listen. He promised himself to never again allow his duties to come before his desire, but old habits were hard to break; especially when Roffius saw the fear in Shem's eyes.

"Of course, Brother, you're right," he replied in a manner befitting of his title Captain of the Royal Guards.

"Good, now I need the three of you to get these men ready," ordered Shem.

Stefano and Julean were stunned to hear that no one was going after Mitzy, and it was clear that they were her only hope of being rescued. Once Roffius and the others were preoccupied with training the men, Stefano and Julean quietly slipped away.

The boys traveled through the tunnels with anticipation on their newest quest to rescue Mitzy.

"Are you sure you remember everything Ithamar said?" Julean asked his cousin.

"Of course I do," replied Stefano confidently.

"Shouldn't we have turned left back there?" continued Julean.

"No, he said to take a right," snapped Stefano. Yet, when the boys reached a fork in the path, Stefano's confidence waivered.

"I don't remember Ithamar saying anything about this," stated Julean as his voice quivered. Stefano took a deep breath before deciding to go right. After a short distance, the boys came to a door just as Ithamar had said.

"Go ahead and open it," urged Julean. Stefano rolled his eyes at his fearful cousin and slowly opened the door. When he did, they sighed with relief upon seeing the familiar kitchen strewn with fresh fruits, vegetables, and a crackling fire beneath Cook's large black pot.

"We made it!" declared Stefano.

The boys wisely checked for any Bara soldiers before entering, but found the kitchen empty. As they passed a long table Cook used for cooling bread, Julean noticed three fresh loaves.

"Bread!" he exclaimed.

"Wait!" scolded Stefano. He snatched the loaf just before Julean took a large bite.

"Hey, what are you doing?" complained Julean. "I'm starving!"

"We're going to need this for the soldiers who are guarding Mitzy," said Stefano. He gathered the other loaves and tucked them under his arm.

"What soldiers?" asked his perplexed cousin.

"Doesn't every prisoner have guards?" continued Stefano. Julean uncharacteristically had no response, and decided it was due to his hunger. Although he'd been denied the scrumptious bread, Julean managed to grab two apples on their way out. He bit into one, and shoved the other into his pocket.

******

Down in the command center while observing the men, Shem realized that he hadn't seen the boys in a while. He looked around, but didn't see them anywhere.

"Where are the boys," Shem asked Roffius.

"Most likely with Jesorath," replied the young captain absent-mindedly. Shem nodded in agreement and dismissed any concerns as he returned his attention to preparing the grossly untrained men for battle.

Dragon Scroll of Nepthali

Chapter 21

United Resolve

Eliab and his men saw the castle in the distance as the first hints of daylight touched the horizon. They were an impressive sight at nearly four hundred strong, although it had been more difficult than Eliab expected to find men willing to fight against fellow comrades.

"Hurry! We must reach the castle before daybreak!" he shouted. Eliab urged them on feeling anxious to see Aykin and Shem freed from their cell. He also hoped that Roffius and Ithamar had been able to prepare the army of unconventional farmers for another battle.

Perez and Luklin were patiently waiting in the large oak tree for Eliab's arrival. When they saw the impressive number of Bara riders approaching, Ithamar's most trusted guards made ready.

"I sure hope that's Eliab," Perez said as Luklin nodded. Moments later, he and Luklin heard the whistle.

"That's the signal!" exclaimed Luklin. He and Perez raced down the tree and hurried through the tunnel to alert Shem.

******

Armed with three loaves of bread, Stefano and Julean traveled through the familiar passageway from the kitchen to the main hallway of the south wing. At the tip of the south wing, Stefano and Julean crouched low and peered around a corner to see the large Bara soldiers posted in front of the door to the Queen's Chamber just as Stefano had predicted.

"How'd you know?" whispered Julean in amazement.

"Ssshhh! Follow me," answered Stefano. He walked confidently into the hallway followed by his not-so-confident cousin.

"What are you little brats doing here?" asked the larger of the two soldiers upon seeing the boys. Stefano quickly pulled out the loaves of fresh bread from under his arm.

"We've brought you some bread," he answered. The soldiers were hungry, but also suspicious.

"Who sent you?" asked the other soldier.

"My Father and Uncle," said Stefano. With that, he delivered a swift kick to the man's shin then stomped on his foot. Julean did the same to the other soldier, and then hit each in the face with his wooden cast. They never knew what hit them as the men fell to the floor face-first.

"Nice work!" exclaimed Stefano.

"Thanks!" replied Julean with a broad smile.

The boys dragged the unconscious men around the corner where Stefano took their swords. He and Julean then ran back to the Queen's Chamber and burst through the door. They each thought Mitzy looked like an angel lying on the bed in the lovely gown from the night before as early rays of sunlight shone upon her. Cora was asleep in the chair beside the bed, but both awoke when Julean accidentally slammed the door. Her look of terror turned to relief when Mitzy recognized the boys. Stefano dropped the stolen swords from the soldiers as he and Julean rushed to her side. The three embraced, laughed, and spoke over one another with excitement.

"Mitzy, we found you!" exclaimed Julean.

"We're here to rescue you!" declared Stefano.

"Such valiant young men!" laughed Mitzy. Cora watched from a distance knowing the special bond these three shared, but Mitzy quickly included her best friend.

"Your Majesties, look who else is here," she said still unaware of their true identity as she pointed to Cora.

"Your Highness'," said Cora straightening her bonnet before offering a respectful curtsy.

"Hello, Cora," they replied politely.

"Mitzy, you look beautiful!" proclaimed Julean as his attention returned to Mitzy.

"I've never seen you like this," added Stefano. She blushed and immediately apologized for wearing his mother's gown.

"Stefano, I'm so sorry; I had to wear this for Narok," she explained.

"It's all right, Mitzy, it looks beautiful on you," said the boy sincerely.

"Are the others here?" asked Mitzy referring to Roffius.

"They're in a secret command center waiting for reinforcements to arrive from Haliel and Belzeeb," answered Stefano. Mitzy was glad to hear they had made it safely, but was disappointed to have Stefano and Julean come for her instead of Roffius. She decided Narok was right; it was foolish for her to think a prince would see her as anything but a servant.

"We've got to get you out of here," urged Stefano. He grabbed hold of Mitzy's hand and pulled her towards the door.

******

Mezrah's hair flapped wildly in the wind as his horse sped back to the castle. His shoulder burned from the wound inflicted by Kenan, but the bulgy-eyed man was certain Narok would inflict far greater pain if he discovered that Mezrah had failed. Therefore, Mezrah completed the details of his plausible, albeit false, story to tell Narok as he entered the inner courtyard. The older man sprung from his saddle with surprising zeal before rushing into the castle. He held his arm close to his side while running directly to the Throne Room. When he arrived, Mezrah found Narok talking with a squadron of Bara soldiers. Narok looked as exhausted as he felt after a sleepless night thanks to Shem and Aykin.

"I shan't tolerate another incident like the one we just had with our special prisoners, do you hear me?!" he

United Resolve

barked. Narok stopped his tirade after noticing his uncle stumbling towards them with blood seeping through his shirt.

"Uncle, what happened?" asked Narok sounding more annoyed than concerned.

"We were ambushed," replied Mezrah.

"What do you mean?" asked Narok.

"Obed lied and led us straight into a trap. I barely escaped with my life to warn you about an army from Belzeeb headed here!" exclaimed Mezrah. He breathed heavily as Narok gave him the same icy stare as Lott used to while pondering his uncle's account.

"Is that so?" asked Narok with a raised brow.

"Yes," answered Mezrah trying to steady his voice. He felt tiny beads of sweat slide down his face as the seconds passed like hours until Narok spoke again.

"Prepare the men at once, and check on my future bride! If those fools are coming, we shall be ready!" he shouted. "Mezrah, come with me to the dungeon. We must check on our special guests." Mezrah sighed with relief and followed after his nephew to the dungeon while Bara soldiers hurried away to check on Mitzy.

******

Stefano placed his hand on the door handle, but Mitzy stopped him from opening it when she heard footsteps and voices in the hallway.

"Check on the girl!" shouted a man.

"Stefano, Julean; hide under the bed!" cried Mitzy. The boys grabbed the swords then slid under the large bed while Mitzy lay down and Cora returned to her place in the chair. Seconds later, a large Bara soldier burst into the room. Mitzy tried to steady her breathing as she pretended to be asleep. Cora acted as if she had been startled awake and sat upright.

"Just what do you think you're doing barging in here like this?" she asked sternly.

"Excuse me, my lady, but I'm here to check on the maiden. The guards posted in the hallway said they were attacked," answered the soldier while looking around the room.

"Attacked? Who would do such a thing to such strong men?" asked Cora facetiously.

"Umm, they said it was two boys, my lady," he replied sheepishly.

"Boys?" repeated Cora.

"Yes, that's the report," answered the soldier with flushed cheeks.

"Well, as you can see there are no boys in here. However, if I see any dangerous looking children, I shall be sure to let you know," continued Cora with an impish grin. The large man looked around the room once more before being satisfied that no one else was there. As soon as he left, Cora walked to the window and saw hundreds of Bara soldiers running through the courtyard. "He's gone, but I have a feeling more shall come," she said nervously. Mitzy joined her friend at the window where

United Resolve

they were soon joined by the boys. They watched in horror as the Bara soldiers gathered into battle formations.

"It isn't safe for the two of you here," said Mitzy. "You shouldn't have come." As they watched more soldiers file into the courtyard, the boys silently agreed.

******

Believing the farmers were as ready as they would ever be, Shem gathered the men to tell them he wasn't their king. Although it would be difficult, the wise former ruler knew he owed them the truth before going into battle. He cleared his throat to begin, but was interrupted by Perez and Luklin entering with good news.

"Your Majesty! Eliab and nearly four hundred men have arrived from Haliel," reported Luklin. Shem smiled and thought it best to postpone his announcement until all the men were gathered.

"Excellent! Ithamar, please show our comrades in," said the former king.

"With pleasure," replied Ithamar. As he started to leave, another scout burst in with more news.

"Your Majesty, a lone rider who appears to be injured has just entered the courtyard," reported the man.

"Did you recognize who it was?" asked Ithamar.

"No, but he had bulgy eyes," answered the guard. "And the Bara soldiers are gathering into battle formations!" Ithamar, Shem, and Roffius knew at once that the rider was Mezrah.

"It's time," said Roffius as the others nodded in agreement.

"We can only hope the men from Belzeeb arrive soon now that we've lost the element of surprise," stated Shem.

******

While Eliab and the men from Haliel waited for Ithamar to open the hidden ramp, the black dragon suddenly flew overhead. Natas had seen the soldiers on horseback and came to investigate. To their good fortune, the beast recognized them as Bara soldiers and continued on his way. Just then, the hidden ramp opened and Ithamar, Perez, and Luklin emerged.

"Did you see that beast?!" exclaimed Eliab.

"The only beast I see is the one in front of me," answered Ithamar in jest.

"I'm serious! We just saw a dragon!" continued the terrified soldier. Ithamar looked up and saw the ominous black figure in the distance.

"We'd better get you inside," he said sternly.

Eliab and his men followed Ithamar through the safety of the tunnels until they reached the room already filled beyond capacity with the farmers from Irvania.

"Nice of you to show up," said Roffius approaching Eliab with a broad smile.

"After seeing that dragon, I was beginning to wonder if this was worth it. But, I didn't want this lug to get all the credit for a victory," replied Eliab. He and Roffius clasped hands while Eliab nudged Ithamar in jest. Aykin came up from behind and enveloped the man who was like a brother in a bear hug.

"It's good to see you in one piece, Eliab," he said heartily.

"And you as well," answered Eliab suddenly overcome with emotion. He wiped his eyes, and then bowed in respect to the former king who'd been willing to trust two Bara soldiers.

"Please, no formalities, at least not for me. Thank you for bringing these men; they're invaluable to us," said Shem humbly. "Aykin and Roffius shall brief you."

Eliab was pleased to hear that he and Ithamar would be leading the charge from the ground, while Luklin and Perez were to take out the archers. Jesorath was given command of the squadrons to secure the courtyard; while Roffius, Shem, and Aykin had the privilege of eliminating Narok and Mezrah. Once everyone was briefed on his duties, Shem gathered the men to tell them that he was not the rightful king. His voice projected throughout the natural acoustics of the room and tunnels as the men from Irvania and Haliel packed in like sardines.

"Gentlemen, I wish to thank each of you for joining in this most noble cause to stop an evil which threatens to destroy our kingdom; but before we begin our attack, there is something I must tell you," said Shem. Eliab looked nervously at Ithamar thinking Shem should wait to reveal his identity until after the attack. Shem continued, "Many unexpected things have occurred as of late, but none having had a greater impact than a truth which I learned about myself." Shem paused briefly and said with a sigh, "I am not your king, which means that none of you is bound to follow me." Whispers and mumblings immediately erupted in the command center and throughout the tunnels.

"If you're not the king, who is?" shouted a man. Other cries followed demanding an answer. Shem raised his hands for silence and the men quieted down.

"Long ago, the wise dragon Orpheus devised a plan to protect the Royal Family from the evil dragon Natas when the time came for the beast to awaken. I have come to discover that the fullness of this plan was also hidden from the people," stated Shem. More restless chatter spread amongst the men, but Shem was quick to continue before he lost control of the crowd. "I shall not pretend to know why Orpheus did this, nor do I fully understand it. Perhaps the wise dragon knows all too well the weakness of a man's heart, or how we are prone to wander even from truth. Whatever it may be, I know that Orpheus didn't leave us without hope. He left us the Dragon Scroll which speaks of hope in his return and better days for our kingdom. I, for one, refuse to give up on this hope without a fight. I believe that if we are united in our resolve, WE SHALL OVERCOME!" shouted Shem. Ithamar wasted no time in his reply.

"It matters not to me the title of a man, but rather the character. I would go to the ends of the earth for you," he pledged.

"You know how I feel, Brother," said Roffius with equal resolve.

A single cry of support floated up from the depths of the tunnel, joined by others until the cries were so loud that the foundation of the castle shook with their vibrations. The army comprised of Royal Guards and farmers raised their swords in wholehearted support of a man whom they were willing to die for, even knowing he was no longer their king.

******

Narok and Mezrah reached the mouth of the dungeon when the cries of support beneath them caused the floor to shake.

"What was that?" asked Mezrah as his bulgy eyes widened.

"I'm not sure, but it can't be good," answered Narok. When they rounded the next corner, they came upon the dead Bara soldiers.

"NO!" shouted Narok. "Quickly, back to the castle!" Narok shoved his uncle out of the way and sprinted through the darkened corridors.

When Narok and Mezrah emerged from the dungeon, they found the courtyard had transformed into a battlefield between evil Bara soldiers, men from Haliel, Irvanian farmers, and Royal Guards. Narok's face lost all its color when he saw Ithamar and Jesorath in the middle of the fighting. He understood that their presence meant Mitzy had lied and Prince Roffius had been in Irvania. Narok was irate as he looked for the elusive prince, but didn't see him anywhere. He suddenly remembered what Nalia had said about Mitzy being in love with Roffius and wondered if perhaps the young prince shared in those feelings.

Dragon Scroll of Nepthali

"Come with me to the Queen's Chamber!" Narok yelled to his uncle.

******

Inside the castle, Roffius ran with Shem and Aykin to the Throne Room hoping to find Narok, but it was empty.

"Where did you say Mitzy was being held?" Roffius asked Aykin with a look of panic.

"In the Queen's Chamber," replied Aykin. He and Shem instinctively knew what Roffius was thinking as they followed after him in a desperate race to find Mitzy.

******

Narok and Mezrah shoved aside the guards posted in front of the Queen's Chamber and burst inside to find Mitzy, Cora, Stefano, and Julean staring out the window. Although Narok hadn't seen the boys since they were infants, he could easily see each one's resemblance to his parents when they turned around in surprise. Stefano had his mother's strikingly good looks, and Julean was a pudgy version of his father Jeru. Their unexpected presence was enough to shift Narok's anger away from Mitzy for lying to him about Prince Roffius being in Belzeeb, at least for now.

"Well, well, well…look who we have here," sneered the evil man as he approached the boys. They wisely passed their swords to Cora before Narok stopped in front of Stefano and slapped the boy across the face without warning. Cora released a deafening scream as Stefano staggered to remain on his feet. Mitzy immediately stepped between Narok and the boys.

"Get out of my way, wench!" he exclaimed while pushing Mitzy to the floor. "Uncle, take these royal brats!" Mezrah firmly took hold of the boys as Narok turned his wrath towards Cora. He raised his hand to strike, but Mitzy grabbed hold of his leg and cried out.

"Wait! Please don't hurt them," she begged. "I'll do anything, just let them go!"

"Don't trifle with me, wench!" snapped Narok remembering his anger at her. "I just saw Ithamar and Jesorath in the courtyard, which tells me that you lied about Prince Roffius being in Belzeeb!" Desperate to save her friends, Mitzy clung to his leg and thought of a diversion.

"Forgive me, Your Grace," she cried. "I am guilty of deceit, but not the one you are accusing me!" Cora wondered what her friend was up to until she saw Mitzy nod. The two had practiced this scenario countless times in the blacksmith shop, and Cora knew exactly what to do without Mitzy having to say another word.

"Tell me then, what is this deceit for which you are guilty?" asked Narok curiously. Her beauty had a calming effect on his burning anger until the only thing he burned with was desire. Narok nearly lost all control while watching Mitzy's voluptuous lips move with her response, and never suspected her to play him so cleverly.

"I lied when I said I could never marry a man like you," she replied seductively.

"Now that's more like it, my dear, I knew you'd see things my way," he said with a wanton grin. Narok then offered Mitzy his hand and helped the maiden to her feet.

Dragon Scroll of Nepthali

Once Mitzy was standing, Cora tossed one of the swords into the air, while the redhead turned the other on Mezrah. Mitzy spun around and caught the weapon with the speed and agility of a master swordsman. Their countless hours of preparation left Narok and Mezrah staring with disbelief at the tips of blades held by maidservants.

"Release Prince Stefano and Prince Julean; and don't move!" ordered Mitzy.

"Well, this is a surprise," snickered Narok. "Handmaidens playing with swords." Finding no humor in his smug comment, Mitzy lowered her blade to Narok's loins.

"Would you care to see how we play?" she asked with a raised brow. Narok scowled at Mitzy for the precarious position he now found himself in, nevertheless, doubted either maiden knew more than how to hold the weapon. With this assumption, Narok foolishly reached for his whip, so Mitzy slashed the side of his face. "I said don't move!" she repeated firmly.

"You do know how to use it…," he said dumbfounded as blood trickled down his cheek.

"GUARDS!" shouted Mezrah tired of his nephew's obvious lack of focus.

The grungy soldiers in the hallway rushed in to find Narok bleeding and two handmaidens wielding swords. Mezrah held firmly to Stefano and Julean while Cora and Mitzy made ready to face their assailants. The Bara soldiers smirked thinking this would be the shortest duel of their lives but, like Narok, soon discovered the error of their assumption. The beautiful maidens possessed skills of master swordsmen, and each killed her first opponent. However, because of a mistimed step by Cora, she was soon weaponless and in the grasp of an angry Bara.

Narok watched with awe as Mitzy continued to fight against two highly trained soldiers single-handedly. He'd never seen someone brandish a sword with such ease, let alone that someone be a woman. Her hair toppled down from the elaborate braid into perfect ringlets falling past her waist as she sidestepped and dodged one strike after another. Narok's desire for Mitzy finally escalated beyond the lustful man's control, and he grabbed a sword from one of the soldiers. With it he backed Mitzy into a corner where one Bara grabbed her sword while another held her against the wall. Narok panted like a dog in heat as he approached the lovely maiden.

"My, that was impressive! I dare say I shan't cross you once we are wed!" he mocked.

"I shall never marry you!" exclaimed Mitzy adamantly.

"And I shan't tolerate this insolent behavior any longer," he said with disdain. Narok raised his hand and struck Mitzy across the face with all the force of his built up anger and desire. Cora screamed as her best friend fell to the floor. The boys tried to break free, but they were easily restrained by Mezrah even in his weakened state.

"We've got to do something," whispered Stefano. Julean thought for a moment before remembering the apple in his pocket. He slyly removed it and passed it to Stefano. His cousin took the apple and glanced down to signal their next move. In unison, the boys stomped on

Mezrah's feet causing the already wounded man to release his grip. Stefano then hurled the apple at Narok as the evil man yanked Mitzy to her feet and pulled her close to steal a kiss. The apple struck Narok in the back of his head just in time and he spun around with a look of pure hatred.

"Take them to the dungeon!!!" he shouted. Bara soldiers grabbed hold of the boys and dragged them across the room while the one holding Cora tightened his grip as she tried to break free.

"No! Please don't harm them," pleaded Mitzy reaching out to Narok.

"It's time you develop a greater understanding of what it means when I say that I'm not to be trifled with," he snapped and pushed her away. Another soldier grabbed hold of Mitzy as Narok walked alongside the Bara soldiers dragging the boys. "I'm going to enjoy killing you more than I had expected," he vowed.

******

Outside in the courtyard, a shower of deadly arrows from the well-trained Bara archers atop the castle wall pierced through Royal Guards and men from Haliel and Irvania. Ithamar knew they must be stopped if any advancements were to occur below.

"Luklin, Perez; get up there and stop those blasted archers!" he shouted. The trusted guards began to scale the wall, but a squadron of Bara soldiers followed after them. Seeing they were in trouble, Eliab rushed to their aid with Jesorath and Ithamar.

"We've got to give them a chance to reach the top!" shouted Eliab. Jesorath immediately grabbed an enemy soldier by the foot and pulled him down. The large blacksmith then swung the man around like a rag doll and threw him into the other soldiers scaling the wall after Perez and Luklin. The would-be pursuers toppled down in a heap of bodies at the base of the wall.

"I'm glad he's on our side!" he exclaimed a wide-eyed Eliab.

Because of Jesorath's handiwork, Perez and Luklin reached the top of the castle wall and managed to slow the deadly shower of arrows. Confusion broke out below after the Bara soldiers realized that Eliab and other comrades were fighting against them. But the momentum gained from this confusion was soon lost when Natas' horrifying image re-appeared. The dragon shot deadly blasts of fire with flawless aim. Ithamar watched with dismay as the entire courtyard looked to be burning. Defeat for the valiant men seemed eminent, even if the reinforcements from Belzeeb arrived, now that the black dragon had returned.

******

Roffius, Aykin, and Shem followed Cora's screams down the hallway of the south wing with increased urgency. Aykin would recognize the beautiful redhead's scream anywhere, especially after her impressive sample the night before in the dungeon. His attraction to the mysterious maiden continued to grow, and he found the thought of her being in danger very unsettling. For Shem, the scene was eerily similar to the night of the attack with his wife screaming while in the throngs of labor. He felt a fresh ache in his broken heart knowing this would be the first time he entered her chambers and Ashter wouldn't be there.

"We must hurry!" shouted Roffius after hearing another scream.

"Wait! We can't just storm in there; we need a plan," warned Shem as he grabbed hold of Roffius' arm. Roffius turned around and easily broke free from his brother's grip.

"Not this time, Shem! My entire life I've done things for the sake of duty, and do you know what's happened because of it? The maiden I love is being held captive by a madman who thinks he's going to marry her!" exclaimed Roffius. "You can plan all you want, but I'm following my heart!" Shem stood in shock from his brother's surprising revelation as Roffius turned and ran down the hallway.

"So...I guess his plan is to act first and plan later?" asked Aykin in jest.

Shem furrowed his brow and hurried after his little brother. Rounding the next corner, they found Roffius with his sword drawn ready to face the oncoming squadron of Bara soldiers.

From inside the Queen's Chamber, Narok heard the commotion in the hallway and grabbed Mitzy before signaling for one of the soldiers to lead them out. However, the man quickly retreated back inside the room after seeing the formidable Captain of the Royal Guards in the hallway.

"It's Prince Roffius!" he exclaimed with terror.

"Block the door!" shouted Narok to Mezrah. Cora released another scream which was muffled when her captor covered her mouth and closed the door.

Roffius ran through the oncoming squadron of Bara soldiers and extended his arm to block the door before it shut, but he was too late. Aykin and Shem drew the fighting to themselves while Roffius remained fixed on his efforts to open the door. It was jammed and his heart raced as he heard more screams coming from the other side. Roffius rammed the door over and over with his shoulder, but it wouldn't budge.

"Shem!" he shouted. "I...can't... get...the door... open!" Shem sensed his brother's urgency and watched as Roffius repeatedly threw himself against the door.

"Aykin, can you help him?" called Shem as he struggled in a duel against two Bara soldiers. Aykin was also fighting two former comrades; however, the young man possessed far greater sword skills than the former king.

"I shall do what I can," he answered.

Aykin grabbed hold of one soldier by the shirt then kicked him into the other. The men were stunned just long enough for Aykin to help Roffius ram against the door. The force of both men working together caused the door to crash down and they tumbled to the floor inside the Queen's Chamber. Aykin got to his feet and looked at Roffius.

"You got this?" he asked.

"Like a rat has the plague," answered Roffius through clinched teeth. Aykin gave the captain a respectful nod before rushing back into the hallway to resume his fight.

"Miss me?" quipped Aykin to his dazed opponents.

Dragon Scroll of Nepthali

Chapter 22

Renewed Strength

Roffius sprang to his feet only to see Cora in the arms of a Bara soldier, and to his surprise, his nephews. He continued to scan the room until Roffius finally saw the one for whom he had come. Mitzy took his breath away in the beautiful pale blue gown with her golden ringlets cascading past her tiny waist. The only thing ruining the image for Roffius was the sight of Narok holding a sword across her neck. Roffius also noticed the gash on Narok's cheek and suspected it was Mitzy's doing.

"Are you hurt, my ladies?" asked Roffius. Each shook their heads to signal no.

"Uncle!" yelled the boys.

"What about you? Are you hurt?" he asked his nephews while continuing to look for any more surprises.

"We're fine; sorry for not telling you that we left to save Mitzy," Julean said with remorse. Narok was quick to interrupt this meaningless chatter.

"Well, well; if it isn't the elusive Prince Roffius," sneered the evil man.

"Let her go, Narok, it's me you want," answered Roffius.

"I wish to kill you but trust me, I want much more from her," continued Narok crudely. "Get him!"

While Bara soldiers surrounded the formidable captain, Mezrah considered his options knowing he could never best Roffius in a duel with an injured shoulder. He decided to make his getaway with his two hostages. With haste, Mezrah hoisted Stefano over his good shoulder and dragged Julean by his broken arm. The soldier holding Cora took a cue from Mezrah and followed the bulgy-eyed man out the door.

"Father!" cried Stefano from Mezrah's shoulder as they sprinted past.

"Help!" added Julean. Shem looked at Aykin with fear in his eyes. Just then, Narok yelled out for reinforcements as Cora's captor entered the hallway with the redhead. She released another terrified scream, but her captor stopped after recognizing Aykin standing beside Shem. The former comrades exchanged icy stares before Shem stepped out of the way.

"I'm going after Mezrah!" he exclaimed. Shem ran after his boys as Aykin charged the Bara soldier holding tightly to Cora.

When Aykin closed in, the Bara pushed Cora into his former commander. Aykin caught Cora in his arms and time froze as they stood looking into each other's eyes. Aykin wanted nothing more than to passionately kiss the beautiful redhead, but refrained after seeing the Bara charging towards him with sword drawn. Aykin placed

Renewed Strength

his hand on Cora's head and pushed her down to protect her from harm. He felt the crunch of bones as Aykin knocked out three teeth after punching the Bara in the mouth. While the man staggered backwards, Aykin picked Cora up and placed her against the wall.

Aykin turned back around in time to block his enemy's first strike as an eerie melody resonated off the stone walls with each clash of their swords. Aykin was too focused on his opponent to notice the soldier who'd been unconscious come to. The Bara staggered to his feet and Cora watched as the man approached Aykin from behind with his sword raised. Without hesitation, the maiden grabbed a sword from beside another fallen soldier and thrust it through the man's side. He cried out in disbelief and slumped to the floor. Aykin heard the cry as he lunged at his opponent and pierced him through the heart. Aykin turned around to see a Bara writhing in pain and Cora standing beside him holding a bloody sword.

"My father was a blacksmith," she said with a shrug of her shoulders. For the first time since his parents had died, Aykin felt like he was home as he looked at the beautiful redhead. He took long confident strides towards Cora and thrust his blade into the already wounded soldier as he passed.

"Are you all right, my lady?" he asked chest heaving.

"I'm fine, but Narok's got a sword to Mitzy's neck!" she exclaimed.

"Don't worry; Roffius can take care of Narok. I've got to get you out of here," declared Aykin. He took hold of her hand and ran down the hallway until they were safely around the corner. Aykin stopped and turned to Cora. "Get someplace safe until this is over," he said intently.

"Thank you for saving my life," she replied. Cora moved a stray hair away from her emerald eyes and Aykin felt as if he could get lost in them. He slowly released her hand and smiled. When he did, Cora noticed how his lips tilted slightly and thought he was the most dashing man she'd ever met. She felt her cheeks flush as she curtsied before running down the hallway. As he watched her go, Aykin hoped more than anything for the chance to see her again.

He paused to consider whether he should go help Roffius or Shem. He guessed that Roffius was terribly outnumbered against the fierce Bara soldiers; however, he knew that Mezrah was an excellent swordsman and had seen first-hand that Shem was not. The decision became an easy one for Aykin as he sprinted down the hallway to help the former king.

******

While Perez and Luklin fought archers atop the castle wall, they noticed a cloud of dust approaching from the north.

"Look there!" Perez shouted.

"I sure hope that's Lamech with more men from Belzeeb!" exclaimed Luklin. Perez looked again and recognized the physician riding at the front of the pack.

"Inform Ithamar that the reinforcements from Belzeeb have arrived!" he shouted. Luklin placed his fingers to his mouth and blew. Ithamar immediately recognized the distinct whistle and looked to see Luklin waving his arms wildly on the top of the wall.

"Ithamar! Lamech has returned with men from Belzeeb!" shouted Luklin.

"It's about time!" exclaimed Ithamar thrusting his sword through another Bara soldier.

******

Obed and Lamech rode hard all night with the men they'd gathered in Belzeeb to reach the castle by morning. On their approach, they watched in horror as the black dragon circled above the castle while smoke billowed from the courtyard.

"I hope we're not too late!" exclaimed Obed. Lamech nodded in agreement and urged his horse to keep up with his youthful comrade.

Obed and Lamech led the exhausted men from Belzeeb into the courtyard where they quickly revived after hearing thunderous cheers of support from the army of farmers. Bara soldiers loyal to Narok suddenly found themselves out-numbered and without a leader, yet the black dragon's daunting presence kept them dangerously confident. Obed charged into the center of the fighting and leapt from his horse in search of Aykin or Shem. Unable to find them, the lad rushed towards Eliab who was fighting a former comrade of much greater strength and size. Before Obed could reach them, the Bara disarmed Eliab and knocked him to the ground. The man then straddled Eliab with an evil smirk as he raised his sword to deliver a fatal blow. The peripheral noises faded away, and the only thing Eliab heard was the pounding of his heart. The

Bara's blade was inches from Eliab's chest when a strange look appeared on the man's face and he fell onto Eliab. Eliab quickly shoved the man off and looked up to see the bloodied tip of Obed's blade.

"Thanks kid! That was close!" exclaimed Eliab with relief.

"Where are Aykin and Shem?" asked Obed as he helped Eliab to his feet.

"They're in the castle looking for Narok," answered the grateful soldier.

With haste, Obed took off for the castle with Lamech following after his spry companion. The physician promised himself that if he lived through this, it would be a long time before he ever rode a horse again.

Once inside the castle, Obed rounded a corner and burst into the Throne Room only to find it empty.

"They're not here!" exclaimed Obed with dismay. As Lamech entered, a woman's screams echoed off the walls.

"That sounds like it's coming from the Queen's Chamber," he presumed.

The two took off running with the old physician leading the way up a flight of stairs and down a long hallway. When they turned the corner where the south wing connects to the east wing, Lamech collided into Mezrah, Stefano, and Julean.

"Ah!" cried the boys as they toppled to the floor in a mound of twisted arms and legs. Obed managed to stop before he, too, became part of the pile.

Renewed Strength

"Lamech!" cried Stefano seeing the physician. Lamech looked up and saw a raised sword behind Stefano's head. He immediately kicked the boy out of the way and miraculously managed to block Mezrah's strike with his sword.

"Get them out of here!" shouted Lamech. Obed hated to leave Lamech alone to face the bulgy-eyed man, but knew they must help Mitzy after hearing another scream from upstairs. When they had gone, Lamech looked at the expert swordsman in front of him and thought he might actually stand a chance thanks to the wound Kenan had inflicted on Mezrah's shoulder in Belzeeb.

******

Obed, Stefano, and Julean heard another terrified scream coming from the south wing as they raced to find Mitzy. When they rounded the next corner, Obed and the boys saw Shem and Aykin running towards them.

"Father!" cried Stefano.

"Uncle!" yelled Julean. Shem happily scooped the boys into his arms for the second emotional reunion in a matter of hours.

Aykin and Obed watched awkwardly as they, too, wanted to express the joy each felt in seeing the other again, but neither quite knew how. Yet Aykin's attention was soon diverted when he realized that Kenan and Lamech weren't with Obed.

"Where are Kenan and Lamech?" he asked.

"I'm sorry, Aykin, but Kenan's dead," answered Obed sadly.

"What?" whispered Aykin in disbelief.

"What about Lamech?" asked Shem with concern.

"He's just around the corner fighting Mezrah," stated Obed.

"He's what?!" exclaimed Shem. "Aykin, go help Lamech while the boys and I go back to help Roffius!"

"It shall be an honor," replied Aykin. Before he left, Aykin took hold of his brother's arm. "Take care of yourself, Obed. I expect to see you in one piece when this is over."

"You do the same, Brother," replied Obed.

******

When Aykin rounded the next corner he found the old physician staggering after a solid frontal strike from Mezrah.

"MEZRAH!" shouted Aykin with authority. Mezrah turned around and smiled at the sight of Aykin's impressive figure.

"You!!" exclaimed the bulgy-eyed man.

"Surprised?" answered Aykin with a raised brow. "Lamech, I believe your assistance is needed in the Queen's Chamber. I shall take care of this rat." The weary physician was happy to comply with the more youthful, and skilled, man's request.

"I shall see you soon, my friend," said Lamech as he stepped aside.

Renewed Strength

"Not if I see you first," replied Aykin with a sideways grin.

Before Lamech rounded the corner, Mezrah engaged Aykin in a duel nearly as fierce as the one between Ithamar and Cain days earlier. Aykin matched Mezrah's first strike with such force that the bulgy-eyed man stumbled backwards down a flight of stairs. Aykin chased after him and their duel resumed on the landing. Mezrah was physically weakened from the wound inflicted by Kenan, so he attempted to weaken Aykin mentally.

"You look just like your father, and fight like him too," said Mezrah chest heaving.

"What would the bastard son of a whore know about my father?" snapped Aykin vehemently. Mezrah's reply came in the form of a swift kick to Aykin's kneecap, which created a painful subluxation. The young soldier cried out as he stumbled to the ground. Mezrah took this opportunity to flee down the hallway. Aykin quickly relocated his knee before chasing after Mezrah who had bolted up another staircase.

In the east tower two floors above where their chase began, Aykin finally caught up to the bulgy-eyed man. The young soldier grabbed hold of Mezrah and slammed him against a wall. Mezrah instantly kneed Aykin in the groin and thrust down with his blade, but Aykin blocked the wicked man's potentially deadly strike. Mezrah faltered as the pain in his shoulder worsened, but he was intent on reaching his destination. He pushed Aykin backwards and continued down the hallway. Desperate to get away, Mezrah knocked over candlesticks and tore down tapestry to slow Aykin until he finally ducked inside a room. Aykin followed after the bulgy-eyed man not realizing that Mezrah had intentionally led him into Kleiko's study. Mezrah thought himself particularly clever to kill both father and son in the same manner from the same room. The older man ran to the far end of the study where he opened one of the large windows. Aykin entered the room as Mezrah jumped out.

"NO!" he shouted. Aykin's cry came not from concern but frustration in thinking he'd been denied the satisfaction of killing Mezrah himself. Aykin hurried to the window and leaned out. But as soon as his shoulders cleared the frame, Aykin felt himself falling.

"You're an even greater fool than your father," laughed Mezrah. The older man hadn't jumped out the window at all, but merely stepped onto the narrow ledge. Once there, Mezrah simply waited for Aykin to lean out so he could throw the young man to his death, just as he had done to Uriah. Mezrah smirked with delight thinking he was one step closer to obtaining the throne, until he saw Aykin hanging onto the ledge. "Perhaps I was wrong; you're far more impressive than your father. I simply threw him out this window and then took your baby brother from your dead mother's arms," mocked Mezrah. His hair flapped wildly in the wind as Aykin looked at him aghast. The bulgy-eyed man projected his maniacal laugh while repeatedly stomping upon Aykin's fingers. His flesh tore away and his bones were bruised, but defeat was not an option for Aykin after finally learning the truth surrounding his father's death. In a bold move, Aykin held onto the ledge with one hand while letting go with the other to grab the dagger tucked inside his waistband. Aykin then reached up and stabbed Mezrah in the calf. The evil man fell onto his side upon the ledge so that he and Aykin were now face-to-face.

"I vowed to avenge my father a long time ago," announced Aykin, "and I always keep my vows!" The bulgy-eyed man cried out in anguish after Aykin thrust his dagger into Mezrah's neck. Blood spewed forth in every direction as Aykin pulled Mezrah's worthless body off the ledge. Serendipitously, Mezrah landed at the base of the east tower exactly where Uriah had twelve years earlier.

Eliab, Jesorath, and Ithamar heard Mezrah's cry and looked up to see one man falling as another clung desperately to the ledge.

"Is that Aykin?" asked Eliab.

"Which one?" asked Ithamar fearing the worst.

"The one dangling from the ledge!" exclaimed Eliab as he pointed to his best friend.

Ithamar felt nauseous watching Aykin cling to the ledge, and was immediately taken back to the night he found Uriah's body against the jagged rocks. But Ithamar was determined to do anything in his power to prevent Aykin from meeting that same fate as he frantically looked around. Suddenly, he got an idea.

"Jesorath, help me with that cart of hay!" he shouted.

The two men sprinted through the fighting with Eliab following after them as Natas released another deadly stream of fire. Once the dragon had flown past, Ithamar and Eliab shielded Jesorath from a barrage of arrows so the blacksmith could position the cart below Aykin. As he did, Aykin lost his grip and fell helplessly down the side of the east tower. However, instead of falling to his death as he had expected, Aykin landed onto a soft pile of hay.

"Nice of you to drop in," said Jesorath.

"Thanks, I owe you one!" exclaimed Aykin. Jesorath and Eliab pulled Aykin from the cart as Natas started another pass over the courtyard.

"Look out!" shouted Ithamar. They ushered Aykin away from the cart and dove behind a row of barrels seconds before the cart exploded into flames.

"That was close," said Jesorath chest heaving after the dragon passed.

"Too close," added Eliab.

"What was that?" asked Aykin.

"Natas," replied Ithamar. "We'd better get out of here; these barrels are filled with oil."

"I've got to get back to the south wing to help Shem and Roffius!" exclaimed Aykin.

"Have you found Mitzy?" asked Ithamar.

"Narok's got her in the Queen's Chamber," answered Aykin with urgency.

"You and Eliab get there as quickly as you can; Jesorath and I shall take care of a nasty black dragon," instructed Ithamar. The men dispersed as Natas started another approach.

Renewed Strength

******

In the south tower, Roffius was once again outnumbered by the fierce Bara soldiers, yet he remained undeterred. And just as in the battle outside of Irvania, Roffius wielded the sword crafted by dragon magic with deadly force and precision. Within minutes, the formidable Captain of the Royal Guards proved himself worthy of the title by killing three of his largest opponents. Enraged by the embarrassment this would surely cause to the Bara reputation, a foolish young soldier charged at Roffius. Assessing his situation, Roffius stepped aside as soon as the young man came within striking distance. To his horror instead of Roffius at the end of his blade, the soldier pierced a fellow comrade charging the captain from the opposite direction. Roffius then executed a forward lunge to impale the foolish soldier. His look of disbelief remained captured in death as blood trickled from the soldier's mouth and he fell to the floor.

With only one Bara remaining in the room, Roffius was eager to finish him off and claim what he had come for. He raised his weapon and their swords clashed together, creating a ghastly melody. Roffius' next thrust fatally struck the Bara and the man dropped to the floor alongside his fallen comrades. Roffius turned around chest heaving and locked eyes with Narok.

"Let's try this again," he stated. "I said, let her go!" Roffius took long, confident strides towards the maiden he loved being held by the man he loathed. As Narok watched Roffius draw near he knew he could never best Roffius with a sword, so Narok would have to disarm the mighty captain with words.

"The only things I shall do, Captain, are kill you and marry this fair maiden," claimed Narok as Roffius continued his approach. "That's close enough!" Narok pressed his sword against Mitzy's neck as a warning and Roffius immediately stopped.

"Release the maiden!" ordered the former prince with authority.

"Nonsense! I shan't take orders from a man who's played the fool for years," snapped Narok. Roffius swallowed hard fearing the evil man had discovered his true identity, or worse, Mitzy's.

"What do you mean?" he asked with trepidation.

"For years you thought I was dead, when in truth I've been alive and plotting your family's demise," boasted Narok. "And you believed it was I who killed your precious brother Jeru, when in truth it was Mezrah."

"I shall gain great pleasure in killing you, Narok," promised Roffius through clinched teeth. He re-started his approach, but the evil man answered by pressing his sword harder against Mitzy's neck.

"Aaahh!" she cried out.

"I warned you, Captain; stay back!" shouted Narok.

"You're a monster," replied Roffius with contempt.

"If you only knew," smirked Narok, "but I think it's time you do know. Even you, dear Mitzy, should find this interesting."

Renewed Strength

"I can't imagine finding anything which you have to say interesting," said Mitzy coldly.

"We shall see about that," continued Narok. "The night you and your mother arrived at the castle twelve years ago was the same night Uriah the guard was charged with treason for conspiring to kill the king."

"What does a traitor have to do with Mitzy?" asked Roffius slyly stepping closer.

"I'm getting to that!" snapped Narok. "As it turns out, Uriah was actually what you would call a hero. He discovered my father's plot to take the throne and went to Kleiko's study to expose him. However, instead of finding Kleiko, Uriah happened upon my father and uncle. Mezrah threw Uriah out the window, and my father concocted the whole story of Uriah being a traitor to keep the truth hidden."

"You come from a family of monsters!" exclaimed Roffius.

"I shall take that as a complement, Captain, but I'm not finished," said Narok callously. "My father suspected Uriah had told his wife of his suspicions, so he wanted the family killed as well. Uriah's wife and daughters were easily disposed of, but as fate would have it, the eldest boy escaped. I believe, Prince Roffius, you've had the pleasure of making Aykin's acquaintance by now, which brings me to you, fair Mitzy. I believe you know well of Uriah's youngest son whose life was spared as an infant. Mezrah brought him back to the castle where the tiny cherub was entrusted to your mother's care." Mitzy's knees went weak as she suddenly realized that Narok was referring to Obed.

"Obed?" she whispered.

"Yes, my dear, the innocent babe whom you and your mother took into your pathetic little home is none other than the youngest son of the faithful guard who lost his life, and reputation, trying to save a king who would label him a traitor," sneered Narok. Roffius would've charged the evil man if not for the sword Narok held to Mitzy's neck.

"You and Mezrah shall pay dearly for these heinous crimes!" threatened Roffius. Narok was pleased with the effectiveness his verbal arsenal was having, but he wasn't finished yet.

"There's one more thing, Your Highness. Did you know that this maiden is in love with you?" he asked. Mitzy was completely mortified and Roffius was taken aback.

"I've no idea what you mean," he replied awkwardly. Narok prided himself in the art of reading people, but he was uncharacteristically baffled by the expression on Roffius' face. The cunning man couldn't tell if the formidable captain was repulsed or enraptured.

"I told her that a man with your royal heritage would never regard her as anything but a servant," said Narok eying Roffius carefully. "But, perhaps I was mistaken…"

Roffius now feared for Mitzy's safety in an entirely new way. He rightly surmised that if Narok suspected Roffius reciprocated in those same feelings of love, Mitzy would be in even greater danger. Because of this reason, Roffius lied.

Renewed Strength

"You are correct only in saying that I could never see her as more than a servant," he said bluntly. "I find your implication of anything more not only absurd, but appalling." His brilliant performance convinced Narok and left Mitzy feeling as worthless as Roffius had described her.

The maiden cried softly and offered no resistance as Narok pulled her onto the balcony while Roffius followed after them. A strong gust of wind blew Mitzy's curls across her tear-streaked face as the black dragon flew over the south tower. When the hideous creature passed, his keen eyesight recognized the Royal Crest on Roffius' cloak. Natas smiled at the sight of a member of the Royal Family and abruptly changed course. From below, Ithamar looked to see why the dragon had turned around, and his heart sank when the guard saw why.

"The beast is after Roffius!" he exclaimed.

"We've got to distract it!" yelled Jesorath. He looked around and saw an unmanned catapult. "Help me load a boulder onto that catapult!"

The large blacksmith and Ithamar wasted no time running for the weapon. Meanwhile, from their vantage point upon the castle wall, Perez and Luklin also saw the black dragon change course.

"Look! The dragon's headed straight for Captain Roffius!" cried Luklin. Perez hastily fired an arrow, but it bounced off the creature's impenetrable scales.

On the balcony, Roffius' sword glistened brilliantly in the morning sun and caused Narok to feel strangely afraid.

"That's a fine sword, Prince, perhaps I shall use it to kill you," he said to mask his fear.

"Never!" shouted Roffius. "This sword was a gift from Orpheus."

"I doubt it, the only dragon in Nepthali is here to defeat your pathetic little army!" mocked Narok. Mitzy's eyes suddenly grew big as the black dragon came into view right behind Roffius. Natas was headed straight for him, and although her heart was broken by Roffius' unequivocal rejection, Mitzy still loved him and had to warn him.

"LOOK OUT!" she screamed.

Roffius heard the sound of a violent, rushing wind and turned around to see two large talons. He arched his back in time to avoid being impaled and simultaneously threw his sword. The blade cut through Natas' scales like butter, but the strike was not fatal. The black dragon pulled back and looked at the sword protruding from his chest with astonishment. Natas frantically tried to remove it with his front claws while struggling to remain airborne. The hideous creature finally pulled it free, and the sword fell into the courtyard.

Roffius started to run, but Natas swiped his razor sharp claws at the man he believed was a member of the Royal Family. Roffius felt the flesh rip from his arm as he was thrown across the balcony. Mitzy watched in horror as Roffius crashed into the marble railing and went limp.

"I'll get you!" roared Natas. The beast flailed through the sky and turned around to make another pass.

Renewed Strength

Down in the courtyard, Ithamar watched helplessly as Roffius lay motionless on the balcony. He knew they must put the catapult to use before it was too late. He and Jesorath worked together to get the boulder over to the weapon; but as they were carrying it, Roffius' sword suddenly pierced into the ground at Ithamar's feet. The guard grabbed the blood-stained weapon and tucked it into his belt. They loaded the boulder onto the catapult and turned it around to face the oncoming dragon.

"Hurry! We must secure that strap!" yelled Ithamar to Jesorath. The rag-tag army of farmers provided coverage as Jesorath pulled back on the lever and waited for Ithamar's signal. Natas' black shadow covered the sun as Ithamar raised his arm and waited until the beast came within striking distance.

"NOW!" yelled Ithamar as he lowered his arm.

Jesorath immediately released the lever causing the boulder to soar through the sky. It struck Natas on the forehead and Mitzy watched as the hideous creature tumbled backwards. She sighed with relief knowing that Roffius was safe for the moment, but she knew Natas would soon return. Narok loosen his grip as he leaned over the railing to see who was responsible for firing the boulder. The clever maiden took advantage of the distraction and bit into Narok's hand as hard as she could.

"Aaahh!" he cried.

Her actions were so unexpected, and the pain was so intense, that Narok dropped his sword and released his grip. Mitzy kicked his weapon away then thrust her elbow into his gut and smashed his face with the back of her fist. The blow broke Narok's nose and caused him to double over in pain as blood spattered everywhere. Mitzy rushed towards Roffius, but she didn't get far. Narok cracked his cat o'nine tails and struck the same shoulder the Bara arrow had days earlier. The jagged ends ripped through her gown and tore open Mitzy's wound. She screamed in agony, and then fainted.

At the other end of the balcony, Roffius stumbled to his knees and shook his pounding head. He ignored the burning pain in his arm as he scanned the skies for Natas. With no sign of the beast, Roffius looked across the balcony and saw Narok's face covered with blood as the evil man lifted Mitzy into his arms. Roffius got to his feet wondering if the dragon had struck Narok as well, and assumed Mitzy had merely fainted at the sight of the hideous creature.

"Let her go!" shouted Roffius pulling one of his daggers from his belt.

"I think not, Captain. If you come any closer I shall drop her off this balcony!" threatened Narok.

Roffius stopped suddenly when he saw blood seeping through Mitzy's dress and knew something was terribly wrong. Roffius also knew that his aim must be true to avoid hitting Mitzy as he turned the dagger around in the palm of his hand. Narok sensed Roffius was plotting something as he stepped closer to the railing. Roffius staggered towards them and Mitzy moaned as she began to regain consciousness.

"I warned you, Captain," said Narok coldly. With an icy stare, he dropped Mitzy over the balcony.

Renewed Strength

"NO!" yelled Roffius. He thrust his dagger across the balcony and hit Narok in the gut with such force that the evil man dropped instantly. Roffius hurdled over Narok's motionless body and sprang onto the railing.

"MITZY!" he exclaimed in terror. Roffius looked down, but didn't see her falling as expected.

"Down here," called a soft voice beneath his feet. "Please, hurry!" Mitzy had managed to grab the base of the balcony to stop her fall, but she knew she couldn't hold on much longer. Roffius climbed over the railing and reached down to pull her up.

"Take hold of my hand, Miss Mit," he said with urgency. Mitzy looked up and reached for his hand. But as she did, Mitzy lost her grip and slipped away.

"RO!" she screamed as she fell.

"MITZY!" he cried out in desperation.

Dragon Scroll of Nepthali

Chapter 23

One Shot

Aykin and Eliab heard Mitzy's screams and looked up with horror to see their queen falling. The men felt completely helpless until they saw Mitzy suddenly stop. She had miraculously managed to once again grab the base of a balcony and found herself dangling two floors below Roffius.

"I'm coming Mitzy!" he shouted. "Whatever you do, don't let go!"

"I shall try not to," she replied in a daze.

Roffius ignored the throbbing pain in his arm as he scaled the exterior of the castle to reach the maiden he loved. But Mitzy was clearly struggling to remain conscious, and Roffius feared he wouldn't reach her in time. He looked for a faster way down, and got an idea after seeing the banners and flags hanging along the castle wall hung to welcome the coming baby. It was a long-shot; especially since Roffius didn't know if the banner could hold the weight of one person let alone two, but he thought it was his best chance to reach Mitzy before she fell to her death.

From their location in the courtyard Aykin, Eliab, Ithamar, and Jesorath watched Roffius hoist a banner over his shoulder before tying it around his waist. The captain gave it a quick tug then swung down using the banner like a long vine. Roffius grabbed Mitzy by the waist and she slumped over his shoulder fainting. He was thankful he'd been able to reach her in time, but Roffius knew they weren't out of danger yet as he watched Natas fly straight towards them. In a desperate attempt to swing away from the dragon's deadly talons, Roffius pumped his legs back and forth. As the swaying motion picked up momentum, the banner tore away from the wall. Roffius and Mitzy fell like sands in an hourglass as another large boulder flew through the sky and hit the dragon in the eye. Natas became disoriented and tumbled backwards, while Roffius and Mitzy continued their downward spiral.

The tail of the banner flapped wildly as they fell and snagged onto one of the jagged rocks protruding from the trim around one of the large windows. This immediately stopped their fall and Roffius held tightly to Mitzy as they jerked upwards. Her eyes fluttered open, and Mitzy wondered if this was a dream as she looked into the hazel eyes of her handsome rescuer. Before she could speak, however, part of the banner ripped and they found themselves falling again. Mitzy screamed and Roffius pulled her close, but the banner snagged once more to stop their fall.

Ithamar and the others watched in disbelief from below as Roffius and their queen continued to cheat death.

"We've got to help them!" exclaimed Eliab. Aykin looked around and saw another cart of hay just like the one which broke his fall earlier.

"Help me with that cart!" he shouted. The four men maneuvered their way through the fighting to get the cart, and then pushed it beneath Roffius and Mitzy.

"Down here, Captain!" Ithamar shouted. At that moment, the banner completely ripped away, sending Roffius and Mitzy downwards at an alarming rate. Roffius wrapped his arms around the Queen of Nepthali to cushion what he feared could be a nasty landing. They hit the cart with such force that the wheels shot out from each side, but it was otherwise quite painless. Ithamar and Aykin fired another boulder to keep Natas distracted while Jesorath and Eliab hurried to help Roffius and Mitzy.

"Nicely done, gentlemen!" said Roffius with relief.

"These hay carts are worth their weight in gold today," quipped Eliab.

"Allow me, my lady," said Jesorath. He extended his hand but after realizing she was only partially conscious, the burly blacksmith ignored protocol and lifted his queen out of the cart. But Roffius sprung over the side and scooped the beautiful maiden back into his arms just as he had done in Irvania.

"Easy now, Miss Mit, let's get you someplace safe," he said tenderly.

"Captain, you're shoulder!" exclaimed Eliab seeing the gaping wound.

"I'm fine, it's Mitzy I'm worried about," continued Roffius.

"We've got things under control here," Eliab assured him.

"Send Lamech to Mitzy's quarters at once if he is able," instructed Roffius.

"He's in the south wing looking for you," reported Aykin as he and Ithamar approached.

"Have no fear, Captain, we shall send Lamech there at once," said Ithamar as he tossed Jesorath a bow. "Jesorath can cover you through the courtyard." The blacksmith caught the weapon and looked it over.

"I'm not used to this. Personally, I prefer a good sword," he replied.

"Not to worry, Jesorath, I trust you," said Roffius. Not wanting to let the captain down, Jesorath fired arrow after arrow with deadly precision while Roffius ran through the courtyard with the Queen of Nepthali.

******

Obed was the first to reach the Queen's Chamber, and he entered expecting to find Roffius and Mitzy. Instead, the lad saw only the backside of a man on the balcony staggering to his feet. Obed watched as the man appeared to pull something from his stomach as he looked intently over the balcony. Obed realized that the man was holding a dagger and raised it to throw at someone in the courtyard.

"No!" yelled Obed. Just then Shem, Stefano, and Julean rushed into the room. When the man on the balcony turned around in surprise, Obed saw that it was Narok.

The evil man broke into a sinister smile at the sight of the man he believed was king.

"Well, well, if it isn't King Shem," smirked Narok. He stumbled towards them with Roffius' dagger in hand.

"Where's Roffius?" asked Shem surveying the ravaged room.

"I was just about to kill him, but I suppose I can kill you first. The fool thought he killed me, but as you can see he failed. I suppose that is to be expected in a family of failures," mocked Narok. He hoped to rattle Shem as easily as he had Roffius.

"I'm afraid you are the one who has failed," replied Shem without flinching. Narok wanted to laugh, but he was too weak. He was sweating almost as much as he was bleeding and struggled to remain conscious.

"I find that amusing coming from the man for whom the black dragon has come to kill!" declared Narok.

"I wouldn't be so sure. You see, before you and your barbaric friends attacked the castle Kleiko discovered something quite intriguing," said Shem.

"What do you mean?" asked Narok to humor Shem.

"He discovered that I'm not the King of Nepthali; in fact I haven't a drop of royal blood in me," reported Shem plainly. "I'm merely a member of the family put in place to protect the Royal Family from Natas…and someone like you."

"How dare you insult my intelligence with such an absurd tale!" sneered Narok. Yet, he felt himself begin to tremble.

"It's true, the rightful heir is actually a queen…Queen Mitzy to be precise," answered Shem firmly. Narok's trembling became uncontrollable as he realized that he had the queen in his grasp, but threw her over the balcony.

"NO!!!!" shouted Narok. He raised the dagger to throw at Shem, but before Narok could release it, Obed thrust his sword across the room and struck Narok in the heart. The evil man died knowing it was at the hand of the boy whose life he had tried so hard to ruin.

"That was for my father… my family… and for me," declared Obed.

******

The black dragon picked up speed and gained on Roffius as he ran through the courtyard. Natas' head hurt, and one eye was blind from the boulder, but the beast remained focused on his target as his chest glowed with an inner burning fire. Aykin felt helpless to stop the dragon and save his friends, until the son of Uriah suddenly got an idea.

"Ithamar, did you say those barrels are filled with oil?" he asked with urgency.

"Yes," replied the guard unsure of what Aykin had in mind.

"Why don't we put one onto the catapult and use that over-grown lizard's own fire to blast him sky high?" pressed Aykin. Ithamar smiled proudly at the oldest son of his best friend.

"It sounds like the best chance we've got to stop that beast. Help me push this catapult closer so we don't risk exposing the barrels!" shouted the guard.

The men ran to the catapult and Jesorath positioned himself at the rear where he began to push. Aykin helped the blacksmith, while Ithamar and Eliab pulled from the front. They were halfway to the barrels when Natas saw them and sent a blast of fire their way. The men jumped to the side and narrowly escaped with their lives as the catapult burst into flames.

"Did the blast hit Roffius and Mitzy?" asked Jesorath with urgency. Ithamar strained to see through the smoke, but sighed with relief after seeing Roffius still on his feet with Mitzy in his arms.

"The beast missed them!" he exclaimed.

"Whew! That was close!" added Aykin as he brushed debris off his pants.

"We lost the catapult," reported Ithamar.

"There's another one over there!" shouted Jesorath. The others looked with dismay at the catapult missing a wheel.

"How do you propose we move it when it's missing a wheel?" asked Eliab.

"Perhaps I can be of assistance," called a deep voice. Eliab turned around and saw the biggest man the soldier had ever seen.

"He's on our side, right?" he asked with head cocked to one side. Ithamar smiled and extended his hand to Cook.

"Am I glad to see you! We need your help pushing that catapult from the rear while Jesorath pulls it from the front," he stated.

"Consider it done," smiled Cook while vigorously shaking Ithamar's hand.

Even with their strength and numbers, it was a struggle for the five men to move the broken catapult. When the weapon was finally alongside a barrel filled with oil, they turned it around to face Natas as the creature started another approach. The dragon roared in frustration watching Roffius draw near to the castle doors.

"Come on! We need to get this barrel loaded before that beast takes another shot at Roffius!" ordered Ithamar knowing that his captain's good fortune against Natas wouldn't last forever.

"We only have one shot men, so let's make it count!" emphasized Aykin. Each understood the urgency of the situation; however, the barrel was more difficult to lift than the boulders had been. Perez and Luklin fired arrows from atop the wall to shield their friends while Eliab and Ithamar held the loading dock steady for Jesorath and Cook.

"Lift on three; one…two…three!" yelled Ithamar. Cook and Jesorath grunted as they hoisted the heavy barrel onto the catapult.

"A little more to the left...hurry!" urged a wide-eyed Aykin as the black dragon closed in on Roffius and Mitzy. Cook and Jesorath let go, and the barrel fell perfectly into place.

"I've got you now!" cackled the hideous dragon. Natas drew a deep breath and his chest glowed ominously.

"Fire away!" yelled Ithamar. Eliab released the lever and the barrel was sent soaring through the sky. It struck the beast's side and ignited on impact. Roffius staggered from the blast and turned around to see a wall of fire headed straight towards them.

******

Lamech entered the Queen's Chamber at the same time the barrel exploded against Natas and the force of the blast nearly knocked the old physician off his feet.

"What was that?" he asked while bracing himself against the door. Shem and the boys turned around, and were happy to see it was Lamech. But Shem immediately returned his attention to Roffius and Mitzy in the courtyard. He tried to see through the smoke, but a blinding streak of light suddenly flashed across the sky.

"Orpheus?" he whispered.

******

Roffius watched in horror as the wall of fire surged closer. He covered Mitzy's body with his own in a feeble attempt to protect the queen from being incinerated. Yet, instead of being consumed by the flames, he and Mitzy were enveloped by the brilliant light Shem saw from the balcony. Roffius would later describe what happened next as being like a hand scooped them up and carried them out of harm's way. When his eyes adjusted following the light, Roffius was astonished to see that he and Mitzy were in the safety of the castle's foyer. Mitzy moaned softly and Roffius quickly returned his attention to the Queen of Nepthali whom he feared was dying in his arms.

******

The smoke from the massive explosion lingered as Ithamar and the others searched anxiously for signs of Natas.

"I don't see the dragon anywhere!" exclaimed Eliab.

"Well done!" said Jesorath as he extended his hand to Cook.

"Thanks, but do you see Prince Roffius?" asked the large man with worry. He was the only one still unaware of their true identities.

"I'm sure he's fine; I've never seen anyone with better luck than he," answered Aykin.

"I agree, if anyone can pull off a miracle, it's Captain Roffius," added Jesorath. Ithamar hoped they were right as the remaining Bara soldiers loyal to Narok ran past attempting to flee now that the dragon was gone. Luklin and Perez scaled down the wall and joined their victorious compatriots. Ithamar turned to his most trusted guards.

"Luklin, I need you and Perez to ensure every lousy Bara soldier who hasn't been with us is either killed or captured," ordered their commander.

"It shall be an honor," answered Luklin. He and Perez ran with swords drawn in pursuit of their enemy.

"What do you want us to do?" asked Aykin.

"Cook, I need you to get back to the kitchen and start boiling water. The rest of you, follow me!" instructed Ithamar.

At that moment, Shem looked down into the courtyard and saw his faithful companions dispersing; however, there was no sign of his brother.

"Ithamar!" he shouted. The guard looked up and saw Shem and the boys waving their arms on the balcony. "Where's Roffius?" continued Shem.

"He's taken Mitzy to her quarters. She is in desperate need of a physician; is Lamech with you?" called Ithamar through cupped hands to project his voice. When Lamech heard his name, he stepped to the railing and waved.

"I'm here! I shall go to there at once!" he exclaimed. Lamech turned to go, but stopped suddenly after realizing he didn't know the way. "Can anyone show me to her quarters?"

"Stefano and Julean can show you, can't you boys?" offered Shem.

"Sure! We practically live there!" answered Julean enthusiastically.

"I know where it is as well," added Obed. Shem leaned over the balcony and shouted down to Ithamar.

"Meet me at Mitzy's quarters as soon as you can!" he said. Ithamar nodded his understanding while Stefano and Julean sprinted out the door with Lamech.

Before Obed followed after them, he stopped beside Narok's lifeless body and nudged it with his boot. He strangely felt no sadness or remorse, only freedom. Shem placed his hand on the lad's shoulder.

"Your nightmare is over, Obed. Never again shall you have to worry about Narok. You are free to become the man you were meant to be; a man like your father," he said.

"Thank you, I plan to," replied Obed firmly.

******

With only a few steps to go before reaching Mitzy's quarters, Roffius encountered yet another obstacle…Nalia. The unscrupulous maiden happened to step into the hallway just as he was passing by and nearly collided with the man she believed was a prince. Her heart skipped a beat at the sight of the handsome young man, and to see her nemesis bleeding profusely only added to Nalia's pleasure.

"Your Highness, thank goodness you're alive! I feared the worst when you went missing!" she exclaimed with an exaggerated bow. Roffius nodded politely in reply while attempting to step around Nalia, but the spiteful maiden matched him step-for-step to prevent his passing. If Roffius had known of Nalia's ill-treatment towards Mitzy, or of her inappropriate advances towards Narok, Roffius would have run her through.

"My lady, forgive me if I appear rude, but as you can clearly see Mitzy's in need of medical attention, therefore, I must get her to her quarters," stated a very frustrated Roffius. Nalia could indeed see Mitzy's dire condition, which was exactly why she continued to stall him.

"It's just wonderful that you've returned to save us from Narok," she cooed. Just then, Cora emerged from the kitchen and gasped at the sight of Mitzy covered with blood.

"What happened?" implored the redhead.

"My lady, I must get Mitzy to her quarters at once," answered Roffius firmly.

"Of course, and we can help you," interrupted Nalia. "Mitzy is such a dear friend." Cora shot Nalia an angry glare which told Roffius otherwise.

"If she's such a good friend, why won't you let him pass?" fumed Cora. "I don't suppose you told the prince about how you threw yourself at Narok in hopes of becoming his queen, did you?" Nalia started to reply, but Roffius cut her off.

"Is this true, my lady?" he demanded. Nalia dropped her head in shame as Roffius continued, "Cora, I'm placing this traitor under your charge until Her Majesty can decide what to do with her."

"But...Queen Ashter is dead," replied Cora softly thinking he was somehow unaware.

"My ladies, you are looking at the rightful Queen of Nepthali," proclaimed Roffius as he pushed his way past. "Bring me some water and bandaging at once!" Nalia's horror-stricken face went white knowing what this meant for her, while Cora giggled at this sweet retributive justice.

******

Roffius had no feeling his arm as they entered Mitzy's quarters, but the queen was his only concern. After laying her gently on the bed in the back room, Roffius saw her eyes were open and moist with tears.

"Have no fear, Your Majesty, help is on the way," he said kindly. Mitzy struggled to remain conscious, but she did hear how he had addressed her.

"What did you call me?" she asked softly. Roffius knelt before his queen and smiled.

"I said 'Your Majesty' because you, Miss Mit, are the rightful Queen of Nepthali," he stated. "I wanted to tell you sooner, but feared such knowledge may put you in jeopardy." Mitzy stared at him in disbelief as he continued, "There's something else I must tell you…" Roffius wanted to profess his love, but stopped once he saw that Mitzy had lost her struggle to remain conscious.

Just then, Stefano and Julean burst through the opened door of Mitzy's quarters with Lamech right behind them. Roffius sprang to his feet with sword drawn, but put it down after recognizing his nephews and the Royal Physician.

"Is it her shoulder?" asked Stefano with concern.

"She isn't going to die, is she?" added Julean.

"Boys!" exclaimed Roffius with relief. "How did you get away from Mezrah? Are you hurt?" They ran to their uncle and he inspected them from head to toe.

"We're fine, but what happened to Mitzy?" asked Julean looking at the maiden covered with blood on the bed.

"Narok must have used his cat o'nine tails on her after the dragon struck me. I fear her wound has re-opened," answered the captain with worry.

"Did you say the dragon struck you?" asked a wide-eyed Julean.

"It's nothing," replied Roffius casually trying to mask his pain. Lamech could see that Roffius was injured, but his main concern was for the unconscious maiden on the bed.

"Let me have a look at her," said Lamech approaching the bed. While the skilled physician inspected Mitzy's wound, the boys informed their uncle about the others.

"You should've seen Lamech; he and Obed saved us from Mezrah, and then Lamech fought Mezrah until Aykin traded places with him," stated Stefano.

"We went to find you and Mitzy, but we found Narok instead," added Julean.

"And Obed killed him!" exclaimed Stefano before his cousin could finish.

"What?" asked Roffius with surprise thinking he had killed the evil man.

"Narok was about to throw his dagger at you from the balcony, but Father distracted him. Then Obed killed Narok before he threw your dagger at Father," explained Stefano. As the boy finished, Mitzy started to moan. Roffius quickly joined Lamech at her side.

"You're safe, My Queen," he said. Stefano noticed the tender way his uncle spoke to Mitzy and finally realized what had been so obvious to Ithamar and the others.

"You love her don't you, Uncle?" asked the boy.

"Yes, I do," admitted Roffius.

"I see," whispered Stefano with head hung low. Roffius was confused by his nephew's sad countenance until he remembered Stefano's proclamation to marry Mitzy someday.

"I seem to recall that you feel the same. Therefore, if you wish, I shall stand aside," offered Roffius knowing Stefano would relent. The boy paused for a moment.

"No, Uncle, I shall be the one to step aside. Besides, I think she feels the same about you," answered Stefano. Lamech hated to interrupt, but he needed help.

"Excuse me, Captain, but I shall need your assistance turning her over," requested the physician. Roffius wasted no time in gently turning Mitzy onto her stomach just as he had done at Jesorath's home in Irvania. Lamech gasped after seeing the extent of her wound.

"She was shot in this shoulder by a Bara arrow on our escape to Irvania, but I believe Narok's responsible for the rest," explained Roffius.

"This is far worse than I had expected," answered Lamech honestly.

"You can help her though, can't you?" pleaded Stefano. The physician's eyes were filled with doubt as he looked at Roffius.

"I think it's best if they weren't here," he whispered. Roffius knew this meant Mitzy's condition was indeed very serious.

"Lamech, there's something you must know," he said. The old physician looked at Roffius with compassion thinking the young man was referring to the news of him not being a prince.

"Yes, I know, my boy. You aren't really a prince...Kleiko told me before he died," answered Lamech with compassion.

"No, it's not that...it's Mitzy. She's the rightful Queen of Nepthali," stated Roffius.

"What did you say?" whispered Lamech.

"While we were in Irvania, I discovered the Mark of Royalty on Mitzy," continued Roffius. Lamech was overcome with both the shock of this information and the considerable amount of pressure it placed on him.

"Oh my, this does change things, doesn't it?" he managed to say. "Fetch me some water, and some bandaging at once. Be sure to take the boys with you."

"Yes, of course. Cora is preparing both in the kitchen now. I shall see what's keeping her," said Roffius. He placed a hand on each nephew's shoulder and continued, "Come, we must fetch what Lamech needs."

Stefano and Julean hated to leave, but not more than Roffius. As he ushered the boys through the doorway, Roffius stopped to look back longingly once more at Mitzy.

******

Shem and Obed ran through the empty hallways towards Mitzy's quarters, but slowed when they heard footsteps approaching.

"Wait," said Shem. He held his hand out to stop Obed fearing they were about to encounter remnant Bara soldiers. He and Obed quickly ducked around a corner. They remained out of sight until the footsteps were upon them, and Shem jumped out with his sword drawn. Instead of it being Bara soldiers as he had expected, Shem found himself looking at the broad smiles of Ithamar, Aykin, Jesorath, and Eliab behind the tips of their extended blades.

"We've been looking for you," said the guard with a raised brow.

"It's about time you showed up," laughed Shem. He and Ithamar clasped hands, but the guard let go when Obed stepped out from around the corner. Ithamar struggled to keep his emotions in check as he approached the lad who looked just like Jenae, and possessed Uriah's unmistakable frame.

"You must be Obed," said the guard. "My name is Ithamar; your father was my best friend." He extended his hand and Obed shook it firmly.

"I'm very pleased to meet you," replied the lad. Ithamar released his grip and turned his attention back to Shem.

"Thanks to the men Obed and Lamech brought from Belzeeb, and those from Irvania and Haliel, the enemy soldiers have been defeated," he reported proudly.

"And thanks to Orpheus," corrected Shem.

"Orpheus?" asked Aykin.

"Yes, I believe the good dragon has returned," continued Shem.

"Good dragon?" asked Eliab not knowing there was such a thing. "Where is he?"

"I don't know; but I do know that if Mitzy dies, Orpheus shall be banished from Nepthali and Natas shall destroy our kingdom," answered Shem plainly.

"What does Mitzy have to do with whether or not Orpheus comes back?" asked Obed with confusion. Shem realized that the lad was still unaware of Mitzy's true identity.

"I'm afraid there's much you don't know, Obed. You see, we've learned that Mitzy is the rightful Queen of Nepthali," explained the former king. Aykin thoughtfully placed his hand upon his brother's shoulder knowing this was a lot for Obed to process.

"What can we do to help?" asked Obed.

"Whatever Lamech asks of us," replied Shem firmly.

"Shouldn't we first ensure Natas is dead?" asked Ithamar anxiously. Aykin, Eliab, and Jesorath nodded in wholehearted agreement.

"In due time," answered Shem. "For now we must go to Mitzy's quarters." Until this moment, Ithamar had always unequivocally carried out Shem's orders, however, now he was relieved to no longer be bound to.

******

When Roffius and the boys entered the kitchen, they found Nalia and Cora tearing strips of cloth for bandaging while Cook added more wood to the fire beneath a large pot of water.

"Cook!" exclaimed Stefano. He and Julean ran to the large man who'd been such a help to the men in the courtyard.

"You're a sight for sore eyes!" laughed Cook.

"Mitzy's hurt," said Stefano.

"She was hit by an arrow, and Narok whipped her!" added Julean.

"I was told she needed help," answered Cook. "You shall soon have all the hot water you need, Captain."

"Thank you, Cook," said Roffius sincerely. Cook could tell by the look on Roffius' face that Mitzy's condition was serious. The large man knew of the attraction the pair had for one another since they were children, and it pained him to see the captain so distraught.

"Why don't you boys help me in here while your uncle and Cora take supplies to Lamech?" suggested Cook. Roffius appreciated the gesture; especially since it allowed him to quickly return to Mitzy.

"Keep a close eye on this one, Cook, she's in plenty of hot water on her own," warned Cora. The redhead nodded at Nalia as she placed one last piece of cloth on the stack for Lamech.

"Is she? Well then, I shall make sure Nalia causes no further mischief," said Cook with a raised brow. Nalia looked to the floor in shame as the large man handed the pot of water to Roffius. As he did, Cook saw the gapping wound on the young man's arm.

"Captain, what happened?" he exclaimed.

"I'm fine, Cook, and thank you for this," answered Roffius hastily as he and Cora left the kitchen.

Dragon Scroll of Nepthali

Chapter 24

Heartfelt Plea

When Obed and the others arrived at Mitzy's quarters, they found Cora assisting Lamech in the back room, and Roffius standing at the foot of the bed covered in blood.

"Roffius!" cried Shem. Roffius turned and smiled weakly upon seeing his brother.

"Shem," whispered Roffius. They walked towards each other and Shem enfolded his younger brother in a tight hug, but this time it was Roffius who winced in pain.

"Brother, what happened to you?" inquired the former king.

"It's nothing, just a little run-in with Natas," answered Roffius casually in spite of the excruciating pain.

"A run-in with Natas?" pressed Shem with growing concern.

Roffius explained to Shem and Obed what Ithamar and the others already knew about Natas nearly killing him on the balcony, and again in the courtyard. When Roffius finished, Ithamar returned the magnificent sword to his captain.

"I thought you might like this back," said the faithful guard.

"Thank you, my friend, I thought I'd lost it," replied Roffius. "Is Natas still alive?"

"I can't say for certain, but I fear he is," answered Ithamar with regret. Although it wasn't the response Roffius wanted, it was the one he had expected.

"I need more water!" Lamech suddenly called out from the back room. "If only I had some Liaspot plant…" The physician's last words did not go unnoticed by Ithamar while Roffius started for the kitchen. But he was immediately stopped by Shem.

"Brother, let us help," said Shem, "Ithamar can fetch the water, can't you?"

"Yes, of course," replied the guard. "Jesorath, you and Eliab come with me." But as he left the room, Ithamar knew he must do much more than simply fetch water to help his queen. Once in the hallway, Ithamar turned to the others.

"You two get the water; there's something I must do," he said before disappearing down the hallway.

"What do you suppose he's up to?" asked Eliab.

"I'm not sure, but he probably shouldn't be doing it alone," answered the blacksmith.

"You get the water for Lamech while I go back and tell Shem," said Eliab.

When he re-entered Mitzy's quarters, Eliab found the former king and Aykin standing near the fireplace while Roffius paced the room.

"Shem! I'm not sure what he's up to, but Ithamar just left saying he had to take care of something," reported Eliab.

"I'm going after him!" exclaimed Roffius. He turned abruptly to go, but Roffius suddenly stumbled to his knees.

"Roffius!" exclaimed Shem. "Aykin, help me!" Aykin rushed to his side and helped Shem steady the wobbly captain.

"It looks like you've got another patient, Lamech! Where do you want him?" called Aykin.

"I'm fine!" snapped Roffius, "Lamech must stay with the queen!" He tried to push Aykin away, but the room began to spin and Roffius dropped to the floor.

"Easy, kid," said Aykin. He held Roffius firmly and draped the captain's arm over his shoulder before helping Roffius to his feet.

"What's going on here?" asked the physician upon entering the main room.

"It's Roffius; he was injured by the black dragon," answered Shem with concern. Lamech remembered Roffius mentioning this earlier and briskly walked over to inspect the captain's arm.

"This wound needs to be closed to stop the bleeding, but it's nothing serious. One of you can stitch him up," stated Lamech matter-of-factly. The men looked at one another with blank stares as each waited for the other to volunteer for the task. From the back room, Cora noticed their hesitation and quickly offered her assistance.

"I can do it; at least I think I can. I closed Narok's wound the other night," she replied. Shem's heart ached knowing Ashter had inflicted that wound. She was everything to him, and Shem missed her terribly.

"I can help Lamech while she tends to Roffius," offered Obed.

"Thank you, my boy," replied Lamech, "Once you've finished, Cora, I shall need you back in here." Cora quickly entered the main room never having imagined that her frightening ordeal with Narok would prove to be so beneficial.

"Bring him over here," she said while pointing to a chair. "I shall need a needle and some thread. You can find both in Meridia's mending basket on the mantel."

Aykin assisted Roffius across the room and into the chair while Eliab retrieved the small basket. Cora felt Aykin's stare as she helped Roffius remove his shirt. The maiden looked up and purposely smiled at Aykin to reassure him that she had no interest in the handsome captain.

"If you two are finished making googly eyes at each other, I'd like to get this over with," snapped Roffius impatiently. Cora blushed as she took the basket from Eliab and got to work.

Heartfelt Plea

"It looks as if the captain isn't the only one smitten with a lovely maiden," teased Eliab. Aykin couldn't deny his friend's accusation as Jesorath returned with more water from the kitchen. The blacksmith was surprised to find a shirtless Roffius sitting in a chair with Cora standing beside him holding a needle.

"Uh...what'd I miss?" he asked with a raised brow.

"The captain just needs a few stitches," replied Aykin.

"May I have some of that water to clean his wound?" Cora asked Jesorath.

"Of course," answered the blacksmith. He held the bucket for Cora while she gathered a small portion of water into a basin. Jesorath took the remainder into the back room for Lamech. Cora meticulously cleaned Roffius' wound before finding the thinnest thread from Meridia's mending basket.

"Are you sure you know what you are doing?" asked Shem nervously as Cora started the first stitch.

"I'm certain, Your Majesty," she answered out of habit.

"She's quite capable, Shem. Let us leave her to her work," suggested Aykin. He and Eliab led the former king to the other side of the room while Roffius sat anxiously in the chair.

"Just hurry so we can catch up with Ithamar!" snapped the captain. Aykin watched with admiration as Cora closed Roffius' gaping wound as easily as if it was a torn piece of clothing.

"You should be as good as new, Captain," she announced proudly after finishing. Roffius immediately stood and put on his shirt.

"Where do you think you're going?" demanded Shem.

"I'm going after Ithamar," said Roffius firmly. He was certain the guard was going after Natas, and Roffius wanted nothing more than to kill a dragon…any dragon. Roffius was furious at Orpheus for allowing harm to come to someone like Mitzy, and couldn't believe that her faithfulness had been rewarded in such a callous manner.

"Can you manage?" Eliab asked while watching the unsteady captain.

"I can handle myself!" barked Roffius. He pushed Eliab aside and stormed out the door.

The others followed, except for Aykin who stayed behind to speak with Cora.

"That was very impressive, my lady," he said sincerely.

"Thank you, Sire, it was my pleasure. I suppose after you stitch one wound, they're basically all the same," she replied with a smile. He was helping her gather up the soiled cloths and found himself holding Cora's hand after they reached for the same one. Their eyes met and she felt her heart skip a beat.

"Is it true what they say about you?" she asked softly.

"I guess that depends on who's saying what," answered Aykin with a raised brow.

Heartfelt Plea

"Some of the men say that you pretended to be an enemy of the king so you could kill Narok. But, others say that was just a way to save yourself," she said. "Which is it?" Aykin was surprised by her straightforwardness, but found it extremely attractive.

"I've been untruthful about many things, my lady, and have made choices for which I shall spend the remainder of my days making amends; but believe me when I say that my intent was never to harm the king," he admitted. "In fact, it is because of Ithamar, Shem, and Lamech that I realized who I truly am...and who I want to be." Although she didn't know him well, Cora believed Aykin. She started to reply, but Lamech called out from the back room.

"Cora, I need you," he said.

"Yes, of course, I'm coming," she replied while realizing that Aykin was still holding her hand. He released it and she looked at him apologetically before turning and walking away. Cora stopped at the doorway to wish Aykin good luck against the black dragon, but the ruggedly handsome soldier was gone.

When Cora entered the back room, Lamech looked extremely anxious as he wiped the sweat from his brow with his forearm. The old physician had seen many wounds like Mitzy's, but rarely did the victim survive.

"How is she?" asked Cora hesitantly.

"She has developed a fever, which means infection is in the wound," reported Lamech. "Nothing I've tried seems to bring it down...I fear I'm losing her, Cora." Cora felt herself go numb, but refused to believe him.

"Don't say such a thing! There must be something you haven't tried," she insisted.

"I've done everything I can think of, but still she worsens," said the physician regretfully. "If only I had some Liaspot plant…perhaps that could save her." Obed listened to the physician's prognosis and couldn't bear the thought of losing Mitzy. He walked in a daze to the small window where he made a heartfelt plea.

"Orpheus, if you're out there, please save Mitzy," begged Obed.

******

On his way to the Royal Stables, Ithamar recalled the night he had tried to reach Jenae and the children ahead of Lott and Mezrah. He failed to save them because of an order, but the guard refused to make that same mistake with Mitzy's life now at stake. Ithamar hurried through the castle, but was soon detained by four Bara soldiers. The men foolishly believed they could easily defeat the single guard, however, they discovered their grave mistake. Ithamar bested the men with little effort and continued ahead to his destination.

Once inside the Royal Stables, Ithamar went straight to Moon Chaser. As he tightened the last strap on the saddle, Roffius burst into the stables followed by Eliab, Shem, Jesorath, and finally Aykin.

"Where are you going?" demanded Roffius. Ithamar hoped they hadn't come to stop him because his mind was made up.

"I shan't stay in that room another minute when I know I can do more to help my queen," he replied firmly.

Heartfelt Plea

"What'd you have in mind?" asked Aykin as he and the others saddled up.

"I'm going to Irvania," stated Ithamar while mounting Moon Chaser. "Mitzy needs her mother and the Liaspot plant; I can find both in Irvania."

"I'm in," said Jesorath grinning broadly.

******

Aykin and Ithamar were the first to burst forth from the stables riding side by side just as the guard had done countless times with Aykin's father. The men urged their horses through the castle gates at top speed under increasingly ominous skies.

"Looks like a nasty storm is brewing," said Eliab stating the obvious. Roffius agreed that something was brewing, but doubted it was a storm.

"Or worse than a storm," he warned. "Be ready for anything." The men understood the risk they were taking if the black dragon was still alive, but each believed no risk was too great for their queen.

After riding for nearly an hour, a sudden flash of light blinded the men and caused the horses to rear in terror. A moment later, the men felt something push against their legs. When Shem looked down, he couldn't believe what he saw. His horse, Hunter, had wings as did the other horses. The animals' legs continued to move in a galloping motion, however, instead of running, the horses were flying.

"What's happening?!?" yelled Eliab.

"It's dragon magic!" shouted Shem as the ground sped past below them.

"At this rate we shall make it to Irvania in no time!" declared Ithamar. Roffius wanted the guard to be right, but dared not hope in something finally going their way. A gust of wind suddenly rushed passed them and the enchanted horses tumbled backwards. The wind was followed by another flash of blinding light.

"Steady men!" shouted Roffius.

"Hold on!" yelled Ithamar. The men regained control of their horses and landed on a plateau facing Og Mountain. When they touched down, a loud roar shook the ground.

"What was that?" asked Eliab nervously.

"Orpheus…or Natas…or both," answered Shem with trepidation. The men dismounted and walked to the edge of the plateau with swords drawn.

Once there, they beheld the mighty dragon brothers together again for the first time in centuries. Orpheus shone so brightly that the men could not look directly upon him, while Natas was covered in the blackness of night. The evil dragon bore the signs of his recent encounters with the humans as blood trickled down his chest from Roffius' sword and one eye was swollen shut because of the boulder. Half of his enormous body was also charred from the barrel of oil. Natas was still a terrifying sight as he stood on his powerful hind legs and shook his head in defiance before shooting a blast of fire directly into the sky.

Heartfelt Plea

"It's been a long time, Brother," cackled the beast.

"Time is a term relative to the humans," stated Orpheus calmly.

"Perhaps, but humans can be quite amusing, and easy to control simply by promising riches," boasted Natas. Orpheus glared at the hideous creature who was once his beloved brother.

"You should've left the humans out of this," he scolded. Orpheus remained stoic as the evil dragon drew closer and puffs of smoke trailed from his blackened nostrils.

"You're an even greater fool than the humans for placing your fate in their hands," mocked Natas. Without warning, the beast swung his powerful tail and struck Orpheus. The white dragon tumbled backwards and smashed into Og Mountain. The force of his impact split the mountain down the center and awakened the dormant volcano causing lava to bubble within.

Shem and the others watched in awe-struck wonder as the dragon brothers engaged in fierce combat. The creatures turned luscious forests into burnt sticks with their sprays of fire, and the rolling hills became flatlands under the weight of their bodies as they threw one another across the terrain.

"You should've killed me when you had the chance!" roared Natas. Orpheus struggled against his brother's strength, and feared Natas might be right. In desperation, Orpheus spread his wings and lifted off the ground into the sky with Natas in close pursuit. Natas grabbed hold of

Orpheus' tail and threw him back to the ground. Eliab looked at the others with fear in his eyes.

"What should we do?" he asked.

"I thought Orpheus was the most powerful dragon," added Jesorath.

"Orpheus' strength must somehow be connected to the Royal Family," Shem said. "I fear this means Mitzy is dying. We must retrieve her mother and the Liaspot plant!"

"Let me go," volunteered Ithamar. He had failed Uriah, Aykin, and even Obed; but Ithamar refused to fail Mitzy…or Meridia.

"I shall go with you," offered Jesorath.

"Very well, the two of you must leave at once. The rest of us shall stay here and try to help Orpheus," said Shem. Roffius wasn't sure if he would help the white dragon, but he definitely planned to kill Natas.

******

Ithamar and Jesorath jumped onto their winged horses and took flight. It wasn't long before the quaint province of Irvania came into view. The men guided their horses to the blacksmith shop where they landed behind the stables.

"You get Meridia and the baby while I stay here with the horses," volunteered Jesorath.

"Good idea," replied Ithamar.

Heartfelt Plea

The guard took the stairs two at a time up to the house. When he reached the small landing where he had last seen Meridia, Ithamar nearly fell backwards as the door swung open and he found himself face-to-face with the tip of a sword. Meridia tried to hold it steady as her hand shook with fear thinking an intruder had come to harm her, or worse the baby. Once she recognized Ithamar, Meridia sighed with relief and dropped the weapon.

"Ithamar!" she exclaimed. The guard thought she looked even more beautiful with a sword in her hand.

"Greetings, my lady, it's good to see you again," he said. "I promised to return this." Ithamar removed her handkerchief from his vest and handed it to her with a bow. Meridia smiled and reached for the token she had given him days ago.

"Thank you, it's wonderful to see you again as well. But, please tell me, is Mitzy with you? I assumed she was in spite of the captain's orders," she said anxiously. The look on Ithamar's face, and his deep sigh, told Meridia that her assumption had been correct.

"I think you might want to sit down for this, my lady," he suggested.

With Meridia comfortably seated beside the fire while Baby Zerah slept in the basket, Ithamar told the worried mother about her daughter. Meridia listened intently, however, she nearly fainted when Ithamar explained that Mitzy was the true Queen of Nepthali and was near death.

"A hope which is pure and true shall not disappoint," she whispered.

"What was that, my lady?" asked Ithamar.

"Nothing," she replied. "I shall gather the baby and some Liaspot plant so we can be on our way."

******

Jesorath greeted Meridia kindly when she arrived in the stables with Ithamar and Baby Zerah.

"You're looking as lovely as ever, my lady," he said with a bow. Ithamar gave the blacksmith a firm stare, but stopped when Meridia suddenly grabbed hold of him.

"What are *those*?" she gasped at the winged creatures.

"Gifts from Orpheus, my lady," answered Ithamar. He assured Meridia of the animals' safety, and how quickly they could reach the castle because of them. Hearing this, Meridia readily agreed and they started back for Nepthali.

As Moon Chaser carried them away, Meridia silently pondered everything Ithamar had told her. She almost laughed out loud thinking that she had been married to the King of Nepthali, and was so proud of her late husband for his unwavering belief in Orpheus even while living as an obscure farmer. Meridia now understood why the Royal Scribe had visited the farm and taught Amalek's great-great-great grandfather Boaz everything about the Dragon Scroll. Knowing that Boaz was actually the son of King Thaddeus also explained Amalek's resemblance to Nepthali's king of long ago. Meridia missed Amalek still, and wished he was alive to discover his true identity. However, she was finally ready to move on, and smiled shyly as she held onto Ithamar. He liked the feel of her arms around him, but knew he must remain focused on getting them safely back to the castle.

Heartfelt Plea

"Don't worry, my lady, we shall be there shortly thanks to Moon Chaser," he reassured her. It was hard to fathom they were traveling on a horse with wings, yet Meridia had always believed that anything was possible with Orpheus.

"I'm coming, Mitzy. You must be strong my daughter…and my queen," she whispered.

The journey from Jesorath's home in Irvania to the castle took hardly any time thanks to the winged horses.

"We're almost there!" shouted the blacksmith. Ithamar was relieved to have made it without encountering Natas as the horses landed inside the courtyard. He sprung from the saddle and helped Meridia dismount with the baby.

"Mitzy's in your quarters, my lady, with Lamech and Obed," he said. Meridia stopped and looked at him with disbelief.

"Did you say Obed?" she whispered. Ithamar suddenly realized that he'd forgotten to tell her about the lad.

"Yes, my lady, Obed's here. I'm afraid much has happened since we last saw one another," answered Ithamar apologetically. Meridia held Baby Zerah close as she ran down the familiar staircase and hallway to her quarters.

******

Stefano and Julean were permitted to return to Mitzy's bedside with strict instructions not to get in the way. The boys proved to be very helpful with one taking a clean cloth and giving it to the other to dip into water before handing it to Cora or Lamech. When Meridia burst into the room she wanted to rush to her daughter's side, but stopped at the sight of Obed.

"Obed?" she said softly. Meridia handed Baby Zerah to Ithamar and approached the lad from behind. He turned around and ran into the open arms of the woman who'd been like a mother to him. "Obed, is it really you? Just look at how tall and handsome you are!" exclaimed Meridia through tears of joy. She stepped back to admire the grown boy.

"Yes, it's really me! I have so much to tell you," laughed Obed. Although Meridia wanted to hear everything, her greater concern was for her daughter.

"And you shall, but right now I must attend to Mitzy," she replied honestly. Meridia released Obed's hands and walked to the bed where she knelt beside her daughter. "I'm here, Mitzy. Be strong, for you must live my daughter," she whispered. "You are the youngest one so brave who shall save the kingdom." Mitzy's eyes fluttered at the sound of her mother's voice. Meridia kissed her daughter's forehead then turned to Lamech. "I've brought this from Irvania," she said handing the physician a tiny pouch.

He opened it and exclaimed, "The Liaspot plant! Thank you, Meridia. I shall need you and Cora to stay and help me, but the rest of you must leave."

Ithamar carried Baby Zerah into the other room while Jesorath ushered the boys out. Once they had gone, Lamech smashed the bushy leaves into Mitzy's wound. As he did, the castle shook just as it had the night of the attack.

Heartfelt Plea

"What was that?" asked Cora nervously.

******

The vibrations caused after Natas threw Orpheus to the ground were felt as far away as the castle. The white dragon cried out in pain as Natas pounced on him and dug his black talons deep into Orpheus' chest. The men watched helplessly until Shem had an idea.

"Roffius, your sword!" he exclaimed.

"What about it?" asked Roffius.

"Orpheus made it specifically for you to save the kingdom! You've seen that it can pierce the dragon's scales, which means we can defeat Natas!" shouted Shem. Roffius looked at the weapon and knew his brother was right.

"If I don't return, tell Mitzy that I love her," Roffius answered stoically. Shem grabbed his brother's arm as the young captain mounted Starlight.

"You shall tell her yourself," he said firmly. Roffius gave a simple nod and a smile as he took flight.

"I'm going with him," said Aykin. Shem and Eliab were quick to follow.

******

Natas dug his talons deeper into Orpheus' chest as Roffius approached the beast from his blind side. When he was directly above the black dragon, Roffius jumped from his saddle and plunged his sword deep into Natas' neck. The hideous creature released his grip on Orpheus and reared on his hind legs in agony. Natas violently shook his head in an attempt to dislodge both Roffius and the sword. But Natas' thrashing only made the incision deeper and longer as the blade sliced downward along the creature's neck and torso.

In a panic, Natas took flight with Roffius still clinging to his sword. The black dragon twisted and turned in a brilliant display of aerial maneuvers hoping to shake Roffius. The captain was steadfast in his resolve, but his grip was slipping. Roffius knew what he must do to prevent himself from being thrown off without the only weapon that could kill the beast, so without hesitation he pulled the sword free. He fell helplessly through the sky and heard a gust of wind before Roffius found himself on the back of Aykin's horse.

"I've got him!" shouted Aykin to Shem and Eliab.

"That was close!" yelled Eliab.

"Too close," sighed Shem with relief.

"We're not out of the woods yet!" exclaimed Aykin. He pointed to the hideous creature with the glowing chest speeding towards them as blood poured forth from his gaping wound.

"Look out!" shouted Eliab. Thanks to Eliab's warning, Shem pulled back on the reigns in time to escape being incinerated by Natas' fiery blast. Seeing the humans in trouble, Orpheus quickly shot his own stream of fire. The flames struck Natas and the enraged black dragon changed course for his brother.

Heartfelt Plea

With Natas now in pursuit of Orpheus, Roffius whistled for Starlight and the trusty steed soon appeared directly below Aykin's horse. Roffius jumped into his saddle and sped after Natas. The black dragon saw Roffius approaching and returned his attention to the human who seemed so difficult to kill. Although Starlight was amazingly agile with wings, the horse was no match for a dragon. Natas' chest cast its familiar orange glow as the beast prepared to release another deadly stream of fire. Aykin was closest to Roffius, and knew what he must do to save the captain from being incinerated. Aykin looked more like a Royal Guard than a Bara soldier when he rammed his horse into Starlight and pushed Roffius out of harm's way. The deadly flames meant for Roffius instead struck Aykin's horse. The impact knocked Aykin unconscious and sent him spiraling downward.

"Aykin!" shouted Eliab.

"Come on, girl, show me what you can do," whispered Roffius into Starlight's ear. Sensing his urgency, the horse tucked her wings close to her side and dove beneath Aykin so Roffius could grab hold of his limp body.

"Get out of there!" yelled Shem.

"Not until that beast is dead!!" exclaimed Roffius. With Aykin draped over the back of Starlight, Roffius turned the horse around. Eliab and Shem were following close behind.

Orpheus felt his strength returning as he flew with lightning speed to help the humans. The glorious dragon snatched Natas by the tail before the beast could release another blast of fire at the men. Orpheus then threw Natas to the ground where the stunned dragon staggered to his hind legs and lunged at Orpheus. Natas pounced upon the white dragon and pinned Orpheus to the ground as he had done before with his black talons deeply imbedded into his brother's chest.

"I shall enjoy killing you, Brother, and your precious Royal Family!" threatened Natas as his chest glowed ominously. However, before Natas could shoot forth his deadly fire, Orpheus took hold of his brother's powerful jaws and snapped them apart like a pair of twigs.

"You're wrong, Natas, the time has come for the darkness to pass away and for Nepthali to become everything I intended it to be," proclaimed the white dragon. With that, Orpheus released a stream of fire directly into Natas' opened mouth.

"NO!" screamed Natas. While writhing in pain as the dragon burned from within, Orpheus lifted Natas by the tail and flew with him to the mouth of the volcano. When they were directly overhead, Orpheus released Natas and he was engulfed by the boiling lava.

******

Roffius landed Starlight on the plateau alongside Shem and Eliab. Aykin's singed body slowly began to move as the brave soldier regained consciousness.

"Thanks, I owe you one," he said to Roffius.

"I'd say we're even," replied Roffius. As he sprang from the saddle to help Aykin, Roffius noticed Shem's face turn pale.

"Orpheus is coming," said Shem reverently.

Heartfelt Plea

"What should we do?" asked Eliab.

"Kneel," whispered Shem dropping to one knee. The others followed suit, except for Roffius who turned to walk away. However, he was forced to stop when the enormous white dragon landed in front of him.

"Forgive me, Orpheus," said Roffius humbly as he knelt before the great Dragon Ruler.

"Tell me, Roffius, for what do you seek forgiveness?" asked Orpheus his scales shimmering brilliantly in the sun.

"I forsook my belief in you because I was angry and afraid; I thought you had abandoned us," answered the young man with his head hung in shame.

"Do not think for a moment, Captain, that you are the first man whose fear and anger have blinded him to truth," said Orpheus in rebuke. "I left the Dragon Scroll with your kind as a pledge of my return, but you saw it only as proof of my separation." Roffius looked up with tears in his eyes.

"I know, and I was wrong. I shall accept whatever punishment you see fit, but please, spare Mitzy," pleaded Roffius.

"Dear boy, today you have demonstrated exceptional courage and bravery, as well as sincere remorse; therefore, I shan't punish you," stated Orpheus with compassion. "As for Mitzy, she shall receive her reward in full."

"Does that mean she shall live?" asked Roffius hesitantly.

"Make haste, Captain, and see for yourself!" roared the mighty dragon.

Roffius felt his heart beat wildly as he jumped into his saddle. He and Starlight were airborne before the others mounted their enchanted steeds. Shem was the next to take flight, followed by Aykin and Eliab who rode in tandem since Aykin's horse had been incinerated by Natas. Nothing would slow the men, or lessen their resolve, as they raced back to the castle to learn the fate of their queen.

Chapter 25

Sworn Allegiance

When Roffius and the others entered Mitzy's quarters, they found Meridia cradling Baby Zerah with Ithamar standing at her side. Shem immediately rushed to the son whom he hadn't seen since the night of the attack.

"Here is your son...Zerah," announced Meridia proudly.

Shem gathered the baby into his arms and gently stroked Zerah's black hair. He marveled at the infant's striking resemblance to Ashter, but the former king understood his place and respectfully bowed before Meridia.

"Thank you, Your Majesty," he replied humbly. Meridia blushed at her new title while Ithamar approached Aykin and Eliab.

"It's about time you got back," he teased and slapped Aykin on the back.

"Easy, I'm a little crisp," winced the young man.

"Nothing that a certain redhead can't fix," whispered Eliab. Aykin looked at Cora who smiled shyly, and agreed.

"Thank you for everything you've done for my family," said Shem as Baby Zerah cooed in his arms.

"It is I who must thank you for saving me from myself," replied Aykin. Shem placed a hand on Aykin's singed shoulder as they followed Roffius into the back room where they were surprised to find Mitzy alert and sitting up. Roffius and the others immediately knelt before their queen.

"So, this is Mitzy," whispered Eliab. "I can see what all the fuss was about." The men stood as Lamech approached them with a warm greeting.

"It's good to see you've safely returned. She shall need plenty of rest, but thanks to all of you, I expect a full recovery," he said with a broad smile.

Everyone was pleased with the physician's prognosis, but none more than Roffius. Yet, he saw a sadness in her eyes as Mitzy looked at him. It pained Roffius to know that he was the cause, and couldn't wait another moment to profess his undying love. Roffius stepped closer and started to speak, but Mitzy's face suddenly lost its color and her eyes welled up with tears.

"Obed?" she whispered. Roffius turned around and saw the lad standing behind him in the doorway. He dutifully stepped aside to allow the long overdue reunion between Mitzy and Obed as Meridia hurried to her daughter's side.

"Mitzy, darling, I wanted to tell you sooner, but I was afraid it might be too much of a shock," she reasoned. Mitzy agreed with her mother's decision to wait; especially since she was still trying to process the fact that she was the rightful queen.

"Hello, Mitzy, I mean, Your Majesty," said Obed as he knelt before her.

"Obed? Is it really you? You're so tall...and handsome," said Mitzy through tears. Obed wanted to hug her, but knew it was forbidden to touch royalty. Therefore, he simply reached into his pocket and handed her something. Mitzy took the object and looked at it for a moment then burst into tears. Roffius took a step towards her with concern, but Aykin stopped him. Meridia sobbed alongside her daughter at the sight of the beautiful little wooden doll in Mitzy's hand.

"Polly?" whispered Mitzy. "Obed...you finished Polly. She's even more beautiful than I ever imagined she could be!"

Obed smiled proudly. In their years apart, he had transformed the piece of wood into an exquisite doll with eyes that seemed to sparkle if you looked closely enough. He also carved out a simple dress with an apron which appeared to be blowing in the wind.

"I made her to look as I remembered you," he said. For the first time in years, Obed felt like he was finally home.

"She's too beautiful to be me, but I shall treasure her always. I don't think this day could get any better," stated Mitzy as she reached out and clasped Obed's hand.

"Perhaps it can, there's someone I want you to meet," he said while turning around. "This is my brother Aykin." Mitzy looked at the ruggedly handsome man and saw something strangely familiar as he approached.

"It's an honor, Your Majesty," said Aykin as he knelt beside the bed.

"Have we met before?" she asked curiously.

"No, My Queen, but perhaps you met my father," suggested Aykin.

"Who was your father?" she asked. Ithamar wasted no time stepping forward with an answer.

"Their father was my best friend, Uriah. He was with me the day you and your mother arrived at the castle, My Queen," he said. Mitzy paused for a moment as she recalled the handsome young guard who had spoken so kindly to her in the hallway with the royal portraits.

"You look just like him," she said sweetly. "He was very kind to me at a time when I was lonely and afraid. I'm certain he would be proud of the both of you."

Aykin felt his eyes moisten from her kind words, but before he could respond a rush of wind blew through the room and a booming roar echoed against the stone walls. Mitzy's heart raced and she instinctively clung to Polly.

"Natas?" she asked her mother. Meridia took hold of her daughter's trembling hand as Stefano and Julean ran to the small window.

"It's not Natas…it's Orpheus!" exclaimed Julean. Mitzy sat up a little taller and looked at her mother wide-eyed.

"Yes, my darling," reassured Meridia. "A hope which is pure and true shall not disappoint."

Although Mitzy was very weak, nothing could keep her from looking upon the great dragon whom she had longed to see her entire life. Meridia helped her daughter walk to the small window where Orpheus bowed in respect to the young queen.

"Shem, Roffius; come out here with your compatriots," he called out.

******

Dead and wounded men lay scattered throughout the courtyard while fires burned all around as Shem and the others emerged from the castle. Luklin and Perez joined them as the survivors from the armies of Irvania, Haliel, and Belzeeb and mixed with a crowd of townspeople gathering around the good dragon. Shem and his companions knelt before Orpheus as the glorious creature addressed the crowd.

"People of Nepthali, today shall be remembered as the day your kingdom was saved from an evil which sought to destroy you," he proclaimed. "And, as the day you met your true queen!" The men from Haliel and Irvania were aware that Shem was not their king, but the townspeople and men from Belzeeb looked around in disbelief. The former king saw their confusion and climbed onto the broken catapult to explain.

"It's true; I am not your king," announced Shem. "But I pledge my service to our queen whom many of you have known for years as a kind and caring maidservant...Queen Mitzy!"

The people erupted in cheers of celebration for their rightful queen, and for Shem who showed them what it meant to be a true leader regardless of title. Ithamar approached the catapult and stood beside his longtime friend and held his fist respectfully to his chest. Roffius did the same, followed by Aykin, Eliab, Jesorath, Obed, Perez, and Luklin. The men raised their swords first to Orpheus, and then to the little window where their recovering queen stood watching with her mother.

"To Orpheus...and to Queen Mitzy!" they shouted in unison. Pleased with their response, Orpheus spread his powerful wings, tilted back his head, and blew into the sky. Every fire was extinguished, and the battered and broken castle was repaired. The stained-glass windows glistened in the afternoon sun. Joyous cries from the people reached a feverous pitch after Orpheus said that all of the gifts had been returned to each of the four provinces.

"The kingdom shall finally become everything I intended it to be," proclaimed the white dragon. "I hereby decree that Shem and his family shall remain in the castle as advisors to our young queen, and Roffius shall maintain his position as Captain of the Royal Guards. Now, go and prepare for a grand celebration!"

"Thank you, Great One, for these most undeserved blessings," Shem said choking back tears of gratitude. He paused a moment before daring to ask what he hoped not to be an offensive question. "Forgive me, Your Eminence, but there is one thing which perplexes me."

"What is that?" questioned Orpheus.

"I am not of royal blood, so how did the birth of my twins mark the appointed time?" he asked.

"My dear Shem, the Dragon Scroll merely stated that the birth of twins within the castle marked the appointed time; never did it say they must be of royal blood. I'm afraid that was an erroneous assumption made by you humans," explained Orpheus. Shem nodded his understanding and felt foolish for ever having questioned the great Dragon Ruler.

"We shall do everything in our power to remain worthy of these gifts which you have so graciously bestowed upon us," he replied humbly. Orpheus nodded his approval before turning to Roffius.

"Now, Captain, there's one more thing I must ask of you," he said.

"Anything," answered Roffius.

"I want you to keep a close watch on Queen Mitzy," replied Orpheus with a knowing smile.

"With pleasure!" exclaimed Roffius wholeheartedly.

******

As they returned to Mitzy's quarters, Roffius and the others met Cook in the hallway carrying a full plate of cookies and some soup for the queen.

"These look delicious," said Aykin. He stopped to grab a delicious treats as Shem whispered something to Roffius as they entered the cozy quarters.

"Wait for me," said Aykin grabbing another cookie. He and Obed followed the others into the crowded back room.

"Obed, come here," called Shem.

"Is something the matter?" asked the lad with trepidation.

"No, in fact, it's quite the opposite. Obed, because of you Narok is dead and the much needed reinforcements arrived from Belzeeb. You've demonstrated bravery and skills in excess of many who already bear the title Royal Guard," stated Shem plainly.

"Sire?" asked Obed. "Are you asking me to be a Royal Guard?"

"I am...that is if Her Majesty approves," answered Shem turning to Mitzy. She was unaccustomed to her title and its responsibilities, but Mitzy was in absolute agreement with Shem's suggestion.

"Of course I approve," she said with a broad smile.

"There's one more thing," continued Shem turning to Aykin.

"What is it?" asked Obed.

"If it pleases Her Majesty, I'd like Aykin to be the new Commander of the Queen's Personal Detail," suggested Shem. Aykin was stunned and slowly knelt before Mitzy.

"It would be my greatest honor to serve you, My Queen. And to do so alongside men such as these is more than I could ever have hoped for," he said humbly.

"I'm certain the honor shall be all ours," answered Mitzy.

"Eliab," continued Shem, "The guards could use someone with your skills as well."

"Just try to stop me!" exclaimed Eliab.

His honest response produced rolls of laughter from everyone in the room. Aykin looked at his younger brother and wished their father was alive to see his two sons become Royal Guards on the same day. He grabbed Obed in a playful headlock and Lamech smiled happily to see them receive such well-deserved rewards, however, one thing still vexed the old physician.

"Perhaps someone can explain something to me," he said. "How were Ithamar and Jesorath able to return so quickly from Irvania, and the rest of you for that matter?" Roffius took a deep breath and ran his fingers through his wavy hair.

"You wouldn't believe me if I told you," he replied.

"Try me," pressed Lamech. Eliab was happy to answer.

"Flying horses," he said plainly.

"I see...," said the physician softly. He briefly pondered the answer until reaching the conclusion that if dragons were back in the land, why not flying horses too.

"Flying horses?!" exclaimed Stefano and Julean over each other. "Can we see them?"

"I shall take you to them, but I can't promise any rides today," answered Jesorath with a wink. The boys ran from the room chattering with excitement ahead of the large blacksmith.

"Well, gentlemen," said Lamech, "I'm afraid I must ask the rest of you to leave as well so that my beautiful patient here can get some rest." Although Roffius hated to leave before telling Mitzy how he felt, he obediently followed the others until he heard a soft voice.

"Thank you for saving my life, Captain," she said. Roffius stopped and turned around.

"It's a life worth saving, my lady, whether a queen or a maidservant," he said honestly. Meridia smiled and motioned for Cora to follow her out of the room to allow Roffius and Mitzy a moment alone. Mitzy watched them leave, but wished they would stay as she recalled Roffius' heartbreaking exchange with Narok. She was certain the pain from his words was far greater than the pain in her shoulder, yet Mitzy knew both would heal in time.

"I'm sorry if Narok made you uncomfortable by saying I was in love with you. But, have no fear, it was just a foolish daydream," she stated softly. Roffius wondered if Mitzy meant what she said as he approached the bed feeling more afraid than when he had faced the black dragon.

"I beg your pardon, Your Majesty, but you're wrong," he said boldly.

Sworn Allegiance

"Excuse me?" she retorted.

"I said you're wrong. It wasn't a foolish daydream; at least I hope not. My only reason for saying such cruel statements was to keep you safe," admitted Roffius. "I thought that if Narok was convinced you meant nothing to me, he would let you go. But make no mistake, My Queen, the only truth I spoke was that of your beauty." He waited breathlessly for a response while Mitzy allowed herself to feel a glimmer of hope as she looked into his hazel eyes.

"What exactly are you saying?" she whispered.

"Miss Mit, I mean, Your Highness," he corrected himself, "I'm saying that from the moment I met you as the daughter of a maidservant, I have loved you." Mitzy looked at him wide-eyed wondering if this was a dream.

"You have?" she asked.

"Yes, and if you shall allow me, I wish to spend the remainder of my days proving it to you," continued Roffius. Mitzy's eyes filled with tears as he looked at her in the same tender way her father used to look at her mother. With just a few honest words, Roffius had proved what she always believed; true love can withstand anything…even a broken heart.

"Well, Captain, I have just one thing to say," answered Mitzy. She paused and Roffius feared his own heart might break until he saw the hint of mischief in her eye. "I prefer to be called Miss Mit." Roffius smiled and leaned in close to the maiden he loved.

"Miss Mit, I am, and always shall be; truly, deeply, and hopelessly in love with you," he confessed.

Her tear-filled eyes sparkled, and Roffius found himself unable to resist the beautiful maiden a moment longer. He gently slid one hand behind her waist and cupped her face with the other. Roffius pulled Mitzy to himself, and the lips which had been denied each other for so long finally came together. Never before had a kiss been filled with such anticipation and longing since no two people had ever been as much in love as Mitzy and Roffius. They were perfectly suited for one another, like sunlight in the spring, and neither could image life without the other. At last, the honorable captain slowly pulled himself away to respect the physician's orders.

"I must leave you now, Miss Mit, but have no fear; I shall return," he said with a dashing grin.

"As your queen, Captain, that's a promise I order you to keep," she replied with a twinkle in her eyes.

Roffius bowed before leaving Mitzy feeling happier than she ever thought possible. He stepped into the hallway surprised to find Eliab waiting.

"Some guys have all the luck," teased the young soldier. Roffius tried to hide another smile as he shrugged his shoulders.

"It's a burden someone must bear," he replied in jest knowing that Eliab was right.

******

Once Mitzy had fully recovered from her injuries, the kingdom celebrated with a grand coronation for their rightful queen. It was the most joyous ceremony anyone could remember, which included the formal appointment of Aykin, Obed, and Eliab to their new positions as Royal Guards.

For her first royal decree, Queen Mitzy granted her mother ownership of the land which her father and his family had faithfully worked for generations. Meridia remained at the castle to be near her daughter, but Obed and Ithamar saw to it that the land was maintained and properly cared for. Aykin and Eliab proved invaluable in their new positions by working tirelessly to bridge generations of hatred between the Bara soldiers and the people of Nepthali. Because of their efforts, old enemies eventually lived in harmony.

Queen Mitzy left the castle as it had been, except for one very important detail. She commissioned the Royal Artist to paint a portrait of her father based upon how the young queen remembered him. It turned out wonderfully, and she surprised her mother by hanging it beside King Thaddeus' portrait in the hallway of Nepthali's former kings.

Finally, Queen Mitzy mercifully pardoned Nalia for her treasonous behavior. However, the mischievous maiden was demoted to polishing boots for the Royal Guards, and was permanently denied inner castle privileges. Although Mitzy faced many adjustments with her new duties and responsibilities, she had never been happier and the kingdom had never been more prosperous.

Dragon Scroll of Nepthali

******

The crisp, fall day finally arrived for the much-anticipated wedding between the Captain of the Royal Guards and Queen Mitzy. Shem and Roffius looked especially dashing in their highly decorated uniforms as they stood facing the pews in the Royal Chapel. Shem felt an overwhelming sense of gratitude for having been asked to reside over the ceremony in spite of his no longer being king. Aykin and Obed stood on one side of him, while Eliab and Ithamar stood beside Roffius in their equally formal uniforms. Meanwhile, at the far end of the platform, Stefano and Julean fidgeted with the collars of their specially tailored suits to match those worn by the Royal Guards. Roffius took a deep breath as he waited anxiously to see his bride.

At last, the rear doors opened and trumpets blew. Cora preceded her best friend in an elegant gown which designated her as the queen's Lady in Waiting. Aykin winked at the beautiful redhead who'd stolen his heart and she smiled happily in return. Roffius strained his neck to see Mitzy, but saw only her silhouette as rays of afternoon sunlight streamed in from behind.

When she finally came into view, Roffius thought Mitzy was a vision of beauty as she walked slowly down the long aisle on Cook's arm. She thought it only fitting that the large man who'd been like a father to her should be the one to give her away. Cook was humbled by such an honor, and looked more nervous than Roffius as he escorted the lovely queen. Mitzy wore a gown tailored from those worn by Queen Ashter and Jeru's wife, Tamar, on their wedding days. Mitzy had insisted upon combining the two as a special tribute to the sisters-in-law she would never truly know. Mitzy also insisted upon wearing the same veil which her mother had worn the day she wed. The delicate lace was secured by her royal crown made of gold from the Cherith River lined with diamonds mined from the mountains in Haliel. Her crown glistened in the natural sunlight streaming through the stained glass windows, but it paled in comparison to the sparkle in Roffius' eyes the moment he beheld his bride at his side. Julean cleared his throat to get the ceremony underway, anxious to partake in the fine feast Cook had prepared. Roffius offered his arm to Mitzy and the young couple turned to face Shem with unsurpassable joy.

"Dear Friends and Fellow Countrymen, we are gathered here today to celebrate the love shared between Captain Roffius and Her Royal Highness Queen Mitzy which joins them today in matrimony," he proclaimed. Shem paused for a moment before turning to his brother. "Roffius, do you take Queen Mitzy to be your beloved wife with the promise to cherish her, and to uphold her needs before your own from now until the day you part in death?"

"I do," replied Roffius with absolute certainty. Shem smiled and turned to Mitzy.

"Queen Mitzy, do you vow in the presence of all gathered here to honor, love, and respect Roffius for the remainder of your days?" he asked.

"I do, with all my heart," she answered with equal certainty.

"Then, by the power bestowed upon me by the great dragon Orpheus, I now pronounce you husband and wife," Shem decreed. "You may kiss the bride."

Roffius smiled as he carefully lifted Mitzy's veil and pulled her close. As they shared their first kiss as husband and wife, Orpheus cast his blessing upon the newlyweds and they shone more brilliantly than the morning star. The guests applauded in celebration as Ithamar winked at Meridia, and Jesorath heartily slapped Lamech on the back. Shem raised his eyes to acknowledge his beloved Ashter, while Julean pulled out the crème puff from his pocket and Stefano shoved him to get moving.

Roffius and Mitzy made their way down the aisle hand in hand and stopped at the doors so Mitzy could throw her bouquet. Maidens pushed one another to position themselves in hopes of catching the prized token, yet Mitzy's aim was true and the flowers landed perfectly in Cora's arms. Ithamar nudged Aykin in jest as the young man's face turned nearly as red as Cora's hair.

With rose petals falling and people cheering, the happy couple climbed into the waiting carriage pulled by enchanted horses. The creatures spread their powerful wings and took flight while guests watched the sweet silhouette of Roffius and Mitzy kissing as the carriage disappeared into the setting sun.

******

Orpheus lived up to what Amalek had taught his daughter as a child in that the promise of a dragon is the one thing to be certain of in this world. Orpheus promised to reward Queen Mitzy for her unwavering belief in the good dragon, and he did. Her reign was long and unparalleled in peace and prosperity. Orpheus also blessed her and Roffius with a son whom they named Amalek in honor of Mitzy's father. After many years of faithful service to her people, it came time for Queen

Mitzy to step down and for Amalek to take the throne. At his coronation, Roffius presented their son with the magnificent sword crafted by dragon magic.

Although no longer serving as queen, Mitzy remained active in the lives of her people. She could often be found telling marvelous stories surrounded by children and flowers in the Royal Gardens. One summer day while Mitzy was telling the next generation about the great dragon brothers, Orpheus happened to fly overhead.

"Is it true what they say about you being the one who brought the white dragon back to Nepthali?" asked a wide-eyed boy. The ever-humble Mitzy blushed, but before she could respond the voice which still caused her heart to flutter answered for her from behind.

"It's as true as the sun shining in the sky, young one," said Roffius.

The children turned around and giggled with delight at the sight of the renowned captain. His furrowed lines forged by the passage of time deepened when he smiled and his hair was as white as Orpheus' scales, but Roffius was still the most handsome man in the kingdom. He joined them amongst the flowers and held Mitzy's delicate hand in his before kissing his wife affectionately, as was his custom each time Roffius saw his beloved. The two were as much in love after being married over half-a-century as the day they had wed.

"What Captain Roffius means to say, children, is that *hope* brought Orpheus back to our land," she said with the familiar twinkle in her aged eyes. "Because as you know, a hope which is pure and true shall not disappoint."

Dragon Scroll of Nepthali
The End

Lightning Source UK Ltd.
Milton Keynes UK
UKHW010940081221
395308UK00010B/1103